REJECTED by the PACK

Other books by Jaelynn Woolf

Circle of Blood Book 1: Lover's Rebirth
Circle of Blood Book 2: Lover's Awakening
Circle of Blood Book 3: Lover's Sacrifice
Circle of Blood Book 4: Lover's Absolution
Circle of Blood Book 5: Lover's Atonement
Circle of Blood Book 6: Lover's Victory

The Last Vampire: Book One
The Last Vampire: Book Two
The Last Vampire: Book Three
The Last Vampire: Book Four
The Last Vampire: Book Five
The Last Vampire: Book Six

(co-written with R. A. Steffan)

Rejected by the Pack

Jaelynn Woolf

Rejected by the Pack

Copyright 2022 by OtherLove Publishing, LLC

All rights reserved. Printed in the United States of America. No part of this book may be used or reproduced in any manner whatsoever without written permission except in the case of brief quotations embedded in critical articles or reviews.

This book is a work of fiction. Names, characters, businesses, organizations, places, events and incidents either are the product of the author's imagination or are used fictitiously. Any resemblance to actual persons, living or dead, events, or locales is entirely coincidental.

ISBN: 978-1-955073-53-0 (paperback)

For information, contact the author at
http://www.otherlovepublishing.com/contact/

Cover by AddictiveCovers.com

First Edition: April 2022

Author's Note

This book contains cursing, descriptions of violence (including bullying), and a couple of graphic sex scenes. It is intended for a mature audience.

TABLE OF CONTENTS

ONE

"COME ON, EMBER. Maybe it won't be so bad," Darby said.

An unimpressed snort escaped my control as I strolled along the well-worn dirt path with my best friend at my side. We were discussing my upcoming wolfbirth ceremony, and despite her comforting tone, Darby still seemed almost as nervous about it as I was.

I breathed in the scent of trees and decaying leaf litter. A weak late afternoon sun cast pale, heatless rays down on the Greystalker lands, a region of dense forests and majestic mountains tucked far away from any of the human cities near the coast. It was usually rainy at this time of year, although today the blue sky was only marred by a few fluffy, white clouds that held no obvious threat of even a light drizzle.

"Why? Do you think the elders have been lying to us all these years about how painful this is going to be?" I shot back.

Darby grimaced and shrugged. "I mean... maybe? You know how these wolf tales get spun out of control. It could just be one of those rite-of-passage things, couldn't it? They get you so freaked out that when it's over, you end up torturing the next generation of wolves with the same bullshit stories just to get a bit of revenge."

I glanced at her skeptically, not sure if I found her optimism refreshing or infuriating.

"I somehow doubt that," I answered.

My twenty-first birthday was looming, which meant that my days of puphood were well and truly coming to an end. Not that I'd been able to enjoy my adolescence like most of my peers had done.

Oh, no.

The carefree camping trips in the mountains… the long nights of swimming in crystal clear river waters… the cozy, sheltered dens filled with affectionate parents and siblings… those were for the legitimate, accepted pups in the pack. Not for me. Not for an orphaned outcast.

I was, not to put too fine a point on it, as low in the pack hierarchy as it was possible to be. I'd never been adopted by another family once I lost my parents, as was customary for orphaned pups. Instead, the pack had forced me to live on the fringes of their society from the time I was ten years old. They kept me alive, but barely. Mostly, I'd been expected to survive on my own.

I set the bitter memories aside as Darby and I wound around the corner of the low dens on the eastern side of the path. The rough-hewn wood that made up the walls and pillars blended so naturally into the landscape that the buildings pressed deep into the side of the mountain weren't immediately noticeable to a casual observer. They were there, though — an entire town hidden among the forests and hills.

The Greystalker packlands might have been the only home that I'd ever known, but I felt little attachment to the place. If it hadn't been for Geneva Padfoot, the eccentric woman who kept a curio shop on the outskirts of the town, I probably would have ended up sleeping under trees or bare, rocky overhangs for most of my young life. Even years later, the thought made me angry.

But there was no use obsessing over it. Not now. For years, I'd agonized over why I was so hated within my own pack. When I'd been little, I'd worried that maybe I'd done something to incur the wrath of everyone around me. My sensitive, childish heart had broken every time a pack member turned their back on me in disgust. It wasn't until I'd grown older that I'd managed to shake off the grief that came with perpetual rejection.

In the end, the 'why' of it really didn't matter—and besides, the eve of my first shift wasn't exactly an ideal time to rehash all of this in my mind.

"You're obsessing over the past, aren't you?" Darby asked, breaking into my dark thoughts.

I shot her a sidelong glance, aware that my musings must have been showing on my face. With practiced ease, I smoothed away the tightness around my mouth and eyes, firmly pressing down the emotions that had, for a moment, bubbled too near the surface.

"Of course not," I said. "Anyway, the wolfbirth ceremony can't be any worse than the rest of this, can it?"

4

My best friend stared hard at me, clearly not buying into my attempt at bravado.

Darby only shook her head at my sarcasm. "You know, in a way, I'm jealous of you."

Taken by surprise, I let out a bark of laughter. "*Jealous*? Of me? Have you lost your mind?"

"No!" Darby insisted, shooting me a quelling look as we passed a dense clump of evergreen trees. "It's just—your ceremony is in two days, and then it will be out of the way."

I frowned. "Out of the way? What's that supposed to mean?"

Darby let out a frustrated sigh. "I have to wait another eleven months until my wolfbirth. And right now, that feels like forever. I want to get *out* of here, Ember."

My pace slowed, pine needles crunching softly beneath my feet.

"What?" Darby asked, looking back at me.

"You're still stuck on that, huh?" I asked, coming fully to a halt.

Darby turned to face me, a faint flush coloring her pale cheeks. "You sound like you disapprove."

I shook my head at her and resumed the trek toward Geneva's shop, where I had an informal job tracking inventory and keeping the books in exchange for room and board. She huffed and fell into step with me once more.

"It's not that I disapprove," I explained, for possibly the hundredth time. "It's just that I don't think the plan will work."

Darby sighed wistfully. "It *could* work. Just picture it! We'll both have our wolfbirths and transform into gorgeous, tawny wolves—beautiful, and with undeniable grace. We'll leave this pack and join another one, where we can find mates that are somewhere in the middle of the pecking order. Mates that are honest, and not cruel. It will be a fresh start and a way to climb up from the bottom rung of this pack."

I met her eyes with regret. "I wish it were that easy. And, I dunno… maybe you should try it. But there's 'low in the pecking order,' and then there's whatever I am. I don't think that kind of fresh start is in the cards for me."

News traveled, even between packs. With my background, I was pretty sure my only shot at salvation would be to get away from wolves completely. And *that*, unfortunately, was something far easier said than done.

Darby grimaced and offered, "Well, on the positive side, at least there's nowhere for you to go but up, right? That gives you some freedom, in a way."

"You think so?" I asked tartly.

Darby snorted in dark amusement and gestured at me. "Well, look at you! Who else could pull off hair dyed half black and half platinum blonde? Who else in the pack is covered in tattoos?"

"I'm not covered," I pointed out. "They're just on my arms."

With a laugh, Darby shook her head at me. "Still. You disappear and come back with tattoos, and no one bats an eye. If I tried that…"

"Your family would kill you," I finished for her.

While Darby was quite low in the pack, she still had a place. Her family might be poorly regarded, but her parents wouldn't tolerate a sin like sneaking off to get tattoos or a human dye-job.

And she had a point. I could do those things. I could steal away in the night, hitchhike to the nearest city, panhandle for human money, and do the kind of stuff that would drag another shifter's reputation through the mud. After all, what else was the pack going to do to me at this point? I was already paying the price for my mother's unforgivable crime. Adding a few minor 'crimes' of my own was no big deal by comparison.

Raucous laughter drifted down the trail from the direction we'd just come, cutting into my thoughts. Darby and I both froze, turning to look with a sinking sense of inevitability.

"Oh, no." Darby let out a low groan.

I set my jaw and said nothing. We both knew those voices. They'd haunted nearly every step of our lives for years now. The gang approaching us was a bunch of pack bullies with hardly any brains to share between them. Unfortunately, being well fed and cared for within the pack meant that despite their disgusting lack of intelligence, they were all well muscled and fast.

God knew, I'd personally tried time and time again to outrun them without any luck.

The group rounded the corner, their attention focusing on us with all the intensity that wolves could muster—even when in human form. But there was one saving grace. Darby might be a target, but I was a *much* better one.

Darby curled in on herself, her shoulder pressing against mine. She was trembling, nervously licking her lips in unconscious reaction to the coming confrontation with more dominant pack members.

"Go," I told her, not wanting my only friend in the world to get hurt when it could be avoided. "I'll be fine, just get out of here."

Unfortunately, while Darby might be terrified, she was also intensely loyal. "I can't leave you here alone," she said, a tiny quaver audible beneath the words.

The group was getting closer, their pupils blown wide with the exhilaration and glee of the hunt. I recognized that expression, and knew it didn't bode well. De-escalation wasn't in the cards today. This was going to get physical.

"You can't do anything," I said, setting my feet shoulder-width apart as I faced the approaching gang. "Or rather, you can. Go get Geneva and bring her here. *Please*, Darby."

My best friend bit her lip, obviously conflicted. I gave her a pleading look, and she finally broke — haring off toward the shop where my ancient and wrinkled boss would be found. Of course, by the time she got back it would all be over, but if it got Darby away from here safely…

She darted off the road and deeper into the woods before disappearing from view. *Smart girl.*

I watched her go, resignation flooding me. The gang descended, and just as I'd hoped, they didn't spare a glance after Darby, who was already long gone.

"What are you doing out here?" Thelen, the boldest of the group spat, stalking closer to me. "I thought I told you to keep your ugly carcass off the public roads."

I stared up at him, my expression cool and emotionless. Of course, my lack of reaction only served to infuriate my attackers. Thelen stormed up and grabbed my jaw, jerking my head to the side so that my eyes were pointed away.

"Don't presume to look at me, you filthy mutt," he snarled, his foul breath puffing against the side of my face. "I will strip your sorry hide of every piece of skin you have."

"I doubt you could figure out how," I ground out, my voice distorted by his viselike grip. "Have you ever so much as caught a rabbit, you useless sack of shit?"

The blow that hit the side of my face seemed to come out of nowhere, and I landed in a heap on the ground at the feet of my attacker. A moment later, I was surrounded by angry shifters kicking and pummeling me, even as I curled into a ball to protect my vulnerable stomach. I couldn't draw breath.

"Time to teach this mutt a lesson," said a shrill female voice. It was Star, a particular nemesis of mine in recent years. I bared my teeth, a low growl boiling up from my chest even as more blows rained down.

"I don't know why they're even bothering with a wolfbirth ceremony," someone taunted.

"You're going to end up the runt of the pack. You'll be half-starved, with patches of fur missing."

"Assuming she can even shift at all!" Star added gleefully. "For all we know, her bitch mother fucked a human!"

I shuddered as the taunt hit home.

Don't listen, I told myself firmly. *None of this matters, it's just one more shitty day like any other.*

I could feel rivulets of blood flowing down my face. More filled my mouth, where my teeth had cut into my cheek. I spat it out, taking advantage of a sudden lull in the attack. At first, I didn't understand why they'd stopped. Then I felt the wind rise. A strong scent of rain swirled across the roadway; the trees creaked and swayed above us. It felt like electricity was crackling through the air, making the hair on my neck stand up.

"Where the hell did that come from?" one of the bullies demanded, looking at the trees bending and swaying around them. "The sky's still clear—"

Through my ringing head, I was aware of the confused murmurs around me, but I only cared that they'd stopped hitting me. The breeze seemed to clear my head—the inexplicable storm-scent strange, but also strangely familiar. I breathed carefully around bruised ribs.

It was only a brief reprieve, though. Star crouched beside me, grabbing me by the hair. I yelped, unable to stifle the noise.

"Stop gawping at the sky and come hold her down!" she snapped.

Hands closed on my arms and legs, even as I struggled. Star grinned maliciously and pulled a knife from her belt. My stomach turned over, but Star still had a handful of my hair, and she had something else in mind other than gutting me, apparently.

"This black and white rat's nest is disgusting," she said, lifting the blade. "It's coming off in chunks. How do you like that, bitch?"

I snarled and jerked helplessly, poised to spit in her face.

"*What are you doing?*" An authoritative voice cut through the sound of wind and mocking laughter.

The odd atmosphere grew even heavier, this time with alpha power. Everyone froze, me included.

No one answered the barked question, but the hands holding me down fell away. I rolled onto my back, intending to get up, but instead I just... stayed there. The newcomer approached, striding confidently down the road to stop just a step or two shy of me. I dropped my gaze, aware of the others doing the same.

It was Cai.

Cai *fucking* Greystalker, the alpha's son. Heir to the Greystalker packlands. Because *of course* he would be the one to see me like this. Anger at the unfairness of it all warred with a desire to sink straight into the ground and disappear.

I looked up at him, almost despite myself. He was tall with dark, tousled hair that fell almost to his shoulders. His sharp, dominating gaze swept over each of the bullies, who all seemed to wilt beneath those piercing amber-colored eyes.

He stared them down, not saying a word. Two of my tormenters began to whimper softly and back away. The rest shifted uncomfortably and lowered their gazes in respect.

With my attackers held at bay for the moment, I pushed myself ungracefully to my feet, staggering a little as dizziness threatened to engulf me. Darkness grew at the edges of my vision, making me think this might not have been such a good plan after all.

A hand gripped my elbow, tugging me to the right. That was when I realized I'd started to fall over. My bleary gaze followed the hand to a wrist, an arm, and finally up to its owner's face. It was Cai. His calloused fingers were warm against my arm. My skin tingled where he touched me.

A shiver skittered down my spine, my pulse picking up. Liquid heaviness settled low in my belly, ridiculous and unwelcome. With difficulty, I ignored my body's betrayal and shook off his touch, looking down to avoid meeting his deep amber eyes.

My obvious embarrassment must have convinced Cai that I'd recovered enough to stand on my own. He turned back to the bullies, who were all looking deeply uncomfortable beneath his piercing alpha glare.

Movement drew my attention to the side of the road. Two of Cai's friends lounged nearby, leaning against the trunks of the largest trees. They looked simultaneously bored and amused by the spectacle. I assumed they didn't think I was worth all this trouble. Still... Cai was the alpha's son. If he wanted to involve himself in the affairs of the pack outcast, it was his right to do so, and neither of them was likely to contradict him.

The silence on the road deepened to truly uncomfortable levels. Finally, Cai dismissed the gang of bullies with a small jerk of his chin, which sent them all scurrying away.

"Are you all right?" he asked in that low, resonant voice of his.

I swallowed, trying to raise some moisture in my mouth. "Uh, yeah."

"You're bleeding." Cai observed.

I swiped at the rivulets of blood on my face. The bleeding was already starting to slow, although the stinging was growing to a deep burn. "It'll heal."

Cai nodded, and I saw the barriers go up, as though my lowly status had suddenly occurred to him. He started to move away; back to his friends and whatever they'd been doing before they'd gotten drawn into my shitshow.

But then, he paused. "Good luck on your wolfbirth. I suppose I'll see you there," he threw over his shoulder.

"Wait. You're coming to my wolfbirth ceremony?" I asked stupidly.

Cai turned back to me. "Sure. It's my family duty to attend all wolfbirths."

I blinked, irrationally disappointed by the answer. "Oh."

Honestly, I didn't know what else to say. I should probably thank him for saving me—or at least, saving my hair—but somehow the words wouldn't form.

And then it was too late. They were gone.

"Ember!" Darby's voice distracted me as my friend hurried up and took me by the arm.

"Did you bring Cai here?" I asked in a dull tone.

"Yeah, I ran into them before I got to Geneva's place." She looked me up and down, a sad expression sliding across her pretty features. "Come on. Let's get you cleaned up."

I let myself be chivvied toward Geneva's shop.

"You were right," I told her faintly, my body stiff and aching. "Maybe we should both leave. Nothing could be worse than this."

14

TWO

AFTER A FEW dozen strides of being frog-marched, I set my heels and balked. "Darby, let me go. I'm fine, I promise!" I insisted, brushing off my best friend's clinging fingers.

"You're all bashed up," Darby said. Her eyes were wide and sad. "I'm sorry I ran away like that."

I shrugged my indifference, hiding a wince as I tried to wipe the sticky blood off of my hands. "No use us both getting beaten into a pulp. I thought you were going to get Geneva?"

Face growing red, Darby chewed on her lip for a moment. "I was, but I, uh, ran into Cai instead."

My glare was accusatory. "So, you *told* him what was going on?"

"He made me." Darby's voice was awestruck, and a dreamy look slid across her face. I snorted and started walking again, a bit disgusted by the whole thing. Still, I dropped the issue. Of course Darby had told Cai everything he wanted to know. You didn't say *no* to an alpha.

We reached Geneva's shop. Unlike most of the dwellings in the Greystalker lands, it was a freestanding building made of logs from the forests, rather than being built partially underground. The roof, instead of the ferns and grasses growing over the other homes in the area, was made of crumbling shingles. The windows were mostly dark in the growing shadows as afternoon gave way to evening, but a few of them were lit from within by insubstantial, flickering candlelight.

Geneva bustled through the door leading to the back of the building as soon as we stepped inside.

"What happened, child?" she demanded, taking in my many gashes and bruises. Even though the bleeding had already slowed, I could feel that dirt and blood caked my face, despite my best efforts to clean up.

"Nothing important," I answered in a curt voice.

Geneva's expression hardened, but she asked no more questions. Within moments she had a warm bowl of water and a washrag in her hands, and she was leading me to the stool that always stood in the front corner of the shop.

"Was it the same group as before?" she asked, as she wiped my face. The cuts stung and burned, making me wince and try to pull away. Geneva's kind, wrinkled face was close to me, her expression reproachful.

I refused to answer, not wanting to talk about it, so Darby muttered the story under her breath into Geneva's ear.

"Well, it's a good thing shifters heal so quickly," Geneva stated, wringing out the now red and brown washcloth. "A few of those gashes are deep, but they should close up soon."

"Thanks, Geneva." I answered, standing up and stretching. I could feel my muddy clothes cooling against my skin.

I looked around the shop at all the trinkets, the potions standing in dusty bottles, and the tightly wrapped bags of tea and coffee. It looked like everything was fairly well stocked, which meant I would have an easy evening, at least. I was grateful, since I didn't feel up to doing much.

"Did anything odd happen while this group was attacking you?" Geneva asked.

I looked around at her, startled. "No. Wait. What do you mean, *odd*?"

Geneva seemed to hover on the edge of speech, her expression turning wary. After a moment, she waved the words away.

What a strange question, I thought.

But as much as I wanted to dismiss it, there *was* something. There was the wind. A storm that wasn't a storm. Still—that was nothing to do with me, or what had happened with the bullies. Pushing those thoughts to the back of my mind, I shook my head and slouched behind the counter.

Geneva narrowed her eyes at me, but said no more on the subject.

"Well, just think—things will be better after your ceremony," she offered. "I'm sorry this has happened to you, but it will be over soon. Perhaps you'll even find a mate."

I smiled and agreed mechanically.

The truth was, I didn't believe the Greystalker pack would like me much better as a shifted wolf than they had as a pup. Still, it might be useful to have the power to transform. Even though my wounds were knitting themselves back together fairly quickly, I knew I'd heal even faster and more completely as a wolf.

At least I had that to look forward to. As for finding a mate, though — I'd rather stab my eyes out with a rusty spoon than mate anyone in this godforsaken pack.

———◆———

The morning of my wolfbirth arrived before I really felt ready for it, with howling wind and cold sheets of rain falling in the forest. I'd been awake most of the night, dreading the part of the following day when I'd be forced to stand exposed before the pack alpha and anyone else who wanted to gawp at me.

There was a long tradition that the one experiencing the birth would be escorted to the ceremony by people dear to them — family or close friends. I had asked both Darby and Geneva to attend my wolfbirth, since there really wasn't anyone else.

Darby was ecstatic. She'd never been to a wolfbirth before, being the youngest in her family, and she was eager to learn what she could expect from her own ceremony.

Geneva had seen many, many wolfbirths over the years, I was sure. Her ancient eyes held none of the curiosity and enthusiasm that Darby had from the moment she hurried through the door, dripping wet.

"Is this part really necessary?" I grumbled as Geneva and Darby stripped the clothes off of my lean frame.

"It's traditional," Geneva replied, shrugging one shoulder. "It's part of the process, no one will think twice of your nakedness."

I pressed my lips together. I had never felt as comfortable with my own nudity as other members of the pack. As everyone over twenty-one had the power to transform their human form into a wolf form, it wasn't unusual to see someone coming out of the woods naked.

It was normal.

So why did I always feel so awkward?

Geneva's fingers traced down my tattooed skin, a strange expression on her face.

"What?" I asked defensively.

After a brief pause, Geneva answered, "Nothing. Are you ready? It sounds like the rain has stopped."

I took a shuddering breath and then let it out with a nod. "Yeah. Might as well get on with it."

We stepped out of Geneva's small den. It was located right next to her shop, and it was where I had lived for the last ten years. I used to think the cluttered halls and musty air were stifling, and I often dreamed of the spacious, bright den that I might have had with my parents.

Not today, though. Even as we all stepped out onto the trail, the cold, wet earth seeping between my bare toes, I wished heartily that we could return to the comfort of the humble den that had become my home.

Wrapping my arms around my naked torso, I shivered as I hurried towards the ceremonial hall, my escorts in tow. Like Geneva's shop, this hall was a freestanding structure — a long roof on poles, mostly open on all four sides. There was a roaring fire burning in the stone fireplace at the center. The smoke wafted out of a hole in the ceiling.

I hesitated just outside, feeling the sudden urge to bolt into the trees rising up from my core. It was like a scream that I could barely contain. Geneva seemed to sense my thoughts and gave me a firm push towards the center of the ceremonial hall. I took a tentative step forward, then glanced back to make sure that Geneva and Darby were following me. They were. We all sat down on one of the benches near the fire, its warmth radiating over my skin. I shivered, pressing my arms against Darby and Geneva, who were sitting close on either side of me.

I kept my eyes locked on my feet, ignoring the babble of voices that surrounded me. It felt like half of the pack had turned up to watch my wolfbirth. I stole a look around, trying not to be obvious about it.

Forget half. Practically everyone was here. *Great.*

But what could I do? Other pack members were always invited to wolfbirths, although it was traditional to only attend the ceremonies of your close friends and relatives. None of these people were my friends, except the two sitting as still as stone on either side of me, and the hard faces of the other onlookers reminded me of that fact in no uncertain terms.

They're here hoping for a show, I realized. *They're not here to support me. They just think something gossip-worthy is going to happen.*

Anger bubbled inside my stomach.

"Are you okay, Ember?" Darby whispered, leaning her head close to mine.

I nodded, not trusting myself to speak.

After several minutes, the crowd stopped growing and most were making their way towards seats on the benches behind us.

A man walked forward, dressed in ceremonial robes. He had a necklace of stone beads draped around his neck, resting over his breastbone. He wore a ceremonial headdress as well, with shiny black feathers and braided strips of shiny material mixing artistically with his hair.

He was tall, with broad shoulders—a powerful man who had passed on his piercing intensity to his son, Cai.

This was our alpha, Bardulf Greystalker. Even though I had not yet been forced to take my wolf form, I could feel the instinctual desire in me to drop my gaze and shy away from him.

To distract myself, I glanced around at the other spectators. The members of the bully gang were in the crowd. Of *course* they were. When they saw me watching them, they pulled grotesque faces and laughed uproariously.

"Good luck shifting," one of them called, "There's a betting pool, you know. Odds say you won't be able to manage it, mutt!"

I threw the guy a flat look over my shoulder and turned back towards the ceremony. Cai had arrived. He'd kept his promise to attend my wolfbirth ceremony. I nodded cautiously to him in acknowledgement.

It didn't exactly make up for the fact that my gang of tormenters had shown up to ogle me like a hunk of meat… but it was something.

The tempo of the ceremonial drums was picking up now. It felt like they were counting down to the end of my old life, the life that was about to be pushed away forever.

I'd left my black-and-platinum-blonde-dyed hair loose, instead of tying it up in a bun the way I usually did. Crossing my legs and wrapping my arms tighter around myself, I let it fall over my chest, serving as an additional cover over my exposed breasts.

Out of the corner of my eye, I felt Cai watching me. Something about his eyes on me made me feel hyper-aware. I didn't like it. That was ridiculous, though. He'd been to tons of wolfbirths. He must know the ceremony inside and out. Why would my naked body be of any more interest to him than someone else's?

Yet, I could feel his gaze lingering on me. A flush of embarrassment stole over my skin. For one wild second, I imagined pulling my hair back to expose myself further, just to shock him.

Before I could make any bad life choices, Bardulf stood up and raised one commanding hand. The gathered crowd fell silent immediately.

"We begin," he said in a deep voice. Despite the gravel of advancing age, it was still powerful.

I didn't know what to do, so I sat motionless between Geneva and Darby. When Bardulf turned and faced me, he gestured with one finger for me to get up.

Before I could consciously make the decision to obey, my legs lifted me to a standing position and were carrying me to his side. Embarrassment flooded me. It looked like I was in a huge hurry to kowtow to this leader who'd never raised a hand to make my life easier.

I was the rebel. Not some simpering pup hoping for scraps from the alpha's table. I resented the power that had sent me scrambling to his side.

The ceremonial hall was quiet as I looked up into Bardulf's face. It was lined and craggy, but not nearly as wrinkled as Geneva's. Yet, in some ways, they looked alike. Maybe it was the eyes. Both of them had dark brown irises, almost black.

Bardulf placed his hands on my shoulders and pressed me towards the ground. I couldn't help but tremble in fear, knowing what he was about to force me to do.

Every one of us was born with the wolf deep in our spirits. It was innate—nothing that we could control. During every wolfbirth ceremony, the alpha would reach within himself and, using his own wolf's power, call the pup's wolf forward. As Darby had discovered the day the bullies had attacked me, you didn't simply refuse a command from an alpha.

24

The ceremony I was about to undergo was a right of passage into adulthood. It was terrifying and exhilarating and painful.

And it was happening. Now.

I squeezed my eyes tightly closed, my breathing shallow as I felt Bardulf's large hands on my shoulders, holding me steady.

Frantically, I scanned my body, wondering what I was about to experience. What would it feel like? How would I know it had happened the right way?

All the worries that I'd tried so hard to ignore for the last few weeks came spilling out of me, almost making me vomit on the floor. A cold sweat broke out across my forehead.

And then, as though there were another presence inside of me, I heard Bardulf's deep voice calling to me. There weren't any words, precisely, but I knew without a shadow of a doubt that it was my time to join him. My body convulsed as a ripping sensation tore down my chest. I brought my hands up, wanting to squeeze myself back together, like I could somehow press my very soul back into my ribcage.

My spine contorted and I fell to the ground, unable to control my arms or legs.

I face-planted in the dirt, screaming in agony as my entire body twisted, wringing my soul out like a dishrag. That part was expected, though still unwelcome. What I *didn't* expect was to rise on four powerful, lean legs. A scream burst from my throat, but it wasn't a human sound that filled the hall. It was a hair-raising howl.

As the sound rose and fell, I became aware of all the other voices of my pack. I could feel their presences, bound to me now that I was wolf as well as woman. Something buried deep inside me sighed in satisfaction. It felt *good* to belong. I'd never felt anything like it in my life, even under Geneva's occasionally maternal care.

This, I realized. *This is what I'm meant to be. I will never be alone again…*

The bullies who had tormented me for so long were looking decidedly surprised. Maybe they were disappointed I'd been able to shift? No doubt they'd hoped for a more exciting show than I'd given them.

I glanced down. How odd it was to see myself standing on four feet. I'd thought the shift from only having two legs would be uncomfortable, but it felt as natural as breathing. I shook my body, feeling every muscle tense and relax under my skin and fur.

"Ember," Bardulf called to me, using his human voice. "Ember, come back."

A thread of panic shot through me. *What? How am I supposed to do that? I don't even know how!*

Yet, the command in Bardulf's voice was unmistakable. As a wolf, I felt my legs start to buckle beneath his dominance.

As I'd transformed from my human form to the wolf, I'd felt like everything was expanding inside me. Expanding to the point of exploding. Now, as I fought to obey his demand, I imagined pulling myself inward. It felt like I was trying to shrink my soul back into the boundaries of my human body.

It didn't work. I could feel my heart racing with the strain.

There was a slightly derisive snicker and I barred my teeth in the direction of one of my tormenters. *I'd make him pay!*

"Ember," Bardulf said again, his voice more insistent. "*Come back.*"

At his words, I sucked in a huge breath and collapsed onto the ground before him. I'd managed to turn myself back into a human, but I was panting and sweating from the effort. It was almost as painful to transform back as it had been to shift in the first place.

Shaking, I pushed myself to a sitting position and found Geneva's eyes. She gave me a knowing look, seemingly pleased.

A moment later, Darby was next to me, helping me into a sitting position.

"Ember!" Her voice dropped to a whisper with the crowd watching us. "Your wolf! There's something... *different*... about it—"

Of course there is, I thought, resigned. *Why am I not surprised?*

"What's wrong with her?" I asked, dreading the answer.

"She's half dark grey and half white!" Darby continued excitedly, oblivious to my less than enthusiastic response. "It's like your hair, kind of. I've never seen anything like it!"

Now that I'd recovered somewhat, I scanned the crowd that had come to watch my ceremony.

They were looking at me, most with their eyebrows drawn together in surprise. There were looks of open hostility on some faces.

I tried to shrug it off. It wasn't like I had any control over my wolf's color.

A flash of pain burned across my chest as I moved my shoulders. I yelped, putting my hand over the puckered scar that had suddenly appeared on my breastbone.

No! A mark? I have a fatemark? Oh, shit...

I glanced down and sure enough, a dark red symbol had etched itself over my heart. The objective side of me was curious—or maybe I was just in shock. The new scar was roughly triangular, but with each side extending beyond the triangle's corners, ending in a stylized curl.

I blinked. This had always been a possibility, but not one I'd taken very seriously. Some people developed a fatemark at the time of their wolfbirth, a sign that their fated mate was out there, somewhere, waiting for them with an identical mark.

I'd seen several marks over the course of my life. For whatever reason, some people manifested a mark and it would take them years, if not decades to discover their soul mate... if they ever found them at all.

Darby gasped as I moved my hand away from the aching scar.

"It's a fatemark!" she all but shouted.

I winced.

There was absolute silence for the space of a handful of heartbeats. Then voices broke out, much louder than the muttering from earlier. My hand clapped protectively over the mark again, trying to hide it even though it was too late.

Bardulf moved to stand in front of me.

"Show me," he commanded in a soft voice.

I wanted to disobey, suddenly and irrationally convinced that letting him see would lead to disaster. I couldn't resist his command, though.

As I lowered my hand, Bardulf's eyes widened. His mouth fell open, and a choked noise came out. It sounded a bit like he was being strangled.

"A triskelion? *That's* your mark?" he demanded, his eyes boring holes into me as I cast my gaze submissively downward.

I lifted one shoulder and let it fall, confused.

Of course it was my mark. It wasn't exactly the kind of thing you could fake, right? It was just suddenly *there*. He'd seen it happen. Why would he start interrogating me like this, when I was huddled naked and shaking at his feet?

He stepped closer and reached down, his fingertip brushing the tender skin. Maybe he actually thought I'd faked it after all. I didn't pull away, determined to show him that I was not a cowering runt. Yet the touch on my bare skin unnerved me. I shivered involuntarily and he pulled his hand back.

"This cannot be," he muttered.

He turned towards Cai abruptly. Cai stared past his father, his burning gaze fixed on my chest... his face expressionless.

Slowly, his hands rose to his shirt, unbuttoning the top of the garment. His amber eyes never left me. As my gaze trailed down his beautiful, smooth skin, I realized in a sudden rush why Bardulf had suddenly started acting like I'd sprouted a second head.

A triangular fatemark identical to mine sat over Cai's heart, etched into his skin.

THREE

THIS WAS obviously a bad joke. And yet, the evidence was right before my eyes. I was staring at Cai's exposed chest, the twin of my mark visible between the edges of his shirt. We were… fated to be mates? How could that possibly be?

The wolf inside me, newly freed, was wild with excitement. I could feel her instinct to leap about, letting her uncomplicated joy spill out into movement. That part of me wanted to race to Cai's side, but my legs and arms were still weak and shaking from my first transformation. I couldn't even muster a smile in response to that upwelling of wolfish glee as I crouched on the ground, looking up at the alpha's son for some kind of reassurance… for answers. The sweat of my recent exertion ran down my sides in chilly rivulets.

Cai stared into my beseeching face for a long moment, his expression conflicted. He took a tentative step towards me, as though unaware of the movement. He raised one hand, only to pause when he realized what he was doing. He looked at me like I was some kind of dangerous temptation, his breath coming fast and hard. Then, he clenched his fist and dropped his hand to his side.

A thrill of horrible dread flashed through me. My breath caught.

"I reject the bond," he said hoarsely.

The words held no meaning to my overwhelmed mind. I stared with utter incomprehension at Cai's pale face, his square shoulders. Now that I fully recognized him as my mate, I could feel the emotional war inside of him. His thoughts were roiling. I could *sense* his conflict as though it were my own. The wolf inside me cocked her head to one side, confused by his reaction. But the human part of me knew. I felt myself wilting as reality returned. The alpha's son could never be my mate. I was an outcast. A freak.

I wasn't good enough in his eyes.

Bardulf's face was impassive, though I could read the relief in his body language. He could never have allowed such a mating to go unchallenged—but if Cai had fought him over me, it might have torn the pack apart at the seams.

Little danger of that, it appeared. I tried to be relieved as well, reminding myself that I'd vowed not to mate any of the assholes in this pack after the way I'd been treated growing up.

The logic rang true, yet the wolf inside me refused to be tamed by this knowledge. I could still feel her desperate need to be close to Cai. To rush to her mate.

The alpha straightened, addressing the murmuring onlookers.

"Let all here bear witness. This bond"— Bardulf gestured between myself and Cai—"is tainted. I order the marks removed at once to put an end to this unfortunate mistake of nature."

My wolf snarled, her anger curling my upper lip in defiance of the alpha command. As far as she was concerned, this wasn't putting things right. This was an assault to nature itself. I knew the politics of the pack would never allow Cai to be paired with me, but my wolf was enraged by the interference. Around us, the wind rose as though echoing my stormy mood. My eyes found Geneva. She looked thoughtful as she gazed back at me, but she didn't rise or draw breath to speak.

At a sharp word from Bardulf, Cai's two friends who had come to my rescue the day before stepped towards me. Their expressions, too, were conflicted.

While it wasn't unheard of to reject one's mate and have the fatemarks burned away, it was not a common practice. In general, the pack held the spiritual connection between mates as a nearly holy bond. Apparently that didn't hold true for pack misfits, though.

As soon as Jace and Finn stepped toward me, Darby, who had been crouched motionless by my side in shock, jumped to her feet.

"Don't you touch her!" she snarled at the far more dominant males. "Stay the hell away!"

Dimly, through the growing distress clouding my mind and making everything around me feel hazy, I was surprised by her boldness. My sweet, timid friend was standing protectively over me, her hands balled into fists as though she might take a swing at the first shifter to lay a hand on me.

Darby hadn't gone through her wolfbirth yet. The two males approaching me vastly outranked her in the pack hierarchy. Yesterday must've had a bigger impact on her than I thought, I mused in a dazed, distant sort of way.

The pair of males glanced at each other, just as surprised as I was, and then turned towards Bardulf for guidance.

"You do *not* get to touch her!" Darby shouted, not backing down even as tears streamed down her face.

I sighed, feeling a great weariness slide over me. Maybe it was the weight of inevitability, but I felt like I could sleep for a week and still not be fully recovered from this day. My wolf whimpered, begging me to fight for this.

There was no point.

Using the last of my strength, I struggled to my feet, swaying. I grasped Darby's shoulder tightly, grateful beyond words to her for being brave enough to defend me.

"Darby," I murmured in her ear, my eyes never leaving Cai's face. "Don't. It's better this way. It'll be all right."

"No, it won't!" she raged, looking up to meet my eyes. "How will this ever be *all right*? You're Cai's *mate*! You can't let them do this to you!"

I clenched my jaw, willing her to understand without making me say the words.

I'm nothing to them. There's no way they can allow this mating bond to exist. I have to accept this, just like I've accepted every other damned thing in my messed-up life.

I couldn't say any of it aloud. The spectators were all watching the exchange with gleaming eyes, waiting for more drama. Clearly, they hoped to see Jace and Finn tear Darby to shreds for her insolence.

Regardless, this shitshow would fuel the pack gossip for years to come—that much was crystal clear.

Something in my expression seemed to convince Darby to let it go. She lowered her gaze in reluctant acceptance, biting her lip as she stared at her feet. At my urging, she backed away from me as Jace and Finn continued forward, flanking me.

Jace proffered a length of soft cloth. I stared at it for a long moment before accepting what turned out to be a simple robe. Relieved to finally be able to cover myself, I slipped my arms in and pulled the fabric tight around me.

Without a word, Finn jerked his head. I followed them away from the ceremonial hall without protest. They walked on either side of me like bodyguards… or maybe prison guards. I felt trapped, even as the cool wind wafted across my face, smelling of rain.

Around us, the moss dangling from the branches of the trees blew softly in the breeze. The sun peeked through the canopy in fits and starts, lighting random patches of ground. In an area usually shrouded in clouds, any glimpses of the sun felt special. It was comforting, as much as anything could be under the circumstances—as though the weather sensed my despair and was determined to prove that light and life lay beyond my present darkness.

The day had started stormy, I reflected, looking up at the sky. Inside me, my wolf rumbled her discontent and confusion.

I hadn't noticed that my feet had stilled until Jace cleared his throat. I glanced between him and Finn. Their expressions were stony — not angry or aggressive, but definitely full of resolve.

"Are we in a hurry?" I asked quietly, wanting just a bit more time to take in the beauty of our surroundings before what was to come.

They glanced at each other before Finn grunted. "We have orders from the alpha."

"I know," I told him. "I just didn't think he'd given a timeline."

They didn't answer. Jace laid his hand on my shoulder. The grip wasn't rough, but he turned me towards the dirt path and guided me along it. Thoughts of escape flashed through my mind, courtesy of my unhappy wolf, but I knew that it was useless to try. I wouldn't make it a hundred yards before they caught me.

The dirt path was well worn and wide enough that we could walk comfortably abreast, not touching. We wound our way around the base of the mountain, which served as the backdrop for our little town. The natural landscape was sharply different than the harsh cities of the human world, with their angular metal, glass, and polished stone.

Our structures were low and organic, most dug deep into the side of the mountain. We had kept with the tradition of our ancestors, first building dark dens that were no more than holes. As we progressed as a society, however, the dens became more elaborate with bright lanterns, fireplaces, and many rooms along the outer wall, where windows brought in the natural light. Tall, wood pillars framed the doorways.

As space decreased, our kind also started building houses similar to that of men, but few chose to live that lifestyle. It felt too much like a betrayal of our history.

The air smelled fresh and clean. I breathed deeply, never having truly appreciated the soft fragrance until now. How many times had I plodded along this path, my head down and mind occupied with the many injustices of my life? I'd never stopped to take it all in. Was it the wolf inside me that made me more aware? Or was it the approach of the end? Because that's what this was—the end of something nebulous that never even had a proper beginning.

Unaccustomed tears pricked at the back of my eyes, and I studied my feet so that Jace and Finn wouldn't see my emotions welling up. I was holding it together—but barely. I'd tried to tell Darby that this would be for the best, and I repeated the argument to myself.

"It'll be over soon, Ember," Finn said in a soft voice.

My head jerked up, causing the tears to spill over. Finn was looking down at me, obviously uncomfortable.

I had no response. Sure, he was probably right, but my inner wolf whimpered in distress. I longed to let out a piercing howl of misery and isolation on her behalf. We were about to be torn from our mate forever. He'd already chosen, and apparently in his mind, a burning iron brand to the chest was more desirable than I was.

"Where are you taking me?" I asked.

"The smithy," Jace answered in a clipped tone, his pace quickening. He was obviously eager for this journey to be over. I didn't blame him.

I didn't understand how it all worked, but I'm sure with the pack psyche, the two stoic figures walking alongside me were at least peripherally aware of the agony my wolf was feeling.

We rounded a sharp bend and I saw the familiar shop in the midst of a clearing of trees. The blacksmith, Gerard, maintained the shop and offered services to all of the Greystalker pack. He and his extensive family did not live in the hut, but in one of the larger dens nearby. As we came into view, I could see him standing out front, drinking from his cupped hands over a basin of water. Sweat plastered his grey brown hair to his forehead.

The muscles on his right arm stood out more defined than the left, giving him a slightly lopsided appearance.

We walked toward him, my every step more hesitant until I felt Finn press me forward with his hand at the small of my back.

"The alpha has need of your service," Jace explained in a low voice, his eyes intent on the blacksmith's face.

My near-nakedness and the fresh fatemark on my chest must have been a giveaway as to what was going on, because he gave a wordless nod before he turned and walked towards the back of his hut. He walked through a wide door to where his forge stood empty. No fire burned inside it, but he pulled a burning brand from a nearby fire pit, his hand wrapped in a thick, leather glove. The kindling inside the forge burst into flame.

"It'll need to heat up for a bit," Gerard said gruffly, leaning back against a table that stood nearby.

Only then did he allow his curious gaze to play over me. I felt faintly sick, and my hands were trembling. I wrapped my arms around myself, trying to block out the world around me and hide the betraying tremor of fear.

I have to be strong, I thought, squeezing my eyes shut.

But I wasn't strong. I was just me, and this was just another blot on the landscape of my life. I would never escape my position in the pack, and wishing so would just make things more difficult for me.

My wolf rumbled her disagreement, the feeling resonating through my chest.

My head snapped up at the sound of approaching footsteps. I knew who it was without looking. That presence felt like it had a thread running straight to my heart.

Cai.

He looked pale, with dark circles under his eyes. Had those always been there? His jaw was clenched. A muscle at the corner ticced convulsively, but I doubted anyone but me noticed. My eyes followed his every move, hungry for him, longing for him despite myself. I could feel the emotion boiling inside him again, our connection growing stronger by the second.

For a fleeting instant, I got the strangest feeling he might stride forward and stop all of this.

That was a ridiculous thing to think, though. From what I knew about Cai, his sense of duty was stronger than almost anything else. He knew he would be alpha one day. That future could not include me, and the idea that he might refuse his birthright for me was a ludicrous notion.

Bardulf followed Cai around the corner, his face grim. The beefy blacksmith dropped his eyes respectfully, dipping his chin as though he wanted to bow before his alpha.

"Gerard, we require your services as a blacksmith," Bardulf's deep voice rang out. "A fatemark has appeared upon this woman's chest—a twin of my son's mark. He rejects it. They must both be burned away at once."

Gerard blinked and nodded, still not meeting the alpha's gaze. He turned away from the group and grasped a dusty branding tool hanging up behind the table.

He fingered the end of it thoughtfully, before proffering it to Bardulf.

"This has been passed down through my family, father to son," he said. "For years it has been used to remove tainted fatemarks."

Bardulf spared a swift glance at it and nodded.

I got the feeling that he'd have let Gerard use a flaming stick to burn away the marks, if that's what it took. He was obviously desperate to rid himself of this inconvenience.

That's all I was to him — an inconvenience to be dealt with and forgotten. Idly, I wondered if the same branding iron had been used on my mother.

I dropped my chin to my chest and closed my eyes, focusing on the breath rasping in and out of my lungs. My fear was nothing compared to the wretched emptiness I felt in the pit of my stomach. Suddenly, I could feel Cai's eyes on me. I was deeply in tune with him even though I didn't want to be, and my eyes snapped up to his face.

Our gazes locked. All at once, I wanted to run to his side… to fall to my knees in front of him and beg him not to reject me. I wanted to make any promise I could think of to save our bond. He was mine and I was his. Couldn't he sense that? Did I mean nothing to him?

I hated those thoughts. I hated myself for thinking them. My wolf whimpered piteously.

As though he heard my desperate thoughts, Cai turned away, looking at his father instead of at me. Gerard placed the brand in the now-roaring fire. After many long moments, he pulled it out and studied the square tip. It glowed red.

"I will wield it," Bardulf said in a dark voice, taking the handle from the blacksmith.

Gerard surrendered it and stepped back, his face hidden in the dark shadow of the corner. I wondered if he wanted to flee the scene as badly as I did.

Cai pulled open his shirt, revealing the raised scar over his heart. It looked exactly like mine, and I ached to run my fingers along it. I wanted to press my lips to it. My pulse quickened, before anger and disgust at myself snapped me free of the pathetic thought.

"My son," Bardulf said in a somber voice. "Speak your purpose."

"I reject the mark. You, my alpha, will burn its traces from me."

Time slowed to a crawl. I could see Bardulf's lips move, but the roaring in my ears made it impossible to hear what he said. My unblinking gaze locked on Cai. He stared grimly into his father's face, his expression frozen with tension.

I watched dazedly as Bardulf pressed the hot brand to Cai's chest. He did not move or flinch, and it was as though my senses turned back on after being far removed from my body. I could hear the sizzle as the flesh smoldered away. I could smell the burning skin, and it nearly made me retch.

A searing pain erupted in my chest, growing and growing until it felt as though Bardulf were pressing the scorching metal to my skin, rather than his son's. The pain was inside me, too—flowing along our bond. My very soul was on fire.

The wolf inside of me pointed her muzzle to the sky and howled out our agony. The noise rose up my throat and burst free as an unearthly scream, neither human nor animal.

I doubled over, clutching at my chest... and kept screaming.

FOUR

THIS WAS insanity. I could feel myself coming apart at the seams, fighting both physically and spiritually for my mate, Cai, who stood as still as stone, his flesh blistering beneath the heat of the brand. The tightness in his eyes told everyone present that he was in pain, but I could *feel* his pain. I shrieked in agony and felt my control of my human body slip. I crouched down between Jace and Finn, their hands still grasping my shoulders, trying to fling myself forward to defend Cai.

No matter how hard I launched myself off the ground, Cai's two friends were bigger and stronger than me. They slammed me back down to the ground, each time with more force.

"Don't be stupid," Finn hissed in my ear, leaning down so that no one else could catch his words.

Bardulf, always proper and formal, turned away from his son to find another brand to finish the job, eyeing me as Gerard pressed another red-hot tool into his waiting hands.

"You need to develop some self control," he observed, leaning towards me slightly as he adjusted the thick glove on his hand.

I sprang forward again, still half wolf, half crazed woman, and my teeth snapped an inch from his face. Bardulf's dark expression would have turned me to mush if I hadn't been wild with desperation, trying desperately to reach Cai.

A blow impacted my cheekbone—the simple cuff by the pack's alpha causing me to spin away from Jace and Finn beneath its force. I landed on the dirt floor, flat on my stomach. A quiet, indrawn breath reached my ears. *It had been Cai.* He'd reacted when his father hit me.

I panted against the pain coming from both within and without, inhaling dirt in my mouth and nose. Spitting out blood, I felt my teeth with my tongue. Nothing seemed to be broken.

Well, that was *one* good thing I had going for me today, I supposed. At least I wouldn't have to learn to hunt with only half my damned teeth still attached.

I clambered around, struggling to rise to my feet. My legs were still mostly in wolf form, not meant to stretch as tall and straight as an upright human. I wanted to get control of myself, but my emotions were seesawing wildly and my head spun from the recent blow.

Bardulf stared at me coldly, his voice steady. *"Be still."*

It was an alpha bark, and I felt myself freeze, obeying against my will. Everything inside me was screaming in agony. I was terrified and enraged. My breath hissed out of my teeth, flecks of blood spraying down my naked chest.

"I thought I told you to hold her," Bardulf said, his gaze pinning Jace and Finn.

Immediately I felt two pairs of strong hands gripping me tightly. Each of them had one hand above and one hand below my elbows. I knew I could kick and fight and they'd simply hold me away from everything, even the ground if they had to do so.

I turned my burning, hate-filled eyes to Bardulf, wishing I could sink my teeth into his throat, rip it away with one smooth motion. My wolf had taken control, and she loathed him for destroying our one chance at a happy life.

I'd never done anything wrong, and he'd treated me like trash in the road, ever since I was a child. I knew I had never really been a part of the pack. It was just a delusion to think that I'd ever had a place here.

When the hot brand met my skin, I didn't scream—determined not to give him the satisfaction. But I did kick wildly, my body finally turning all the way back to human beneath the searing agony.

As soon as it was done, my captors let go of my arms at a nod from Bardulf. I was shaking so badly that I immediately collapsed to the ground again, one hand hovering over the wound bubbling on my chest. It was pain like I had never felt, but I clenched my teeth and remained silent.

To distract myself from the searing burn of it, I searched deep in my heart and mind. The bond with Cai was still there—I was sure of it. It was tattered, almost completely shredded, but it was there. I could feel the pull of his mind and my wolf longed to rush to his side, even after all of this.

I said nothing. I didn't want them to know that it hadn't worked. For one thing, who knew what they'd do next to try and break it? The thought made me shudder.

My wolf had other ideas, though we were in accord when it came to protecting this secret. I could feel her hope that the bond might re-grow somehow... that our mate might realize he'd made a mistake and magically decide to accept us. I stared at the dirt floor in front of me, shivering.

"My son," Bardulf's strong voice called.

I looked up quickly to discover that Cai had backed away from me while Bardulf burned out my fatemark. He was as pale as I was, and his deep amber eyes were sparkling with a strange light. He stared at me and I didn't look away, my wolf hoping against hope.

I knew better.

"Cai," Bardulf called again, breaking into the moment.

"Yes, Alpha?" he replied, his voice even despite how pale and sick he looked.

"What do you want to do with her now that the tainted mark has been removed?"

Something flickered deep inside Cai's eyes. Through the connection that still existed between us, I could sense the flow of his thoughts. It was extremely confusing for me, as I was so full of my own terrible emotions. Yet, I could clearly sense that Cai was conflicted, angry, and in pain. A surge of strong, protective feelings filled him, and for a moment, Geneva's face flashed into both of our minds. He shook his head, obviously trying to clear the mental images.

"Exile her from the pack," he said in an absolutely flat tone. "I never want to see her again."

I blinked, not certain I'd heard correctly. Surely, he couldn't mean to exile me. Exile was for criminals in the pack. Criminals... like my mother.

My stomach churned.

Banishment from the packlands was a vanishingly rare sentence. Despite our wild ways, shifters had always been able to co-exist more functionally than our human counterparts. Normally, punishments were meted out *within* the pack. Only a few people had managed to put themselves into such poor graces with the alpha that they'd been forced completely out of the Greystalker lands. Of those who had, no one knew or cared if they'd lived or died afterward.

But I... hadn't done anything wrong. What possible crime could I have committed that would justify this response? *All I'd done was shift and gain a fatemark!* My internal voice was rising in hysterics. Frustrated tears of pain and confusion burned behind my eyes.

I looked desperately into Cai's face, yet he refused to meet my gaze. Without a word, he turned and stalked away from the smithy, disappearing into the trees.

Bardulf hesitated. He was quite clearly relieved that the mark had been burned away, yet it was obvious he thought Cai was going a bit too far.

After a moment, though, he turned towards Jace and Finn, barking out the order. "You heard my son. Take her to the holding den. She will be exiled tomorrow."

So that was it. My life in the pack was over, worth no more to this great alpha than a shrug of his shoulders as he indulged his son's whim. Anger burned inside me, and I found myself growling, even though I was still in my human form. My inner wolf was baring her teeth and clawing for freedom.

Jace and Finn gripped my arms tightly this time as they marched me away from Gerard's smithy. I was a prisoner, soon to be exiled. They had no room in their loyal hearts for pity or mercy, and I wasn't stupid enough to ask it of them.

The holding dens that served as a jail for the pack's few troublemakers stood far away from the rest of the town, nestled in a dense bunch of trees that almost entirely blocked out the light.

Jace and Finn walked me inside, where they were met by a shifter on guard duty. At his direction, they led me into the depths of the damp subterranean structure. I could hear the guard following us, practically vibrating with curiosity. Without a word of explanation, I was placed in a dark cell, dirt walls all around me. There was a wooden bench in the corner that smelled of urine. I wrinkled my nose and crossed my arms, but I couldn't stop the beseeching look on my face as my two captors backed away.

"Why?" I croaked.

Neither answered, but it was clear that they were unhappy with what was happening.

"Just answer me!" I pleaded. "I'm nothing to you! Please, just *tell me why.*"

Jace shook his head and turned away. The guard waylaid him, and they moved out of hearing range, speaking in soft tones that I couldn't make out.

"Finn," I tried, raising my sad, tear-streaked face to his.

He chewed on his lip, looking horribly uncomfortable.

"You don't understand," he finally said. "It's complicated."

I waited a minute but he didn't continue.

"What don't I understand?" I demanded.

Finn seemed to hesitate, as though choosing his words with care. "Cai has always been drawn to you. Always. I don't believe he really wanted this, but you can't be his and he can't be yours."

And, it was just that simple, wasn't it? I nodded darkly in understanding, already painfully aware of the difference in social position between the two of us.

"It would be too much for him to see you every day," Finn insisted. "But… maybe this is for your own good, as well as his?"

The feeble question wasn't even worth answering, so I turned towards the wall, studying the cracks that he grown through the dirt foundation. I stepped closer, wondering just how many people had fantasized about escape through one of these cracks.

Despite the sickening smell, I sat on the edge of the bench, feeling the rank dampness of the wood against my still naked legs. I wrapped my arms more tightly around myself as the chill crept deep into my bones. I knew that it was no use to beg for mercy or a second chance.

My thoughts drifted to Darby. She had wanted to leave the pack. I'd been afraid to. I snorted derisively. That was irony for you—I was getting what she wanted most in life. A chance to leave.

Of course, *she'd* wanted a fresh start somewhere else with a new pack. It was an open question whether that option would be available to me. It had been a long time since I'd studied the packlands in school. I'd never dreamed that I would be separated from the Greystalker clan. Not... *permanently*. Not like this.

Whenever I'd snuck off, it had been to the human towns—my curiosity about their strange ways and seeming freedom drawing me to risk the ire of a pack that already hated me. Contact with humans was discouraged. Allowing humans to learn about the supernatural world was *forbidden*, on pain of death. And that was one line I'd never even come close to crossing.

Could I flee to the human world, rather than to some other pack that might treat me just as badly as this one had? An exiled wolf would not be welcome anywhere, and even between far-flung packs, gossip traveled.

I stared unseeingly at the wall as my thoughts drifted further and further. The hours melded into one long, shapeless stretch, but it felt like it had been a very long time when a low burn of discomfort in my chest shook me out of my trance.

Cai! My wolf whined in distress, and I jumped to my feet.

Something was wrong. I could feel pain along our bond. Instinct pressed me to go to him, the wolf heedless of the torture he'd already subjected us to.

Pulled along for the ride behind her emotions, I walked to the door of my cell and rattled the bars. They were made of heavy iron, no doubt the work of Gerard.

"Hey! You can't keep me here," I yelled. "I'm not a criminal! Let me out!"

My words fell on deaf ears, as I'd known they would. It was so frustrating to be locked up for the simple sin of existing, because that was sure as hell what this felt like to me.

If they wanted me gone so badly, they shouldn't have locked me up in this cell, I thought. The irony really was too much for me, and I started laughing. My giggles began to turn hysterical and I wondered if I was losing my mind. Could a person go crazy from having their fatemark burned away?

Right on cue, I could feel the ghost of the pain flare again, deep in my chest. I looked down and studied the blistering, raw skin. Maybe it was just residual pain from the burn? Then pain started flashing across other areas of my body — first on my shoulders, moving up towards my neck.

Heat pooled in my stomach, causing me to break out in a sweat despite the dampness of the cellar jail. My heart rate quickened, and it was a long moment before I realized what was happening to me.

52

Desire.

That strange heat in my belly was sexual desire.

But... that was ridiculous. I'd just experienced a major psychological trauma, being wrenched away from and rejected by my mate, then thrown in jail for no reason, and facing banishment from the pack. How could I possibly be turned on right now?

I shook my head sharply, trying to clear it. I wasn't turned on. There was no way I could be—as sad, miserable, and scared as I was feeling in that moment. Cai could have been standing naked in front of me, pleasuring himself, and I doubted I'd be able to muster any great enthusiasm under the circumstances.

Yet the aching, tingling sensation was growing, filling my body. There were parts of me that throbbed more insistently, and slick heat formed between my legs.

What was happening to me? Would Cai be able to feel this? Would he know?

I froze.

I couldn't have said how long I stood there, my mouth open in horror as realization dawned on me. I still didn't understand how, but just as I had known Cai was in pain earlier, I knew now that Cai was mating.

Mating *someone else*.

Someone... who was *not me*.

In that instant, my mind fractured—separating the analytical part of me from the emotional one... the part of me that contained the wolf. The wolf's emotions were whirling and collapsing, her pain and rage so overwhelming that I couldn't stand it. I had to escape.

But I couldn't escape. She was me. I was her. We were the same.

I clung to human reason, trying to remain calm in the face of her madness. What I was feeling proved that the severing of the bond hadn't been successful. Not entirely, anyway. I glanced down at the wound over my heart. I couldn't tell if there was any trace of the mark, which had formed a similar whirl in the fur of my wolf's coat.

Maybe there were little pieces of skin left, I thought, trying to see through the darkness, which was only broken by a single, flickering torch on the wall beyond the bars.

I fought to ignore the burning ache between my legs, the soft sensations of pleasure that was rising in me, a counterpoint to the wolf's fury. But it *wasn't* in me, I reminded myself, over and over. Cai was the one experiencing pleasure, not me.

The wolf needed to accept this terrible, horrific fact. Otherwise I was afraid I'd be stuck here, frozen in place forever as the two halves of me fought each other. Yet, I could feel the raw, animal emotions inside me overflowing, taking over my human rationality.

He's destroying the last of our bond, I realized numbly. I gritted my teeth at my body's weakness in the face of this last and final insult. The wolf inside of me growled, snarling and cowering as if I had struck her physically by even *thinking* the words.

When Cai's climax rocked my body, leaving me kneeling in the middle of the floor and panting as if I'd just run several miles, the sense of pain and betrayal took over. My wolf form was nearly hysterical. Biting at herself and running in circles from the agony of it. I was enraged on her behalf, and, to my own disgust, also deeply jealous.

He cheated on us, I thought. Tears welled in my eyes as my emotions synced with the wolf's. *He's our mate, and he cheated.*

I shook my head, trying to clear it. He must have been trying to burn out the remnants of the bond. Why else would he *do* something like this? You didn't *cheat* on your *mate*. You just… *didn't*.

It was pack taboo. Bad things happened if you broke that taboo — I had more cause than most to know that. After all, I was the product of cheating, and I knew bitterly well what it was like to be at the bottom of the pack. My very presence was a curse… a physical representation of that terrible act between bonded mates.

My mother had been with her mate for years — but as sometimes happened when one partner or the other was infertile, they had been pupless.

I had no idea what prompted my mother to break her sacred vow of fidelity to her mate. But, as the story was told, he'd sensed her betrayal through their bond, and it had sent him mad. When he found out later that my mother was pregnant with me, he'd left our village and climbed the mountain alone. That night, he threw himself from a precipice. Pack members found his body the next day, shattered and broken on the rocks below.

Because of her part in his death, my mother had been exiled as soon as I was considered old enough to fend for myself—at the ripe old age of ten years. The pack elders removed me from her care, and the alpha cast her out.

Like mother, like daughter.

When it became clear that the pack wasn't going to lift a finger to help me, Geneva had stepped in to make sure I at least had food and a roof over my head. But she wasn't family. She'd always been eccentric and hard to pin down. Despite living with her for almost sixteen years, I still felt like I barely knew her.

I wondered if she'd miss me when I was gone.

The wolf howled her outrage, still circling restlessly inside of me.

This pain is what my mother's mate experienced, I realized. *Only his was even worse, because they'd been bonded for years.*

I'd never given much thought to him, growing up. He wasn't my father—just an unknown, faceless figure. Now I felt my heart go out to him, my punishment coming full circle, yet again. My mother broke her bond... so my mate broke ours, rather than be saddled with the bastard offspring of a pariah.

My evil thoughts swam in tighter and tighter spirals as tears streamed silently down my face. Unable to stand it anymore, I wrapped my arms around my naked torso and collapsed into angry sobbing.

FIVE

I SIGHED, staring at the depressingly small stack of paper money being pressed into my hand. I'd hoped for nearly double that amount. Triple would have been nice.

"Is that all?" I grumbled to Frank, the slimy owner of the run-down home for old and mentally ill humans.

He grunted at me, which was his usual response for nearly everything. Closing my fingers over my pathetic pay, I left his cramped office with its old, mismatched furniture covering almost every available inch of the floor. I'd often wondered if he had so much junk in his office to hide the suspicious stains soaked into the carpet.

I wrinkled my nose more out of habit than actual distress as I passed into the common area of the house. There were twelve residents, all with blank, pale faces. The smell of highly processed food crept out of the kitchen, despite my best efforts to keep the area clean and sanitary.

Having been literally raised among wolves, the average human would doubtless assume that I'd be a slob. The reality was quite the opposite. Humans really were disgusting, and the burning smell of the bleach and cleaning products at least helped to mask the odor of stale urine that seemed to permeate everything in this building.

It was after eight o'clock in the evening, with the residents' dinner and cleanup already completed. Everyone was settled in front of the television, ready for the night crew to come on duty.

I yawned widely, eager to get home.

Home. It was hard for me to think the word when there was nothing homelike about my run-down studio apartment in the slums of Rockville. Not for the first time, I shook my head and marveled at how I'd ended up here at all. The last six months sometimes felt like one long blur.

The morning after I'd been exiled, I woke up in the dark, underground cell. Bardulf had crouched awkwardly as he thumped down the stairs towards me, so tall that his head would have smacked the ceiling had he stretched to his full height.

I'd had a different guard that morning—one who'd never spoken to me once, or even bothered to check on me and see if I was still alive. Despite my frustrated yelling, he'd ignored me, until I'd eventually been forced to relieve myself in the corner of the cell.

Now, however, he tagged along at the alpha's heels with a sycophantic expression on his face. At a swift word from Bardulf, he'd released me from my cell.

Bardulf's face was grim. He held a dark cloth bag in his hands.

"Your belongings," he said in a gruff voice, thrusting them at me.

Freezing cold after my night in the cell, I opened the brown sack with numb fingers and pulled out boots, socks, underwear, one of my old shirts, and a long pair of hiking pants.

Bardulf looked disgusted as he eyed my attire. The clothing had been purchased in a human secondhand store after I'd spent the day panhandling for money in the city. It was clear enough he'd realized that, and didn't approve.

I followed him up the steps, out of the holding den, and into the bright sunshine. It was another unusually nice day, but my soul felt like it was muffled in fog.

As I stumbled through the door, I caught sight of Geneva and Darby standing silently outside. Darby's father stood a few steps removed, watching. They were the only ones who'd come to say goodbye, it seemed. Geneva's face was grave — almost calculating — as she appraised me.

"Survive," she murmured, touching my elbow as I passed her. "Make sure you survive."

I looked at her, wishing somewhere deep inside for a more affectionate parting. She was the closest thing to a real mother I'd ever known, and the best advice she could give me was to survive?

I shook my head in disgust.

Darby, however, had tears streaming down her face. She threw her arms around my neck, her face buried in the black side of my hair. "I tried to sneak away so I could join you," she choked out between sobs. "But my parents caught me packing to leave. I'm *so sorry*, Ember! None of this should have happened!"

Knowing well her desire to leave the Greystalker lands and start her life over, I clutched her tight. "I'm sorry, too. Find me when you can," I whispered against her ear.

I let her go reluctantly as Bardulf, now in the form of his wolf, let out an impatient growl. In this guise, he was a giant, black beast with a graying muzzle. He herded me away from the only two people I'd ever called friends—a low rumble of warning in his throat as he drove me relentlessly south, out of the Greystalker lands. I remained in my human form the entire time, my bag of possessions slung over my shoulders.

When we reached the border of the pack's territory, Bardulf slowed. This wasn't the farthest from home I had ever traveled, by any means, but I knew this time there would be no coming back. All those times that I had snuck away, getting tattoos, dyeing my hair—it seemed like a lifetime ago. What I'd thought of as a grand adventure had been nothing more than childish rebellion.

Bardulf bared his teeth at me in a fierce snarl. I left him behind without a word, wandering through the dense forest until I found the road that would take me south, towards the human city of Seattle.

Afterward, I hitchhiked my way farther south, passing by the large, bustling city. The man I was riding with chatted idly, telling me about how all the tourists insisted on visiting a building he'd called the Space Needle, while he'd never actually been inside despite being a native.

I glanced at him surreptitiously—taking in his long, dirty blond hair and the soft fuzz of beard around his jaw line. I knew I wasn't doing a very good job of keeping up my side of the conversation.

"You seem kind of lost," he observed in a soft voice.

I'd only been able to shrug, not sure what to say to this human.

When I didn't answer, he nodded sagely and continued, "Eh. Don't take things too hard, okay? Life can be like that sometimes. You just gotta roll a fresh joint and go with the flow. Speaking of which, do you care if I smoke?"

Smoke? I blinked in confusion, but then comprehension dawned.

"Oh. No. Go right ahead," I replied. I'd forgotten that some humans liked to wreath themselves in the sweet smelling smoke that dulled their senses and made them sleep, while others liked the sharp-smelling smoke that made them jittery.

As long as it didn't make him crash the car, it didn't bother me. Besides, the man seemed to be in a good enough mood to start with. He continued to talk during the entire drive, though I never really answered beyond vague noises of agreement. Apparently, he didn't need any reciprocation from me to keep up his steady flow of words.

He dropped me in a smaller city about an hour and a half south of Seattle. I wasn't sure why I decided to stop there, rather than continuing on. The city seemed good enough, I suppose. What was the point of going any farther?

I wandered the streets, listening to humans talking to one another. This had always been how

I'd gathered information—trying to take in as much of my surroundings as possible, so I'd know what I needed to survive.

It wasn't a long list.

Shelter.

Food and water.

I could get all of those things easily enough as a wolf—but it would be risky spending time in my wolf form when I was still so near to the places where shifters lived. I didn't *think* they'd go out of their way to hunt me down, just because I'd been cast out of my pack. It wasn't a sure thing, though—lone wolves were vulnerable, and anyone caught shifting where humans might see would definitely be a target for pack retribution. All in all, it was best if I spent most of my time human.

Once I'd seen the lie of the land, I spoke with a few people until someone finally pointed me in the direction of a homeless shelter.

Part of me wanted to roll my eyes at the very idea. Finding a den wouldn't be hard, even in a place like this. But I stopped myself. In reality, I was an outcast now. I did not, in fact, have a home. I needed to leave that kind of pack-based shifter mentality behind me.

Once I found the shelter—having scraped together a few dollars begged from strangers along the way—I walked up to the front desk, nervously clutching the straps of my bag.

Swallowing my pride, I told the pretty young woman with blonde hair and a pert nose that I needed a place to stay. She'd taken a long look at me and asked a few pointed questions.

"Is there a chance that someone might come looking for you?" she asked.

Biting my lip, I cast my eyes to the floor. Surely no one would come look for me as long as I didn't start trouble with the humans. That was, after all, the whole point of being banished.

Wasn't it?

A terrible thought occurred to me, clenching my stomach in a frozen grip. Killing me would be a surefire way to completely eliminate the bond between two mates. Cai had wanted me gone. *I never want to see her again*, he'd said. Was there a chance he'd send someone after me to finish the job?

Shit.

"It's possible," I whispered, my voice hoarse—and tugged my neckline down far enough to reveal the top of the ugly burn scar over my heart.

After that, I was redirected to a domestic violence shelter. I didn't challenge the decision. For one thing, it seemed like this place was smaller and quieter—much more to my liking than the noisy shelter where I'd first sought a place to stay.

In the end, I'd stayed at the women's shelter for about three months, slowly building up a stash of clothing and supplies. Some of the human women staying there knew about employers and landlords who would be willing to accept cash, and look the other way regarding my lack of any I.D. or background documentation in their world.

From what I'd seen so far, humans placed an unnecessary emphasis on a strange concept called 'credit history.'

Anyway, that was how I got connected with the seedy nursing home on the outskirts of town. The man who ran the place didn't care if I had three heads, let alone a legal I.D. He just needed someone who could cook large amounts of cheap, low-quality food without burning down the building in the process.

I... sort of met those requirements? After much trial and error, I'd gotten the hang of cooking for the dozen people that called the place home. And while there might have been a bit of smoke in the beginning, nothing had required a visit from the fire department. I'd even managed to mix in some more nutritious options from time to time, when the local food pantry was giving away vegetables.

After saving enough cash, I moved out of the women's shelter and got myself a tiny apartment in a run-down building a couple of miles from the nursing home. Objectively, I could tell that it was in what the humans would call *a bad part of town*, with drug dealers and prostitutes prowling the streets as soon as the sun started to set. Yet I was not afraid.

I probably should have been, but in my heart, I knew that my wolf form could tear the head off anyone who tried to bother me. Of course, actually *doing* that was a terrible plan that would likely lead to discovery by the humans. But that same aura of self-confidence seemed to dissuade problems before they even started.

Human predators didn't like difficult prey.

As it was, my inner wolf was utterly miserable living within the noisy city limits. I had to get out of town every now and then so I could shift, simply to ease the strain on my mind and soul.

That part was bad enough. Even worse, I could sense things through the bond between myself and Cai—mostly intense emotions and strong physical sensations. It seemed like he was spending more and more time miserable and conflicted. His infrequent nights spent with other female wolves burned dully inside me, bringing tears to my eyes in the darkness—but his affairs were always followed by an empty, sick sensation through the bond that was almost worse.

That feeling was grief, I thought. Horrible, pervasive, never-ending grief.

Still, I was learning how to manage it, and I could make it through the day most of the time without problems, which was an improvement. During my weeks at the shelter I'd been prone to crying spells, both from the terrible agony deep in my soul at the cruelty of the world, and the searing pain I occasionally experienced through the bond with Cai.

I couldn't tell if it was fading, or if I was just getting used to it.

A cheerful voice interrupted my thoughts. "Hey, Ember, are you ready to go?"

I flinched in surprise, realizing too late that I'd been staring vacantly through the window while my mind whirled around in the same, familiar circles.

"Sorry, Anna," I said quickly, trying to play it off. "I was zoning out a bit, there. Yes, we can go."

Anna was my only friend in the human world — a tiny, sweet girl a year older than me who had been on her own for a while. She had left the domestic violence shelter a few weeks after I arrived, and she was the one who'd helped me most with finding a job and a place of my own.

"I know a landlord that never asks too many questions," she'd assured me.

We often walked home together when our shifts coincided, striding through the dark streets side by side. I got the impression she appreciated the sense of increased safety that came from traveling together in a pack — even a pack of two.

This night was particularly dark, with the moon hidden behind heavy clouds that threatened rain at any moment. There was also a cold chill in the air, making us clutch our ragged jackets around our shoulders more tightly and hurry quickly towards home. We usually saw pedestrians along the way, but it seemed like no one wanted to venture out in the unseasonably cold weather.

I glanced around warily. Something was off. My wolf could sense it. She paced nervously, her hackles raised and her teeth showing.

As a human, I was only slightly larger than my companion. I knew I appeared gaunt and frail from infrequent meals. Appearances weren't everything, however. Even in this form, I was stronger and faster than the average human, my body able to adapt to the strength of a wolf easily. In this world, I had to be careful not to draw attention to myself by running too fast or lifting something too heavy.

A quiet noise broke into my thoughts and I realized that Anna's teeth were chattering as she walked beside me.

"I don't like this," I finally muttered, quickening my pace. "Something feels off."

"What's wrong?" she asked. I could see the glow from the nearest streetlight reflecting in her wide eyes.

Part of me wanted to tell her the truth. I could almost hear my voice in my mind, explaining my heightened senses, my connection with the earth.

I'm not human. At least, not fully. I'm part wolf and I can feel that something is brewing tonight.

Even by my somewhat crazy standards, I could tell that the words sounded ridiculous. Anna would probably think I was off my meds.

Rather than answer directly, I grabbed her hand, dragging her along behind me.

"Come on," I said tightly. "We need to hurry. It's not safe here."

She stumbled as I increased our speed, and tried to twist her hand free. "Ember—"

Before she could protest further, a dark figure stepped out from an alley just behind us, matching our pace.

"Too late," I breathed. Before I could decide what to do, two others stepped out from a doorway just in front of us.

We came to an abrupt halt. The men closed in around us on both sides of the sidewalk. I glanced around the area, trying to find a way to escape, but one of the men in front of us broke into a harsh laugh and veered into the street. We were boxed in on all sides, trapped against the wall of an abandoned warehouse.

I took a deep breath, tasting the humans' scents on the air. Over the past six months, I'd worked hard to develop my wolf's senses. It seemed to ease her anxiety when I was more vigilant about my surroundings.

The smell was like an assault. All three had recently smoked cigarettes. Their clothes reeked with the foul fragrance of tobacco, strong enough that even Anna would notice it. My nose was much more sensitive than hers, and to me it was almost overpowering.

The one on our left also had the lingering scent of cheap perfume clinging to his skin, along with the musky odor of sex.

Prostitute. I identified, mentally noting that if his base desires were satiated he might be more sluggish in an attack.

The one that had come up behind us had recently vomited. I studied him closely and noticed that his hands were shaking, and he looked at us with an expression of sheer desperation. A trickle of sweat dripped from his hairline despite the chill in the air.

The last man, the one who had laughed at us, was obviously the leader.

"Nice night for a stroll, ladies?" he asked, giving us a cheeky wink. "Now, what would two fine young things like you be doing out so late at night?"

Anna squeaked in fear, pressing herself against my side.

"Going home," I snapped, barely able to keep my wolf's snarl under control. "So… if you'll excuse us, please?"

"Not so fast, pretty girl," The man replied, ignoring my statement. "I want your money. *Now.*"

I planted my feet shoulder-width apart, bending my knees so that I could spring at him in an instant, if I needed to.

"No," I told him, without hesitation.

I lived from paycheck to paycheck, barely able to keep up with my utilities. Too often I had to go hungry when the money ran out early. There was no way that I was handing two weeks' worth of my earnings over to these junkies.

I'd finally recognized the other scent rolling off two of the men, and I knew exactly what they wanted. Heroin.

While the allure of the drug to humans was a mystery to me, I'd learned a thing or two while living in the domestic violence shelter. The man on my right was dope-sick, and I knew he would stop at nothing to make his next score.

As soon as this thought passed through my mind, he pulled out a gun and pointed it straight at my face.

Anna let out a muffled shriek—a choked, breathless noise that told me she was panicking.

"Just give it to them," she begged me, shaking my arm.

"No! This is all I have," I countered, never taking my eyes off the man's hand. I could launch the distance between us faster than the blink of an eye, shifting to my wolf form at the same moment.

Before he could even realize that I had moved, I would tear his arm off with my teeth in one clean bite. Would that be enough to make his friends flee? I bet it would. They were both laughing and enjoying themselves. It was the man with the gun who was desperate.

As I contemplated my options, barely taking one second of time to process all of this, my eyes fell on Anna.

Internally, my wolf gave a brisk, full-body shake. Sanity reasserted itself. I couldn't transform right in front of someone who knew me. I'd be breaking one of the most sacred wolf laws, revealing my secret to a human. The junkies might not be believed—assuming I left them alive. But Anna could never know about my true nature.

If she did… if she told anyone, I'd be risking my entire pack. *Every* pack.

And while I wasn't feeling overly generous towards Bardulf and his kin at the moment, I knew that bringing a horde of angry, paranoid humans down on all of the shifters in the Pacific Northwest was not the ideal solution to my current problem.

"Maybe this will persuade her," the man on my left said, stepping forward suddenly and snatching Anna's arm.

She screamed and tried to pull away, but he wrenched her forward until she was pressed against his body. I could see her standing stiffly, obviously terrified.

A flash of silver caught my eye and before I could move, the man had a knife pressed to Anna's throat.

Anger at the unfairness of life bubbled up inside me, feeling like it had been building for months… for *years*. I was like a volcano, waiting to erupt. My vision turned red at the corners as I took in Anna's petite frame—wide, terrified eyes pleading with me to save her. Her lips pressed hard together, as though she were trying to hold back the whimper of terror that wanted to break free.

I lifted my hands in front of me, reaching toward her. My burning eyes flashed to the man with the gun. He was steadying it, still aimed at my head. His finger trembled on the trigger.

A blast of wind hit my body.

My hair blew wildly around my face, but the wave of pressure didn't stagger me as it did the others.

All three of the men fell beneath the onslaught, landing heavily as the wind blew them several feet down the sidewalk. Anna fell to her knees and pressed herself flat against the ground, covering her head as torrential rain burst free from the heavens.

The rage continued to burn inside me and I took one deliberate, furious step forward. The men were blasted backwards yet again, flying through the air as if the wind itself obeyed my command.

Around me, the screech of folding and tearing metal came from the surrounding buildings, as though the walls were ripping themselves apart. I'd seen similar scenes on the news, after a hurricane hit one of the southern states.

Was this a hurricane? I wondered, in some distant corner of my awareness that wasn't overcome with righteous anger. Was this... *my* hurricane?

SIX

MY SENSES WERE on high alert. Anna's slight form still huddled on the ground next to me, trembling. What was happening? I could see the wind's effects, but it didn't seem to pull on *me*. I might as well have been a tree, with a vast root system holding me fast to the ground as the storm raged around me.

The junkies writhed on the ground as dirt, rocks, and bits of debris peppered them. I could still see the knife in the hand of one of our attackers. Another wave of anger ripped through me at the sight of the weapon he'd intended to use on my friend. An instant later, the ground heaved beneath us, as though in answer to my vengeful thoughts.

My eyes grew wide. I knew that *earth quakes*, as the humans called them, were not unheard of — although I didn't think they were a regular occurrence in this area. I'd certainly never felt one while living with the pack.

The fresh sound of screeching metal assaulted my ears, but I didn't dare take my eyes off of the junkies. They were still being blown around, tossed to and fro on the heaving ground.

Finally, one of them managed to pull himself to his feet using the light pole near the corner. It was the one who'd held the gun on me, though there was no sign of the weapon now.

"Run!" he screamed, his eyes wild. "*Run!* It's the end times!"

His companions needed no further encouragement. They weren't shrieking, but their faces were studies in horror.

Stumbling and staggering across the ever-shifting ground, they all hurried off without another backward glance. The wind and shaking earth showed no signs of abating, and I began to worry that the nearest structures wouldn't be able to withstand much more of this. The taller ones were starting to sway ominously.

"Come on!" I yelled over the din. "We need to get away from the buildings!"

With a tug, I tried to pull Anna up and away from the danger. Unfortunately, it seemed like she'd forgotten how to use her legs, and she sank to the ground with a terrified whimper after only a couple of steps.

I hauled her up with easy shifter strength. In the end, I had to half-drag, half-carry her. We stood in the center of the street, watching the destruction with sick fascination. I took a few deep breaths and felt myself beginning to calm.

At which point, the wind eased, and the shaking ground settled.

Anna's frantic, fearful panting filled the growing stillness instead.

"Wow," I murmured, looking down at her. "That was some storm."

In my peripheral vision, I could see the clouds rolling away. For a half a moment, I was sure I saw something else swirling at the edge of my awareness, as though the clouds themselves were whirling around in a vortex the size of a skyscraper. I blinked, but it was gone the moment I tried to focus on it, leaving me unsure if I'd truly seen anything at all.

Pushing the odd moment from my mind, I focused on Anna again.

"Are you all right?" I asked.

She rose shakily to her feet. Tears ran from her eyes, leaving salty streaks down her face. "All *right*? No! I'm not all right! Ember, we almost *died*!"

I nodded and tried to look sympathetic, even though I was confident that those men could not have overpowered us.

… Probably.

At least… not if I had decided to risk my anonymity and shift form.

We walked the rest of the way home in silence, except for the occasional hitching, stifled sob coming from Anna.

Eventually, she gave a final loud sniffle and turned red-rimmed eyes on me. "That weather. What on earth *was* that? I've never seen anything like it!"

I had no real answer for her.

"Um," I hedged, not at all sure how best to comfort a terrified human. "Climate change, I guess?"

To my surprise, however, it seemed like this was the right answer.

"I guess so," she agreed, shuddering. "My god. I don't know whether to say we got lucky or not."

I shrugged, feeling pretty lucky that I hadn't needed to shift and risk exposure after all. Once I'd walked Anna to her own apartment in our shared building and made sure she was safely locked inside for the night, I jogged to my own door and unlocked it with fumbling fingers.

Maybe I was a bit more affected by what had just happened than I'd thought. Even though the wolf inside me recoiled at spending another second in this cramped, run-down place, I still felt a sense of relief to have the deadbolt locked behind me. At least I could take it easy for a few hours before I had to return to work and face humans again.

Even so, sleep was a long time coming that night.

The following day, some inner voice convinced me to take a different route to work. It only made sense, I told myself. If those junkies were still around, they might be keeping an eye out for me. There was no point in borrowing trouble, after all. Anna and I were on different shifts today, so I headed in alone. The walk to the nursing home was quiet and peaceful.

Later, as I was cleaning up the residents' breakfast dishes, I overheard one of the nurse's aides muttering about *'crazy end times stuff'* under her breath in the other room. I'd learned to disguise my better-than-the-average-human senses, so I wandered in as though I'd simply been bored in the kitchen on my own, drying a plate with the clean dishtowel in my hands.

She was watching the news, with a worried scowl on her face.

"What's going on?" I asked, nodding towards the television when she glanced at me.

"There was some really weird weather last night, not far from here," she said.

"Oh," I replied, not sure what else to say.

She didn't reply, but continued to stare at the screen. On it, a reporter was walking down a very familiar-looking street. The whole area was in shambles, the damage far more striking in the daylight than it had been in the dark. Wow. Had things really been that bad after the storm? Words like 'microburst' and 'significant damage' buzzed at the edges of my brain as the man on the television continued to drone on about it.

After the wind and shaking ground had subsided, I'd mostly been focused on getting Anna home safely — distracted by her obvious emotional distress. I hadn't paid much attention to the buildings around us, once I was confident they weren't likely to fall on our heads.

Thanks to the local news crew, I was getting a good look at them now. I'd seen images from hurricanes on the other side of the country. This looked much the same.

"So, I take it this kind of thing doesn't happen often around here?" I asked, even though I knew the answer. There were no records of a hurricane ever hitting the coast in all of our pack's history. Yet, I still felt the need to ask. To confirm it.

"*Never*," she said with feeling. "That's why it's such big news. Plus, only a block away, everything is untouched. They're saying it didn't even rain outside of that one little area. And there was an earthquake, at almost exactly the same time! Did you feel it?"

I thought back to the heaving ground... the swaying buildings.

Clearing my throat, I said, "Yeah, I might've felt something, I guess."

I was preoccupied for the entire rest of the day. My thoughts swirled in ever tighter circles—memories of the last time the bullies in my pack had decided to teach me a lesson about being a bastard, and the way the wind had howled around me as my desperation rose. It had to be a coincidence, right? What else could it possibly be?

With a deep sense of misgiving, I readied myself to walk the same route home as last night. It was my night to leave early, so Anna would have to find her own way. Hopefully she'd beg someone for a ride, since she'd seemed so shaken and upset by the previous night's events.

But... I had to see the damage for myself. I had to try and figure out what had caused it.

When I was finally able to clock out, my nerves were stretched far more tightly than when I'd realized that the men last night had us surrounded. It made no sense. Why would this possibly be more frightening to me than the prospect of being shot or stabbed?

Unbidden, a memory of Geneva came into my head. It was from just after I'd been beaten up. '*Did anything odd happen while this group was attacking you?*' she'd asked me.

It had almost seemed as though she'd known something about me that I didn't even know myself.

But what could that mean? Did it mean anything at all? I was nothing. Nobody. The bastard offspring of a mate-killer, as far as the pack was concerned. I would never know what Geneva had been thinking that day. The ache of loss that I'd held for so long for her and Darby yawned beneath me like an endless chasm, no less painful now than it had been the first day I'd been cast out.

My feet carried me closer to the spot where Anna and I had been attacked. Abruptly, I found myself entering a crowd of people. They were all milling about, staring at the buildings. Here and there, windows had been blown out—glass strewn in glittering shards across the sidewalk. Parts of the metal roofs were bent back on themselves, which explained the screeching noises I'd heard.

I approached the edge of the crowd, people gathered just on the other side of a ribbon of yellow police tape. The block where Anna and I had been ambushed the night before was completely roped off. There, the damage appeared truly catastrophic. The images I'd seen on the television at work were a cheap impersonation of reality. They'd been nothing in comparison to this. Several buildings were completely destroyed. Only the fact that it was a largely deserted warehouse district would have prevented mass human casualties.

The more I looked around, the more it seemed like there was to see. The road, which had been perfectly smooth the night before, was now buckled and wavy, as though a meteor had landed in the center of the street, with the shock waves expanding in every direction.

I noticed that a light pole was bent in the middle, twisted into a bizarre spiral. What could have caused that? Surely that wasn't done by the wind. Even stranger were the pieces of rough wood jutting out of crumbling walls, like they'd been hammered into place by a giant's mallet. They were clearly pieces of trees, although in such a commercial area the lack of green space was conspicuous. Had the storm pulled up trees from further away and blown them here? Was that even possible, when the news had said that no other areas were damaged?

Shaking my head, I started to back away. I didn't want to see this anymore. It was too much to take in at once. A deep part of my soul—a part untouched by logic and reason—insisted that this was my fault. *You did this*, it whispered. *You caused this destruction.*

But that was impossible. I was just one wolf who'd happened to be caught in the wrong place at the wrong time.

My feeble mental argument did nothing to erode the growing certainty that something irrevocable had happened to me last night. In some ways, it was like my wolfbirth—once the feeling awoke inside me, there was no going back.

I hurried home, glad that I'd decided to take a different route to work that morning. I would never have been able to get through the day if I'd had all of these thoughts whirling around inside my head.

Through the haze of my preoccupation, I felt something prickle at my awareness. The hair on the back of my neck rose. I tried to shake off the odd sensation, attributing it to my shattered nerves. After a minute, though, awareness turned to alarm. I was being followed. I could *feel* it—the whïsper of quiet breath behind me, the soft rustle of clothing.

I whirled around. There was no one to be seen. No human could move with such stealth—I was sure of it. They blundered along, slapping their feet carelessly on the concrete. No, I was certain that the creature following me was something inhuman.

Again, I turned, moving in a slow three-sixty as my eyes raked my surroundings.

This is ridiculous, I thought. *Just because you're spooked about what happened last night, it doesn't mean that someone is following you. There's no one here — they're all busy gawping at a bunch of destroyed buildings.*

The wolf inside me growled, unconvinced by my inner monologue.

Certain that I was being stupid, I darted around the next corner, taking a different street than I normally would. If there was something following me, I sure as sin didn't want to lead it straight to my apartment. My wolf rumbled her agreement.

As soon as I was around the corner, I broke into a dead run and ducked into the first alley I came across. Glancing around in the low light, I climbed a set of concrete steps and backed into a dark doorway recessed into the side of a building. I was confident that I had not been seen, and I wanted a chance to be the observer — the hunter, rather than the prey. I would wait here for a few minutes. If no one walked by, I'd chalk it up to my overactive imagination and go home.

After the events of the previous night, it was almost certainly nothing more than my own paranoia. Because if it wasn't, and someone — or something — really was after me for the second night in a row, I was the unluckiest person in the damned city.

Attempted mugging, earthquake, freak weather incident, and now I was being followed by something that didn't feel human? For fuck's sake — maybe I'd have had better luck staying with a pack after all.

I shook my head in disgust but kept my eyes trained on the street.

At first I could hear nothing, even with my ears straining to pick up the slightest whisper of sound. The longer I stood there, however, the more I became convinced that someone was close on my heels, even now.

How was that possible, though? I'd slipped away so quickly that no one could have seen me. Why did I still feel like I was being watched?

The hair on the back of my neck was standing up. Something was coming for me—I could feel it. Something with immeasurable power. Cold sweat broke out across my skin.

Movement deeper in the alley caught my attention, and I whirled to see a tall figure looming in the darkness. Instinct took over. I snarled and dropped into a crouch, poised to spring at my pursuer. Deep in my soul, I knew this was the creature that had been tracking me all along.

My eyes adjusted to the deeper darkness, taking him in. A breeze whispered through the alley, stirring locks of long, white-blond hair. I caught a familiar scent an instant later, and my wolf froze, entranced. It was intoxicating—full of a richness unlike anything I had ever smelled before, yet it still somehow felt like home.

The animal part of me wanted to run to the man and bury my nose in his neck to get more of that scent, in hopes of understanding what it might mean.

Even with this embarrassing realization, I didn't relax my stance. I knew better than to trust some random creature who smelled like the primeval forest made incarnate, and I certainly wasn't going to let my guard down until I found out why he had been following me.

He stepped further into the light, revealing sharply sculpted, beautiful features. His intense, pale blue eyes were focused on me to the exclusion of all else, as though he could see into my very soul.

My wolf began to pant as my gaze raked over his perfect body—lean and muscular, wrapped in clothing made of buckskin and linen. He stood still as a stone, regarding me in turn.

His head cocked slightly to the side, a look of mild disdain sliding across his features as he took in my appearance. The wolf bristled at his expression, pressing against my control—trying to break free. She wanted to test herself against this male, who both drew her interest and provoked her unbearably. Under her influence, my lips pulled away from my teeth in a silent snarl of challenge.

A smile ticked the corners of his mouth upward, though I got the impression it had very little to do with amusement. "Well now, Little Wolf," he said. "Here we are at last."

SEVEN

SHOCK ROOTED ME to the spot for the briefest of moments. He'd called me *Little Wolf.* How could he have known? It was impossible… unless he, too, was a wolf — then I supposed he could have scented me.

I inhaled experimentally, trying to place the aroma that was making my blood feel too hot in my body. No, there definitely wasn't any wolf scent coming from him.

Something about him smelled so familiar, yet I couldn't figure out why.

I didn't answer him, feeling a surge of energy rising within my wolf-form. She could barely seem to contain herself. How could we simultaneously want to fight him, to tear him to shreds… and also to lick every single inch of his lithe, athletic body? It didn't make sense.

The wolf itched to tackle him to the pavement and pin him there. I had a sneaking suspicion she was being overly optimistic about our chances against him. These thoughts passed through my mind so quickly that it probably seemed like I'd only paused to take a breath.

I opened my mouth and forced some words out.

"Who are you?" I demanded, since that seemed like the most relevant question.

The man let out a low sound of amusement. It sounded like the first thaw of spring after a long winter of doubt. My heart raced, but I remained frozen, unmoving.

"Does my name matter so much to you, Little Wolf?" he countered. "I know who *you* are."

I didn't argue. He'd already sensed that I was no more human than he was. It seemed stupid to deny it.

"Why are you following me?" I tried, bringing the full weight of my wolf's stare down on him. I had no more patience for this.

Apparently, something about my expression convinced him to speak. A wry smile twisted his full lips, and he gave me a faintly ironic half-bow. "Since you insist, my name is Tamlain of the Seelie. I am here to transport you to the fae realm of Elfhame."

I blinked at him, completely thrown. My people told stories of Elfhame and the fae folk to their pups, just as the humans had done with their children for generations. There were so many old tales that it was hard to pick out truth from fiction. These days, many in the younger generations had started to believe that the fae realm was only a myth.

Personally, I hadn't been so sure of that. And it looked like I'd been right, since the preternaturally attractive man standing before me seemed real enough. Something Darby had once said shifted to the forefront of my memory.

They say that people go mad in the fae lands, she'd told me, her face shining with delight in a mystery.

It wasn't unusual for her — Darby had always been fascinated by what she couldn't have.

Why do they go mad? I'd asked her, curious and skeptical in equal measure.

Her eyes had glowed with fascination. *There's too much magic in the faerie realm. It's just too strange — some people can't handle it and they go insane. It's like a sickness.*

I hadn't truly believed it at the time. We'd been two young pups whispering to each other in the branches of our secret tree — the place where we went when we wanted to hide from the rest of the pack. She'd been leaning back against the trunk, staring at the leaves above us as they rustled in the light breeze. It has been a perfect afternoon... one of the few I cherished from my youth.

Of course, at the time I'd scoffed at her. I hadn't known if I believed in Elfhame or not — let alone in the stories of magic and madness. Now, faced with this obviously magical hunter who'd tracked me down in a human city, I had to admit that there appeared to be some merit to the stories.

"I can't go with you," I told him, my gaze still locked with his. I stood poised and cautious in the alley — not immediately ready to spring, but certainly not relaxed either.

"Oh, Little Wolf. I assure you — you can, and you will," he replied.

There was so much certainty in his voice that I found myself bristling, my wolf's hackles rising at his confident tone.

"*Excuse* me," I snapped, "but you don't get to just waltz in here and demand I go somewhere I don't want to go. I've spent a lifetime being yanked around by other people's whims, and I'm done with it. This is *my* life."

I packed as much authority into my tone as I could muster—knowing full well that while my strength was more than enough to deal with a human, that didn't mean I could fight one of the fae folk. Tamlain of the Seelie was a warrior. A hunter. That much was painfully clear.

The fae's expression went stony.

"One life, yes," he said in a hard tone. "A single life, while my entire world hangs in the balance. So, no. Given what is at stake, you do not, in fact, have a choice in this matter."

"What—you're going to kidnap me?" I demanded in disbelief. The wolf inside me rose up, incensed… threatening to escape her bonds.

"Think of it less as an abduction," he said, "and more as the next step toward your destiny."

I blinked at him. "My… what, now?"

"Your *destiny*, Little Wolf. You were always supposed to be in this place, here and now, so that I might transport you to where you need to be."

I chose to ignore this in favor of something that seemed a bit more immediate. "They say people go mad in Elfhame. Even if I believed a word you were saying, it doesn't seem like I'll be much use to destiny if I'm drooling and rocking back and forth in the corner."

"That will not be an issue. Not for you," Tamlain insisted in a cold voice. "Now, come. We must hurry."

"Go to hell," I replied, planting my feet firmly. There was no way I was moving an inch with him.

I ignored the little voice that urged me to throw caution to the wind and follow him. But all this talk of destiny? I was an outcast. What kind of destiny could I possibly have, beyond trudging back and forth to the nursing home, making barely enough money to scrape by in the human world?

Tamlain wasn't a shifter… but he seemed to know about us, the unhelpful little voice whispered. Maybe if I went with him, I would have a chance to transform more often? Maybe in Elfhame, I wouldn't have to worry about other shifters coming for me? Maybe I could just be left alone?

Don't be ridiculous, I chastised myself. *Things don't just work out like that. At least, not for someone like me.*

I studied the man before me, wondering how old he might be. His face and body were youthful enough—well muscled and smooth-skinned. But something behind his blue gaze appeared incredibly old. Weary, even. He looked like he'd seen too much during his life. There was a grimness present in him that made me think his white-blond hair might be hiding some grey.

Tamlain appraised me silently in return. Suddenly, I just wanted to be somewhere else, away from the intense eyes now boring into me. *Anywhere* else.

His blue eyes narrowed. "I will not be going anywhere except back to Elfhame. *With you.* Now, come," he commanded.

My wolf's self-control snapped. Before I could stop it, she exploded into being with a snarl. My clothes ripped as my body twisted, unexpectedly changing form.

My hind legs were still tangled in my torn jeans, which gave me just enough of a pause to regain a hairsbreadth of control. Had I not been effectively hobbled, I probably would've lunged straight for Tamlain's throat.

Instead, I wrested back control from my animal nature long enough to wriggle free of the remains of my human clothing and flee. Scrabbling toward the mouth of the alley, I turned and charged flat out down the street, as fast as my four legs could carry me.

Although she was still angry at the loss of control, my wolf rejoiced at the freedom to run. I was stretching my body in ways that I hadn't in a very, very long time. I could feel the asphalt under the pads of my feet as I pushed myself even faster.

Mouth open, tongue lolling as I panted, I could taste the air. To my relief, there were no humans nearby. No one would see a lone wolf racing through the middle of town. The fact that this was a bad area worked in my favor— most people around here only came out for nefarious purposes this late at night.

There was no way Tamlain would be able to pursue me at this speed. Not on two legs. I was flying, racing for the trees on the edge of town. I was willing to risk spending more time as the wolf to ensure that I got away from Tamlain. With that distinctive scent of his, I was sure I would be able to smell him coming for miles.

As soon as I'd thought it, I became aware of another form coming up fast behind me. Glancing over my shoulder without breaking stride, I saw an eerie white glow. Blinking hard, I let out a growl and squinted back towards my pursuer.

It was another wolf. As the glowing white animal closed the distance between us, loping with an easy grace, I caught a whiff and immediately recognized Tamlain's *primeval forest* scent on the wind.

I almost stumbled, so great was my confusion. Wait, so he was a shifter after all? My wolf pushed the thought away, her instinct to fight rising once more, now that flight was obviously impossible. I was running as hard as I could, my breath coming in rapid pants, even as he drew up to my shoulder, as though this was nothing more than an easy stroll for him.

Maybe my wolf had a point. With a snarl, I lunged sideways, trying to snap my teeth around the scruff of his neck. I was so angry at this point, I would have liked nothing more than to put him on his back with my jaws around his throat. I wanted to see him grovel on his belly, and then shift back to human so I could tell him to crawl back where he belonged and *leave me the fuck alone.*

To my surprise, my teeth closed around thin air with a sharp snap. He'd been *right there.* But the instant I'd moved, he'd leapt away from me as quick as lightning, spinning around and colliding with my shoulder.

I stumbled, but managed to keep my feet underneath me. I ran wide before turning back and leaping at him once more, intent on slamming my full weight into his white flank.

Again, I met nothing. I landed hard and off balance against the pavement, my claws making a terrible scraping noise against the asphalt as I wheeled around, ready to charge again.

To my fury, he was sitting calmly, not even panting as I hurtled forward, my teeth flashing as I opened my mouth wide, trying to grab his leg. He sprang effortlessly straight into the air, while I tumbled over and over across the ground.

I landed on my side, the wind knocked out of me as a mass of white fur and sharp teeth landed on top of me.

I was completely pinned down, despite the frantic scrabbling of my back legs. There was no way I was wriggling free of his incredible strength.

My wolf recognized the defeat an instant before I did. With an instinctive movement, she bared our throat, surrendering to him. With a whimper, our gaze dropped. A moment later, I felt his weight shift off me.

He was in human form again, his pale hair mildly disheveled after our tussle. He was fully clothed, and unlike his hair, the buckskin and linen clothing looked as fresh and clean as it had in the alley. Crouching next to me, he reached out and placed one hand on my furry head.

I had only a second to think disjointedly that it felt kind of nice. Then, a surge of energy passed through my body, and with a twisting wrench, I, too, was back in human form. Unlike him, however, I was lying on the street, covered in bruises from our fight.

"I thought you weren't a wolf," I accused breathlessly.

"I am not," Tamlain answered. "At least, not unless it is convenient to be so."

He seemed entirely indifferent to my plight as I lay battered and humiliated on the ground. At least he was no longer holding me down—small mercies.

At that moment, it occurred to me that I was completely naked, having ripped my way out of my clothes when I shifted. Apparently, I'd already spent too much time among humans, because I felt distinctly uncomfortable as he glanced over my body with a frown.

He reached out again, and I flinched away. At that, he paused, his brow furrowing.

"I have need of you, Little Wolf, it is true—but not for that," he said, and reached his hand toward me more cautiously this time.

I held myself still with an effort. With a complicated gesture over my body, he spoke low words in a language I didn't understand. When I glanced down, my clothing had reformed around me, perfectly clean and undamaged.

"Thank you," I said cautiously.

He gave a single nod of acknowledgement and stood, pulling me to my feet with him. His unexpected kindness surprised me. For as cold as he'd acted, I'd expected him to drag me away naked, even if he didn't intend to actually assault me.

Right now, though, I had more pressing problems.

"If you're not a wolf then how — ?" I began, but he interrupted me.

"I told you. I was a wolf because I needed to be. I am fae. I can change form to suit my needs, but that does not truly make me a wolf or a tiger or an eagle." The words were clipped.

I blinked. "You can become an eagle?"

"This discussion is not relevant to the task at hand," he said sharply, as he raised a hand in front of him. "We are leaving now."

With a slow, deliberate motion and a muttered word in that same strange language, he passed his hand in a circle in front of him. At first it looked like nothing would happen, but then a swirling vortex opened up in midair.

I shuddered in sudden fear. Were all the myths of my people actually true? The elders had told us stories of powerful magicians who could travel between Elfhame and the normal world, kidnapping shifters and taking them away as slaves to a land that might drive them mad. I had always scorned the notion of that kind of magic. Yet, before my eyes stood an impossible portal.

I gaped at it, frozen in place. Without another word, Tamlain gripped my elbow and pulled me into the vortex. The swirling currents surrounding me made my stomach churn. I opened my mouth to cry out in fear, but the sound never reached my ears. The rushing wind sucked it into the void the moment it left my lips.

I clamped my eyes shut, wanting to throw off Tamlain's powerful grip, but terrified that doing so would leave me trapped in this chaos forever. Instead, I clenched my fists tight.

As quickly as it had started, it was over. My feet slammed into unfamiliar soft turf. We were no longer standing on a street in the human city of Rockville.

Terror gripped me, so intense that I didn't dare open my eyes. Instead, I reached out with my other senses, trying to understand my surroundings without truly having to acknowledge what had just happened.

Wind carried the sweet smell of nature to my nostrils. The scent made me want to breathe it in deeply, and I realized that it reminded me of Tamlain.

Carefully, I peeled open one eyelid and glanced around.

Shock rooted me to the spot, and both eyes shot open, taking everything in. I blinked rapidly, but the vision in front of me remained unchanged.

Everything was... *so green*. The Pacific Northwest was a lush area by any measure, with evergreens standing high on the sides of mountains, marching down to the sea.

This made everything I'd seen on Earth seem pale by comparison—a lifeless landscape shrouded in dust. Elfhame was beautiful. Not just beautiful, but *stunning*, in the literal sense of leaving me stunned speechless.

The rich golden light dazzled my eyes, and I found myself squinting, as though I were trying to stare directly into the sun. Everything *glowed*. The smell of flowers was so intense it was making me dizzy.

I turned to find Tamlain standing at my side — watching me watch his world.

The question that I had been about to ask died on my lips as he waved a lazy hand towards the open portal. It snapped shut.

Wonder at my surrounding faded beneath the growing realization that I was now trapped in this strange, disorienting world of Elfhame.

I was Tamlain's prisoner.

EIGHT

DESPITE THE grim realization that I was trapped in the fae realm, the wolf inside me was overcome with delight. The world around me was stunning, painted in colors I had never imagined and with sweet fragrances floating on the wind. I wanted to run, wild and free, until my four legs could no longer carry me. I imagined flopping down in the soft grass and letting the sun warm my pelt. No more cold, dreary Rockville skies.

I shook my head sharply, trying to banish the fantasy. I needed to concentrate. The human in me knew that I was being held as a prisoner, or maybe more like a hostage. I had to keep my wits about me.

"Come," Tamlain said solemnly. "I have a place arranged where you may stay in safety."

He led me towards a tall hill covered in blowing grasses. The shimmering sea of green before us was mesmerizing, and for a moment, all I could do was stare.

"No," I replied, my eyes never leaving the scene in front of me.

I felt him stop and tore my eyes away, taking in his stony expression.

"*No,*" I said again, my voice stronger. "Not until you explain some things. Until you do, I'm not going anywhere with you."

"You don't have much choice, Little Wolf," he reminded me. "Unless you plan on wandering around an unfamiliar realm with no way to return to the other side?"

My gaze drifted towards the sky, which was tinged with colors like the northern lights—if the northern lights happened during daylight and came in every shade of the rainbow at once.

"Maybe I will. It's an interesting place. I wouldn't mind having a look around," I retorted.

Tamlain didn't laugh, exactly, but there was definitely a note of amusement in his tone. "I suppose I shouldn't be surprised. Stubbornness has always been a shifter trait."

"Regardless," I said, tearing my attention away from the mesmerizing play of light in the sky, "I want to know the truth. What did you mean before, about your world hanging in the balance? What does Elfhame have to do with me?"

Tamlain stared at me for a moment, appraising. Then he walked over to a large boulder and sat down.

"Tell me about your control of storms," he shot back, rather than answering the question.

"That's not—" I started to say, but Tamlain held up a hand to stop me.

"No—no deflection. You know of what I speak. Answer the question," he said.

I floundered for a moment, off balance. "There's nothing to say."

He raised an eyebrow. "Nothing? Really? So you've never noticed storms descending when you're upset? And here I thought wolves were supposed to be canny."

I opened my mouth to deny it, and couldn't. To my annoyance, there was a knowing look in Tamlain's crystal-blue eyes. It made me want to snarl at him.

Instead, I shrugged my shoulders. "It's nothing. Just a coincidence. What else could it be? I'm nothing and nobody."

His lips thinned as he stared at me. When I didn't speak, he gestured impatiently. "Then perhaps you can tell me more about these *coincidences*." His tone dripped irony.

I hesitated... but maybe this would be the quickest way to convince him it wasn't the huge deal he seemed to think it was.

"One time when I was being" —I paused, not sure how to explain without sounding like a pathetic runt of the pack—"*annoyed* by a group of shifters, it got a little windy all of the sudden. We were living on the side of a mountain; the weather was unpredictable."

He pinned me with a flat stare. I could tell he knew there was more, and I scowled.

Who *was* this guy? *What* was he? It felt like he'd seen every corner of my life and already knew all the answers I didn't want to give... like he just wanted to hear me say it out loud. I couldn't figure out what any of it meant, and I was growing frustrated with the games.

Why wouldn't he answer any of *my* questions?

"Fine," I snapped. Inside me, the wolf growled low. "I was with a coworker the other day in the human city where you found me. We were attacked by a group of drug addicts. They were looking for money, and they threatened to kill my friend. I was going to transform into a wolf and rip their throats out, but an earthquake and a storm hit at the same time, saving me the trouble. End of story."

He nodded slowly, as if I was confirming all of his suspicions.

"*What?*" I demanded, feeling irrationally defensive.

He didn't answer, but continued to nod as he stared out over the horizon, pursing his lips thoughtfully.

"The other day?" he pressed. "That's oddly non-specific."

"All right, *yesterday*," I admitted reluctantly. "Why are you asking me this? I answered your questions, now you need to answer mine!"

He looked into my angry, determined face and sighed.

"Those were no storms, wolf. They were Earth and Elfhame colliding."

I blinked, in hopes that his matter-of-fact explanation might start making sense if I replayed it in my head a few times.

Nope. No such luck.

"Colliding?" I finally asked. "What does that even mean? They're separate realms, right? Like, different dimensions? It's impossible."

"I assure you, it is not. You were pulling our two worlds together in your anger, and where they touched, it caused damage."

I stared at him, remembering how the wind had blown fiercely, but hadn't seemed to affect me. As though I were somehow a part of it.

"The damage done on Earth yesterday was extensive," Tamlain said in a soft voice. "The damage here in Elfhame was catastrophic."

I watched him for several long moments, waiting for the punchline of the joke. It reminded me of a stupid show I would put on the television for the nursing home residents where humans would play pranks on each other, resulting in varying degrees of humiliation.

He stared back at me, his face impassive.

Finally, I shook my head in negation. "Bullshit."

He cocked his head at me, curious. "You think I'm lying, Little Wolf?"

"I *know* you're lying." I squared my shoulders. "I admit it—I've accepted Elfhame isn't a myth, okay? But the idea that the two worlds in different dimensions can somehow slam into each other, and that *I* was the one who caused it? That's ludicrous."

"Fae cannot lie." The words carried the weight of an unbreakable maxim. "I am fae. Therefore, my words are truthful."

In my pack, the pups were told stories about the magical inhabitants of Elfhame. It was true that the fables insisted fae couldn't lie, but the point was to teach youngsters the value of honesty. Not that it was actually *real*.

"Then you're just mistaken," I replied. "Because listen, Tamlain—like I said, I'm nobody. I don't think you really grasp that. I'm an illegitimate shifter exile living in the human world, working a dead-end job with too much month left at the end of the money. The only reason why I haven't starved to death yet is that I can go into the forest and hunt rabbits for food."

He looked at me without the slightest trace of pity.

"I'm nobody!" I repeated to emphasize my point. "Why would someone like me have that kind of power? The only logical answer is that I couldn't. I *don't*. So, sure. Maybe fae can't lie. But you can obviously be wrong about things, because you are one-hundred percent wrong about *me*."

"Foolish wolf. This power is in your heritage." Tamlain said, his tone growing clipped. "It's in your very blood. Now, I have answered your question, and it is not my concern if the answer is not to your liking. Come with me."

He rose to his feet and started walking, not even bothering to glance at me to see if I was following.

The reality was clear enough. I could either go with him, or I could wander around lost in a dangerous and unfamiliar realm. Bravado aside, that didn't sound like it would go well for me, despite what my wolf seemed to think.

The whole thing was insane. Fine—Elfhame existed. It wasn't as though I could deny that part, under the circumstances. But the rest of it?

A rustle off to my right made me jump, brushing into Tamlain as I spun to meet what I assumed would be an attacker. A figure moved through the trees, half-seen. My wolf's senses prickled in interest.

"The creature is not concerned with you," Tamlain said, sparing me a quick glance. "Do not be concerned with him."

"Him?" I asked, confused.

The shape emerged into a shaft of light and I stared in fascination at a large, horse-like beast.

Yet, how could a horse be that tall? I'd seen human riders in the mountains a few times. I'd even petted a horse once. It had been afraid of me at first, its nostrils flared and snorting. But I'd had some human candy in my pocket and shared a peppermint, making a fast friend in the end.

None of the horses I'd seen before had been anywhere near this large.

Dark, luminous eyes turned towards me, and that was when I noticed the most amazing feature of all. A large, white horn stood out three feet from the horse's head. It was pearly and spiraled, glistening in the odd light.

"A unicorn," I breathed in shock.

The unicorn stared at me for a long moment, tore off a mouthful of grass, and meandered on his way.

"Is every myth we were told as pups actually true?" I demanded, whirling to face Tamlain.

"Probably not," he said, and continued on his way.

I trailed behind him, letting my gaze wander over large, pink mushroom rings and trees with purple leaves the size of my face.

Soft, bell-like laughter reached my ears, and I saw glittering figures flying through the air, weaving in and out of the tree branches. They were small, just slightly larger than my hand. Their voices were high pitched as they giggled and chatted together in a language that I couldn't understand.

With my mouth open, I watched as they buzzed around like insects.

"Do try not to get distracted," Tamlain called in a dry voice.

The wolf inside me was jumping around, delighted. I felt the instinct to transform and allow myself to run around, my nose to the ground. I wanted to explore every inch of this world with my heightened animal senses.

I couldn't say how long we walked, but we trekked deep into the heart of the forest. The leaves above us were purple and yellow here, complementing each other as the light flickered through them.

A deep blue stream, crystal clear, wound its way along the path we were taking. I wondered if it was safe to drink. Could there be anything poisonous in Elfhame? This place seemed so much like Heaven that it seemed wrong for anything to be truly dangerous. And yet, I couldn't help wondering how many visitors had felt the same way, only to come to some horrible end.

Elfhame drives humans and shifters mad, the stories said.

"We're here," Tamlain finally said, several long minutes later.

I looked up, shaken free of my distraction. Ahead of us, a beautiful cottage made of white stone nestled between the boles of two huge trees. They were easily twice as big as any tree I'd ever seen on Earth. The cottage fit so perfectly between them that it was as though it had grown there right along with the rest of the forest.

"Okay, wow," I breathed.

"This will be your safe harbor, for now," Tamlain said. He approached without hesitation and pushed open the door without knocking.

I hesitated, suddenly nervous, but Tamlain shot me an impatient look. With few other options, I followed him into a cozy, perfect little front room. A fire in the hearth crackled merrily, giving off the perfect amount of warmth.

"Dianthe," Tamlain said, as though in greeting.

With a jolt, I realized we weren't alone. Disquiet flooded me. How had my wolf not noticed the tall figure, who rose from a chair in the corner to approach us? She was female, and moved with a sort of lethal elegance that made my heart ache. Her long, fiery red hair hung in a simple braid tossed casually over her shoulder. Her eyes, a bright green, studied me with the same intensity I was using to study her.

"This is your wolf?" she asked, no expression in her voice.

"Yes," Tamlain said. "Dianthe, this is Ember Valentine, formerly of the Greystalker pack. Ember Valentine — this is Dianthe."

I didn't know Elfhame's courtesies, so I lowered my chin in cautious acknowledgement.

"Dianthe has been a loyal comrade of mine for many centuries," Tamlain explained. "She has graciously agreed to assist me in this matter."

"In other words, he'd be lost without me," Dianthe said, with a wry twist of her full, red lips. "That's what I'm hearing, anyway. Is that what you're hearing?"

Tamlain didn't roll his eyes, yet somehow his impassive expression managed to convey a sense of fond exasperation. "How fortunate you agreed to assist me, in that case." His blue gaze returned to me. "She will be remaining here with you as a guard."

"Guarding me from other people? Or guarding me... like a prison guard?" I asked sharply, once again growing annoyed. "And where are you going to be while she's busy *guarding* me?"

Seriously, if you were going to kidnap someone from another realm, it only seemed polite not to dump her at the first opportunity afterward.

To no one's surprise, Tamlain ignored me. "You will be safe here for the time being. I have cast wards around the forest to ensure that there is no surveillance. You cannot be tracked while you are here, and your presence will not be noticeable to the average being."

"*Average being*?" I echoed blankly—only to be ignored again.

"Do not set one foot outside this forest," he said, very seriously. "However, within those bounds, you may come and go as you please."

"Great," I observed flatly.

Tamlain turned towards Dianthe and grasped her shoulder. "Take care. I cannot overstate the importance of keeping her out of Oberon's hands, and I want both of you safe when I return."

Dianthe raised a wry eyebrow. "Of the two of us, I think you face the greater peril, Tam."

And, okay. That sounded... ominous.

"Perhaps," Tamlain replied, pensive. He turned to me. "Dianthe will be your protector and guide, Little Wolf. The woods are your haven, but they can still be perilous."

I blinked at him. "So, just to make sure I have all of this right... you break into the human realm, track me down, chase me, fight me, and then ultimately kidnap me into another dimension without a way for me to return. Then, you decide to just leave me here in a cute little faerie cottage with your girlfriend?"

Tamlain looked mildly irritated, but Dianthe smiled widely at me. Her eyes darted back and forth between the two of us.

"Ooh, I like this earthling, Tamlain." she said.

I wasn't sure whether to be flattered or freaked out, so I continued glaring at Tamlain instead.

"This may come as a shock," he drawled, "but with my world falling into chaos and *you* standing at the epicenter, I currently find myself rather busy. There are many important people with whom I must consult."

"Consult... about me, you mean?" I shot back. "If that's the case, then it seems like I should be there, too, don't you think?"

Tamlain didn't smile. "Believe me when I say, to call such a thing 'ill-advised' would be a considerable understatement."

With an economical gesture of one hand, he opened a portal in mid-air, exactly like the one that had brought me to Elfhame in the first place. For one wild second I considered diving through it, just to see what would happen. Before I could act, however, a firm hand closed on my arm. Tamlain stepped through the portal and vanished. It snapped shut an instant later.

I slumped, defeated. I'd missed out on my opportunity.

Dianthe studied me as she removed her hand from my arm. "Are you well, Ember Valentine of the Greystalker pack?"

I pressed my lips together, feeling the frustration of the moment building up inside of me. I wasn't really sure how to answer her. I blew out a slow breath.

"Yeah, *terrific*. This is just a lot to take in, as you can probably imagine. Who the hell is Oberon? And, I mean, what is all of this even *about*?"

Dianthe turned and started moving around the cottage, hanging a pot of water over the fire to boil. "In his defense, Tamlain truly *is* very busy," she said absently. "He was tasked with obtaining you and bringing you back here. To answer your first question, Oberon is our king. You do know what a king is, right?"

"Well... yes?" I replied. "Obviously."

She smiled in relief. "Oh, good. Humans and human-adjacents are a rather strange bunch, so I never know for sure."

"Right..." I said uncertainly. "So, why would this king guy take an interest in me? Is this about Tamlain's crazy theory?"

Dianthe smiled, but her eyes held disquiet. "It is better if you learn the details from him. You must have patience."

I eyed her. "Well, since I'm trapped in a strange dimension with fae, a handful of pixies, and one very large unicorn, you can hardly blame me if I'm a little less than tolerant."

Dianthe took this in with a nod. "I understand."

I hadn't expected her to give in quite that easily, so I didn't press my luck about what I really wanted, which was to explore until my wolf was satisfied, and then be allowed to return home.

"Are you hungry?" Dianthe asked.

"Famished," I told her. It was true—my stomach was aching with hunger.

"Then let's go find some food," she suggested.

"Sure," I agreed, in the absence of better options. I started towards an area of the kitchen and opened one of the shelving doors, only to have a huge puff of dust hit me in the face. I coughed and sneezed, waving my hand around and trying to clear the air for me to breath better.

"No, no, my dear," Dianthe said with a laugh. "I was thinking something a little fresher."

I wrinkled my nose against the dust. "What do you mean?"

"You are a wolf, are you not? Do you feel up for a hunt?" she asked, a twinkle of excitement kindling in her green eyes.

My wolf perked up in response. "That sounds… good?" I said cautiously.

Inside, however, the wolf was excitedly dancing the canine version of the conga. The wild part of me was so excited and eager to shift that I could feel the ripples through my body. I was about to burst from my clothes and I needed to pull myself together.

This could be useful, I told myself. I could do a little bit of exploring this way. Reconnaissance, for lack of a better word.

I nodded my agreement.

"Okay, then," I told Dianthe, more enthusiastically than before. "Let's hunt."

The glint of enthusiasm shone brighter in Dianthe's eyes, and she grinned at me. Her teeth looked a little sharper than human, and I couldn't help but smile tentatively back, recognizing a fellow predator when I saw one.

"Let me show you where you'll be staying first," she said, waving for me to follow her.

We walked down a narrow hallway with fieldstone walls. I could feel the drastic change in temperature from the warmer front part of the cottage. I ran my hands along the rough edges of stone, wondering who had built this cottage here in the heart of a fae forest. The unfinished rock felt the same as rocks on Earth, yet the whole structure had a distinctly magical feel.

"This is where you'll sleep," Dianthe told me, pushing open a heavy wooden door. "You can undress here before you shift, since I know you only have one set of clothes with you."

Something about the door reminded me of the jailhouse I'd stayed in the night before I was exiled, and I had to repress a shudder.

"Thanks," I managed, and disappeared inside.

Fortunately, the inside of the room was cheery and bright—completely different than my earthen cell, even if it was also a prison of sorts. After changing out of my clothes and into my wolf form, I padded out of the room, using my nose to push open the door.

In this body, the scents surrounding me were overwhelming. It was nothing like Earth, and I longed to explore more of it. In some ways, it was harder to control the instinctual desires of the wolf now that I'd ceded physical control to her, but I pushed forward and found Dianthe standing at the front door. She was armed with a bow and a quiver of arrows. She stared at me as I stalked forward, giving me an approving nod.

I cocked my head at her.

'You'll do," she said, and led me outside.

Without any further warning, Dianthe launched across the carefully tended yard and plunged into the trees. My claws tore into the ground as I streaked after her, feeling a wild happiness as the brightly colored forest blurred around me in a dizzying display of hues and fragrances.

The hunt was on, and my wolf was exactly where she wanted to be.

NINE

I CLOSED THE distance between us as Dianthe circled around a clearing, her body crouched low to the ground. Even to my wolf senses, she was barely making a sound.

I panted silently, tasting the air and taking stock of the animals in the vicinity. Although things on Elfhame were similar to Earth in some ways, the differences were still significant. I could hear animals that resembled squirrels scurrying up and down the trees, leaping above our heads from branch to branch, yet they remained in the air far too long. Everything here breathed magic and power. We had tracked a beautiful golden panther for a long time through the trees, until Dianthe got a good look at the creature and shook her head.

"Too powerful," she'd whispered to me, turning away.

In my wolf form I stared across the riverbed separating us, watching the massive predator slip away. I let out a soft whine and Dianthe laughed.

"You'd be turned into panther food in two seconds, my piebald canine friend," she informed me, jerking her head in the opposite direction.

I could hardly argue that, especially given how little time I'd spent in wolf form as opposed to human form. It felt amazing to stretch my legs, to really give free rein to my abilities and my senses.

I'd spent so much time terrified of being discovered as a wolf that I had only hunted when it was unavoidable—taking only enough prey to keep from starving, and no more.

This was different.

I wanted to speak to Dianthe, but transforming back into a human would mean I'd have to stand before her naked. There was something so coolly intimidating about this fae shield maiden that I couldn't bring myself to do it.

But I *really* wanted to hunt a unicorn. Not for food… not to kill… just to see if I was good enough. Strong enough. *Powerful* enough.

As though my thoughts had transferred directly into reality, Elfhame provided. We walked towards the river and I could hear galloping hooves on the other side.

As the herd passed us by on the opposite side of the water, I could only stare. The brilliantly white creatures with pearly horns tossed their great heads, manes flowing easily down their necks.

The magic around them was palpable.

I watched them go, twitching a bit as Dianthe raised a hand in a clear gesture to stay hidden. In my human thoughts, I knew she was right. Like the golden panther, they were too much for a lone wolf and one fae hunter.

In the end, we tracked a heard of ordinary deer. Well, I *say* ordinary. Their coats were deep red, the color of autumn leaves.

With an economical movement of one hand, Dianthe gestured me to skirt around the clearing. I crept away, my belly almost touching the ground as I made my way to the back of the herd.

She hadn't said a word, but I had grasped her plan immediately. It felt as though we had hunted together for years. We were two parts of the same whole, working seamlessly together on the hunt. It was almost like being part of a pack again. Out of nowhere, the loneliness that I had suppressed for months reared up. I longed for the sense of wholeness that came from being a part of something larger than me.

I reminded myself forcefully that I was a prisoner here on Elfhame, held against my wishes. These were facts I knew as a human, but as a wolf it was more difficult to keep priorities like that at the forefront of my thoughts. I became more instinctual, working on emotion rather than logic.

Centering my thoughts, I shook myself and heard the soft sound of my fur rustling in the still air. One of the deer looked up, and I froze. Eventually, it lost interest since I was downwind, and went back to its meal. I needed to focus, or we would lose this kill.

After several long minutes, I was finally in position, directly behind the herd.

I gathered my powerful hind legs underneath me, teeth bared in anticipation. With a powerful lunge, I sprung forward. I was flying through the air, my front paws outstretched as I landed a mere yard or two from a large deer at the edge of the herd. It startled in surprise and bounded away.

An instant later, the entire herd scattered in terror—but most were headed towards Dianthe, still hidden among the trees.

As I pressed them forward, I saw her swing around and release an arrow. It pierced the heart of a young buck, and the animal was dead before it hit the ground.

My tongue lolled out appreciatively. It wasn't a cheeseburger, but it would do. I was so hungry that I could have gorged on the entire carcass myself, but I sat back on my haunches and watched as Dianthe field-dressed the meat.

Her hands were quick and deft, completely sure of every cut.

After spilling the contents of the chest and abdominal cavity, she reached out with bloody hands and held up the heart to me, steaming in the humid air.

I tugged it free of her fingers delicately and wolfed it down in one swallow.

She smiled at me as I wagged my tail, licking my lips. I thought about sitting up on my haunches, just as I had seen dogs around town do when they wanted something. It would be good to make her laugh. Maybe it would mean we could be friends.

My wolf definitely felt like we were bonding over the experience, especially when she offered me the liver next. The organs were packed with nutrients, which, as I'm sure Dianthe knew, had been absent from my diet for many months. I knew I was a shadow of my former self, thin and drawn from near-constant hunger.

Wolves aren't meant to be alone, I had often thought whenever I'd gone to bed with an empty belly — wondering if my failure to provide for myself meant I'd failed as a human as well as a shifter.

With the meat properly dressed, Dianthe swung the heavy carcass over her shoulders, tied together at the feet by a length of rope.

"The cottage is this way," she said, satisfaction at a good hunt evident in her tone.

I trotted after her, leaping up to sniff at the delicious aroma of the meat she carried on her back.

She laughed at me and swatted at my nose.

"Stop that, or I'll make you carry it," she threatened, a half-smile lifting the corner of her full mouth.

Despite the heart and liver I'd eaten, my stomach was rumbling again by the time we made it back to the cottage. My hunger had even driven my fascination with the forest out of my mind as I trotted quickly back to my room.

Once there, I closed my eyes and took a deep breath, mentally pulling my human skin back over myself. Muscle, bone, and tendon crackled and shifted. I stood up on my two human legs and hurriedly grabbed my clothes.

I examined them thoughtfully, remembering the way that Tamlain had waved his hand and made them reappear on my body. These clothes barely fit me, I'd gotten them from the shelter I first lived at when I landed in my human life. They were thin from frequent washing, but they smelled as fresh and clean as if I'd just pulled them out of the dryer at the laundromat.

Tamlain's powers were very... odd. Impressive, certainly—but still odd.

I slipped on the clothes and walked out into the hallway, spying a small washroom with a basin of deep blue water.

The same sweet smell that clung to my clothes hung in the air and I splashed water on my face and neck. I rinsed out my mouth—never quite having gotten used to the aftertaste of raw meat as a human—and dried with a towel I found rolled up on a set of low shelves.

I ran my fingers through my black and white hair, trying to loosen the worst of the tangles. Feeling somewhat refreshed, I walked back to the kitchen, where I found Dianthe chopping up small roots that resembled potatoes and dumping them into a pot. She'd lit a fire in the low grate. Strips of venison were sizzling and popping as they cooked over the flames.

The smell was delicious—so much better than the pathetic meals I served the residents of the nursing home. There were unfamiliar herbs floating in the pot of water, which hung next to the meat over the fire.

"This smells *amazing*," I said, sitting in a chair near the fire. I wasn't cold, but there was something comforting about the familiarity of a merrily burning hearth in such a strange land.

"I'm not as good of a cook as many of my people, but I think you'll find this satisfactory."

Dianthe said with a nod. "The bread is a day old, so it may be a bit stale."

I didn't care. Stale bread or not, this was a feast.

I sat, watching Dianthe work. She was silent except for the occasional sound of an absently hummed tune. It wasn't uncomfortable, exactly—I could sense that this fae simply preferred the quiet.

"Dianthe," I finally said, my thoughts long ago having strayed back to my predicament, "what am I doing here, really?"

She lifted her eyes casually to me and then turned back to her stew. With a pair of tongs made of green wood, she carefully transferred the strips of meat into the boiling pot.

"What do you mean?" she finally answered. "You are here because Tamlain thinks this forest is the safest place for you."

"You *know* what I mean," I replied, frowning. "Tamlain tracked me down on Earth to bring me here. He came to an *entirely different realm* for the sole purpose of kidnapping me, on the basis of a story that sounds totally crazy."

I waited, hoping that my silence would prompt her to speak. To my surprise, it worked.

"He already told you that our world is in peril, and that you are in a unique position to save us. Countless lives are at stake, wolf."

"So he says," I said, waving my hand in the air. "But no one will say *how*."

She glanced up at me before returning her attention to the food. "I'm sure Tamlain will explain everything when he gets back."

"You think so?" I countered. "Don't you think I have a right to know *now*? I was brought here against my will, in case you've forgotten."

Her eyebrow flickered, though she didn't meet my gaze. "Let's just say, I think this is a cause you'll be willing to get behind, once you understand."

"That's a pretty bold assumption," I snapped. "And one that's getting less likely the longer I'm kept in the dark."

Dianthe sighed and pinched the bridge of her nose between her thumb and forefinger.

"I am not the person to explain it to you," she said, looking me squarely in the eye, "it's not my place. Tamlain must be the one to explain about your heritage."

"My *heritage*?" I scoffed. "I'm a disgraced wolf. That's it. That's my heritage. So what?"

Dianthe shrugged and took the large pot full of steaming stew off the fire. Pouring me a bowl, she tore off a chunk of bread and handed everything to me, along with a spoon.

I huffed in frustration, but it was like trying to get information out of a brick wall. I felt like we had the potential to be friends, but obviously we were nowhere near the kind of friendship that included confidences like *'why the hell did your crazy hot boyfriend bring me here?'*

For lack of any better options, I started on the stew. After one spoonful, I was shoveling large bites in my mouth as fast as I could chew and swallow. Dianthe stared at me, but I ignored her, intent on getting as much food into my stomach as

I could in the shortest amount of time possible. After all, there was no way of knowing when I would have another meal this good.

When the edge of my ravenous hunger started to dull, I made a few more attempts at probing her with questions, but got nowhere. I finished my stew, thanked her for the meal, and returned to my room in irritated silence.

It wasn't *fair*. How dare that fae bastard kidnap me, hold me here, and not even give me any answers about how I was supposedly going to save their world? I was just *me*—I couldn't even save myself. Had Tamlain not noticed that I was barely surviving as a human? There was no way that they could—or *should*—trust the fate of their entire world to me.

I needed to understand more. I needed answers.

I kept my clothes on, but took my shoes off and placed them neatly next to the bed before climbing in. With a sigh, I rolled so that I was facing the small window with my back to the door. My breathing grew slow and deep, yet all the while I was listening intently to Dianthe with my heightened wolf senses. I could hear her every movement in the kitchen as she cleaned up her cooking utensils. I heard her take the rest of the stew down into the cellar of the cottage, where it would be cool enough to keep it from spoiling for a day or two.

After she was done with that, she stood silently for so long I wondered if I hadn't missed her leaving. The sun had long ago set behind the hills, multi-colored stars winking in the dark sky, visible through the gaps in the trees.

Dianthe finally made her way down the hallway into the washroom. A few minutes later she stopped outside my door, and I heard the slight creak of the hinges as she pushed it open. I stayed perfectly still on my side, my back still to the door. I let my breath ease in and out of my lungs, slow and deep like a real sleeper.

She stayed long enough that I started to wonder if she could tell I was awake. To my relief, she finally backed out of my room with a sigh and softly pulled the door shut.

I waited until her footsteps disappeared into the other bedroom and the door closed behind her before I sat up, still fully dressed under the blanket.

Okay, screw this. It's past time for some answers, I thought, removing my clothes and standing naked in the middle of the floor.

I couldn't leave yet. Dianthe would hunt me down in no time and drag me straight back here, I was sure. So I sat on the bed and counted slowly, waiting until I was certain the fae huntress was asleep. When I reached five thousand, I held my breath and listened for any sound of movement in the house. There was nothing except for the slow, steady breathing in the room next to mine. Dianthe was soundly sleeping.

Perfect.

The bedroom window would be small for my human form, but the wolf could wriggle through. Thankfully, there was a latch on the inside, and the hinges made only the faintest of creaks as I swung it open.

There was an interruption in the soft breathing next door, but it resumed again moments later. I counted to a thousand again, just to be safe.

Once I was fully confident that Dianthe hadn't woken, I transformed silently into the wolf, gritting my teeth against the discomfort of the shift. I leapt nimbly onto the bed and through the open window. When I dropped onto the earth, I looked around with my enhanced senses. It was quiet except for the chirp of insects and the scrabbling of small night creatures.

My wolf was wildly excited.

Twice in one day!

Her joy was intoxicating, but I rolled my eyes at my own ridiculousness. I shouldn't get used to having the freedom to transform at will— it would make returning to Earth that much more difficult. And I *would* be returning to Earth.

I trotted away from the cottage, my ears cocked for sounds of pursuit. There weren't any.

Problem number one—I didn't know where to go. I had a vague notion of doing some serious reconnaissance, but nothing more useful than that. Mostly, I couldn't stand the idea of being caged, even if it was a very comfortable cage.

Sitting back on my haunches, I looked up at the sky to study the two large moons hanging above me. I suppressed a thoroughly self-destructive urge to throw my head back and howl for my pack.

There were no other shifters here, and if there had been, they wouldn't have helped me. I was still exiled, even in this strange land.

Tamlain and Dianthe said that I had to stay within the bounds of the forest for my protection, I mused. *I wonder if that was a lie? Maybe they just don't want me to see what's beyond the forest?*

I had no idea what that might be, but in my mind's eye I pictured a large city.

Could I disappear in a crowd? Find someone who would help me get back where I was supposed to be? Or would Tamlain sense me and track me down again?

Did he already know I was gone?

But that kind of speculation was pointless. I couldn't sit here worrying about Tamlain finding out I'd snuck away. He knew that I was a rebellious wolf. If he was smart, he probably would have expected something like this.

Which would make the rule about the forest that much more plausible.

I shook myself sharply and took off, following the same track we'd taken to go hunting earlier. There had been a point where the trees had grown thinner ahead of us before we'd changed direction, and I thought I'd been able to see light peeking through.

I returned to that spot, tracking our scents. To my wolf nose, the trail was as clear as day. Once I saw the thinning of the trees ahead, I left the path that Dianthe and I had used and crept forward, seeking the edge of the forest. To my surprise, I was only a hundred yards or so from where the trees came to an abrupt end. I stayed back, still hidden among the underbrush, and considered my options.

There was nothing stopping me from following along the edge of the forest, just to see how far my confines went in every direction. Despite my frustration with being a captive, I was, in fact, hesitant to set foot outside of the warded forest. Tamlain hadn't explained—not properly— but he'd made it clear that I would be in danger if I left.

I stared out through the trees, noticing flickering lights in the distance. Maybe they were campfires, or torches.

Tamlain hadn't really explained the living arrangements of his people. Were they city dwellers? Rural? Did they build castles? All of the above? None of the above?

There was something on the horizon, that much was certain—a large structure that glittered with many flickering lights near the foot of a mountain. Or maybe it was just the cliff face reflecting the light of the two moons?

I didn't think so, but I couldn't tell for sure from this distance, and curiosity was starting to get the better of me. Whatever it was, it was mesmerizing. It felt like the lights were calling to me. I inched my way forward, step by step, leaving the trees behind me. Despite the lure of the distant fires, I felt horribly exposed beyond the edge of the tree line. The hackles on the back of my neck stood up in alarm.

I had the unpleasant feeling that I was being watched.

No sooner than I'd decided to turn around and head back to the cottage, two loud, electric noises ripped through the air. A pair of magical portals opened before me, and I backed away, crouched low and growling.

Two male fae stepped through, each holding something that resembled a crossbow. I froze as both weapons were leveled at me. The threat was obvious — if I moved a muscle, I was dead.

"This was almost too easy," one of them said, sounding delighted.

"I'd heard shifters were little more than dumb animals," the other purred. His smile was more like a leer. "Looks like it's all true."

They stretched out their free hands, weapons never wavering as they muttered words I couldn't understand. A shining blue net appeared faster than a blink of an eye, surrounding me on all sides. I leapt sideways, trying to force my way over or through, but I couldn't get past it as it shrunk around me like a shimmering cage.

"Don't try to transform, wolf," the first man advised with a harsh laugh. "It'll be worse in your human form."

Stupid, stupid, I swore at myself, looking around in desperation for a way out.

There was none. The net had even stretched over my head. I wondered for a brief instant if I might be able to dig my way out, but that would take far too long.

A female shout of anger echoed from the forest behind me. I turned to see Dianthe launching herself from the trees. Her mighty leap carried her in a graceful arc above me, her arm stretched behind her. Her hand held a blazing dagger, and her face was focused with determination as she sliced it across the top of the trap.

It crackled and sizzled, like an electrical transformer that was about to blow up. With a flash that nearly blinded me, the strands of power forming the cage disappeared, fizzling to nothing.

Dianthe landed in a crouch beside me, She pulled out a longer sword blade from a sheath strapped to her back. Wielding both blades at once, she stepped forward, drawing herself up to her fullest height and facing my would-be captors without a trace of fear.

I was in awe, but before I had even a moment to consider what to do, Dianthe spoke over her shoulder, never taking her eyes off of my attackers.

"Don't let them catch you, Ember—the survival of both our worlds depends on it!"

TEN

A FLASH OF light flooded the grass and trees around me, illuminating the brilliant colors for just a moment before the world faded back into the muted grey tones of nighttime. In the next instant, both of the blades in Dianthe's hands were ablaze with an icy blue fire.

"Run!" she shouted, charging forward and meeting the first blow.

I wheeled around and darted back into the trees, trying to remember the rules about the protection of the forest. Would it hold now that they knew I was here? I wasn't so sure.

With no better options, I stayed back, hidden by the darkness, peeking around the large base of a tree to watch as the fight went on and on. One of the attacking fae was armed with a heavy sword, and the other with a spear. Dianthe moved as gracefully as a dancer, ducking and parrying every strike.

A growl rumbled up in my chest. I wanted to be out there, helping her. Despite my questionable status as a prisoner here in Elfhame, I still felt the fragile bond of friendship with Dianthe tugging at my instincts. My wolf was eager to rush to the aide of my new fae packmate, but the human part of me knew that I would only make things worse by emerging from the questionable protection of the woods.

The wolf huffed in irritation, as our eyes remained glued to the battle in front of us.

Dianthe was a powerful fighter, but the two-on-one battle was stretching her capacity — especially since she was constantly trying to reposition her body between her opponents and my position hidden among the underbrush.

The fae with the spear used the base of his weapon to launch himself high into the air, like a pole-vaulter. At the top of the arc, he jerked his spear around so the point was aimed directly at Dianthe's heart.

With a spring as fast as lightening, Dianthe flipped backwards, her arms and legs extended in graceful flight. The thrust fell short, but it was far too close for comfort. I held my breath. It felt like everything around me had turned to slow motion, even the pounding of my heart sounded sluggish in my ears.

Dianthe's feet touched the ground and she raised her flaming blades in a flash.

I blinked as time sped up again, sucking in a gasp. Dianthe rushed forward, her hair flying behind her, slashing at the air where the fae's head had been a moment before.

He dodged away from her, but nowhere near as gracefully as she had done. His spear remained lodged in the ground, now several feet away from him. As I watched, his face fell and he registered that he'd been disarmed. He leapt backwards again, in full retreat now.

Instead of pursuing a weaponless opponent, Dianthe fell back, moving closer to the edge of the forest. I couldn't see the expression on her face, but her hands were tight on the hilts of her blades. She held them up, crossed defensively in front of her.

"You will go no further," she said in a low, commanding voice.

"Traitor," the remaining fae hissed. "You defy our king! You will die upon my sword, and then we will take your wolf."

Dianthe let out a low, musical laugh—a sound of pure derision. My admiration for her courage swelled, even as my humiliation at my own cowardice grew. What kind of predator was I, huddling here in the forest while my new friend fought for both our lives?

"So, I'm to die on your blade, am I?" she said with false sweetness. "You know, it's actually kind of cute how you think you can catch me."

With that, her remaining attacker snarled and lunged for her. Dianthe swung her blades to block every strike of his sword, spinning the blows away from her body with sharp motions.

In the next instant, the other fae appeared behind her. He was using magic, I was sure—I hadn't even seen him move. Too late, I howled out a warning, but Dianthe had already sensed the movement at her back and ducked, the fae's recovered spear thrusting inches above her head.

Before the two fae registered what she was doing, Dianthe rolled to her right through the grass, coming up on her feet.

"You have betrayed Oberon!" one of the men yelled, his face darkening with anger. An orange glow like flames lit his eyes from within.

"*I* am loyal to Elfhame," she snapped. "Can you say the same? Why do you fight for a mad king bent on an unwinnable war?"

I gaped at her from my hidden position. A… *what now*? Goddamn it—I *seriously* needed to drag some answers out of these people.

"All I know is that there are traitors in our midst," the first fae snarled. "All who betray Oberon will pay the price!"

The pair attacked again. Dianthe leapt between them, barely evading the blows they tried to land.

I was starting to wonder if fae ever got tired, because the battle had already dragged on long enough that I was exhausted merely from watching. The powerful blows continued to rain down, and I wondered how long Dianthe could withstand them.

As though my thoughts had summoned the reality, Dianthe gradually began to flag. Her flips were slower and when she landed, she staggered a little before righting herself. The spearman, too, seemed to be wearing out, and his attacks went wide as often as they landed true. Despite her growing exhaustion, Dianthe finally landed a slash across his chest.

With a cry, he fell backwards, stumbling as he clutched at the injury. A look of shock painted his features, as though he hadn't believed she might actually best him.

The other fae shouted in rage. After a crushing sword blow that Dianthe barely managed to parry in time, she spun away from her attacker and tried to kick out, only to be caught in the air by her outstretched foot.

The fae swordsman brought her down to the ground with a horrible, fleshy thud. The breath caught in my throat when she did not immediately fight free and roll to her feet.

Get up, I willed her silently, fear flooding my chest. *Get up!*

With my sensitive wolf ears, I heard a low moan escape from her lips. She kicked out weakly, but her flailing attempts to rise were useless and uncoordinated.

She got the wind knocked out of her, I thought, fighting against the urge to race to her side. *Or maybe a concussion?*

Her entreaty not to let myself be caught, no matter what, was the only thing that held me in place. *The survival of both our worlds depends on it*, she'd said. The other fae crouched over her prone body as she writhed, sneering down at her. The one she'd injured had his hand clamped across the slash in his chest. He murmured low words, and a golden glow emanated from the wound. A few moments later, he dropped his arm. There was no sign of the ugly gash except for the drying bloodstains on his tunic.

"You won't catch her," Dianthe rasped weakly.

The one on the right laughed at her. "Oh, I think we will, traitor."

"Yes," the formerly injured one agreed, hatred twisting his features. "You see, we've just figured out the right bait to use."

He reached down and grabbed a handful of Dianthe's hair. She choked on a cry of pain as he jerked her head back with a violent motion, exposing her throat.

I watched, horrified, as the other fae lifted his weapon. The blade of the sword swung down toward her neck, stopping a hairsbreadth from her skin. The Fae's hate-filled eyes trained on the trees where he knew I was hiding.

"Wolf!" he called, his voice echoing around the forest. "Come out, now, or I'll cut her throat while you watch. We'll see just how long it takes for her to bleed out from the jugular!"

The other fae crouched over Dianthe, laughing down at her as he held her in place. She was panting rapidly through her mouth—her expression unafraid, but gray and pinched with pain.

"Such a fierce little traitor," he observed. "A pity you strayed from the path—Oberon could have used a warrior like you."

"Come out now, Wolf!" The other snapped, his grip tightening on the sword. "Or I *will* hack off this traitor's head."

I couldn't stand another second. I charged forward, heart thundering with fear and anger, pulling my form inward until I rose on human legs and stumbled out of the woods.

"Stop!" I cried, emerging from the trees with my hands raised.

Dianthe jerked, struggling against her captor's grip. "*No!* Ember, get back!"

I ignored her and walked forward slowly, my breathing ragged… my hands held at shoulder height, unthreatening. This was the wrong thing to do. I knew that. But I couldn't just stand by while these fae sliced my friend's throat open. What would I tell Tamlain?

"Don't hurt her," I said. "I'm here, okay? Just… let her go. *Please.*"

The fae with the sword sneered at my naked, human form. "Not much of a predator now, are you?"

"Let her go," I said again, unable to keep my voice from shaking slightly. "You've got me. You don't need her."

The swordsman let out a harsh bark of laughter. Dianthe's glassy eyes burned into mine. *Run,* her expression said. *Don't do this!*

"I'm right here," I said desperately. "I'm the one you want, right? There's no reason for anyone to die."

"No reason?" the fae pinning Dianthe said in an incredulous tone. "Traitors die, wolf. No other reason is needed."

I met Dianthe's gaze, feeling like all the air had been punched from my lungs. She was staring at me with large, reproachful eyes. There was something accusing there, and it was obvious that she thought I was a fool for giving myself up.

What did you expect me to do? I tried to communicate with my expression. *I couldn't just stand back and watch them kill you!*

Dianthe gave a tiny, frustrated shake of the head, and I wondered for a crazy instant if she could somehow understand my thoughts.

The fae with the sword stepped toward me, his face alive with malice. He raised his free hand and murmured an incantation, his fingers curling in the air.

My arms and legs froze into rigid stiffness, locking me in place. The magic net fell over me again, but this time my invisible bonds grew tighter and tighter until I was gasping.

"What did you do?" I demanded, relieved to find that at least my jaw still worked.

"A little something to ensure you can't escape again," the fae explained. "Don't fight it, Wolf Girl. It will go the worse for you if you do."

I ignored his words, struggling to no avail against the magic trapping me.

To my horror, the fae lifted his sword once more, poised to bring it down on Dianthe's neck.

For the briefest of moments, Dianthe turned her head so that she and I were looking at each other. There was resignation in her eyes that frightened me. I continued to fight the bonds holding me in place, as the sword began its downward arc toward Dianthe's throat.

"*No!*" I screamed, channeling all my strength into that single cry of negation.

Complete silence fell over the forest for the barest instant, as though the very rocks and trees were holding their breath in anticipation.

The fae halted his swing, his head jerking up. An expression of alarm slid over his features. For a brief moment, I had no idea why—but then I felt the wind around us pick up. It tugged at the fae's clothes, which snapped and blew in the sudden gale.

"What in Mab's green garden?" The crouched fae murmured, looking around with clear apprehension.

I gritted my teeth, anger pulsing through my body. My hair flew wildly around my face. Around us, the grass blew flat against the ground. The wind surrounded me, placing me at the eye of the storm. Eyes burning with rage over what had almost been done to my friend, I allowed more and more anger to flow through me.

The storm intensified in response. Trees uprooted and flew through the clearing, some of them missing us by mere feet. In the next moment, the fae were knocked backward by the force of the gale. My two attackers tumbled through the air, hitting the ground with heavy force. The roar in my ears grew deafening, even as the magic holding me captive snapped.

I narrowed my eyes, watching with something very like glee. The ground beneath us trembled and heaved. I rode it like a surfer cresting a wave, but Dianthe rolled and tumbled across the grass for several moments before she managed to push herself unsteadily to her feet.

She swayed as the earthquake raged on, but made her way towards the other fae, both of whom were being tossed around like rag dolls. The ground heaved and split, and she went tumbling again. For some reason, the earthquake barely seemed to touch me. I crossed to Dianthe's side and helped her to her feet once more. She clung on to my arm, keeping herself upright as she stood on unsteady legs.

With an explosion of noise that made us all look around, a crackling portal opened up before us, and a blinding white figure stepped through. The light was so all-consuming that I had to shield my eyes.

"Cease this at once!" a familiar voice thundered.

Squinting up, I followed Dianthe's tug on my arm as she pulled me down to the ground. As I lifted my face to the brilliant light, I recognized the silhouette as Tamlain, descending on us like an angry god.

"Oh, *shit*," I whispered, meeting Dianthe's wide-eyed gaze with my own.

ELEVEN

TAMLAIN CROSSED the short distance separating us without so much as losing his footing on the heaving ground. He crouched and grabbed me by the throat, shocking me so badly that I didn't even think to resist as he pulled me upright. I was vaguely aware of Dianthe rising as well, placing herself between us and the fae guards who'd attacked us.

Tamlain's blue eyes snapped fire in the moonlight as he yanked me forward until only inches separated us. "If you cannot control your emotions, I will kill you where you stand," he said, with frightening coldness.

My lip curled, as my barely controlled wolf contemplated snapping at his face. She still responded to him with the same contradictory mix of aggression and interest—neither of which was terribly helpful when my human half was abruptly aware of how big and male and *close* he was... coupled with how exceptionally naked *I* was.

I gulped, my throat working against the pressure of his hand. As though a switch had been flipped, my panicked fury over the threat to Dianthe's life drained away. Around us, the wind began to calm. The earth beneath our feet quieted.

"Better," he spat, his hand jerking away from the skin of my neck as though I'd burned him. He made a sharp, irritated gesture, and the familiar fabric of my clothes melted into existence around my body.

I looked down, took in what had just happened, and looked back up to take stock of the situation. Horrible thoughts lurked just below the level of my consciousness, and I didn't dare examine them directly. Not yet.

The two fae had managed to regain their feet. Both of them were looking at Tamlain open-mouthed.

The one with blood on his tunic spoke, disbelief coloring his tone. "It's true, then. I could scarcely credit that Oberon's greatest general had turned traitor."

"You serve one fae king," Tamlain said. "I serve our entire world."

"You are harboring property that belongs to your ruler," said the other fae.

The words pricked at me. I knew they were important. I should have feelings about them—about being called *property*—but I couldn't focus on them past the growing sense of horror that seemed to be opening up beneath my feet like a pit.

Several things happened all at once. Dianthe gave a warning cry as the fae with the spear reared back to hurl it. At the same time, the other one called forth a ball of fiery magic and blasted it toward us. I had no idea if they were aiming at me or at Tamlain, but he swiped his hand out with a growl, and the magic slid past us to the side. The spear missed us by inches in the other direction, its owner toppling to the ground as he clutched at the hilt of Dianthe's short blade—now protruding obscenely from his chest, where she'd hurled it.

Meanwhile, a terrible chill had crept over me, and I barely registered it when the second fae cursed and called a portal into existence.

"Stop him!" Dianthe cried, flinging her sword at him an instant too late. The portal snapped shut, and he was gone. The blade buried itself in the ground a few feet past where the hole in reality had been an instant before.

"Damn and blast!" she shouted, the sound echoing around the suddenly empty meadow. She whirled on Tamlain. "He'll report straight back to the throne about this!"

Tamlain could have been carved from ice. "I left you in charge of watching her. You *knew* she was unlikely to stay where she was supposed to." The tone was caustic enough to strip paint.

"And I was only seconds behind her," Dianthe shot back, equally cold. "You might have mentioned that Oberon had guards monitoring the wards and ready to strike at a moment's notice!"

"Had I known that was the case, I most certainly would have." Tamlain bit the words out.

Under any other circumstances, I might have been mildly amused or at least temporarily entertained by the sight of the two powerful fae bickering like an old mated couple. As it was, I couldn't stop looking around us at the scene of destruction.

Destruction *I* had caused.

There was no more avoiding it. I might have been able to delude myself back in the packlands, and again in Rockville when the junkies had threatened Anna—but apparently, the third time was a charm when it came to my brain and its powers of self-deception. My knees stopped holding me up and I sank to the ground, staring wide-eyed at the torn earth, downed branches, and crazily tilted trees surrounding us.

Both of the fae had turned to look at me when I collapsed beneath the weight of what I'd just done.

"What am I?" I asked, barely recognizing my own voice. "What's happening to me?"

Panic prickled at the edges of the numbness blanketing my brain, and the wind around us rose in muted threat. Dianthe hissed out a breath and came to crouch in front of me. Her strong hand closed on my shoulder in what felt like reassurance.

She craned to look up at Tamlain.

"Enough of this," she said. "You cannot expect her to understand if you will not *speak!*"

"Speak of *what*?" I whispered. "What's going on? *Why is all of this happening,* Tamlain?"

The fae still looked angry enough to spit nails. But after a long, pensive moment, he breathed out a sigh. "It seems like a cruelty to place this on her shoulders, when she is not truly responsible for her own actions," he said, directing the words to Dianthe. "But perhaps you are right."

All I could do was stare up at him, still lost to the horror of the thing.

The damage done on Earth yesterday was extensive, Tamlain had told me after Rockville. *The damage on Elfhame was catastrophic.*

"Come, Little Wolf," he said, extending a hand down to me. He still appeared to be reining in his temper only with difficulty—but now, I thought that his anger might not be directed at me, but rather at someone or something else.

I let myself be hauled onto rubbery legs, supported between his grip and Dianthe's. A moment later, he opened a portal large enough for all three of us to enter. The two fae led me through, steadying me when I stumbled over uneven ground. The glowing ring snapped shut behind us, and I had to blink away the afterimages before I could make sense of the panorama before me.

Elfhame's two moons illuminated a vast wasteland stretching out into the distance. It was barren and churned, resembling nothing so much as the aftermath of an attack by an angry giant that had crushed everything into rubble. I stared at the jumble of rock and bare earth, my mouth agape.

"You are a child of two realms, Ember Valentine." Tamlain's voice was grave. He stretched a hand out to indicate the carnage covering the land. "And this devastation is your legacy."

TWELVE

A CHILD OF two realms? I blinked out across the wasteland of destruction, feeling like I'd been hit over the head by a brick. This was nothing like storm damage spread over a few city blocks, or branches and trees damaged in a single section of forest.

"What does that *mean*?" I demanded. "Damn it, Tamlain! No more beating around the bush! You already know what I am! I'm just a wolf without a pack—an outcast. I don't have a fucking *legacy*!"

I don't want a fucking legacy. Not if it looks like this.

Tamlain appeared suddenly as old as the ravaged hills in front of us. He sat down heavily on a flat-topped boulder, staring out at the devastation the same way I was.

"You are not just a wolf," he said, the words falling to the ground between us with the weight of exhaustion. "Tell me what you know of your father."

"My sire?" I took a step back, a sick feeling roiling in my stomach. "I don't know anything about him—except that he was a no-good loser who thought it would be fun to break up my mother's mate-bond and then disappear afterward."

Dianthe swallowed a choked sound, but when I looked, her face could have been carved out of marble.

"He has killed people for lesser insults than the one you've just leveled," Tamlain said, still in a monotone.

I caught my breath, because Tamlain spoke like it was someone he knew personally. "My father… is fae?" Try as I might, I couldn't make the words settle into place in my mind.

"Little Wolf," Tamlain said, "your father is the *king* of the fae."

That was enough to drag my eyes away from the lifeless wasteland. I gaped at him, my jaw hanging loose.

You are harboring property that belongs to your ruler, one of my would-be kidnappers had said to him.

The king of the fae. King… Oberon?

"That… makes absolutely no sense," I managed. "The fae king has nothing better to do with his time then pop across the veil to Earth and play home-wrecker with a female shifter?"

"It's a bit more complicated than that," Tamlain said.

Anger began to rise from beneath the sea of my confusion and disbelief. "My mother's mate *committed suicide* when he found out she was pregnant with me!"

A sigh. Tamlain lifted his hand, fingers squeezing at the bridge of his nose as though the entire conversation pained him. "Oberon has long possessed a cruel streak. This entire fiasco began as nothing more than petty revenge."

"Revenge against who?" I demanded. "Revenge for *what?*"

"Against his wife, for protecting the child of a friend," Dianthe said, disgust evident in her tone.

"So he has a mate, too?" I asked in disbelief. With a sharp shake of the head, I muttered, "Of course he does. Why respect someone else's mate-bond if you don't even respect your own?"

"Our king respects very little," Tamlain said grimly. "Because there is very little that he does not feel is beneath him."

"Titania—his queen—saved a female shifter who'd been exiled from her pack while pregnant," Dianthe said, taking up the story. "They became friends, of a sort. She took the shifter into her household as a servant and close confidante, and I imagine Oberon resented that fact."

"Our esteemed ruler desired to take the shifter's pup as a slave," Tamlain continued. "A plaything, so that Titania would not possess something that he did not. But she genuinely cared for her servant. She hid the babe away as soon as he was born. I know not where. Neither does Oberon, evidently."

The pieces began to fit together, slowly revealing a picture. My stomach roiled, the wolf circling restlessly inside my mind.

"He decreed that if he could not have the slave he desired, he would create his own." Tamlain looked thoroughly disgusted.

"Two birds with one stone," Dianthe said, face dour. "With a single act, he humiliated Titania for her moment of rebellion, while also bringing into being that which he so selfishly desired."

I watched them both unblinkingly. "You're telling me the king of the fae sired me because his wife wouldn't hand over her friend's newborn pup for him to use as a slave?" The words emerged flat. It felt like I was hearing myself speak them through a tunnel.

"Yes," Tamlain said simply. "That is what we are telling you."

I shook my head slowly back and forth. "But that's…" I began, only to trail off. "What does any of this have to do with storms and earthquakes and huge fields of broken rocks?" I flung a hand toward the destruction.

Tamlain sighed again. "It should not come as a surprise that Oberon had no interest in actually raising a child. Doubtless if he'd acquired his original prize, he would have pawned the infant off on someone else until he was of age. The king was content to leave you on Earth with your pack, though he did send a spy to watch over you until he was ready to pluck you away to Elfhame to serve him."

An icy chill trickled down my spine. "What spy?" I asked, barely recognizing my own voice.

Tamlain shrugged. "Her name is Pavia. An oathbreaker with little choice but to perform any function the king asks of her, lest she be cast out and thrown to the Wild Hunt. I do not know what identity she took in your pack."

He might not, but *oh*… I did. And the realization had me about two breaths away from puking up the remnants of Dianthe's venison stew.

"*Geneva*," I breathed.

The mother-figure who'd kept me from starving or freezing after my mother had been exiled, but who'd always seemed so odd and distant. Had she ever really cared for me at all? My entire history was crumbling around me, like the broken rocks in the wasteland before us.

"Ah. Clearly you have an idea," Tamlain observed. "But whatever the case, Pavia was tasked with keeping you safe until you came into your shifter powers. After which, she would report back to the king that you were ready to take your place as his slave."

Growing horror slid through my veins like icy flames. I staggered to another convenient rock and sank onto it. My breath was stuck in my throat, but around me, the wind rose, tugging at Dianthe's clothing and Tamlain's long, pale hair. The female fae crouched before me and took both my hands in hers. Her skin felt warm… or was mine cold? Her wide green eyes bored into mine.

"Ember," she said. "You must control your anger and fear. It's better to know the truth, even when the truth is painful."

With a jolt, I remembered that when my emotions took over, I caused things like the wasteland before me… like the torn and gutted forest behind me. I swallowed hard, my breath releasing with a gasp.

"You still haven't explained about the destruction," I rasped.

Tamlain nodded reluctantly. "Originally, Oberon was only interested in his trifling revenge against Titania. But then Pavia reported back to him about your strange powers."

A small, punched-out noise escaped my chest. *Geneva.* She'd seemed so interested in the odd windstorm that had appeared when the pack of bullies cornered me on the road.

"When Oberon heard her story, his plans changed." Tamlain looked grave. "He thinks to use you as a weapon—a threat against Earth unless the shifters and the humans submit to his rule."

The fae closed his brilliant blue eyes, his head bowed. "I have served my king faithfully as his general for centuries. But now, I am convinced that Oberon is going insane."

I swallowed, licking my lips to moisten them. "So you decided to kidnap me and hide me away to keep Oberon from getting his hands on me?" I asked.

He nodded. "I was tasked with retrieving you and bringing you to his palace. But doing so would place a weapon that can destroy worlds in the hands of a madman."

"I don't understand, though," I said. "If that's the case, why bring me to Elfhame? Why not hide me on Earth."

Tamlain looked me in the eye, unblinking. "Because you are growing stronger, and because your emotions pull the worlds together. Wherever you are when you exert this pull, there is damage.

But in the other realm, there is" — he indicated the barren wasteland — "*this*."

"Elfhame is our home," Dianthe said softly. "If such damage must be done, we chose for it to be done… elsewhere."

It felt like Tamlain had closed his fingers around my throat again. "So, just now — I made something like this happen… on Earth?" I could barely get the words out.

"Yes," Tamlain said simply. "I had thought that perhaps bringing you here would negate the effects of your powers. It hasn't. It has merely shifted the destruction elsewhere."

I stared at him, aghast. "So, what happens now? Since that hasn't worked?"

His face was granite. "I am consulting with those I can trust, in hopes of finding a solution to the problem. However, if none can be found, I will kill you myself before I allow the two realms and all of their inhabitants to be destroyed by your powers."

THIRTEEN

TAMLAIN'S THREAT should have frightened me. Instead, I found myself gazing across the wasteland again. Every living thing had been crushed and buried, condemned to die in the blind destruction that I'd unknowingly left in my wake.

I will kill you myself before I allow the two realms and all of their inhabitants to be destroyed by your powers.

The fae warrior's words echoed in my mind. And for that moment, I didn't care about the very real threat to my life. Of course he would kill me rather than see worlds die.

"There were people here?" I asked shakily. "People… lived here?"

I read the answer in Tamlain's expressionless face. Bitterness surged in my throat; a scream too large to claw its way out of my mouth. I covered my face with trembling hands, breathing heavily.

"How many people died in this destruction?" I demanded, not caring that my voice quavered.

Tamlain and Dianthe glanced at each other, a look passing between them. For some reason, the silent exchange made me even more afraid of the answer.

"The precise number does not matter," Tamlain replied, brushing some dirt off his sleeve. I could tell that he didn't want to have this

154

conversation. And that was fair. Neither did I. But still—

My voice was barely a whisper. "I want to know."

Silence fell for a long moment.

"Knowing the answer will not help you," Tamlain replied eventually, in a tone of finality. "Those deaths were not your ethical responsibility. The blood is on Oberon's hands."

The number must be huge, I realized with growing horror. If it had only been a handful of people, he would have said, wouldn't he?

Swallowing back my nausea, I looked away from Tamlain and Dianthe, not wanting to see their expressions of censure… or compassion.

My whole life had been a lie. I'd truly thought that Geneva had been the closest thing to a mother that I would ever have, but now I could see that she was just a pawn. She was just another tool used to orchestrate the horrors in my life.

I'd been told for as long as I could remember that I was a waste of space. I was the product of something shameful, a stain on the pack. I was a bad influence on the legitimate, honorable pups that had been born after me. My only friend was another outcast, barely higher in status than I'd been.

In that moment, I wanted nothing more than for Darby to be here, so I could fall into her soft arms and weep for everything I'd just learned.

How many times had my tormenters insisted that it would have been better if I were never born? It was too many to count. And as my eyes roved over the pits of broken ground, the burned and torn remains of large trees with round trunks sticking up like abstract art, for the first time in my life I truly agreed with the sentiment. It would have been better if I'd never existed.

I wondered how many lives would have been saved if Oberon had never barged into our world and ruined my family forever by siring me. There was my mother's mate, for one. He would not have committed suicide because I'd been conceived. My life had brought the world nothing but suffering.

A chill swept through me, so cold that I imagined my body turning to a sculpture made of ice. I couldn't move, could barely draw breath. Through it all, my heart beat traitorously in my chest—a steady drum that spelled life for me, but doom for others.

I'm in shock, I thought, a detached portion of myself taking stock of the strange sensation of cold. *That's strange*.

With difficulty, I dragged my gaze back to Tamlain's haughty face. He was looking down at me, his expression unreadable. Maybe he was debating killing me here and now. It would probably be the safest course of action, in his mind.

"I don't blame you, you know," I murmured. "It would be the right thing to do."

His brows drew together. "What are you saying, Little Wolf?"

I didn't answer. My eyes strayed to the distant horizon, barely illuminated by the light from the two moons.

A moment later, Tamlain stepped close in front of me, blocking the mesmerizing vision. I jerked in surprise, leaning back to put more space between us.

"What would be the right thing to do?" Tamlain demanded again.

I blinked, having no choice but to look at him. He was... so beautiful. Dianthe was a lucky woman, in many ways.

"It would be right for you to kill me," I said in a monotone. "My life is not as important as the lives of all the humans and fae I might accidentally kill. Their safety means more than mine. Plus, killing me would mean that Oberon couldn't have his crazy war."

Tamlain cocked his head to one side, his expression unchanging. Something complicated kindled behind his blue eyes.

When he spoke, his words were measured. "That is true."

"*No.*" Dianthe's voice was steely. "Don't say things like that, Ember. We will find another way to fix this."

When neither of us moved or spoke, she sighed and crossed her arms, glancing back and forth between us. "Well, I think the first thing to do is obvious."

I blinked. "Is it?"

She glared at me. "Very. *You*, Little Wolf, need to learn self-control."

If the situation had been less dire, I would have snorted. Shifters in general were not particularly well known for their emotional self-control. And I didn't even have the support of my pack to help keep me on an even keel.

"That seems a rather significant undertaking," Tamlain observed, his tone dry as dust.

I frowned at him, annoyed despite myself.

"Perhaps," Dianthe agreed. "Yet it is straightforward enough. Ember needs to avoid getting angry or frightened at all costs — even when provoked."

Sure, no problem, I thought. *I'll get right on that.*

Tamlain appeared similarly skeptical. "She is a shifter. Self-control at that level isn't really in her nature."

Even though he was right, I still threw Tamlain a dirty look. He ignored it.

"You don't give her enough credit," Dianthe observed, staring pointedly at me. "Does he, Ember?"

I turned my scowl on her. "Yeah, it's no biggie. I'll just hang out here in a completely different world after being kidnapped from Earth, contemplating the fact that the king of the fae wants to use me as a weapon in a massive war between the realms. I mean, there's no reason at all for me to feel anger or fear, right?"

Dianthe narrowed her eyes at me. "Very funny."

I glowered back. "I'm not laughing."

"Neither am I," she said.

We glared at each other for a long moment.

Tamlain cleared his throat with the air of someone whose patience was running dry. "I don't think either of you realize the bigger problem that we face."

"Bigger than her temper, you mean?" Dianthe asked, jabbing her thumb in my direction. I growled at her, probably not helping my case.

Tamlain only looked at her. "You are forgetting Oberon."

Dianthe winced. I could tell she understood what he was implying, even if I didn't.

"What about him?" I asked, resigned.

"By now he knows of my deeds, and he will name me a traitor to the realm. He certainly knew already that you were here on Elfhame. The fact that guards were posted at the edge of the warded forest is evidence enough that he expected to find you here."

"You think he'll send more guards to search for her," Dianthe said.

"I imagine those two were just a test," Tamlain continued. "Neither of them were particularly powerful, but they worked well enough to flush us out. He will send *specialists* next time."

I cringed a bit at Tamlain's careful emphasis on the word. I had no idea of the extent of fae magical powers, but I suspected that I'd be happier not knowing what a 'specialist' was capable of doing. I was beginning to understand that the king would stop at nothing to get what he wanted.

Namely, *me*.

I shivered, rubbing my hands up and down my arms.

"He won't give up, will he?" I whispered.

Both Tamlain and Dianthe looked at me, something like pity in their eyes.

"Is there nowhere that's safe?" I asked, glancing back and forth between them. "Nowhere at all?"

Dianthe looked uncomfortable and Tamlain sighed again. It was answer enough.

I thought back on my life, wondering how it was possible that it had been demolished so thoroughly in such a short span of time. Was it really only a couple of days ago that I was minding my own business, going to work at the nursing home? Was it only a few months ago that I'd still had my place—such as it was—among my pack?

My pack. I hadn't allowed myself to really think about them during my months of exile. It was too painful to be separated from others of my kind. Now, though, my grief was tainted with something else.

Betrayal.

I thought of Geneva. I thought of all the years that she had protected me; insisted that I was fed and cared for, even in the most rudimentary way. I owed my life to her, and I'd thought it was because she'd cared for me. Now I realized that she was trading my life for her own.

I didn't recognize the burn in my stomach or the heat that flooded through my body until the wind around us started to pick up.

"Wolf! *Control yourself!*" Tamlain snapped, but I was already taking deep, steadying breaths.

Within seconds, the wind retreated to a mere whisper. I looked around, distraught. What would a gentle wind here be like on Earth, though?

"I think we should return to Earth," I blurted, as though I hadn't just nearly destroyed the world again.

Dianthe sucked in a breath between her teeth. Tamlain scowled.

"Why?" he asked me, skepticism written all over his face.

I took another calming breath, feeling my emotions ebb and flow inside of me. None of my mysterious power spilled out, though—and I felt safe enough to speak.

"We can question the king's spy in the Greystalker packlands," I said, trying to sound reasonable. "Geneva Padfoot—the one you call Pavia. We need to know exactly what she told Oberon and what her orders were. That way, we can at least know what he knows."

Tamlain looked grudgingly impressed. "It's not a completely terrible idea."

I shrugged, striving for an air of indifference. "Do you have a better one?"

"No," Tamlain said. "At this point, I'm sorry to say I do not."

"Then I think it's our best option right now."

He nodded silently, his expression growing thoughtful. "Will you be able to control your emotions when faced with reminders of your past?"

I stared at my feet. For a moment the pain and rage of my exile threatened to overwhelm me. But instead of the wind whipping around me, I felt the hot sting of tears behind my eyes. I blinked them away. These fae would not see me crying like an injured pup.

"I understand the consequences now," I assured him when I could be sure my voice was steady. "I will not fail. I know there are lives at stake."

He tilted his head to the side, studying me for a moment before he nodded. "I suppose it's the best plan we've got right now."

"I'll stay here," Dianthe offered. "I can try to gather as much information as possible from my contacts at Court. My presence will draw less attention than either of yours would."

"In a hurry to get rid of me?" I asked, trying for lightness and falling far short. The terror gripping my stomach was threatening to take control again... and I couldn't afford to let it.

"Oh yes. You're the worst shapeshifter I've ever shared a cottage with, by far," Dianthe replied, deadpan.

I managed a slight smile for her. "Really? How many others have there been?"

"None," she said promptly. "You're the only shifter I've ever met." Her gaze flicked to Tamlain. "Are we agreed on this course of action, then?"

Tamlain nodded. "Yes. I will contact you in the usual way."

"The... usual way?" I asked, confused. "You two do this kind of thing often, then?"

Tamlain didn't answer. Instead, he raised his hand and cast a portal into the air in front of us. For a moment, I stared into its depths, trying to make out the world of my birth through the foggy mists. All I could see was a swirl of green and flashes of bright blue, the same color as Earth's sky.

Abruptly and achingly, my heart longed for home. Despite my fascination with Elfhame and my deep desire to explore the new world I had just discovered, I could feel the call of the forest in my very soul.

"Go," Tamlain said. "There is little time."

I wanted to growl at him for being so cold and harsh all the time, but instead I turned to Dianthe, unsure what to say. She had nearly sacrificed herself to save me, and I needed to thank her.

I couldn't bring the words to my lips, however. She smiled at me, a little sadly, and raised her hand in farewell as I let out a sigh of defeat and stepped through Tamlain's portal. As before, it felt like I was being dragged forward through space and time, the air sucked out of my lungs.

As soon as my feet found dirt again, I gasped for breath, looking around at the shockingly familiar setting. I was indeed home. I recognized the path twisting through the tall trees. I had been forbidden from returning to the Greystalker lands under pain of death. Would they believe me that there was a traitor in their midst? Would Tamlain's glowering presence at my side convince them of the truth?

Somehow I doubted it. But before I'd formed any conclusions regarding the best course of action, he stepped through the portal behind me and closed it.

"I wasn't sure you'd really bring me back," I admitted to him, my gaze wandering over my surroundings.

As soon as I looked toward the west, my heart skipped and stuttered. Where there had once been a thick forest marching down the slope toward the coastline, there was now a deep scar gouged into the earth. It was plain to see what had happened here. This was another place, just like on Elfhame, that had been destroyed in one of my fits of rage.

I stared around with wide eyes. Acrid bile rose in my throat.

"This is why you must learn control," Tamlain said tightly.

"I did this?" I breathed. "My god. How could I have done all this and not even known?"

"You draw the two realms together with your fear and rage. Earth and Elfhame were never meant to inhabit the same reality."

I shook my head slowly, as though in negation of his words. "So this happened when—"

"When you believed that Dianthe was in danger."

"All the trees," I murmured, my eyes feeling hot all of a sudden. "All the wildlife that was here. Did I kill them all?"

Tamlain's blue eyes slid closed for an instant. When he opened them, they were burning with conviction. "As I said earlier, you are not to blame."

"Well, I can't really blame Oberon, can I?" I demanded, my shocked gaze still snared by the fresh destruction.

"You should. I do," he said in a hard tone. "This never would have happened if my king had not behaved selfishly and thoughtlessly."

"Or if I had learned some self-control in the beginning," I replied.

"You're young yet," Tamlain said. He, on the other hand, sounded old and exhausted despite his youthful features.

I swallowed hard. "It's hard not to feel responsible when the desolation is right in front of me."

To that, he had no reply. We stood shoulder to shoulder in silence for a long moment, staring out over the sea of flattened trees and cracked boulders.

How could I ever make this right?

FOURTEEN

THE ENORMITY OF the task felt like a boulder dropping into the pit of my stomach, leaving me breathless and reeling.

Tamlain must have seen my reaction. His voice was gruff as he stepped close to me. His large frame loomed in my vision, blocking the destruction that lay beyond. "Remember, you must maintain control."

He grasped my arm with one callused hand. Unlike the previous times he'd grabbed me, there was no threat in the gesture. It was almost like he was trying to remind me that he was there… that I was not alone.

I took two ragged breaths and nodded, ruthlessly blinking back the tears that tried to well up.

"Okay," I said hoarsely, when I finally felt in control. "I'm okay. I'm fine."

Tamlain nodded his approval at my show of control and let me go, stepping away from me. I dragged my attention away from the destruction, wanting to shield my inner wolf from the horror of it. Somehow, the idea of protecting her from all of this steadied me, so I clung to it.

I could do this. I could maintain control.

With a deep breath, I oriented myself to the rest of my surroundings. This patch of wilderness was familiar to me. Relief poured through me, turning my legs to rubber. These were not the Greystalker homesteads. This area would have been entirely devoid of human or shifter habitations.

"No one lived here," I said. "Unless someone happened to be out here hunting, no people will have died, I don't think."

Tamlain regarded me for a beat, then offered a silent nod.

"All the wildlife, though," I said, my throat clenching painfully.

It was stupid, being upset like this over rabbits and birds that my wolf would happily have eaten for lunch, but the shifter mentality was so deeply rooted in my heart that I couldn't help it. We treated every animal with respect, even when we were hunting them. It did not escape us that we were part of a delicately balanced system, one where we paid for a life with a life.

It was sacred, even down to the smallest living creature.

Tamlain lifted a hand to his brow, massaging his temples as though they pained him. "You didn't know. You couldn't have known, because I chose not to tell you."

I blinked at him, a bit shocked that the stubborn fae would say something like that.

His hand dropped to his side. "I should have explained things sooner."

My jaw clenched, but I couldn't afford to let the anger escape. "Yes." I bit off the word. "You damn well should have."

In a way, it *was* his fault. His and Oberon's both. Too bad that didn't actually change anything.

"It's still a tragedy, either way," I managed.

He nodded. "It is, yes."

I turned to face the mountains, trying to focus on the immediate task in front of me. Standing very still, I reached out with my wolf senses, attempting to get my bearings in the forest. I recognized the general area, but everything looked and smelled different with the earth churned up behind me. Even so, I could hear the faint sound of rushing water, so I pointed in that direction.

"We need to go that way," I said, not meeting Tamlain's eyes. "And while we're walking, we need to discuss our next problem."

He raised a slanted eyebrow. "Oh? Which one shall we start with?"

I'd never heard Tamlain make a joke before — not even a dark one.

"The most immediate one," I told him, and led the way deeper into the trees. Large ferns brushed our hands and arms as we passed. The vibrant purple flowers scattered along the forest floor reminded me of Elfhame's forest, albeit a less spectacular version. "I've been exiled from my pack," I explained patiently. "We'll have to be stealthy about this. If they realize I've returned, then Bardulf — the pack alpha — will kill me."

"He will not," Tamlain replied, as though that were the end of it.

I turned on him, and he came to an abrupt halt to avoid walking into me. Damn it, why was he following me so closely?

"Uh... *yeah*," I said flatly. "He will. You can't just break exile. Nobody does that. *Ever.*"

Tamlain's brows drew together. "You need not fear, Little Wolf. No harm will come to you."

Says the guy who just threatened to kill me half an hour ago.

"I'm not scared," I said through gritted teeth, ignoring the little voice chanting, *liar, liar.*

His unblinking blue gaze pinned me. "Yes you are. After everything you've learned in the last day, how could you not be afraid?"

I considered his words for a moment, and whirled away rather than answering. We walked in silence, until finally I couldn't stand it anymore.

"Maybe you're just saving yourself the trouble of having to kill me personally." The words were out of my mouth before I could second-guess them.

"Don't worry," Tamlain replied tartly. "If I decide to kill you, you'll know it. Until then, I will not permit anything to happen to you."

I wasn't quite sure what to do with that reply, so I stayed quiet. We passed the next hour or so in silence, winding our way alongside the river, getting closer and closer to the Greystalker settlement.

I was now in familiar woods, seeing places that I had explored with Darby in the early years of my life—back when I knew nothing of the way the world worked, or of my own life. Nothing about fated mates, or Elfhame, or Oberon. Nothing of my terrible power. I could practically picture us running through the trees in our blissful ignorance, laughing and sharing secrets in the uninhibited way that only wolf pups can.

My heart ached for Darby. She was my best friend in the entire world, and I'd left her alone in a place she hated. All because of the stupid fate mark.

I wondered if her life might have been better without me, though. Had things been easier for her after I'd left? Self-loathing rose up in me, and I felt unwanted power crackling through me. Before Tamlain could notice, I redirected it inward.

Think. Don't feel.

That would have to be my new mantra from now on.

I glanced back at him, scanning his impassive face. My eyes started drifting lower, across the muscular planes of his chest. I quickly turned away, facing forward. Those feelings were just as distracting, albeit less destructive than the anger and rage I'd felt earlier. I needed to concentrate, despite the powerful fae following at my heels. Besides, Dianthe would probably kick my ass if she caught me ogling her boyfriend—even if the pair weren't exactly what you'd call demonstrative.

He said he'd protect me. Despite my best efforts, a little seed of something was germinating in my chest.

He also said he might kill you, I reminded myself firmly.

Irritated, I gave myself a little shake. The internal debate was pointless; I needed to move on. If I could just change into a wolf, everything would be simpler. We hadn't tested to see if my powers to draw Earth and Elfhame together still worked in my wolf form. Everything seemed tied to my emotional state, which was raw and unbridled as a human. As a wolf, things were much more straightforward.

My wolf still felt anger and fear, but it was different. While human thoughts still passed through my mind, in that form we lived very much in the moment. The problem was, how did you test something like that without risking more destruction and loss of life if the theory was wrong? I didn't know the answer.

Still, being a wolf would make this whole thing easier. As I considered shifting, I remembered that I only had one set of clothes, and I didn't want to have to ask Tamlain to do some more clothing repair magic. I wasn't sure how many times a fae could remake one set of clothes before they randomly dissolved into oblivion.

And I sure as hell wouldn't be showing up to see my old pack naked.

"I'm half fae, right?" I asked suddenly, inspired by my dilemma.

"Yes," Tamlain replied cautiously.

I hesitated, wondering how to word my question. "Do I have fae magic?"

His footsteps slowed for a moment as he considered this. Then he started walking again. "Beyond your destructive powers? I really have no idea. Why?"

"I was just thinking about your ability to repair things and summon clothing through the ether," I said, "it seems very useful for a shifter."

He hesitated. "We can attempt to find out, if you like."

Surprised by his offer, I glanced back at him. "Do you mean it?"

"I am fae," he replied. "We do not lie. But perhaps now is not the time for such experiments."

My heart sank, as I realized how close we were to my old home. Despite Tamlain's reassurances, I suspected there was no way I would be getting out of this completely unscathed.

With nothing else for it, I pressed on. This had, after all, been my idea in the first place. I'd just assumed we'd be doing more *sneaking* and less *casually walking in like we owned the place*. We reached the outskirts of the settlement, not far from the jail where I had spent the night suffering through the destruction of my mate bond with Cai.

The memory made me shiver as we approached the building, my keen ears alert for the sound of any of my pack mates.

"No one's around," I said, keeping my voice low.

He nodded his understanding, his sharp eyes scanning the trees. Ushering me forward with a hand barely brushing the small of my back, he indicated that we should continue deeper into the settlement. His body so near mine did not make it easy to keep my mind on our task.

We have to find Geneva. Focus on that, Ember — not the hot fae who promised to protect you from your former pack.

As we approached the main gathering place where I'd had my wolfbirth ceremony, I felt unfriendly eyes on my back and froze.

Spinning around, I saw a figure dart off into the trees in wolf form.

I thought I recognized the wolf's coloring, but he was off so quickly I couldn't be sure.

"Well," I said conversationally. "I expect the shit will hit the fan shortly, if that's what you were after."

The fae gave me an odd look. Maybe they didn't have rotating fans on Elfhame. Too bad—I'd always found that human expression rather evocative.

We continued along the main path at a purposeful pace, and I looked around the Greystalker settlement with new eyes. In many ways, it was as though I'd never left. Everything appeared just as I remembered it. *I* was the one who'd changed.

Surprised muttering followed us. The pack was shocked to see me back, breaking the terms of my exile. They were probably just as surprised—if not more—by the presence of the powerful fae warrior at my side.

More and more people followed in our wake. They mostly hung back on the winding path behind us. Some crept through the trees in near-silent wolf form, pacing us.

"Still think there's nothing to worry about?" I asked through gritted teeth. Tamlain gave me a haughty glance and didn't deign to reply.

We'd just reached the center of town when a low growl met my sensitive ears. I froze in place. Tamlain stood at my side, the picture of unconcern as a large figure burst through the trees across from us, flanked by several people.

It was Bardulf, the pack alpha himself. The one who'd exiled me... who'd ordered my fate mark burned from my chest. His rage upon seeing me was palpable, and had I been in my wolf form, I would have been on my belly in front of him, groveling.

Still, Tamlain showed no evidence of concern as he stood next to me, shoulder to shoulder.

My attention fell on the group of shifters that had entered the square behind Bardulf. I recognized some of his lieutenants, as well as a white-faced Cai.

I didn't need the sickening lurch in my stomach to remind me of our destroyed mate-bond. And he seemed every bit as viscerally aware of my presence as I was his. I tried not to take vicious satisfaction in that fact.

In fact, the alpha's son looked like he'd just seen a ghost.

I studied his stricken face, a surge of conflicting emotion rising as my wolf stirred in response to his proximity. Despite everything that had happened, she still longed to race to his side and try to comfort him in any way that she could. She found it maddening to be separated by the rocky square and the crowd of angry shifters.

But with Bardulf standing between us, we might as well have been in different realms. *Oh, the irony.*

Unhelpfully, my damaged fate mark decided that this was the moment to flare to life. I could feel the echoes of our bond, still not dead despite Bardulf's and Cai's best attempts to kill it. My wolf practically leapt with joy at the connection's resurgence. My human heart leapt with anger.

No, no! I thought, frantic to keep my emotions in check. I had no idea what that kind of primal, soul-deep betrayal would do to Earth and Elfhame.

I took several deep breaths, exhaling slowly as I controlled my trembling.

Tamlain looked down at me sharply, sensing my emotional upheaval. His eyes darted around to the trees nearby—but thankfully, they remained completely still. He gave a barely perceptible nod of approval at my control, and it shouldn't have meant as much as it did to my shattered nerves.

All of this happened in the space of a few heartbeats, and none of the pack noticed a thing. Bardulf stormed forward. Several of his shifters stalked after him, awaiting his command—death in their eyes.

My death.

Well, I thought in resignation, taking in just how badly outnumbered we were. *I did warn Tamlain this would happen.*

"Approach no closer," Tamlain commanded, his powerful voice rolling around the town square. A part of me couldn't help but admire his appearance of utter nonchalance in the face of the alpha pack leader and his enforcers. I knew all too well what a pack of determined shifters could do when they worked together.

Shock of shocks—no one listened to the fae's command. Several of the men threw off their robes and transformed into their wolf forms, snarling at us in clear threat as they closed in, ready to spring.

Tamlain sighed and waved one hand in a casual gesture. Fog swirled from his fingers, whipping around in a gray vortex above his head before descending on everyone in the approaching group.

Or rather, everyone except Bardulf.

The attacking shifters stumbled and fell to the ground, humans and wolves alike.

I gaped at the bodies around us, all of them lying still and silent—Cai among them.

"Are they—?" I broke off abruptly as a loud snore emanated from one of the men in human form.

"Asleep," Tamlain assured me dryly. He raised his voice to be heard all around the square. "And asleep they will remain, Bardulf Greystalker—until our business is concluded."

Bardulf looked astonished for the briefest of moments. If I hadn't been staring at him, I would have missed the expression. Then his features hardened into lines of fury. I took a reflexive step backward, eager to put some distance between myself and the enraged alpha bracing to attack.

It was as though Tamlain's display of power meant nothing to Bardulf. Or maybe he was too furious to think rationally. Either way, instead of pausing to consider his options, his eyes fixed on Tamlain, glowing copper-gold with rage.

"*How dare you*," he growled, his deep voice echoing off the trees and cliffs.

The shifters who had followed us at a distance were still hanging back, unaffected by Tamlain's spell. They, too, seemed to sense that their leader had lost control—not a comfortable notion for a pack.

Bardulf couldn't back down now, or he'd lose his dominance over the others. And indeed, he brought his hands to his chest and ripped his ceremonial robes off, exposing a muscular, gray-haired chest.

With a bellow of rage, the alpha dove forward. His wolf form exploded into being mid-leap, huge and grizzled, slavering with rage. He snarled, saliva flying through the air as he snapped his powerful jaws towards Tamlain, a clear challenge.

Tamlain gave the giant alpha a cynical half-smile, stepping forward to close the distance separating them. An instant later, an explosion of light burst from his body. I cried out and shielded my eyes against the dazzling glare, but not before the image of a white wolf and a dark wolf clashing in the center of the square burned its way into my retinas.

FIFTEEN

IN THE MIDDLE of the town square, Tamlain and Bardulf's wolf forms crashed together in the explosion of light. Bardulf's wolf was a black silhouette within the flare of brilliant magic. By contrast, Tamlain's wolf was a blinding, vivid white. Together, they became a blur of ripping teeth and flying fur as they tumbled over the rocky ground.

Their enraged snarling made the human part of me want to cover my ears against the cacophony as the sound echoed off the nearby mountain. My inner wolf, on the other hand, was crouched as though to spring forward into the middle of the brawl.

Bad idea, I told her firmly. *Bad, bad idea. Literally the worst idea ever.*

My eyes darted to Cai against my better judgment, and away again an instant later. It was desperately painful to be this close to him, like the wound where my mark had been burned away was fresh and blistered again. He, like the other guards, was still fast asleep on the hard ground — utterly undisturbed by the terrible noise coming from the fight.

Dragging my attention back, I watched in something like awe as Tamlain bit and tore at Bardulf's larger wolf-form. I'd seen him fight before. Hell, I'd fought him myself when he'd first tracked me down in Rockville. Now, I realized that he'd purposely used his magic during that scuffle to gain the upper hand over me without hurting me.

Well, without hurting anything except my pride, at least.

That was decidedly not the case now. Every move Tamlain made was clearly intended to cause as much damage to Bardulf as possible. He body-slammed the alpha shifter into a tree, smashing him between the unforgiving wood and Tamlain's own teeth and claws. The fae warrior tore mercilessly at Bardulf, his white muzzle streaked red with fresh blood.

It hit me rather abruptly that Tamlain was King Oberon's top general—or he had been, before his betrayal to save both Elfhame and Earth. He could well have been ancient beyond measure. His experience was obviously giving him the upper hand... but his utter ruthlessness held hints of something more personal, too. It felt like he was unleashing all of his tightly controlled frustrations on the unlucky Greystalker alpha.

Bardulf's counterattacks grew less fierce, and his lunges, less precise. He tore free of the fae, and the two wolves circled each other warily. Tamlain snarled, his teeth bared. Bardulf panted hard, clearly approaching the end of his stamina.

Despite the fact that my ex-mate lay on the ground about thirty yards from me, I couldn't help the way my gaze played over Tamlain's powerful wolf form. His coat was glossy, light shining off of the individual strands that fluttered gently in the breeze. Just as in his human form, smooth muscle rippled beneath his white pelt— bloodstained though it currently was.

Caught between two males she desired, my inner wolf whimpered in longing. I clenched my jaw and mentally shook myself.

Tamlain was obviously with Dianthe, even if they weren't exactly into public displays of affection. I couldn't let my feelings run away with me—no matter how impressive Tamlain's wolf was as he lunged again, seizing Bardulf by the scruff of the neck and whipping him around before tossing his larger opponent away. Blind with rage, Bardulf pushed to his feet and barreled straight into the shifted fae.

I frowned, seeing the alpha wolf I'd always feared in a completely different light than I ever had before. Bardulf simply lost himself to the battle. There was no strategy. No higher thought process. He was just hurling pent up aggression at a superior foe—and he was losing. *Badly*.

Had he always been like this? Had he always been so *pathetic*? Why had I never seen it until now?

These questions made me uneasy. It was against my nature to question an established alpha wolf. It simply wasn't done in shifter society—the only time anyone challenged an alpha was if they were willing to fight him for dominance, possibly to the death.

Bardulf's lack of strategy was turning the fight into less of a battle and more of a beating.

Tamlain's viciousness startled me. More than winning, he seemed to delight in the chance to cause even more injury to the alpha.

With a final ferocious lunge, Tamlain pinned Bardulf on his back by the throat. The alpha lay bleeding from several torn spots on his body.

There was a piteous moan and then, finally, stillness. It was over.

Tamlain shook his massive wolf form. Magic swirled around him, healing the few blows that Bardulf had managed to land early in the fight. When it faded, Tamlain's white fur flowed smooth and pristine, completely unmarked. It was as though the injuries had never existed in the first place.

I couldn't keep my mouth from dropping open in shock. I would never cease to be amazed at Tamlain's abilities.

Could I learn to do that? It sure would have been a handy skill to have when I was younger and constantly getting kicked around by the pack. Talk about missed opportunities.

I blinked, and Tamlain shifted back into his fae form. He hunched over Bardulf's crumpled body, still pinning him down by the neck.

"You," Tamlain said in a steely tone, "will transform to your human form. *Now*."

Alpha or no, it was a command, not a request. Bardulf looked up at the fae with fear shining in his dazed eyes… and shifted back into a man.

Tamlain released his hold on the alpha's neck with a sneer of disdain, but Bardulf did not get up. He raised a bleeding arm to swipe at the mud and blood on his face. The fae stood, towering over the former alpha's prone form. The power difference between the two was so drastic that it brought a strange lump of feeling to my throat. Bardulf had led our pack—yet in the end, he was weak.

Turning in a slow circle, Tamlain searched the faces of the wolves and humans in the crowd for any signs of imminent attack. There were none. The others hung back at a safe distance.

"Here is your alpha," the fae said, still in that same cool voice. "Lying beaten in the middle of your town square with all of his lieutenants—defeated by a single man."

There was a slight rustling of discomfort, but no one moved or objected.

Tamlain gave a careless shrug before turning his attention back to me. The skin at the back of my neck prickled under that blue gaze, and my wolf gave a delicious shudder.

Thoughts of Cai, lying insensible with the others, instantly brought me back to reality. I chewed on my bottom lip, suddenly nervous. Clearing my throat, I said, "Actually, I think you should release Cai—the alpha's son—from the sleeping spell now."

I gestured towards my former mate, who was curled up like a pup taking a nap.

Tamlain raised an eyebrow.

I blushed furiously. "He probably knows where Geneva is," I hurried to add.

I didn't have to explain further, but the way that Tamlain gazed at me made me feel like I was naked again. During our brief acquaintance, I hadn't shared the details with him. But was it possible this fae knew the story of my exile? The *whole* story?

"If you insist," Tamlain said after a long moment, his tone studiously indifferent.

With a casual wave of his hand, Tamlain reversed the spell. Cai immediately began to stir. He blinked several times and pushed himself to his feet, staring at the carnage around him, his eyes growing wide.

I drew breath to say something, but the words died in my throat. Cai's gaze narrowed, taking in the crumpled, bleeding figure of his father — still on the ground at Tamlain's feet.

Slowly, he raised his head, his disbelieving gaze falling on the fae.

Tamlain lifted his hand, examining his fingernails as though he didn't have a care in the world. "If you would like to fight me, too, wolf, that can be arranged."

Cai straightened to his full height at Tamlain's words, but he didn't attack — demonstrating far more sense that I ever would have expected from him.

"No," he said. "Perhaps we should go somewhere quiet and have a conversation, instead of a battle?"

Tamlain smiled — that cynical half-twist of lips that I'd seen several times now. "How terribly civilized of you. I see that you do not take after your sire."

Cai's jaw muscles clenched, but he didn't rise to the bait. Instead, he gestured toward the prone figures. "What about my packmates? Have you harmed them permanently?"

The fae made a tiny scoffing noise. "*Please.* They will awaken just as you did, once I release them from the spell."

Cai gave him a guarded nod and turned towards the crowd. Many of them were clustered together, whispering into each other's ears. "You and you," he said, pointing at two men. "Take my father to the healer's den."

Without a word, the pair hurried forward and hauled their fallen alpha to unsteady feet. Even though he was clearly in pain, I could tell that Bardulf was furious at being sent away from the situation. I wondered what Cai made of all this.

Bardulf had lost the fight fair and square, though. An alpha who lost to another was no longer an alpha. He had no right to attend this meeting.

I felt torn watching Tamlain and Cai move closer together, preparing to depart the scene. It was horribly conflicting to see them like this, as if two parts of my life were crashing together. Past and future. Old and new.

"Please," Cai said courteously, dipping his gaze before the fae who had bested Greystalker's leader. "Allow me to conduct you to our den."

Tamlain gave a single, regal nod of acknowledgement. We walked through the town with Cai. My sensitive ears picked up several members of the pack trailing behind us, murmuring to each other. I wondered for a moment if Darby was one of them, and without warning my heart began to ache for my sweet friend.

I pushed the thoughts away. If she'd been among the crowd, she would have called out to me. I was sure of it. Besides, this was not the time for personal concerns—as much as I might wish it was.

By the time we reached the alpha's extravagant dwelling, night had fallen. Cai opened the door for us and I was surprised that no one greeted us at the entrance. Although I'd never been inside, I knew that there were members of the household guard that served as protectors for the alpha's family when he was away. There were also servants.

Cai, however, didn't miss a beat at having to play host without support. "Let me take your things."

He accepted Tamlain's cloak and hung it up in the hallway, before offering us refreshments. We murmured our thanks, and he led us into a large sitting room. The richly furnished space included several comfortable chairs situated around a fireplace carved into the natural stone of the mountainside.

As he efficiently nursed a fire to life, I caught Cai throwing glances in my direction from time to time. His eyebrows were drawn together in thought, or perhaps concern. At one point our eyes met, and Cai quickly turned away, saying something about returning with food and drink. My stomach rumbled hopefully at his words. The meal that Dianthe and I had shared seemed like a lifetime ago.

He returned a short time later with a platter heaped with simple honey cakes, blocks of cheese, and fruit. Cai set it before us, and went to poor us large, cold drafts of water from the mountains. I drank deeply and stuffed food in my mouth, hunger and thirst overpowering my curiosity about Cai's oddly obsequious behavior—not to mention, any desire I might have had to appear either dignified or polite.

With his host duties completed, Cai sank into a chair across from us. "Why have you come here?" he asked Tamlain. His gaze flickered to me and away again. "Why bring *her*?"

I probably should have been offended. Instead, I took another giant bite of honey cake.

Tamlain steepled his fingers together—a thoughtful gesture. "Perhaps Ember should be the one to explain."

I froze, my hand halfway to my mouth as my eyes flew to the fae's accusingly. How was I supposed to explain this situation to Cai? Wasn't it meant to be a secret? Besides, I barely understood it myself. How on Earth was I going to convince him?

Replacing the food on the plate, I swallowed a gulp of water and sat back in the chair, considering what to say. The silence stretched for a long moment, growing heavy. Finally, I steeled myself and looked straight into Cai's eyes.

The ghostly burn of the mate bond bubbled up in my chest again. By the strain I could see in Cai's face, I guessed he was experiencing something similar.

Good. It served him right.

"Earth and the fae realm of Elfhame are on the brink of war," I began. "There's a lot to explain, most of which I barely understand, but I'll try my best."

I paused again, cleared my throat, and continued, "The story that the pack tells about my birth isn't the whole truth. I'm not some random shifter's bastard. My father is the King of Elfhame."

Cai blinked, an expression of disquiet sliding across his handsome features. "Who told you that? Your father was a lone wolf who shattered the mate-bond with your mother. You're the result of a crime against nature."

These words had been hurled at me my entire life, but hearing them out of my mate's mouth stung. I had to cover a flinch, gritting my teeth to keep from snapping at him.

"No doubt that is the story you've been told," Tamlain said. "It is not, however, the truth."

Cai's gaze shifted back and forth between us. I found that it was hard to look him in the eye. Tamlain seemed content to let me explain, so I gathered myself with difficulty and continued. "The fae king Oberon grew jealous of his wife Titania, who was friends with a shifter and her pup."

"But shifters can't travel to—" Cai cut in.

I glared him into silence. It felt good. "Yeah, so people say. But *I've* been there, and anyway, the how and why of a shifter being in Elfhame with her pup isn't important. The point is that they were."

Cai looked like he wanted to argue more. In his defense, the notion was a pretty wild one... but he gave a curt nod and lapsed back into silence.

I continued before anyone could come up with another interruption. "Oberon wanted to take the pup as his personal slave, but Titania hid him away to protect him. So the fae king came to Earth and impregnated my mother as a way to get some kind of twisted revenge against his wife for her interference, while also getting what he wanted—a shifter to keep as his own. He was indifferent about me as an actual daughter, so I guess he left me here with the pack until I became old enough to be of interest to him."

Anger, confusion, and bitterness warred inside me as I spoke, fighting to spill out. But there was too much at stake. I refused to let them wrest free of my control.

Tamlain was looking at me with a satisfied expression, presumably at my unexpected emotional mastery. When he caught me staring back, he gave me a fleeting smile and a nod of encouragement.

I took a deep breath. "While I was with the pack, Oberon sent a spy to report back about me. Turns out, she gave him some very, *very* valuable information... and now Earth and Elfhame are on the brink of war—because of me."

"Why?" Cai asked. He'd gone pale again, I couldn't help noticing.

I shifted uncomfortably in my chair, glancing at Tamlain for help. He jerked his chin toward Cai

188

in a way that said I should just get it over with and tell him.

Right. "Because apparently I have fae powers and shifter powers, since I'm from both worlds. The kind of power that destroys things."

Cai looked alarmed, and I wondered if he was thinking of the ravaged forest at the edge of the packlands. "What does that even mean?"

I smiled grimly. It felt like a rictus. "You know exactly what destruction I'm talking about, Cai."

"The forest," Cai breathed. "The council has been meeting about it. The humans are saying it was caused by a meteor—a rock falling from space and exploding on impact."

"No," I said simply.

"There was also a terrible storm not far from here," Cai went on. "They seem to strike at random."

"Well." I grimaced and dragged a hand over my face. "Not *entirely* at random."

"That was you." He looked positively ill.

I shrugged helplessly. "Sort of. When I get angry, Earth and Elfhame get pulled together, and somehow that causes the storms and the destruction. I only just learned about this myself," I added, with a pointed glare at Tamlain.

"Indeed," he said—rather unhelpfully, in my opinion.

"Anyway, now that I know"—my glare intensified—"I'm doing my best to prevent it from happening again."

Cai's complexion was the color of curdled milk by this point. I saw him swallow convulsively, like he was fighting back nausea. The bond between us throbbed painfully. We both reached up at the same moment to clutch at our chests, where the marks had been burned out of us.

As soon as he noticed the mirrored motion, Cai jerked his hand away and clasped it firmly with his other. He appeared angry at his own lapse. I let my hand fall slowly to my side. Was he as drawn to me as I still was to him? He clearly felt the ghost of our bond, just as I did.

There were so many questions that I wanted to ask him. At the same time, I could feel my inner wolf straining to reach out and nuzzle into Cai's neck. She desperately wanted the bond, even now.

And I couldn't afford to think like that. I *couldn't.*

With so many questions swirling around in my head, I reached for the one that was most important, and least likely to plunge me into emotional quicksand.

"I told you Oberon sent a spy here," I said. "We need to speak with Geneva Padfoot right away. Where is she?"

His eyes widened in understanding and his breath escaped in a huff.

"Geneva Padfoot?" he said blankly. "She's gone."

"What?" I exclaimed, surging to my feet. "You *let her go?*"

He only stared at me. "What grounds would we have had to stop her? Besides, she just disappeared. It was right after the destruction that hit the edge of the packlands."

Tamlain and I exchanged a look. My expression was horrified. His was grim.

SIXTEEN

WITH A SNARL of frustration, Tamlain rose to his feet and glared down at Cai. "Did she take anyone with her? Is *anyone else missing*?" he demanded, tension rolling off him in waves.

Obviously out of his depth, Cai glanced at me for the briefest of moments. He steeled himself to meet Tamlain's burning gaze, squaring his shoulders.

"Just one other—a young, low-status shifter who used to hang around with…" His voice trailed away as if my very name burned his lips. Instead he gestured lamely and said, "With her."

I blinked at him. My mind was frozen in denial, but my body felt like it was in free fall.

A young, low-status shifter who used to hang around with me. Who used to hang around with… me.

The words played inside my head on an unhelpful loop, drowning out everything else. I could feel myself starting to tremble, and Cai's next words seemed to come from a long way away.

"Her family has been searching for her, but they haven't had any luck finding her."

"*Darby.*" The name escaped my throat as a whimper, so low and soft that I was sure neither of the two men could hear me. I was wrong, however.

Tamlain's face filled my vision. He gripped my shoulders with firm hands and gave me a sharp shake. I blinked his blue eyes into focus, barely able to think past the horror and rage growing inside me.

"*Stop*." Tamlain's voice demanded my attention. "Ember. This person is obviously important to you, but my homeland and the lives of my kinsman all rest on your ability to control your emotional reaction."

I dragged in a gasping breath as the sense of his words registered. Even as I continued to tremble beneath his warm grip, I remembered the barren wastelands I had seen on both Earth and Elfhame. I could *not* be responsible for more lives lost... more lands destroyed. My emotions were burning me from the inside out, but I took another longer, steadying breath and pushed my feelings down deep, burying them inside a vault of iron control.

The whisper of breeze blowing ominously around the room stilled. My eyes were damp with frustrated tears. I let the air in my lungs out slowly, nodding at Tamlain when I felt like I had regained control.

"Good," he said, rubbing gentle circles on my shoulders with his thumbs. "Thank you, Little Wolf."

A low growl sounded from behind me. I twisted in Tamlain's grip to find Cai on his feet now, as well—the ghost of the wolf in his gaze, alight with possessive jealousy.

Jealousy? I looked at my former mate in sheer disbelief. How dare he? How *dare* he act as though he still had some claim over me, after what he'd done?

The shock of it was enough to temporarily banish the lingering terror and anger that I felt for Darby, as I stared him down.

Tamlain, too, had heard the noise rumbling in the back of Cai's throat. The fae narrowed his eyes in menace. It was very clear that he would have welcomed the chance to deliver the alpha's son the same kind of beat-down his father had just suffered at his hands.

We didn't have time for this.

"Enough, both of you!" I said. Didn't they see that we had more important matters to deal with than a pissing match over who held some ridiculous claim over me?

Anger tried to rise again—anger over the fact that I couldn't even control my own damned life—but that wasn't helpful, either.

"Tell us everything you know about Geneva and Darby's disappearance," I demanded. "There must be something that can help us find them."

I kept my emotions under control, but I couldn't hide the intensity in my voice and body language. I—a lowly, exiled lone wolf—was demanding answers of the presumptive alpha of my former pack. But maybe that was the point. He wasn't *my* alpha. Not anymore. Maybe he never really had been.

"There's nothing more I can tell you," Cai said. He, too, seemed to be working hard to control his emotions. "Their possessions were untouched, no one saw them go. They just disappeared in the dead of night. No reason to think the disappearances were connected, except for the timing. Darby's family has been making inquiries, thinking that maybe she ran away and joined another pack."

"Darby. Who is she to you, exactly?" Tamlain asked, turning towards me.

"She was my best friend," I responded without expression. I could say no more without threatening the shaky control I held over my feelings of horrified dread.

Tamlain nodded his understanding and turned back towards Cai. "It's as I feared, then. *You*. Tell me everything you know about Geneva Padfoot."

It was clear that Cai didn't appreciate being ordered around by the fae, even after seeing what had happened to Bardulf.

He scowled and folded his arms. "What makes you think I know anything of use? She was an outsider. A wanderer who settled here and mostly kept to herself."

My own growl rose in my throat. "You're lying. Cai—I swear I will let him tear off your limbs one by one if you don't tell us *every single thing* you know."

I barely recognized my own voice. It held an unaccustomed power that I'd never heard there before.

Cai clenched his jaw, but something in my expression seemed to convince him to speak. "It's true that I did speak with Geneva a handful of times over the years. Mostly about you, as it happens." It sounded like the words were being pulled from him.

The wolf inside of me perked up at the idea that he'd thought about me over the years, but I did my best to ignore the feeling. "About *me*?"

He nodded. "She warned me that you were... different."

"Explain," Tamlain demanded. "What exactly did she say?"

"She wouldn't tell me any more than that," Cai replied, shaking his head. "All she would say was that you were special in some way that was related to magic. I admit that I didn't take her seriously at first. She was just this crazy old lady that lived at the edge of the village. I didn't have a reason to investigate her outlandish claims."

He sounded defensive, but I hardly noticed. I felt a fresh wave of anger building at the idea that so much had been kept from me all these years, and shoved it down hard.

"She called you a threat to the status quo, or something like that," he said. "I do remember that part."

My head snapped up, and my bewilderment must have been etched across my face.

Cai gave me an apologetic look and continued. "She always encouraged me to look out for you. To protect you. She said it was important that your... *differences*... were never discovered."

Tamlain tapped his fingers thoughtfully on the table. "That is telling. What did you do?"

"Not very much, really," Cai admitted. "I did my best to keep the pack from being too harsh with her. As the alpha's son, that was my duty, regardless." He turned to look at me. "But you didn't really seem to need protecting from much else."

"Hold on a second. Your *duty*?" I spat. "You thought keeping the others from beating the shit out of me was *your duty*?"

Cai grimaced. "You were just a pup. Hell, Ember—we both were. What was I supposed to do? Let them beat you for having the misfortune of being born a bastard?"

"Why would Geneva ask *you* of all people to watch after me?" I retorted. "Because, *news flash*, you did a terrible job at it!"

But that wasn't exactly true. As I thought back through the early years of my life, I remembered many times that Cai would seem to magically appear and distract the bullies from their attack on me. He'd come onto the scene just as I was being bloodied up and demand that they go hunting with him, or he'd order them away and shuffle me off to Geneva. Even as recently as the eve of my wolfbirth ceremony, Cai had been instrumental in stopping the attack that resulted in that first strange windstorm.

Maybe I was being unfair. The realization stung.

As though he could read my thoughts, Cai's face flushed pink and he said, "I did the best I could. Geneva always said the most important thing was that you needed to avoid close scrutiny, otherwise you'd end up dead."

"But why did she ask *you*?" I pressed.

His skin turned an even brighter shade of red and he glanced away, breaking eye contact in a very un-alphalike manner.

"*Tell me,*" I demanded, leaning forward to press my unexpected advantage. I was desperate for any information that might give me answers.

"Geneva knew my secret," Cai said, still looking away.

"Your secret?" I asked, even more confused than before.

"My feelings for you," he said reluctantly. He rubbed his forehead as he spoke, pinching the skin together as if it was causing him pain. "She could tell when I looked at you that I was attracted to you."

The swooping sensation in my stomach nearly made me gasp aloud. It felt like the solid flagstone floor had suddenly dropped out from underneath me, and I was in free-fall.

Tamlain had been quiet, letting me pull the story from Cai one painful word at a time. "*Ah,*" he breathed, in the tone of one experiencing a revelation.

It was probably a different revelation than the one *I'd* just experienced.

"Y-you were?" I stammered.

Tamlain shifted next to me, but I ignored him. My eyes bored into Cai, willing him to speak.

"*Yes.*" The word was a hiss. "During your ceremony, when our mate-bond was revealed, I panicked, all right? I knew that we could never be mates. Talk about scrutiny—every aspect of your life would have been picked apart and examined. I didn't know what else to do, so I rejected the bond to protect you."

If ever I were going to fly into a rage, this would have been the appropriate moment. I took several deep breaths and pictured the destruction that I'd already caused, willing myself to stay calm as my pulse thundered unchecked in my ears.

It was all so completely and utterly ridiculous. Why would Cai believe Geneva in the first place? She wasn't even a part of the Greystalker pack—not really. She'd always been an outsider, tolerated because she had a business that sold trinkets people wanted to buy. Why would Cai believe her so easily? Why had he let her manipulate him so transparently?

And why hadn't he simply told me the truth instead of having me banished from the pack... from my home?

These questions battered at me until I felt a throbbing headache bloom between my eyes. I pinched the bridge of my nose, trying to stay calm.

"*Why?*" I breathed, the single word encompassing all of my questions.

"I was afraid," Cai said, sounding defeated. "I didn't know if what she was saying was true, but I couldn't risk it. Not with you."

"But you could have told me!" I snapped. "So much of this could have been avoided if you'd just talked to me! It was *my life* you were playing with!"

Tamlain laid a warm hand on my arm, reminding me again of everything that was at stake in that moment. I gritted my teeth and pulled in the power that had started leeching out of me as my temper flared. Was it getting easier to do so, with practice? I couldn't tell for sure, but I supposed the absence of wind rising around me boded well.

"I don't know why I didn't tell you," Cai said. His brow furrowed, but his eyes were vacant and distant as he spoke. "It makes perfect sense now that I should have, but at the time I just... *couldn't*."

Tamlain snorted. "No mystery there. You were fae-touched — simple as that."

Cai and I both turned to him in surprise before glancing at each other uncertainly.

"Fae-touched?" I asked, prompting him to explain.

Tamlain gestured towards Cai and said, "Geneva needed this one to comply, so she told him her story and wrapped it up in a spell to bind his mind."

"She did *what* to my *what*?" Cai demanded, looking genuinely alarmed.

"What did she tell you would happen if Ember's secret was ever discovered?" Tamlain challenged, his eyebrows raised.

Cai fell silent, but a queasy expression slid across his face. "She said my father would kill her on the spot."

"And you believed her," Tamlain replied curtly. "Because it played into your deepest fears. The spell needed a place to land in your mind, so she wrapped it up in a story that you deemed plausible. That's how she was able to take such a firm hold on you, overriding your rational thinking."

"So it was the power of the spell that convinced you to have me banished?" I asked Cai tentatively.

Tamlain replied before he could. "Yes and no. He might have chosen some other response, but it still would have been something in line with the suggestions Pavia—or Geneva, if you prefer—planted in his mind."

Cai bristled. "I don't appreciate all this talk of someone controlling me, fae. I'm not some weak whelp to roll over for an old woman."

An emotion washed over me that wasn't anger, exactly. Rather, it was an odd sort of supreme confidence in both my own rightness and Cai's utter cluelessness. I channeled that feeling into my burning glare.

Instantly he backed down, almost shrinking in his seat. His eyes darted away. I was aware on some level that I should never have been able to cow the alpha's son with a single glance... but that was a concern for another time.

Tamlain shot me a speculative look. I cleared my throat and tried to redirect the conversation to the most important topic.

"I get why Geneva would leave. She has to report back to Oberon. But what does Darby have to do with any of this?" I asked the fae.

Please tell me her disappearance is just a crazy coincidence, I thought, already knowing it wasn't true.

He gave me a pitying look, and I knew then that whatever he said next would be bad.

Tamlain sighed heavily. "My best guess is that Geneva has already told Oberon that your powers are triggered through powerful negative emotions like anger and fear. She will also have told him about your friend's existence. I suspect that she took Darby straight to Oberon to use as leverage against you."

I staggered backward into the chair I'd vacated earlier. Tamlain lifted his hands in a calming motion, but I didn't need his wordless warning.

I could feel power coalescing inside of me. Ice and fire were blending together inside my soul, forming a growing sea of energy. I didn't let it spill over to pull Earth and Elfhame together. No wind picked up outside, yet I could feel the terrible, raw power expanding under my skin as though my body might split open and pour it all out in a wave of unstoppable destruction.

"Ember, you must stay calm," Tamlain said. "Many lives in both realms depend on it."

"I know." My voice sounded strange in my ears. Resonant.

Cai's expression was half horrified, half fascinated.

"Your eyes," he said. "They're *glowing*."

I blinked, taken by surprise. The buzzing sensation that had filled my body faded and vanished. Just like that, I was *me* again, my body slumped heavily in the chair. A great weariness pressed me down, but I needed to know the truth.

"What will Oberon do to her? What's his plan?" I looked up at Tamlain pleadingly, demanding answers.

Tamlain crouched in front of the chair and took my hand. He squeezed my fingers as though to impart courage.

"If Oberon succeeds in capturing you and bringing you back to Elfhame, he will use Darby to force strong emotions from you, pulling on the Earth and causing widespread destruction here. You are the weapon he covets—the one that will give him dominion over both realms… or at least, whatever is left of them when he's done. Your friend is the lever. You are the weight that needs to be moved."

"But what does that *mean*?" I whispered.

Tamlain shook his head, his eyes narrowing in sympathy. "There are many ways he could use her against you. Just as the threat of Dianthe's death during the battle caused you to lose control, so might a threat against your childhood friend. A threat, or… worse."

Ice crawled through me as his meaning became clear. With Darby as a hostage, Oberon could master me. He could force me to do anything he wanted. If the choice was between destroying the world of my birth, or standing by as Darby was tortured or killed, which would I choose?

SEVENTEEN

"WE HAVE TO go rescue my friend," I insisted, my throat growing tight.

Cai shifted in his seat and threw a look at Tamlain, as though he couldn't believe his ears. But the fae only gazed at me steadily, giving a single, slow blink.

"That will be impossible," he said.

I laughed bitterly and replied, "Oh, *hell*, no. It's definitely not. If I've learned anything over the last few days it's that *nothing* is impossible."

Maybe that was stretching things a bit, but Tamlain got my point. I'd been dragged between realms, discovered that I was the daughter of the fae king Oberon, and also that I had the power to destroy worlds with my emotions.

He tilted his head in grudging acknowledgement of my words, but didn't back down. "While the last few days seem to have pressed the boundaries between possible and impossible, I assure you that rescuing this shifter from Oberon is not feasible."

"Why not?" I demanded.

Tamlain sighed in frustration. "You clearly don't understand what it means to be Oberon's captive. Your friend will be kept in the deepest dungeons at the very heart of the palace. She will be heavily guarded by the best warriors in the realm, not to mention all the rest of the security around the entire royal complex."

"Which you know all about, I take it?" I said, my voice icy.

"I trained most of them," Tamlain snapped, biting off the words. "I designed Oberon's defense strategy."

"Then you should know exactly how to get around it," I pointed out.

He didn't look impressed. "There is no such thing as a perfect defense, but if there were, it would be that design. That castle is functionally impenetrable."

I tapped my chin for a moment, thinking about my next argument.

"Fine," I conceded, "but not trying isn't an option either, since Oberon has basically figured out that he can use her as emotional leverage against me."

Tamlain stared me down. "Clearly. In case you hadn't noticed, he's doing so right now."

I ignored that. "Doesn't matter. Think about the big picture. We don't want him having that kind of control over my emotions, do we?"

"No," Tamlain agreed. "We don't. Which doesn't negate the fact that it has already happened."

"The other thing," I said, trying to keep the fear bubbling up in my stomach at bay, "is that we can't forget how easy it was for you to find and capture me on Earth."

His brow furrowed. "Your point being?"

"It was *nothing* to you. You didn't even break a sweat. Practical upshot—me being here is no safer than me being on Elfhame. If Oberon wants me, he'll just send someone to come and get me again."

Cai turned towards Tamlain, scowling. "You captured her and took her to the fae realm? You could have driven her mad!" He glanced at me. "Well... *madder*, anyway."

I waved him off, still focused on my argument with Tamlain. "Shut up, Cai. I'm half fae—*apparently*. My sanity wasn't in any danger. Now, *focus*. We can't just sit here and do nothing. Darby is my best friend! I will *not* simply give up on her like that."

Tamlain blew out a breath, obviously annoyed by my stubbornness. "The best I can do is take you back to Elfhame and keep you in hiding there. I will make contact with Dianthe and find out what she was able to discover from her acquaintances at the palace. After which, we will discuss our next steps."

I smiled despite the anger boiling inside of me, showing teeth. It wasn't a nice expression. No, that was *not* enough. I would not surrender Darby to Oberon's cruelty so easily.

"It's a start." I replied sweetly, knowing both men saw the hardness beneath the facade.

Cai looked between us. "And what do you expect me to do now? In case you've forgotten, you just deposed the pack alpha and threw our clan into chaos."

Tamlain and I shared a mystified glance.

"I don't expect you to do anything, whelp," Tamlain said. "Your petty shifter power struggles hold no interest for me."

"That's the point I'm trying to make, you sanctimonious fae asshole," Cai said through gritted teeth. "Because apparently, I accidentally contributed to the world maybe ending soon, not to mention the fact that one of my pack members is now the prisoner of a psychopathic fae king who wants to start a war. I'm asking if you want me to come with you."

"Wait. You'd do that?" I asked, taken aback.

Cai shrugged. "The pack will be in an uproar after my father's defeat. The power vacuum will lead to problems, it's true—but that's my father's issue, until and unless I decide to make it mine by challenging him for control of the pack. I will come with you if you ask."

He stared straight into my eyes as he said the final words. The intensity of that amber gaze sent a shiver down my spine, rousing my wolf. Warmth spread through me despite myself, starting from the pit of my stomach.

Tamlain gave Cai a pitying look. "You'd go insane the minute you set foot on Elfhame, pup."

My pleasurable bubble burst abruptly.

Reminding myself that Cai was still the asshole who'd rejected our bond and sent me away, I pushed everything down, determined to stay focused on Darby. The hazy memory of her face swirling in my mind made my stomach churn. If shifters went crazy on Elfhame, was she already lost to me?

I shook the unwanted thoughts away. It didn't matter if she'd succumbed to the fae realm's magic or not, I would not abandon her to the whims of Oberon. She was still my friend, even if he'd already broken her.

Cai remained focused on me, ignoring Tamlain's dismissive words. "It's your choice, Ember," he said, his gaze never wavering. For a moment, it felt like we were the only two beings in existence.

Stop, I told myself harshly. *Think.*

It was too much, after all the betrayals I had suffered. I tore my eyes away from him despite my wolf's silent howl of protest. He didn't deserve to see into my heart like that. He didn't deserve to see how much pain I was hiding.

There was no way I would allow him that kind of connection with me. Not now.

"You should stay here," I said, as though it meant nothing to me. "There will probably be a lot of alpha wannabes running around, right? Can't let leadership of the Greystalker pack fall to some random asshole with a chip on his shoulder."

Cai might as well have been turned to stone. When he finally answered, it was through lips that barely moved when he spoke. "If that's what you want."

Had my rejection upset him? *Oh, the irony.*

"You'll need to keep the pack from splintering," I told him. "That is, assuming you're ready to challenge your father for his place as an alpha. And you probably should."

"I hadn't given it much thought until today," Cai admitted, his voice low. "I never considered that he might lose his status in such a…"

He trailed off, not finishing his statement.

"Stupid way?" I suggested, not pulling the punch. "Well, just do me a favor. Try not to lose any more pack members like you lost Darby."

With that vicious parting shot, I stalked towards the front door. Tamlain was a silent shadow at my shoulder. I was determined to escape my ex-mate's presence after getting the last word. Then, I would put him out of my mind for good.

Yeah, right, I thought sourly.

"Ember—" Cai said, before I could make good on my hasty exit.

Damn.

I stopped, but couldn't bring myself to turn around. My shoulders were a tight line of tension as the silence stretched between us. I didn't know what to say, so I shook my head without looking back and slipped outside.

"Let's just get back to Elfhame, please," I told Tamlain, surprised by how steady my voice sounded.

Tamlain's expression gave nothing away as he waved his hand in a slow, circular motion. The portal opened right on the doorstep in front of us. I stepped through the magical gateway and felt the disconcerting lurch as I landed in the fae realm.

It took my eyes a long moment to adjust to the sudden darkness of my surroundings. My last visit to Elfhame had been in a part of the world that was bright and colorful, the vibrant hues slightly muted during the hours of darkness but no less distinctive. This, however, was entirely different. The landscape was shrouded in a heavy, black mist, and a faint smell of sulfur hung in the air.

I hadn't heard Tamlain step through the portal behind me, but his low voice came at my shoulder an instant later. "Let's go, Little Wolf."

I gestured around us. "Go where? What is this place, anyway? There's nothing but darkness and mist in all directions."

"And shadows," he answered gravely. "One mustn't forget the shadows."

He seemed to know where he was going despite the lack of visible landmarks. With little choice, I followed him through the disorienting landscape. As we passed through the mist, every glimpse I got of our surroundings looked nearly identical to the last one.

"Tamlain, seriously—what *is* this place?" I asked again, pressing closer to him. Out of the corner of my eye, I saw one of the larger shadows shift between the trees, and the hair on the back of my neck stood up. My wolf whined, and I could feel my heart thrumming nervously against my ribs.

"There is a place nearby," he said. "Dianthe and I used it to pass messages to one another, back when we were both young. It's a very large tree. Very old, and full of magic."

"Oh?" I asked. Another formless shape moved, somewhere off to my left. The wolf growled in alarm, her hackles rising.

Trying to keep the conversation moving to hold my fear at bay, I jabbed Tamlain with my elbow and said, "I still don't understand why this place is so different from the other forest I saw."

"It's a different part of Elfhame," Tamlain replied evasively. "It's not really important for you to know every single detail about the magic of our world... but not all of this world is drenched in light magic. Some of it is dark."

I couldn't really argue with that logic under the circumstances, since I knew nothing about how magic actually worked. I was, however, eager to keep talking. I'd noticed another shape rising up in the darkness and irrational fear was clawing at my throat.

I pressed on. "Fine. In that case, tell me how long you and Dianthe have been together. We're trying to save two worlds, and I feel like I barely know you."

Tamlain stopped so suddenly that I nearly crashed into him. "I *beg* your pardon?" he asked, sounding incredulous.

"Uh," I said, looking at him in confusion. "It's a simple enough question, surely. You and Dianthe — how long have you two been lovers?"

Tamlain stared down at me in the murky darkness, looking at me as though I'd grown a second head. "We are not lovers. We are cousins. We grew up together."

I stared right back at him, trying to reset my brain to take this new information on board. *"Cousins?"*

Tamlain let out an annoyed sigh. "I am certain that humans and shifters also use that term. It means that our mothers—"

"Were sisters?" I finished for him, astonished.

"Precisely." He was still peering at me, his face an almost comical picture of offense. "You really thought—?"

I let out a huff of shocked laughter. "I thought you were together, yeah. You've got that whole 'old mated couple' vibe going on."

He made a disgruntled noise. "*Hardly*. Don't be offensive."

Still wrestling with this unexpected revelation, I fell silent as we continued our trek toward Tamlain's mysterious destination. Curious, I allowed my gaze to flit over the powerful fae guiding me through the darkness with sure, confident steps, watching him from the corner of my eye. He had protected me—so far, at least. At times his blinding power frightened me, but that had more to do with the scope of his abilities. I didn't feel like I was personally in danger with him.

Stupid of me, probably, since he'd said outright that he would kill me if that was the only way to save the realms. And yet... he'd also promised that if it came to that, I would know it was coming. I believed him.

I studied his face with covert glances, comparing his noble appearance to Cai's rugged features. By contrast, the fae was ethereally beautiful—an enigmatic combination of youth and great wisdom.

At last, the gloom parted as we approached a massive, twisted tree that rose high into the air. It was far taller than the tallest tree I'd ever seen on Earth. I gaped upwards, trying to see to the top in the weak starlight.

"Okay," I managed. "*That* is a huge freaking tree, all right."

"We used to play here as children. We were the ones who left the silks," Tamlain explained. He gestured to the lowest branches, where strips of fabric in all colors hung. Some were faded and dirty, obviously having been exposed to the march of time. Others were brighter, more recent additions. Baubles and glittering bundles were also there, some with only a dull shine remaining to them.

Tamlain moved to the nearest branch and untied a blue silk sash from around his belt.

"This will let Dianthe know that we have returned—without letting anyone *else* know," he said, tossing it over one of the branches and tying it into a complicated knot with the ends hanging free.

A moment later, he froze. His right hand moved in a flash, reaching for the blade sheathed at his side. Quick as lightning, he stepped between me and the base of the tree. Starlight flashed on his polished iron blade as he whipped it out and brandished it towards the darkening shadows at the base.

"You," he breathed as I peeked around his shoulder.

To my utter astonishment, Geneva Padfoot stood where the shadow had been a moment before. She regarded us coolly. Wind rose, whispering through my hair, and I took deep breaths to calm my flare of anger.

I had to remain in control.

The breeze quieted. Everything was totally silent for a beat. Then, she moved with a swiftness that was astonishing for such an old woman. Darting forward, she spun past Tamlain, who swung his blade through the empty air. It whistled, but did not find its mark. Geneva lunged straight at me, her hands held in front of her, balled into fists.

I staggered away from her, the suddenness of her attack throwing me off balance.

In a flash, she tossed a handful of dust in my face. It coated the inside of my nose and mouth as I gasped in shock. Coughing and choking, I tried to expel it, but I couldn't avoid inhaling the particles. I expected pain, because surely this had to be some sort of weapon meant to hurt me. Was it poison? Some kind of chemical?

What I did *not* expect was the cloying, sweet smell and taste, or the low, liquid heat kindling in the pit of my stomach.

"What the *fuck*?" I sputtered, frantically trying to wipe the dust from my eyes and mouth.

I charged after her clumsily, gritting my teeth to keep my emotions in check. I knew that she had information about Darby and I was damned well going to drag it out of her—whatever it took. I didn't care. Geneva's betrayal of me still stung, and I wanted answers. Maybe a bit of revenge, too.

Had it all been a lie? I longed to ask. *Did you ever care for me at all?*

My voice didn't seem to be operating properly, because rather than words, all that emerged was a deep growl.

This all happened so quickly that I never saw Tamlain move. I had been blinded by my desire to lay my hands on Geneva—not to mention by the sparkling dust—so I didn't realize that Tamlain intended to use his magic to capture her. As he was conjuring his spell, I crashed into him.

The net that had been forming in the air imploded into green sparks that faded before they even reached the ground. A sudden crackling noise rent the air, and I looked up from where I had sprawled on the ground at Tamlain's feet.

Geneva had just opened a portal and was already halfway through it. Her expression was triumphant as she paused and looked back. "Oh, well *done*, General. You should know that after inhaling the dust, our little half-wolf will be in heat within the hour. I trust you'll be a good mate to her, Tamlain. Make Oberon proud!"

With a final cold smile, she disappeared from view. The portal snapped shut with a crackle, and an ominous silence fell across the clearing as Tamlain and I stared at each other in shock.

EIGHTEEN

WITH DAWNING horror, my hand dropped to my belly, where the heavy warmth was spreading outward, moving steadily throughout my body.

Heat, she'd said.

As a female shifter, I was subject to heat cycles, but I'd never had one. It wasn't unusual for the cycles to begin only once they'd been triggered by finding a mate. My mate-bond had been damaged the moment it appeared, so I'd been able to enjoy my new adulthood without the strain of undergoing mating cycles.

Until now, apparently. The dust must have been imbued with some sort of magical property that forced my body to begin the process.

"*No*," I gasped, wrapping my arms tightly around my stomach. As though such a simple denial could stop what was happening.

"Oh," Tamlain said blankly. "I'll admit, I did not foresee this."

I stared at him, wondering how he could remain so calm—and simultaneously wanting to smack him for it. For the first time in what felt like days, my simmering anger entirely vanished. Now, the only emotion I was trying to control was a very primal kind of fear.

I'd never done this before. And if childhood gossip was to be believed, in the absence of a mate to satisfy me, the experience would be akin to physical and emotional torture.

To make things even worse, the bond with Cai had sprung to life right after the dust began to take effect. Unthinkingly, I tugged the front of my shirt away from my chest and glanced down. Impossibly, the triangular fatemark had reappeared in the exact shape and location as before. It was as though Bardulf had never burned it out in the first place.

How could this be?

Panic welled, pushing me to the breaking point. Only the knowledge of what would happen if I succumbed to my fear allowed me to keep control over the power flowing through me... threatening to spill out in the form of destruction. Thankfully, with practice it was becoming easier to keep it within my command. Otherwise, this would have meant chaos back on Earth when my control shattered.

I couldn't allow that. I *could not*.

"Pavia's actions make no sense." Tamlain was still staring at me, his expression intense. After a long moment, he turned back to the tree and finished tying his sash to the branch. "Unless..."

"Unless *what*?" I asked, my voice cracking from the strain.

"I have a theory."

Gods above, I was going to strangle the man. "Okay...?" I prompted.

"Such a magical attack might be logical—but only if Oberon believes that mating you will seal the protection for the world that your mate inhabits. Perhaps forging that connection with a fae ensures you cannot become a danger to the fae realm."

I stared at him. "That's crazy."

He only raised an eyebrow, and the desire to punch the expression off his smug fae face now warred with the desire to lick him.

Not good.

"Is it?" he asked. "It would also explain why Pavia—or rather, *Geneva*, as you know her—worked so hard to prevent you from mating that shifter whelp whose fatemark you carry. If you had, your power would be primarily linked to Earth, and only Elfhame would be in peril. That would make you worse than useless for Oberon's plans—it would make you an active threat."

I probably would have been super-interested in hearing all this... about fifteen minutes ago. Now, Tamlain's detached, scientific interest in my shifter mating biology was too much. Within minutes, the insatiable lust of a heat cycle would take over my body. I'd be helpless with the instinctive need to mate.

I would need relief more than I needed to breathe the air around me, and the only one present to help was Tamlain.

Tamlain. The gorgeous and powerful fae who had fascinated my inner wolf from the very beginning.

These thoughts made the heat in my stomach spread like wildfire. *I couldn't do this.* I needed, with terrible immediacy, *not to be here with this man.* The thought of seeing him pull away in disgust when I threw myself at him was unbearable.

Mindless instinct shrieked at me to escape. Wide-eyed, I whirled away from him and ran, shifting into wolf form mid-stride. Clothing ripped and tore. I struggled free of it and ran blindly around the massive tree, disappearing into the dark, mist-shrouded woods.

Light flashed behind me, and my animal senses picked up the sound of another wolf hot on my trail. I longed to turn around to meet him. Instead, I ran faster.

In the tiny part of my mind that was still my own, I knew that I needed to get far, far away from Tamlain. If he was right about this, I would have to ride out my first heat in solitude or risk playing straight into Oberon's hands.

The urge to turn around and throw myself at Tamlain's glowing white wolf-form was nearly all-consuming. With my instincts at war, I did the only thing that my wolf knew to do in such a moment — I kept running.

So did he. We ran together through the shadowy woods. On some level, I knew Tamlain's magical prowess could have ended the chase at any time. Perhaps he sensed my need to expend some of the nervous energy that was coursing through my body. Whatever the case, he let me run, my paws flying over the uneven terrain.

I could sense him right behind me, nipping at my heels. Eventually, though, his patience wore out. The glowing white wolf surged forward, shouldering into me. We had been running at such a great speed that we crashed together through the trees, our bodies rolling together in a tangle.

The wind was knocked clean out of my lungs as we came to a stop, but I fought to get my paws back underneath me. Tamlain seized me by the back of the neck and pressed me to the ground, growling softly against my fur.

The hunger inside of me sparked to life. His warm body pressed on top of mine, holding me down as I writhed against him.

Without warning, the pressure let up and he transformed back into a man. His strong arms wrapped around my wolf form, preventing me from immediately fleeing again.

"I'm not having this conversation with an animal," he said, grunting with strain as I tried to wriggle free. "Shift back."

The moonlit clearing where we had crashed was warm; the fragrance of flowers hung over the bushes and mossy earth where we had fallen together. I whined, afraid of what would happen if I changed form. Panic was lurking beneath the desire. Would I be able to control it?

"I'm here, Little Wolf," Tamlain murmured, sending a frisson of need down my spine. "All will be well. I will not allow it to be otherwise. Just...please. We need to make a plan, while you're still able."

I closed my eyes and pulled inward, reaching for my human skin and realizing too late that I would reappear naked beneath him.

And so I did — face down on the soft cushion of moss with his strength pinning me in place. The sensation was delicious, but I didn't have a chance to stop and enjoy it. Tears trickled down my face as the blazing heat under my skin became unbearable.

"Please," I begged, pressing my body against his. I wanted his clothes off so that I could feel his hot skin against my back. Would I be able to feel the tingle of his magic between us, flesh to flesh?

Tamlain's grip gentled, his weight lifting away from me. His large hand settled against the center of my back, a reminder not to flee. I couldn't bring myself to turn and look at him.

"I don't know what to do," I whispered, as the tears streamed down my face. "I'm a v-virgin and I've never done this before."

His hand moved away quickly.

"Ah," he said. "Of course. Your mate-bond was destroyed. Stupid of me. I had assumed—" The words cut off with a sharp huff. "Never mind."

If only my mate bond *had* been destroyed. Instead, it was wide-awake and throbbing like a fresh wound inside me.

Tamlain moved to crouch in front of me. My fingers gouged furrows in the mossy earth beneath me, as I clutched at it to prevent myself from fleeing or shifting again. I forced myself to look up at him, but I couldn't speak. I was lying in a naked heap on the ground, within arm's reach of the most beautiful creature I had ever seen, and my hormones were raging. Slick heat pulsed between my thighs. My head swam.

Worst of all, through the throbbing connection with Cai, I could tell that he was aware of the change in me. I was sure I could feel his answering arousal ghosting through our bond, even though we were in different realms. In some part of my frenzied brain, I could sense that he'd gotten to his feet and was pacing restlessly back and forth, frustrated anger blazing inside of him.

I shook my head sharply, trying to clear it.

"Please don't leave me like this," I begged. "Please help me! It *hurts…*"

For the first time since I had known him, Tamlain appeared completely caught off guard by events. My frustration and terror spilled over, the wind rising around me.

"*Ember,*" he said, that single word reminding me yet again of everything that was at stake.

Keeping my powers under control was like trying to hold water cupped in my hands — while also missing a few fingers — but after a few deep breaths the wind died down. My stomach lurched at the thought of the devastation I might have just caused on Earth.

Tamlain seemed to read my mind. "It was only for a moment. It's all right, Little Wolf. Perhaps you spawned a thunderstorm on Earth. That's all."

I squeezed my eyes shut and nodded, hoping desperately that he was right.

"I can't fix this with magic," said the fae. His warm hand closed on my bare shoulder.

So strong, I thought hazily. His hands were callused. I wondered what they would feel like, trailing up my legs… between my thighs.

A painful cramp of need hit me low in the belly. I moaned, rolling onto my side, away from his touch. Gritting my teeth against the agonizing emptiness, I clutched at my naked flesh, hands clamped over my womb. My thighs slid together restlessly, but the friction wasn't enough. Nothing was *enough*.

"I can't do this," I whimpered, hiding my face in helpless shame.

Maybe I could just take the edge off? I let my fingers explore lower despite my utter mortification—much as I had done as a growing pup, experimenting in the dark with whatever felt good.

Now, though, my body craved more. *Demanded* more. I moaned in distress, rolling onto my back and looking up at Tamlain, luminous in the starlight. Like a light switch flipping, I felt the moment when my need overcame my rational mind.

"You promise you're really just cousins?" I asked, my voice a pathetic, breathless thing.

"What?" he asked, obviously mystified.

I shook my head in frustration. "*Dianthe*. She's your cousin, right? You promise that's the truth?"

Confusion painted his features. *Fae can't lie*, I remembered him saying.

"Yes, of course. Why would you think—"

I never let him finish. Instead, I rolled upright and pounced—a predator seeking prey. I had to touch him *that very instant*. To smell him... to feel the heat of his skin against mine.

He drew in a startled breath, but did not push me away. My lips sought the place where his neck met his jaw. I mouthed at it with a low growl, my tongue darting out to taste his skin.

My hands pushed his buckskin vest out of the way, and before he could stop me, I'd already unbuckled the heavy belt around his waist as well. It clattered to the ground, his weapons clanking together.

Strong hands captured my upper arms before I could attack his shirt or trousers, easing me back. His troubled blue gaze held mine.

"I'll help you," he said. "But you must give me control over what happens. Do you understand?"

"*Please*," I panted mindlessly, straining forward in an attempt to get my mouth on him again. I wanted his clothes *gone*, damn it—but when I reached for the crisscrossed laces of his leather breeches, he captured my wrist.

"No," he said in a tone that conveyed there would be no further debate on the matter.

I pulled my hand away and collapsed to the ground again, stung by his rejection. First Cai, and now Tamlain? Did *no one* want me?

But not even that painful question was enough to dampen my body's need. The slickness between my legs had long since become a heavy trickle, soaking me and dripping down my legs. Unable to control myself, I found my hand drifting once more toward the thatch of hair at the apex of my thighs.

"Don't," Tamlain whispered, crouching before me on the soft moss. He caught my fingers in his own and squeezed. "*Don't*. I'll take care of you. And I will ensure Pavia's plan doesn't come to fruition so easily."

Hope pricked at me. Maybe he wasn't rejecting me totally?

"Hurry," I begged him. "Tamlain, please. It aches."

"I know." His voice was a low, soothing rumble. "I'm sorry, Little Wolf."

Strong hands eased me down to lie on my back. Tamlain lowered his body to cover mine, caging me beneath him as I writhed restlessly.

"Shh." He kissed down the side of my face and neck, avoiding my mouth. Trailing down, his lips brushed my collarbone and continued lower, over my chest.

I arched my back, blind with desire as he nuzzled along my breasts. When he took one nipple in his mouth and sucked, I cried out—almost at my peak from that alone. He let it pop out of his mouth and blew cool air across the damp skin. Gooseflesh erupted all over my body, my nipples hardening to painful points.

I was losing control… unraveling. All I could think about doing was ripping the fae's clothes off of him and letting him bury himself inside of me to the hilt. I needed his cock. I needed his bite. Did fae bite? I needed to claim him, and be claimed.

Through the damaged mate-bond, I could feel Cai, frantic with lust and jealousy. In the absence of my higher brain functions, an animal snarl of satisfaction escaped me at the idea of him suffering the way I'd suffered the night after he rejected me.

Tamlain continued to kiss his way down my body with a patience that seemed positively unholy. My legs fell open, making a space to cradle his lithe form as he reached my belly. By the time his tongue traced along the crease of my hip, I was shuddering.

No one had ever done anything like this to me before. In my right mind, I might have had second thoughts. Would I taste bad? Would he hate it?

But in the throes of heat, I didn't care. I grabbed handfuls of cornsilk-soft hair and dragged Tamlain's wicked mouth the final inch to where I wanted it. He made a low, male noise in his throat and *devoured* me, as though he was the wolf in reality, and I was his meal.

A wailing cry tore free of my throat, wavering in time with the long strokes of his tongue along my soaked folds. I couldn't tell exactly what he was doing as he varied his movements and rhythm. I only knew how it made me feel, and I was coming out of my damned *skin*.

My climax crashed over me within minutes, every muscle locking solid as pleasure crested and slowly ebbed. It did nothing to ease my need, and Tamlain must have sensed that. His tongue curled deeper, not letting up for an instant.

Through the bond, I could sense Cai—in wolf form, now—howling at the moon. He could feel the pleasure I was taking from another male, and it maddened him.

Part of me mourned what Cai and I might have had together. He'd thrown that future away, though—tossed me aside like garbage the moment things got complicated. My revenge now was sweet. I'd never forgotten the first night when I'd felt him mating with female after female in an attempt to exorcise the remnants of our connection.

He'd at least had a choice. This was different. Geneva had thrown the magic powder at me and brought on my heat before I even knew what was happening. I wouldn't have chosen voluntarily to do this to Cai, but I couldn't stop biology. He'd just have to deal with it, the same as I had.

Lips closed over the most sensitive part of me and sucked. Tamlain ran the flat of his tongue over the delicate nub and I came again, groaning, my vision whiting out.

When I regained awareness of my surroundings, he was looking up the length of my body—his silky hair mussed where I'd tangled my fingers in it. His lips were shiny with my slickness.

"Roll over, Little Wolf," he said. "Get on your hands and knees."

Fresh lust flooded me, short-circuiting my brain as I remembered the feeling of him pinning me beneath him in wolf form. The she-wolf inside me panted with need, desperate to be filled and mated.

He sat up and steadied me as I scrambled into position. A heavy hand closed on the back of my neck, pressing me down until my cheek rested against my crossed arms on the ground, ass still in the air. I cursed, weak but heartfelt, certain that I would die if he didn't fill me up *right the fuck now*.

Still pinning me in place with one hand, he reached back with the other, running it over my flank and buttock. His fingertips stroked my soaking wet folds.

"Is this what you need, little one?" he asked, teasing a place that gave way beneath his exploring fingers.

I wanted to rock back, to take *more*, but the hand on my neck prevented me. After what felt like a small eternity, the blunt finger pressed into me, sliding in with little resistance.

"Yes!" I yelped. "Yes yes *yes!*"

It was what I needed, all right—though it still wasn't *enough*. Even though the unfamiliar intrusion burned as my muscles clenched around it, I wanted more.

"Please," I begged. "I need more, give me more!"

"Yes, Little Wolf," he said. "Take it all. It's yours."

A second finger joined the first, stretching me wider. I keened as the fingers fucked in and out of me, stars exploding behind my eyelids when a third entered me. Tamlain twisted his hand, changing position, and now his thumb brushed over my nub with every deep stroke.

My body melted beneath the overwhelming sensations. In the deepest part of myself, I longed for the feel of his cock in me. Still, the constant overload of pleasure as his fingers massaged me inside and out kept me from focusing too much on what I didn't have. His unwillingness to take pleasure as well as giving it felt like a rejection of sorts... but at least he was here. Helping, as he'd promised.

He hadn't left me to face this nightmare alone.

I sobbed my way through another orgasm—this one originating from somewhere deeper inside me than the ones he'd licked out of me earlier.

"That's it," he murmured. "Let go and feel, little one. I've got you."

I let go of the last of my rational mind, and *felt*.

Finally, after hours had passed in an endless, hazy cycle of need and release, the compulsion began to ease. In its place came bone-deep exhaustion. With a final moan, I went limp, curling onto my side in the starlight. A soft rustle of shifting cloth came from behind me, and I felt the heat of a body as Tamlain seated himself next to me, a few careful inches of space between us.

"Tamlain?" I slurred, scooting back until my spine rested against his thigh.

"Yes?" he asked. "What is it, Little Wolf?"

I swallowed and licked my lips. "Thank you."

He said nothing, and before long, sleep stole across my awareness. I wasn't sure if the feeling of rough fingers stroking my hair away from my face was real, or my imagination.

NINETEEN

CONSCIOUSNESS RETURNED slowly. First, before I ever opened my eyes, I could feel soft, fragrant moss underneath me. Was I back in the Greystalker packlands? But that didn't seem right. All of my memories were jumbled together, nothing making clear linear sense.

Oh.

Wait.

I remembered the storms, the revelation of Geneva's betrayal, and Darby being captured. A series of flashing images from the day before assaulted my brain. I remembered Geneva's magic powder and my spontaneous heat.

I remembered Tamlain's dutiful assistance, even though my humiliating condition had seemed to disgust him. He hadn't let me suffer, but my heat hadn't touched him as a male. Shame pressed heavily on my soul. I moaned and stirred fitfully, my body still hot and aching.

"Try to rest," a low voice murmured nearby.

My eyes flew open and I looked around the clearing, not having sensed Tamlain's presence nearby. At first the bright sun blinded me, and I wondered how I'd managed to sleep through its piercing light. When I could finally focus my eyes, I saw the fae sitting upright and regal on a large boulder a few feet away.

He looked neat and composed, in contrast to my perfect representation of a hot mess. Even his hair was smooth and sleek, though my grasping hands had pulled at his intricate braids like they'd been all that was tethering me to the world.

Clapping those same hands over my face to hide the stain of embarrassment on my cheeks, I rolled over and groaned.

"How am I supposed to rest?" I asked, my voice muffled by the moss. "That was *awful.*"

It had been awful… and wonderful. *Gods above, somebody please kill me now.*

Tamlain's reply was hesitant. "Well, I suppose fae and shifters differ in what is, um, pleasurable to them. I didn't realize, but I'm sure that there are biological differences between—"

When I finally realized what he was jabbering about, I pushed myself up and glared at him from my undignified spot on the ground, sticks and leaves no doubt tangled in my hair.

"*Tamlain,*" I said, holding up my hand. "Stop. Please. Just *stop.*"

He looked nearly as embarrassed as I felt, which was saying something under the circumstances. I groaned again.

"It's not that it wasn't, uh, good," I started, pushing myself to my feet and feeling sore muscles scream in protest. "It's just that, well, oh never mind."

So lame, I thought, cringing inwardly. *Way to play things cool there, Ember.*

As I tried to brush the mud and dirt from my aching body, I realized I was wearing Tamlain's grey linen tunic. He must have slipped it onto me after I fell asleep. Although my imagination temporarily went into overdrive picturing that moment, I couldn't afford to dwell on it. I might have wanted it to be a tender gesture, but it was more likely he was just repelled by my nakedness.

"Thank you for this," I said, plucking at the long garment. "And for everything else, too."

He nodded in acknowledgment and didn't answer. I was grateful to him—but mostly, I never wanted to speak of the incident again.

"I'm going to bathe in the river, then I'll need my own clothes back, please," I said, turning and walking through the trees.

"Of course," Tamlain said.

The fae stayed nearby but out of sight, giving me privacy while I undressed and lowered myself into the stream.

The water was icy cold, easing the pain radiating through me from head to toe. I shivered as I plunged my head below the surface and scrubbed my tangled, matted hair with my fingers. It took me a good ten minutes to pluck out all the debris and pull apart all the tangles. By the time I was done, I was shivering violently and every joint was stiff from the cold.

I climbed out and lay on the fresh, clean grass in a patch of warm sun. This place that had seemed so dark and threatening at night was a lot more agreeable in daylight, happily.

It seemed rude to use Tamlain's borrowed tunic as a towel, so I air-dried instead. Letting the water evaporate off of my naked body took longer than I thought. By the time I was dry, my skin was warm and pink beneath the sun.

I stood up and called for Tamlain, my bi-colored hair tickling my shoulders in the breeze. He came walking through the trees, glancing at me and quickly away. I saw him swallow hard and wave his hand through the air.

My clothes rematerialized over my body, yet again. What was this—the third time he'd done that? The fourth? I wrapped my arms around myself, feeling the familiar fabric against my skin.

"Thanks," I breathed in relief.

"You're welcome," Tamlain replied neutrally.

He still looked slightly awkward but was obviously fighting to keep his voice normal. "Come, we must move on."

"Move on?" I asked, falling into step beside him. "We aren't meeting Dianthe here at the tree?"

"It's location and significance have been compromised. We can't risk remaining here. Pavia—or Geneva, if you prefer—will probably return at some point to see if her mission was accomplished."

"I wish I understood what that mission was," I muttered, irritation bleeding through in my voice.

"I think the theory is fairly straightforward," Tamlain observed.

I shot him a side-eyed glance, pushing aside a bush as we walked through the trees under the bright sunshine. "Is it really?"

Tamlain sighed. "I'm sorry. I should explain from the beginning."

"Yes, that would be helpful," I agreed, making no real attempt to hide my sarcasm.

"Geneva meant for us to mate last night."

I sent him an incredulous look. "Yes, I already got that part, thanks."

Tamlain let out a huff of frustration. "When two shifters mate, a strong psychic connection forms. This connection is powerful enough to transcend the physical realm and leach into the spiritual realm. Fae are not exactly the same, but we still form deep bonds. By mating me, it's possible you would have formed a connection to all of Elfhame, channeled through my psychic connection to this realm."

"So our bond would live within us and... also within this world?" I asked, my eyebrows furrowed in confusion.

"Exactly. I believe Oberon is counting on such a bond protecting our world from your powers, since a part of you would be one with Elfhame. You do not harm yourself during those outbursts of energy. That's why you can withstand the wind and earthquakes unharmed."

Thinking back to the first big storm that had developed around me on Earth, I remembered standing firm as things were destroyed, my hair flying but my feet planted beneath me while other people were tossed around like dolls.

"Holy shit. That's true," I whispered.

Tamlain shook his head. "The storm is around you, not within you. The emotions pull the two realms into each other, but you are not crushed between them."

"The reverse of that is… kind of how I control it. It's hard, though—like trying to hold back a hundred sneezes at once."

Tamlain huffed and pushed his way through some thick undergrowth. "*Sneezes*? Little Wolf, perhaps we should work on your similes."

I scowled at him. We walked in silence for several long minutes, each of us absorbed in our own thoughts. Tamlain's theory made a certain amount of sense, but there were still holes where the picture didn't seem complete. I shook my head. Despite his insight into Oberon's state of mind, I still felt woefully in the dark.

"It doesn't make sense," I admitted, continuing the conversation as if we hadn't just walked in silence for such a distance. "Not completely."

Tamlain shrugged. "It's just a theory, although it's one in which I'm reasonably confident."

"I expect you're probably right," I stated, "but what does this have to do with me as a weapon? Isn't that Oberon's ultimate goal? Yet, having me form a mate bond would make me…"

My voice trailed away and I felt the flush erupt across my cheeks again. I busied myself brushing some stray burrs off of my clothing, as if this could cover up the awkward moment.

Tamlain took my shoulder and stopped walking, turning to face me. I couldn't meet his piercing, beautiful eyes.

"What? It would make you… what?" he asked.

"I don't know," I said, raising my hands and letting them fall back to my sides. "I was going to say happy, but that's stupid. I was just thinking that if I was content, I wouldn't make a very good weapon when my powers are fueled by rage and fear."

His brow furrowed. I pushed past him, not wanting to continue this conversation. He let me go, silence again stretching between us as we walked. This time it was Tamlain who broke it.

"He still has your friend," he said in a low voice.

I threw him a sharp look. But he was right. Of course he was right.

"The crux of it all is that with you bound to this world in such a deep and permanent way, Oberon believes that your powers would protect this land while still allowing him to decimate Earth," he continued.

My stomach soured. I wasn't quite ready to admit his theory about mating was correct, but it was still a horrific thought.

"I'll never escape his slavery, will I?" I asked quietly. "Not while I'm alive, anyway."

"That is yet to be seen," Tamlain replied.

I didn't want to face this next part. "What does all of this mean for Darby?"

"I don't know. Not exactly."

I grabbed Tamlain's forearm and pulled him around with a snarl. Although I was several inches shorter than him, the ferocity of my grip yanked him to within a few inches of my face.

"You're lying by omission, fae," I snapped, the air around me starting to whip my hair past my face.

Again, I reeled in my power before it could escape my control. There seemed to be more of it told back each time I tried. While the wind faded to nothing within seconds, I maintained the grip on Tamlain's arm, my fingers digging in like claws.

"No more secrets," I said flatly. "Just *tell me*."

But Tamlain was examining me with a thoughtful frown. His eyes dipped to my hand on his bicep. "Your powers continue to grow. You are becoming stronger with each day that passes."

But I wasn't ready to be distracted. "*Tell me about Darby.*"

His lips thinned. "Oberon's mind is twisted and dark. I fear once you are in his power, he will torture your friend in such a way that it will make you lose control entirely."

I gritted my teeth, jerking my head in a swift nod of understanding. I'd asked, and he hadn't pulled any punches. It wasn't as though his answer was unexpected.

"Why does my power impact the other realm more than the one I'm currently in?" I said, trying to distract myself from horrible thoughts about my friend.

"I cannot answer with certainty."

I glared at him darkly. "Have a guess."

Tamlain sighed. "You are entirely unique, Ember. My *guess* is that it's because you are part of both realms, but not fully connected to either one."

"Keep talking," I said.

"I am fae," Tamlain explained. "Elfhame is my home as well as a part of me. My power grew from this world. But you? You are both fae and shifter, not fully belonging to either world. You are a piece of both, but your connection shifts depending on which place you currently reside. Right now, you are on Elfhame, so your connection to Elfhame takes precedence. When you pull the realms together, the same power that protects your physical body also offers a degree of protection to the world with which you're more connected in that moment."

"You've really considered this at length, haven't you?" I said.

He eyed me cautiously. "It was a long night."

A fresh surge of blood rushed to my cheeks, heating them. The idea that this whole thing was somehow linked to my pathetic sex life was unbearable. Doubly so, when something new occurred to me.

Tamlain had been desperate to save Elfhame. So desperate, in fact, that he'd insisted on bringing me to his world, despite the obvious danger of having me in the same realm as Oberon.

And what if Oberon had been right about the mating bond? Tamlain could potentially have saved his entire world and all of his people by mating with me last night. Had he taken me and claimed me as his own, Elfhame might have been protected from my powers for good.

Why had he refused? It didn't seem consistent with the cold-blooded, self-sacrificing soldier I was coming to know. I couldn't make sense of it. As I allowed Tamlain to resume walking, leading me further into the darkness of the trees, I studied his back.

Was I really that repulsive to him?

Crap.

Emotions swirled inside of me—confusion and hurt. Yes, I was attracted to Tamlain, damn it. And not in a just-recovering-from-a-chemically-induced-heat sort of way, either. My wolf had been intrigued since the moment she scented him. That sense of connection had only grown as time went on.

He'd stuck by me, too—even when I was crawling all over him trying to get him to mate with me. If ever there was a time to abandon his mission to keep me out of Oberon's hands, that would have been it.

Yet he hadn't. He hadn't mated with me, true—but he also hadn't run screaming for the hills. The pain of rejection combined with gratitude for the help he *had* given me warred in my chest.

As I wrestled my emotions back into obedience, the mate bond that was supposed to have been destroyed throbbed painfully awake.

Oh yeah, I thought sourly, *and then there's that.*

"I can hear you thinking, Little Wolf," Tamlain's resigned voice called back to me. "Why don't you simply ask your questions, rather than choking on them?"

I blinked, looking up to find Tamlain some distance in front of me. Evidently my pace had slowed to a crawl as I mulled my growing collection of problems.

"Why didn't you mate me last night?" I blurted, before I could lose my nerve.

He stood completely still for a moment, then retraced his steps to stand in front of me.

"Why would you ask such a thing?" His tone was wary.

I shook my head in frustration. "Just listen! If it's true that mating me would have protected Elfhame—"

He blinked down at me. "That's only a theory."

"You're convinced it's true," I accused." You had an opportunity to seal protection around your world! All you had to do was mate with me and that would have been it. Why did you hold back? Fear? Disgust? *Why?*"

My voice wavered. Tamlain's lips curled back, showing gleaming white teeth that could have easily pierced the skin of my neck to seal our bond.

"You demanded that I be truthful with you, yes?" His eyes burned.

"Yes!" I said emphatically, while thinking maybe I didn't want to know the truth after all...

Tamlain regarded me, forcing his expression back to its normal cool facade. "I have learned that you do better with the truth."

"So tell me," I insisted.

He drew breath and paused before speaking.

"You were forced into heat by means of magic. It wasn't natural. You could not give consent—and though I may be a killer when it's called for, I am not a rapist. Yet... I could not bear to watch you suffer, so I aided in what way I could, but without tying you to me permanently."

I stayed silent, digesting his words.

"Also," he continued, "it would have played straight into Oberon's hands. I will not give Elfhame's mad king a weapon to cause havoc across other worlds."

"But—" I began, only to be cut off by a sharp shake of his head.

"My loyalty may be to Elfhame, but that doesn't mean I'm ready to stand by and watch Earth be destroyed and subjugated. No, I could not give him that power."

He really was the most bizarrely noble creature sometimes, I reflected. I still had trouble believing it wasn't some sort of act that he put on. It couldn't be, though. Not when the stakes were so high.

At that exact moment, an idea struck me from out of the blue—terrible and wonderful in its simplicity.

"What is it?" he asked, frowning at me. "You've gone pale."

"Nothing," I replied quickly. "It's nothing. Let's keep going. Thank you for, uh... for answering my questions."

As we walked, I clenched my fists at my sides, trying to think things through. Would it be possible? And could it really be so simple?

I couldn't answer my own questions. The idea that had so forcefully knocked its way into my brain was essentially the reverse of Oberon's plan. If he could bind me to Elfhame by forcing me to mate with someone here, and thereby protect his world from my powers, then logically, I could mate with someone on Earth so that Elfhame would be the only world in jeopardy.

If I were mated to someone from Earth, then Oberon wouldn't dare harm Darby. Doing so would risk destroying his own realm. He'd have to let her go to appease me. I could threaten him; tell him that I would unleash the full wrath of my powers against Elfhame if he didn't immediately release her and return her safely to Earth. Any attempt to manipulate me would immediately be turned against him.

I couldn't let Tamlain know about my idea, though. Just because he didn't want to mate me if it meant Earth's destruction, that wasn't to say he'd stand by quietly while I put his world at risk instead. I needed to figure this out on my own.

So I allowed my mind to wander down the path of this new possibility. As far as I was concerned, Cai could fall into a deep dark pit and rot there for all I cared, even if my inner wolf whimpered at the idea. If I were going to mate, it would have to be someone else.

But who? I wasn't any keener on the other male shifters I'd grown up with than I was on Cai. It didn't have to be my pack, though, did it? It could be… well, anyone, really. This might even be an opportunity for a fresh start.

If I was really going to do this, I would have to find passage back to Earth without Tamlain's help. There was no way he would go along with this plan voluntarily.

As he'd said earlier, his first loyalty was to Elfhame and his people. It always would be.

No, Tamlain would never agree to this. I'd have to sneak back somehow and hope that Darby could hold on a little longer, until I could find someone who would be willing to mate with me.

As we continued walking into a part of the forest that appeared to be growing rockier, I tried to come up with some cover story for returning to Earth, especially after I had insisted on coming to Elfhame in the first place.

If only I'd thought of this plan yesterday.

If only I'd *known*.

Eventually, Tamlain slowed. "We're here," he said, the first time either of us had spoken in nearly an hour.

I glanced around, confused. "Okay? Uh, what's *here*, exactly?"

He jerked his chin toward the jagged cliff face to our left, leading me toward an outcrop of rock that stood about ten feet high. On the ground in front of it lay a small ring of stones, half-buried in the dirt. It appeared to be an old fire pit, long disused and abandoned. I wouldn't have even noticed it if I hadn't tripped on one of the stones.

"Tamlain, this is even less sheltered than the tree was," I pointed out.

"Not inside," he said, and slipped out of sight. From my position by the fire ring, it almost looked like he disappeared.

Frowning, I walked around the face of the rock until I reached the place where Tamlain had vanished. The rock wall was smooth except for a bundle of vines draping from the top of the outcrop down to the forest floor.

"Tamlain?" I called uncertainly.

His face appeared through a gap in the vines. They were not growing against the rock face, as it had first appeared. Instead, they efficiently camouflaged a split in the stone, just wide enough for someone to shimmy through if they pushed the vines aside.

"Wow," I said after I'd squeezed inside to find a small cave with a soft dirt floor. There was a second fire ring inside that looked much more recently used than the one outside. In an alcove near the back, a small stash of supplies was visible—blankets and cooking vessels. "Okay, I take it all back."

I leaned against the wall, searching for a way to bring up my need to return to Earth without giving away my plan.

"So, I've been thinking—" I began, only to be cut off by an electric crackle a few feet behind me. I whirled around as a travel portal opened right inside the cave. Dianthe stepped through it, her face grim as she glanced around and registered our presence.

"Cousin. What is it?" Tamlain demanded. "You obviously have news. What have you learned?"

Dianthe took a deep breath, her eyes falling on me. I couldn't read her expression, but something about it made my stomach dip.

"I've received word from one of my contacts in the palace," she said. "Oberon has issued a new decree. Ember is to appear in the public square before dusk tomorrow. Otherwise he will publicly torture and execute the shifter female known as Darby Adalwolf."

My eyes slid closed in horror, the breath exiting my lungs in a rush.

TWENTY

DARBY. MY DEAR, sweet-natured Darby. She was a complete innocent. She knew nothing about this war, or the truth of my identity. Darby had been my one true friend and had wanted nothing from me but my own friendship in return. We'd been confidantes. We'd been *everything* to each other.

My throat tightened with emotion, and I turned to Tamlain with a look of pleading. The words formed on my tongue without my bidding, because I already suspected the answer before I spoke.

"Would Oberon really do that? Torture and kill an innocent?"

He hesitated, exchanging a look with Dianthe. "Yes, he will torture her. It will be cruel and your friend will suffer, but I do not believe that he will kill her yet."

Dianthe snorted in disgust. "Think our dear leader has gone soft, do you?"

I couldn't help but look hopefully at Tamlain.

But he was shaking his head. "No. It's only that he will need to keep his hostage alive if he is to have any hope of controlling Ember."

"This whole thing is crazy," I said. "We have to save her."

Tamlain looked grave. "We will do all we can, but there is very little time to plan."

Plans. All of mine flew abruptly out the window at Tamlain's reminder. My deadline to save Darby was barely more than a day away. There was no way that I could return to Earth and secure a mate in such a short window of time. Even if I'd been the daughter of a famous, rich alpha male from a huge pack, I imagined I'd still have trouble finding a mate who was willing to become involved in an inter-dimensional war between Elfhame and Earth.

I shook my head, trying to clear it. I had to focus on what was most important.

"And that's not all," Dianthe said in a tone of voice I *really* didn't like.

Fresh dread welled up inside of me. I'd been through so much over the last few days... I wasn't sure how much more bad news I could take.

The female warrior shot me a worried look, as though she could tell I was close to the breaking point. "You must try to stay calm, Ember... but Oberon has dispatched Pavia back to Earth with a new mission."

I wrinkled my nose at the mention of the woman I knew as Geneva Padfoot. "Back to Earth? Why? She'll have no place in the Greystalker pack now that Cai knows who and what she is. She'll be banished, just like I was."

Dianthe came over to me and took my hand. Her skin was cool and smooth; her features perfectly composed. I was not comforted by her attempt at reassurance.

"What is it?" I asked, pulling my hand away sharply. "What are you not telling me?"

Dianthe sighed. "She has been given orders to kill the Greystalker alpha's son—the one called Cai."

I blinked at her, sure that I'd heard her wrong. As the words sank in and understanding blossomed, I realized that Oberon might have already anticipated my plan to mate with someone on Earth. He was eliminating the most obvious choice, since I'd already manifested a fate-bond with Cai.

Geneva would destroy him, just like she'd destroyed every other goddamned part of my life.

It felt like the floor of the cave was falling away, and I was plunging downward into the heart of Elfhame. My head spun and my breathing grew ragged. The horror that was clawing up inside of me started to spill out and the wind whistled shrilly around the narrow entrance to the cave.

"Ember!" Tamlain barked, coming to stand in front of me and gripping my shoulders.

The familiarity of his touch soothed my whirling emotions. The wolf inside of me calmed slightly, although I could barely resist the instinct to transform and pace back and forth in the cave with my hackles raised and a growl rumbling in my chest.

That would achieve nothing.

The quieting of the wind around us told the fae that I had regained control of my emotions. I drew breath through clenched teeth, making a faint hissing sound.

"I don't understand why he would set Pavia on the shifter," Dianthe said. "What would Oberon hope to accomplish? Unless it's merely another way to manipulate you and cause you to lose control…"

Tamlain took a deep breath and explained his theory about the potential protection a world would gain should I mate with a member of its population. Meanwhile, I stood silent, my cheeks burning with embarrassment.

"He's trying to prevent her from mating with someone on Earth, which would be catastrophic for his efforts," Tamlain concluded.

Dianthe raised a sharp eyebrow, evidently hearing what remained unspoken.

"Has Oberon tried to force her to mate with someone here, to give our world that protection?" she asked, watching Tamlain closely.

Tamlain threw the briefest of glances at me, but I remained stubbornly quiet. My jaw was set as I stared at the strip of light peeking through the vines that had hidden the entrance to the cave.

"Yes," he finally said in a low voice. "Yesterday, Geneva attacked Ember with a magical powder that forced her to go into heat."

Dianthe's expression looked far too knowing for my peace of mind. She glanced back and forth at us, as though she could picture all that had passed between us the previous night.

"*Ah*," was her only response, seeming to notice the awkwardness in the cave.

I turned away from the speculative eyebrow that was now pointing in my direction, walking to the back of the cave where some blankets and food parcels were stacked neatly on a natural rock shelf.

I pulled one of the blankets down and pretended to examine the fabric, but I wasn't really seeing what was in front of me. Desperate to regain my focus, I tried again to consider my options and come up with a plan to save Darby. She didn't deserve any of this.

I will not allow her to be harmed because I sat back and let the deadline come and go, I vowed, comforted by my own determination.

"We must not play into Oberon's hands," Tamlain said, watching as I paced restlessly back and forth.

I needed him to be quiet so I could think, damn it. I draped the blanket over my shoulders and pressed my fingers to my temples, trying to force away the lingering effects of the unnatural heat I had experienced the previous day. Nausea churned in my gut.

"Oberon wants to use me as a weapon," I muttered, ignoring Tamlain and Dianthe leaning against the cool stone walls of the cave. "And he wanted me to mate with Tamlain to protect Elfhame."

Maybe that was it. Maybe *that* was the key. I spun on my back foot and faced the two fae. "He has no idea if his plan has worked or not, does he?"

"Oberon?" Tamlain asked, a confused expression on his face.

"Yes—he has no way of knowing that we didn't mate, right?" I clarified.

"None that I know of." Tamlain's face was set. It was obvious he had deduced the general direction of my thoughts.

"Don't give me that look. I haven't even said anything yet!" I protested.

He stared me down, unblinking. "You don't have to." His tone was as dry as the desert.

I glared back. "He has no way of knowing that we didn't mate, and that Elfhame isn't protected. We *need* to use that to our advantage, Tamlain. In case you haven't noticed, we're kind of short on advantages at the moment."

"She's got a point there," Dianthe agreed wryly.

I stepped back, putting additional space between us. "You have to let me go to Oberon by myself. I have this one piece of leverage over him. I can use it to keep him distracted while you two sneak in and save Darby."

"You want us to save her while you do…what, exactly?" Dianthe asked, sounding deeply skeptical.

I shrugged. "I'll be the distraction. That's all. He'll be so preoccupied with the prospect of bending me to his will so he can use me that he won't be focused on who else is slipping away. If he doesn't have Darby to manipulate me, and I'm not mated to anyone on either planet, he has to behave himself, right?"

Dianthe and Tamlain exchanged another one of those speaking looks that I was growing to hate.

"Or he could just drag you off to his dungeon and do whatever it takes to break you," Tamlain retorted.

And… okay. As plans went, it was maybe not the most fully formed. But I'd only just thought of it, damn him.

I shrugged again. "Well, I am hopeful that you can rescue me, too—but Darby is the priority. You must see that both of our worlds depend on getting her away from Oberon."

"I don't like it," Tamlain said flatly.

"I'm open to suggestions," I told him… and waited out the resulting silence.

Neither fae spoke.

"Well, with that resounding chorus of alternate plans, I think we can safely say this is our only option."

"What about the alpha's son?" Dianthe asked, as though she thought I'd forgotten about him.

The crushing guilt over Cai that I'd been resolutely ignoring reared up inside of me. My wolf howled her distress at the reminder of our fated mate, and I bit my lower lip hard in an attempt to maintain my composure.

"I can't help him," I whispered.

It was the plain truth.

Cai *wasn't* my mate, no matter what my wolf wanted to believe. There was only one of me, and I had to focus on saving Darby. Cai was strong—an alpha male with an entire pack around him. He stood a greater chance of surviving a confrontation with Geneva unscathed than Darby stood as Oberon's prisoner.

"I will go to Earth and see what I can do in the time we have," Dianthe offered gently. "I promise I will return to help with whatever you have planned to rescue your friend tomorrow."

I lifted my eyes to the ceiling of the cave in an attempt to hold back tears, wishing that I could release any of the complex emotions roiling inside of me. Cai had made a choice to have our bond destroyed. He'd listened to Geneva and chosen the easy way out instead of trusting me enough to simply *talk* to me. My old self-doubt rose up, whispering that even without Geneva's guidance, he probably would've destroyed the bond anyway.

There was no way that someone of his station could be mated with someone of mine, I thought angrily. *He still would have rejected me.*

But what if he hadn't? For the first time since the day Bardulf had the connection between us severed, I allowed myself to daydream about what being Cai's mate would have meant for me. I'd most likely be nearing the end of the first of many pregnancies by now, working and living within the safety of the Greystalker lands. I would be automatically respected as the alpha's mate. I could have been a leader… a guide for my people.

And Oberon would have no hold over me. I would have been mated to someone on Earth, protecting the entire planet.

The bitter irony was not lost on me as I shook the thoughts away angrily. Cai had believed he was protecting me, but in reality he'd put two worlds in horrible danger.

The realization was enough to make anyone go a bit crazy, except I couldn't afford to fall to pieces. I needed to stay focused.

"Thank you," I whispered, wrapping my arms around Dianthe and squeezing.

She hugged back, patting my shoulder. "I'll do what I can," she said again, and let me go before opening a portal in the center of the cave. After she disappeared through the doorway to Earth, I leaned against the smooth wall of the cave and allowed myself to slide down into a seated position, my elbows propped on my thighs.

"You must try to rest," Tamlain said gruffly. "I will make you a bed."

I didn't argue as he pulled down the remaining blankets and arranged them in a cozy nest on the floor. I lay down fully clothed and curled into a ball, hoping that I'd be able to doze off despite the buzzing thoughts in my brain. An hour later, I lay staring at the ceiling of the cave, my mind chasing itself in circles and keeping sleep at bay.

"Sighing like that every few seconds won't help you go to sleep any faster," Tamlain muttered from across the cave, where he sat with his eyes closed and his back propped against the wall.

I threw him a dirty look. I'd been trying so hard to ignore his presence, since the memories of the previous night sure as *hell* weren't going to help lull me to sleep.

Finally sitting up, I stared over at the dim outline of the fae keeping watch over me.

"I'd like to try something," I said in a decisive tone.

His startling blue eyes snapped open. "Try what, exactly?" The question sounded decidedly wary.

I paused, not sure how to explain. "Well, I'm half fae right?"

Tamlain didn't reply, probably because the answer was obvious.

"On one hand it would be logical that my magic would be different than other fae," I continued, "but that doesn't seem to be the case with my shifter powers. Except for my wolf being half dark and half white, I'm a pretty normal shifter, actually."

"Go on," Tamlain replied, obviously curious where I was heading with this.

"I think it's logical that I'd have normal fae magic as well, especially given who my father is."

Tamlain looked thoughtfully towards the ceiling, considering that.

"Perhaps. And how would you propose to test this theory?" he finally asked, sitting forward and examining me with his piercing gaze.

I pushed myself up to a sitting position as well, mirroring his stance. "So, the fact that you can manifest clothing at will would be pretty useful for a shifter, right?"

I glanced away, rubbing the back of my neck awkwardly as I tried not to think about the circumstances where I'd needed him to manifest and repair my clothing for me.

His lips quirked in a way that I recognized as him trying not to smile. "As it happens, that is a fairly simple task, magically speaking."

"So, can we try it?" I asked eagerly.

He nodded and jerked his head towards the slight crack in the wall leading to the outside world. Dusk was beginning to fall and I knew that it would be dark soon. I rose and hurried forward eagerly, pushing my way out between the vines. He joined me outside.

"Remove one of your boots," Tamlain instructed.

I hopped around awkwardly for a moment before handing him the muddy footwear. He tossed it away into the trees where it thudded softly in the underbrush, out of sight. I'd watched him replace my clothes enough times that I knew the hand motion to use.

"Like this?" I waved my hand over my foot, concentrating on bringing my boot back.

Nothing happened.

I glanced at him in question.

He shook his head. "Concentrate on the source of power that you feel within yourself when your emotions are at their most tumultuous."

I nodded, allowing some of the carefully controlled emotion to rise up inside of me. As a faint breeze rustled the tree limbs, I waved my hand forcefully over my foot, mentally commanding the boot to appear.

Nothing.

Tamlain stood nearby in the growing darkness, watching my many attempts to make the boot appear in vain.

"Okay, so maybe I was wrong about having magic," I grumbled.

I was disappointed, to say the least. There was no doubt that my chances against Oberon would be better if I could use *both* fae and shifter powers.

"There may yet be a way," Tamlain said thoughtfully. "But I'm not certain of the best method to attempt it."

"What?" I demanded, perking up.

He stepped closer to me, raising a hand slowly towards my face.

I reared back, suddenly nervous. "What are you going to do?"

Something passed across his expression so quickly that I couldn't catch it. When he spoke, however, his voice sounded completely normal. "I'm merely going to guide you. We use this as a way to guide fae children as they learn to control their powers. In some ways you are no different than them."

I knew my expression betrayed my opinion of that statement.

"Trust me, Little Wolf," he said.

I nodded and took a slow breath. Tamlain raised his hand again and traced his fingers along my face. Suddenly my nerves were alight, glowing inside of me as the fae gripped my hand with his free one. I could feel power flowing between the two points of contact, from brain to fingers.

It was immediately clear that the magic had always been there inside of me. I had simply never been able to pin it down before. With Tamlain guiding my mind, I could feel the rush of an energy field around both of my hands, one held in Tamlain's and the other hanging loose at my side.

The power pulsed in my mind and my hand trembled with the sensation of my own native magic. I thought about the boot I wanted and with a slight zapping sensation along my nerves, it reappeared on my foot. The laces were neatly tied and everything.

"Wow," I breathed.

Tamlain started to pull away from me, drawing my mental focus towards him. Abruptly, my mind teemed with unfamiliar thoughts and memories. I could see myself on the floor of the cave, tossing and turning, unable to sleep. A strong feeling of affection rolled through me as the eyes I was seeing through roved hungrily over the curve of my hips.

Tamlain jerked back, breaking the physical contact between us. The images vanished as suddenly as they had appeared.

I stood completely still, not even breathing. Had I just read his mind?

It seemed so. He looked more awkward and discomfited than I'd ever seen him before.

"Do you feel fatigued?" he asked, too quickly. "Perhaps we should return to the cave now that you've grasped the basics."

"Yeah. Sure thing," I replied, not looking away from him.

I couldn't help but replay the image in my mind. What was hardest to ignore was the sadness that tinged the memories. Tamlain was obviously attracted to me, but he was also devastated that he couldn't protect me from what was coming. As I slipped through the crack to the cave and returned to my bed, I wished desperately that I could get another glimpse of Tamlain's mind before tomorrow.

I needed to know what was coming for me.

TWENTY-ONE

THE FOLLOWING day dawned faster than I could have possibly imagined. Tamlain was quiet throughout the morning and early afternoon as we made our way resolutely towards Oberon's palace, the epicenter for all the troubles in my life.

With my newfound emotional self-control skills, I was able to stay calm—at least on the surface. I was sure that Tamlain knew it was all an act, but we didn't discuss it. I couldn't have kept my composure if we had, and he probably knew that, too.

By the time evening began to fall, I could no longer bring myself to speak, even the brief, one-word answers that I'd been snapping at him throughout the day. It felt like something terrible—some silent, existential scream of horror—was clawing its way up from the depths of my chest. My breathing was ragged and any time I stopped moving, I began to tremble.

"Are you ready for this, Little Wolf?" Tamlain asked me as we came over a hill and saw the beautiful, large palace nestled in a valley before us.

I nodded curtly even though it was a lie, averting my eyes from his piercing gaze that always saw too much. I marched down the hill, not even bothering to try to hide myself from the scouts that I knew must be present. They knew who I was and why I'd come. There was no reason to chase me any more.

Tamlain didn't move from his position on top of the ridge. I turned to look back, expecting him to follow me.

He shook his head. "You will soon be within sight of the palace walls. Walk straight through the gate and follow the main road towards the setting sun. In the center of the royal quarter, you will find what you seek."

I nodded again, forcing myself to meet his eyes and hold them for a brief moment.

A look of understanding passed between us, but before he could say any more, I turned my back and began walking away. This was between me and my father now. I had to keep Oberon distracted long enough for the others to act.

Sure enough, shouts went up as I walked boldly towards the open gates. I stole sidelong glances at the fae lining the city walls, some with bows and arrows trained on me. A shiver went down my spine. I knew that all it would take was one slip of a finger, and I would die at someone's hands.

But I had to stay focused. I had to ensure Darby was rescued. That goal would give me strength to push the fear away.

I held my head high and strolled in like I owned the place. There was probably a law somewhere that said I *would* own it someday, after all. There must be some sort of succession clause laid down in fae history. Did Oberon have other kids? Now *there* was a disconcerting thought.

As I strode forward, the afternoon light waned as the sun approached the western horizon. Twinkling lamps shone in many of the windows lining the rustic street. Most of the buildings were shops, along with a few houses that surrounded the palace. The walls shimmered with pale colors that gleamed and twinkled from every light source. It would have been beautiful if I hadn't been so busy fighting to keep my terror under control.

What was I going to say to the fae king who'd ruined my life and my family by siring me? *Hey, Dad. Glad to finally meet you after so many years! I understand that you don't like my friends, but let's not kidnap and torture them, 'kay? Thanks, bye now!*

I snorted. Tamlain would smack me upside the head if I led with something like that. He'd urged me repeatedly to act humble and cowed before the king, hoping it would stroke Oberon's ego and perhaps pique his curiosity to buy us some extra time. Personally, I wasn't a fan of the plan, and didn't think it had even a slight chance of working.

I could see a large open area, which I assumed was the square outside the palace. The entire area was bathed in a bright, white light, presumably illuminated with magic. People milled around, talking and pointing towards the far corner of the open space.

I passed a group who must have recognized me as a shifter. They began whispering excitedly to each other and fell into step behind me.

Soon the crowd following me grew to at least fifty people, some laughing and shouting as I made my way towards the raised platform that dominated the far end of the square. There, I could see a small, dark-haired figure chained against a stout wooden pillar.

My heart thundered, a dangerous rage building inside of me despite my best efforts. I could barely control my fury. The wind rose, whipping around me.

Taking several deep breaths, I tried to settle my spirit and control my powers. As I got closer and saw the extent of Darby's injuries on her swollen and battered face, my hold on the storm growing inside me wavered. I wanted to let it loose to destroy the palace. I wanted to force Oberon to watch everything he had made crumble before his eyes.

The wind teased my hair, and I thought of all the innocent lives on Earth that might be lost if I didn't regain control of myself. As much as the need for revenge clamored inside of me, I couldn't justify the loss of lives in another realm.

On his throne across from the execution platform, the fae king appeared to be too engrossed in a conversation with a tall figure in a long, black robe to notice the shifting winds swirling around me as I approached.

I took a moment to examine this man who'd allegedly contributed half of my DNA. His hair was raven-black, swept back in intricate braids similar to the ones Tamlain favored. He was dressed finely in silks and furs, a long ermine-accented cloak draped over his shoulders. A crown of woven holly twigs encircled his brow. His eyes were oddly colorless, as though a light inside him were shining through clear glass.

"Hey, Dad!" I called, waving frantically over my head to capture his attention. "I, uh, heard you wanted to talk to me about something, so I'm here!"

I grinned at him, baring my teeth as my inner wolf snarled in rage. I had such a strong desire to shift form and try to rip the powerful fae apart that I could hardly hold back the tremors through my limbs.

Oberon turned his gaze towards me, his expression steeped in disdain. Something shifted in the air around me, and I became aware that I was one small figure surrounded by an ancient magical power strong enough that it had spawned my own.

Kneel before him, Tamlain had insisted. *He will be intrigued by your deference, since he would never dream of lowering himself before another. You are not yet his prisoner, and still you act like one? That will be a mystery to him — one that he will wish to unravel. Perhaps it will buy some time.*

As I stood before the throne, feeling the strange, ethereal vibration of fae magic shimmering through the air, I couldn't bring myself to do it. Maybe I was my father's daughter after all.

"Your insolence is noted, but misplaced," Oberon said, in the clear voice of someone used to public speaking. "Had I wished to speak to you before now, I would have ordered you brought before me the moment you arrived in my realm."

"*Oh,*" I replied, drawing the word out obnoxiously. "Well, then I guess I'll just be going.

Things to do, people to see, you know? I'm a busy person."

He examined me with his disconcerting pale eyes, like one might examine an unfamiliar insect that had crawled inside the house. "You claim to be my offspring, yet you are *weak*. A single threat against a worthless shifter female, and you crawl to me on your belly like a craven worm."

I clenched my jaw, but the taunts weren't unexpected. I was destined to be Oberon's slave... his means of revenge against his disobedient wife. Why would he ever treat me with respect?

I shoved the unwanted thoughts aside.

His guards were moving, hemming me in, but I didn't look at them. I didn't want to betray my fear in front of this so-called *king*, even though I could guess what was coming next.

"Halt," Oberon thundered, and I froze despite myself in response to the power behind that voice. So did the guards.

A shiver worked its way through my body. Oberon rose to his feet and sauntered towards me without a care in the world. He raised his hand and slowly lowered it.

A magic cage appeared from thin air above me and dropped without warning, forcing me to the ground.

"That was uncalled for," I gritted out, knowing my knees were going to bruise after hitting the unforgiving cobblestones beneath me.

I was trapped, but I was also exactly where I had expected to be. I looked around hopefully, waiting for Tamlain or Dianthe to emerge from the crowd and rescue Darby while Oberon was focused on me.

The swish of a fur-trimmed velvet cloak caught my attention, and I looked up to find Oberon approaching with an expression of cold satisfaction on his chiseled face.

"You must be quite a miserable creature," he drawled. "Neither fish nor fowl, as the humans say. How interesting that your new mate isn't here to share in your captivity. A pathetic lover indeed, leaving you to face me alone. And to think, I once let him lead my armies."

He tutted softly as the crowd around us looked on in interest, muttering among themselves.

Tamlain had been right, though. Oberon didn't know we weren't mated. I let out a low laugh, knowing that it would only incense my father more. He stopped, cocking his head to the side.

"You find this situation amusing?" he asked, his tone a clear warning.

"No," I replied. "It's not that. You're just an idiot, is all."

The vibration of barely leashed magic surrounding the king seemed to grow in intensity. His eyes blazed.

"You dare insult me?" he said in a low, dangerous tone. "The king and lord of Elfhame?"

I shrugged. "It's no insult, just the truth. You truly think your *honorable* general would mate someone without their permission during a magically induced heat? You fool. Do you even know Tamlain *at all*?"

Oberon's face darkened with rage.

"Tamlain would never force himself upon a woman like that," I told him. "So, *newsflash*—I remain as dangerous to Elfhame as I do to Earth. Piss me off, and I'll wreak havoc on your world, too. Your plan to safeguard Elfhame from your new weapon has failed."

Unfortunately, despite my needling, Oberon wasn't *actually* stupid, and he immediately latched on to the flaw in my plan.

"No matter," he said, his eyes narrowing. "I still hold you prisoner here. You are far more dangerous to Earth than to Elfhame while your remain in my realm. If my general was too soft to mate you, I'm sure I can find someone else to do so."

He glanced around at his guards, many of whom let out dark chuckles, not even bothering to hide their lustful gazes.

I shuddered, my skin crawling at the mere thought of it.

Several of the guards and a few men from the crowd were creeping closer, as though they expected Oberon to make good on his threat at this very moment.

I bared my teeth in warning, trying not to think about what was likely to happen to me if Tamlain and Dianthe didn't show up soon. Where the hell *were* they?

As though my thoughts had summoned it from the ether, a familiar voice echoed across the square.

"That will not be happening, my liege."

With a small gasp of relief, I scanned the square until I saw Tamlain striding toward us, seeming completely at ease. He looked neither troubled nor surprised to find me in this predicament.

"Traitor." Oberon's voice hissed like an angry snake. "You *dare* to approach me? To look on your king—the one to whom you swore eternal loyalty and service?"

Tamlain stood silent, staring at his king with blank, expressionless eyes. This seemed to enrage Oberon even further, and he stalked closer, his hoarse voice low and furious. "You would come here to my palace, defying your ruler and betraying your race... for this *creature*?"

"Shifter," I grumbled, just loud enough for Oberon to hear me.

Oberon's look of disgust was answer enough. He turned towards his guards, pointing a shaking finger in their direction.

"You there! Do your duty and slay this traitor!" He gestured at Tamlain, who still hadn't moved.

The guards rushed forward en masse, drawing their swords as they converged on Tamlain. It was clear they expected him to fight and their pace slowed slightly when he made no effort to defend himself.

Why wasn't he defending himself?

The first guard to reach him aimed a wide arcing stroke that would surely cleave Tamlain's head from his neck. I squeezed my eyes shut with a gasp, unable to watch the fae die such a gruesome death, but the sound of metal meeting flesh and bone never came.

I opened one eye in time to see the guard stumble, his missed strike carrying him forward to the ground in a heap. He rose clumsily to one knee and swung a backhand swipe toward Tamlain's unmoving form, attempting to slice his hamstrings. This time I opened both eyes and saw the blade pass cleanly through Tamlain's body, which merely shimmered in response to its passage.

What the... *what*?

Ghost-Tamlain's face twisted into an amused smirk as he folded his arms in front of him.

"Did that make you feel better?" Tamlain's voice called from somewhere behind Oberon. "Because it didn't look terribly satisfying from over here."

A second Tamlain strode forward, an identical amused expression on his face. In moments, four more Tamlains had surrounded us.

"Are you all idiots, to be fooled by these feeble magical projections?" Oberon demanded, raising his voice to be heard over the shouts of the crowd. "Find the real one and kill him, you fools!"

In the same instant, the magical bars around me flickered, crackling as a different kind of energy pulsed through them. I tried to push through, desperate to get free while Oberon was distracted—but the cage remained too solid for me to escape.

It was all I could do not to unleash a massive storm on the palace. I wanted to level the damned place to the ground, if only the backlash wouldn't endanger Earth. I looked around, searching for any possibility of help. Where was Dianthe? She must be here somewhere. My eyes fell on a figure at the edge of the crowd—one that wasn't shouting and milling around like all the others. It appeared to be an old man, stooped and hooded, leaning on a stick. At first I didn't know what about him had caught my attention, but then a pair of vibrant blue eyes met mine and held.

My breath caught. It was the real Tamlain, hiding in plain sight.

Ember. His voice echoed inside my head. I recoiled in shock, my back impacting the bars of the cage with a sharp crackle of magic.

"What the *actual fuck*?" I yelped.

You forged a mental connection with me when I was attempting to teach you fae magic, said the eerily familiar voice in my head. *I am using all of my power to project so many images of myself. I can't break the cage around you without your help.*

I wasn't sure if he could also hear my thoughts, so I mentally yelled as loud as I could. *I don't know how to break the cage! And how did this even happen? Where is Dianthe?*

He winced. *Please stop shouting, Little Wolf. I can hear you perfectly well. To answer your questions, this most definitely should not have happened, and Dianthe has not returned from Earth. Now focus. I will guide you to use your innate magic to break free.*

Around us, chaos reigned as the guards attacked Tamlain's projections. My mouth had fallen open, but I snapped it shut and nodded slowly, allowing him to mentally light my magical way. Just as in the forest, I could see the path illuminated for me, leading me toward my own powers.

The cage began to vibrate, rattling against the ground. Oberon whirled toward me and thrust his hand out, his fingers moving in a complicated gesture.

My muscles froze, completely paralyzed. I couldn't even breathe.

"Oh, no. I think not, little shifter." He turned and called for the two nearest guards. "You two! If the bars around this creature so much as tremble, remove the hostage's head."

He flicked his fingers again, and the paralysis instantly lifted. I gasped in a breath. My eyes flew to Darby, still chained on the execution platform.

Oberon leaned in close. "I know he's here," he snarled. "My traitorous general… your *lover*, if not your mate. You will both yield, otherwise your little friend on the platform will pay the price."

I watched as the two guards unchained Darby from the post and wrenched her away, making her cry out in fear and pain. One pressed her down to kneel with her head on a wooden block, as the other picked up the large axe that had been leaning against it. He looked from me to her and back again, his message clear as day.

It's you or her.

No one moved. No more shouts rang out through the crowd. All I could hear was my own ragged breathing and the frantic beating of my heart. Time seemed to slow as Oberon stared down at me.

The heavy silence was broken by an electric crackling noise. Flames ripped through the air and a portal opened near the platform.

I stared, open-mouthed, as a female figure emerged, stumbling as though she'd been pushed. It couldn't be Dianthe, could it? She leapt through every portal with the grace of a deer.

This woman staggered and fell, her hood sliding off to reveal her face. Geneva Padfoot, the *true* traitor, fell to her knees a few feet away from me. Her wrists and neck were chained with iron shackles.

Another figure stumbled through the portal and came to an abrupt halt. Cai's amber eyes flickered over the entire scene, including me on my knees inside a magical cage.

In the next second, a sheen of madness turned his gaze glassy as the exposure to Elfhame crashed down on him. He was a shifter—he should never have come to this world. *What had Dianthe been thinking?*

Cai roared with rage, grabbing hold of Geneva's chains and dragging her roughly to her feet. Shocked gasps rang out, as the fae around us regarded the angry shifter and his iron-bound captive with trepidation.

There was nothing sane in Cai's expression as he whirled back and forth, taking in the crowd's presence. "You fae fuckers!" he shouted. "I'll kill *every single one of you!*"

TWENTY-TWO

THE WORLD FELT like it was moving in slow motion. I watched in shock as Cai lunged forward, shifting into his large wolf form with a rippling snarl. He shook his head violently, then took a long, flying leap into the crowd, chasing after the onlookers who ran screaming in all directions.

Movement caught my eye as Dianthe leapt through the portal behind Cai, an odd look on her face as she surveyed the chaos spreading in expanding waves throughout the square. Geneva Padfoot had fallen to the ground and remained there, covering her head with her chained hands.

I was frozen in place, watching as Cai charged through the square, his sharp teeth bared in rage. He looked like one of the monsters from a human horror movie — rabid and deadly.

This wasn't the real Cai, I reminded myself. *This was Elfhame's madness.*

While my fated mate had rejected me, he wasn't cruel, or a murderer. Seeing him like this, with blood spattering his gray muzzle and mindless rage in his eyes, made my stomach turn.

Listening to his anguished howls shredded the last remaining self-control I possessed, and as the cage quivered around me, I shifted into my own wolf form. The growl that escaped my throat made the few fae that had remained nearby spring away as if afraid I, too, would turn on them.

Maybe I would, I thought as I snapped at the cage holding me back.

Cai stampeded through the open square, snapping and biting at anyone slow enough to remain in his path. His eyes rolled wildly, the magic in Elfhame clearly causing him terrible suffering.

My wolf was frantic to get to him, whining and pushing on the magical bars of the cage.

The sound of metal clashing against metal drew my attention, and I watched as Dianthe charged through a group of guards, cutting them down as she moved in a wide circle around my cage. As soon as she launched her assault, Tamlain threw off his concealing hood. Under the cover of Dianthe's attack and the raging wolf, he quietly leapt onto the platform where Darby knelt bound and gagged.

In a flash, he brought a blade around and cut the throat of her would-be executioner.

A relief so powerful that I felt almost giddy crashed through me. As my immediate terror for her safety eased, I concentrated on my own nascent magical powers, which I was surprised to find were much easier to grasp while I was in my wolf form.

Before I had a chance to wonder at that, I became aware of a great upwelling of power building around Oberon and his remaining guards. Their attention was not on me—nor on the two fae in league with me — but rather, on the crazed wolf now nearing the edge of the palace square.

I didn't know what they were going to do, but I guessed that the power I could feel building in the air around us would *not* be beneficial to Cai's health, to put it mildly. Oberon would kill him, as he'd intended Geneva Padfoot to do when he'd sent her back to Earth.

Grinding my fangs together, I let my newfound magical powers extend outside my own body. It felt in some ways like I was bursting through my own skin, and the explosion of invisible force shattered the bars of my cage.

My claws scraped along the paving stones beneath my paws as I charged through the falling debris of my enclosure. With one quick look towards Cai, I let out a long howl and flung a shield of power around us both.

The human part of me was surprised at my own ability, but the wolf's instinct to protect our mate had taken over — an instinctive need beyond rational thought. I couldn't have stopped myself from creating that shield if I'd tried.

If I'd had more time to explore the ability, I felt like I would have been able to mold and shape the sphere now protecting us. I could have pushed it outward so that it was big enough to cover an entire building, or shrunk it down to protect only one finger on my hand. As it was, it expended to exactly the size needed to enclose us both.

Fleeing crowd members were able to pass through the shield, but guards carrying weapons were rebuffed by the intensity of my power. It appeared in my mind's eye like a radiant, pure heat.

The well it was drawing from felt limitless.

Yet no sooner than I'd had the thought, I felt the defense begin to weaken. I'd pictured a giant bubble surrounding us, which repelled the magical blasts coming from Oberon and his guards. That was indeed what I'd created, but in some ways the bubble felt as though it had a life and a will of its own. The amount of energy I had to exert to keep the shield in the configuration I wanted was weakening me. I had access to the power I needed to *create* it, but trying to *control* it was draining me of all the energy I possessed.

More magical blows rained down on the shield, and I desperately wished that I could steal the energy from Oberon's attacks somehow, instead of using my own.

Wait. Maybe I could?

I'd created this shield by simply picturing the bubble around us and using the power of fae magic to make it real, because I'd needed it so badly. Maybe I could imagine it absorbing and using the power of Oberon's attacks the same way?

In the next instant, the shield began channeling the energy from every attack directly to me, restoring my vitality with each blow Oberon tried to strike.

Ha! Take *that*, Tamlain. So what if I couldn't make a boot reappear without help? This was *way* better.

But unfortunately, the protective sphere around him was not enough to ease Cai's madness.

He was still lunging and snapping at any fae that got too close to him. In between attacks he threw himself to the ground, rubbing his face frantically against the stone as though bugs were crawling on him.

Even in his wolf form, I could tell he was screaming inside. One of the fae guards had stopped just on the edge of the square and turned back towards the mayhem. He appeared to hesitate, obviously torn as he glanced back and forth between his path to safety and the staggering Cai.

Run, I urged silently. I didn't want to see any more people suffer for what Oberon had done. The fae fled into the darkness, and I breathed a sigh of relief.

Even with my new influx of stolen power, I needed to stay focused. I searched for any familiar faces among the crowd streaming past me. After a few moments, I located my two fae allies. Dianthe had joined Tamlain on the platform and was kneeling down behind Darby, struggling with the bindings around Darby's wrists. Meanwhile, Tamlain fought off any guards that dared approach. During the lulls, he would turn his eyes towards Dianthe, muttering instructions I couldn't hear through tight lips.

"Enough!" A thunderous voice boomed out, so loud that everything in the square shook and rattled.

It was Oberon. He stood in the center of the fleeing crowd, his arms outstretched as they parted around him like a river. Overhead, dark purple and blue clouds formed in the sky, looming ominously low over the crowd. A fork of lightning flashed above us, illuminating the scene and bathing Oberon in an unearthly, flickering light. The wind howled around us, reminding me unavoidably of my own unwanted power over the elements.

With a commanding gesture towards the platform where my friends were battling, Oberon sent another bolt of lightning towards the ground. I froze in horror as it crashed into Tamlain, who fell as though pole-axed and lay still.

No!

Could a fae die from being electrocuted? My internal scream of denial emerged from my wolf in the form of an anguished howl.

I looked around wildly. Where was Dianthe? Surely she could help him—

After scanning the crowd, many of whom were moving away as quickly as possible, I found her standing just off the platform. She was supporting Darby, who appeared to be barely conscious.

Pandemonium erupted around us as the remaining members of the crowd ran shrieking in all directions. More lightning flashed down, the bolts throwing small explosions of rock and dirt in every direction, peppering everyone with the shrapnel. The thunder was so loud that I felt like my canine eardrums were about to burst.

Through the din, I caught the sound of a shrill, female cry of warning. Whirling around, I found Dianthe again. She had cast an open portal a few feet away from me, but the lightning dancing around her and the power that crackled through the air appeared to be on the verge of causing the opening to collapse.

I knew in that instant we had to reach it before it disappeared. We *had* to get everyone to safety. But… *Tamlain*. There was no way to get to him! I stood frozen, unsure what to do.

"*Go!*" Dianthe screamed over the din, dragging Darby forward as the crowd buffeted around them. Everyone was pushing and shoving to get away from Oberon's rage. She met my eyes frantically. "*Get Cai and go!*"

I moved without thinking, diving forward to sink my teeth into the thick fur around Cai's neck. He snarled and tried to bite me, but his madness was weakening his reflexes.

I avoided the clumsy attack and dragged him towards the open portal, even as it flickered and almost went out. I could see Dianthe and Darby about the same distance away.

Supporting Darby with one arm, Dianthe paused and stretched out her other arm towards the portal, her fingers splayed open. She took a deep breath, closing her eyes, and the portal seemed to stabilize.

I knew we had only seconds to get away. I could sense Oberon's gaze upon us, and the night air echoed with his deafening commands for his guards to stop us.

Still half-dragging Cai, I lurched through the portal and into a mercifully quiet forest on Earth. With a final mighty heave, I pulled Cai the rest of the way through with me, shifting back into a human form just as we both landed in a tangled heap on the ground.

I turned back towards the magical doorway, ready to help Dianthe pull Darby through. It was essential that we got them all out. But would the portal remain open long enough for Dianthe to get Tamlain, too?

As I surged forward, only able to see a small sliver of the battle through the opening, I heard a distant wail, echoing across the planes between Earth and Elfhame. Before I could do anything, the portal snapped shut, all trace of the nightmare on the other side cut off.

"No!" I screamed, my hand outstretched uselessly towards the friends I could no longer reach.

TWENTY-THREE

TERROR AND RAGE tried to claw their way up my chest, choking off the air from my lungs. But I couldn't let the emotions get free. I *couldn't*. I closed my eyes and forced a huge gulp of air past the lump lodged in my throat.

Think! Stay focused or you'll only make things worse!

I wasn't simply beating myself up for failing to get everyone through the portal. I knew that if I didn't get my reaction under control, I ran the risk of accidentally killing the very people on Elfhame that I was so desperate to save.

With no other alternatives, I sat on the ground next to Cai, who was still out of his mind and writhing on the grass. He was shifting rapidly back and forth between a wolf and a man, his intermittent screams and howls cutting each other off.

I needed him to *stop*, damn it all. I couldn't handle the current disaster and his madness, as well.

Withdrawing deep inside myself, I pulled inward as though I was preparing to shift. Just as I felt the power beginning to spread through my limbs, preparing to shed my human skin and pull on my wolf form, I stopped pressing everything in.

Teetering between the balance of human and wolf instantly quieted my mind. It felt as though I could access all of my powers while in transition between the two competing parts of myself.

Almost.

I breathed deeply and forced myself to concentrate. I had to take stock of my situation so that I could fix this terrible mess.

I was stuck on Earth, with no handy fae around to portal my lame-ass shifter self anywhere else. I focused on the soft sound of my own breathing, trying to drown out Cai's guttural noises of despair and rage. I needed Cai on my side, but he was still suffering from the insanity of Elfhame. We shared a bond, though—as much as he'd tried to break it. Was there a way to snap him out of his madness?

I paused for a moment, exploring the environment around me with my inner senses as well as my outer ones. Cai had stumbled away from me in wolf form and was scratching frantically at the ground.

A mental voice that sounded suspiciously like Dianthe's suggested slapping him silly to see if that would work.

Tempting.

Although my wolf was deeply invested in preserving our fated mate's safety, it would be pretty damned satisfying to take out some of my frustration on him right now.

He can't even defend himself, chided an inner voice that sounded more like Darby. My heart ached at the reminder of my sweet friend's predicament, but the ghostly voice had a point.

Cai's madness was torture to listen to. I knelt silently on the forest floor, willing my heart rate to slow and my breathing to return to normal.

When I again felt in command of my own emotions, I opened my eyes. Glancing around, I studied Cai. His huge gray wolf was rolling on the ground and thrashing, paws kicking wildly in the air.

Pity welled up inside of me. I couldn't stand watching him suffer any longer. Plus, I needed him in his right mind to help me rescue my friends.

Steeling myself, I explored the fragile mate-bond. I needed to reach beyond the hysteria sparked by his exposure to Elfhame — to his true self. I could feel the hollow, painful place where our mate bond had been buried inside my chest. It ached and seared with neglect, as if a part of me had genuinely been burned away. But beneath the scars that Bardulf and Cai himself had inflicted, I also could feel the connection between us. It was deeply damaged, but it was from this part of me that I received phantom impressions of him in my mind and heart.

I pressed onward, trying to reach him through the connection, but it felt hopeless. I could sense some deeply buried part of his wolf straining feebly to reach my wolf. But his humanity was entirely blocked out by the madness of Elfhame hijacking his thoughts.

Before I was truly aware of what I was doing, I'd shifted into my wolf form. Cai stopped growling and stilled his frantic thrashing on the ground. He lay panting, his gaze lolling towards me, his bright red tongue gathering dirt on the ground. He looked completely spent and exhausted.

Something about his weakened state brought a part of me alive that I'd never known before. I felt protective. *Possessive*, even. My wolf needed Cai, and he needed me. All of the things that had happened between us weren't gone or even forgotten... but they paled before what needed to happen next.

Our world was at stake. Cai had made mistakes... *so many* mistakes. But he'd also been manipulated into thinking his actions were the only way to protect me from a terrible fate. He'd listened rather than losing his temper when confronted with his shortcomings and errors, and he hadn't dismissed my claims about Geneva, or about the risk to Earth.

Somehow — and I couldn't even imagine how he'd pulled it off — he'd managed to capture Geneva despite her powers of magic and mental influence. He'd come to a hostile world despite the danger to his life and his sanity, and his presence had *almost* been enough to turn the tide of the battle in our favor.

I rose on four legs and padded toward him with a gentle whine, nudging his shoulder with my nose. In my heart, I was certain I could bring Cai back to himself. I could *fix* this... if I surrendered my human will to my wolf's.

It was more difficult than it should have been. I'd always held part of myself back from my true shifter nature. The human inside of me fought against giving in to my most basic animal instincts. Yet I recognized that my human self was unlikely to ever reach Cai, no matter how long we were stuck on Earth together.

I gave my body a hearty, head-to-tail shake and surrendered—allowing my humanity to fade, and the mind of the wolf to surge up and take over.

We nuzzled Cai's thick ruff of fur, whimpering at the feel of his madly racing heart.

My wolf settled our body against his so that he, too, could feel our heartbeat. It was slow and steady, and before long, our rhythms began to synchronize as his wolf reacted to us. He raised his head and licked our face with exhausted affection. We nipped playfully at his chin, receiving a low rumble in return.

With our bodies pressed close like this, it occurred to me that it was the most intimate position we'd ever been in with him. It felt nice, curled up against his side as our breathing fell into sync.

My wolf knew exactly what she wanted, and now that I'd ceded control to her, she would no longer be denied. As Cai's madness ebbed away to calm and stillness, we nuzzled at him again, rubbing our body provocatively against his. Fur slid against fur, the scent of our arousal growing until he lurched to his feet and shouldered into us, nosing along our side and flank.

My wolf yipped happily, dipping into a play bow and wagging our tail as we circled and jostled each other good-naturedly. Between the madness and the battle on Elfhame, Cai had clearly been exhausted. He'd rubbed all the blood off his muzzle and fur when he was thrashing around in the dirt, but I could still scent it faintly, clinging to him.

He fought for us.

That was my wolf's thought, but it was just as true for my human self. Cai had come for us. Cai had fought for us.

The scent of blood faded beneath the scent of Cai's answering arousal, and his playful nips grew heated. He'd been sliding his body against our side, but now his jaws closed around the fur at the back of our neck and held tight as he mounted. Despite being on four legs rather than two, my body flashed back to Tamlain's callused hand closing over the back of my neck and pressing my upper body gently to the ground.

Tamlain must have trained me well, because lust flared instantly in response. Cai's body covered ours, and he entered us in a single swift stroke.

It was pleasure and completion—but it was also more than that. Our souls were connected, despite all that had happened between us. At the connection of our bodies, that bond flared into life like a supernova, burning away all of my human uncertainty like ice melting beneath a blowtorch. We were *together*. There was no other word for it.

Underneath his wolf's instinctive drive to mate and bond, I felt Cai's human self stirring. The madness was gone, replaced by the white-hot connection weaving together between us.

With his growl muffled by the fur of my ruff, he snarled and pumped into my body, shuddering through a release that dragged me right along with him. When the pleasure finally faded, reality asserted itself. I sent a suggestion along the bond, knowing enough about wolves mating to know that if we stayed in this form, he'd knot me and we'd be stuck together for longer than either of us could afford.

Our bodies shifted form in tandem, the quality of the pleasure changing as fur became skin. His teeth were around my shoulder now, sending fiery tingles down my spine as we collapsed onto our sides in slow motion.

Cai kissed the bite mark tenderly as we lay curled against each other, panting and flushed. He was still inside of me, and I was trembling so violently I could barely lift a hand to shove my tangled hair away from my face.

The mate bond between us throbbed and hummed with life, no trace left of the twisted scar tissue of fear and rejection that had muted the connection up until now. His soaring emotions thrummed through the bond, filling me with such a sensation of love and belonging that I burst helplessly into tears. His soul-deep adoration was a balm soothing my frayed edges. The burning sense of betrayal I'd been harboring was gone, along with the bitterness I'd held close to my heart since my exile.

"What is it?" Cai asked. His softening cock slipped out of my body, but he cradled me close to him, our warm skin pressed together. "What... just happened? Ember? Please don't cry..."

Despite the passion of our wolves' lovemaking, he held me gingerly, almost awkwardly against his chest. He seemed shocked by what we had just done, as though he couldn't quite believe it was real. He didn't appear to know exactly what to do with his hands.

After gathering me a little closer, he repeated his question in a low murmur. "You're upset. Please tell me what's happening."

"I've never felt like this before," I whispered, trying to wipe the tears away. My nose was running, and I was sure I looked like a complete emotional wreck. He didn't even seem to notice as he nodded and pressed his cheek to mine.

"Me either," he admitted, his fingers twirling a strand of my platinum-bleached hair absently.

The tender moment couldn't totally chase away the reality of what was happening back in Elfhame, though. My fear for my friends surged anew, causing the wind to pick up around us.

I dashed away my tears and dragged myself back under control when Cai abruptly sat up, staring at the freshly blown leaves settling around us.

"Strange," he observed, "I didn't even feel that breeze. Was that you?"

I nodded, still dabbing my eyes when his words fell into place.

"Wait," I said, sitting up, too. "You didn't feel the wind just now? *Really?*"

TWENTY-FOUR

CAI LOOKED AT me like he wasn't sure why I was asking about the wind when everything else around us was going crazy. "Not really, no," he said. "Why do you ask?"

My lips parted in shock as I tried to process the implications of what I'd just done. I remembered the attackers that had cornered my coworker and I as we made our way home from work in Rockville. They'd been blasted off their feet by the power of the storm I'd brought down on us. Meanwhile, I'd been able to withstand the wind with no problems. The same thing had happened during the storm in the forest on Elfhame.

This kind of thing was Tamlain's territory, not mine. He was the expert on fae magic—but it seemed like when Cai and I mated, my power had, in fact, connected to him somehow. Intuitively, it felt like the power flowing through my soul was now also flowing through his.

I badly wanted to test the theory, but could I risk more devastation on Elfhame while my friends were still there?

I needed to know if I'd done it. Had Tamlain's theory been correct? Now that Cai was connected with me through the revitalized mating bond, was Earth protected from my powers?

I wasn't sure there was a way to safely tell—at least, not without some guidance from someone who knew what the hell they were doing. I didn't feel brave enough to experiment with my newly awakened fae powers in an attempt to test it.

"Hey… Ember. You still with me?" Cai's voice broke through my reverie. I wondered how long I had been staring wide-eyed at him, lost in the implications.

"Yeah," I said, too quickly to sound casual. "I was just thinking. It seems like you have protection against my fae powers now."

He pursed his lips. "That could come in handy. How does it work?"

I lifted my hands helplessly. "I wish I knew."

"So am I, like, fae by marriage now? That's how the humans do it, right?"

He was only teasing, but I still hesitated. Did he fully understand that I was half fae and half shifter… the daughter of Elfhame's mad king? Did he truly know what kind of person he'd just mated?

I strove for the same light tone. "I don't think so. You'd be a pretty lousy one, what with going crazy the minute your feet hit Elfhame."

It felt good to tease each other. While I still felt the overwhelming love and acceptance flowing across our mate bond, it was a relief to also feel humor and a little mischief from my mate.

My *mate*.

Holy crap. That was going to take some serious getting used to… but unfortunately, there was a laundry list of more important things I needed to focus on first. I still needed answers. There were certainly things that needed to be worked out between us—especially surrounding my banishment from the Greystalker pack—but I had bigger priorities right now.

"How did you capture Geneva? And how on *Earth* did you convince Dianthe to drag you to Elfhame?" I demanded. "Sorry, I should've asked you that right away, but... uh... one thing led to another and..."

My voice trailed off, and my face heated. I was probably bright red with mortification, because *damn*, but my inner wolf was a serious hussy. Cai reached over and squeezed my fingers reassuringly.

"Some of the scouts spotted Geneva slinking around the Greystalker lands," he said. "They let me know about it, and when I came across her scent while I was out hunting, I tracked her. I've been carrying an iron blade with me ever since you and your blond boy toy explained that the fae were involved, and told me what she'd done to me."

"Smart," I said, blushing harder at the reminder that Cai had felt every moment of my night spent with Tamlain.

"Anyway," he continued, "when I found her, I knew there was no way I'd managed to sneak up on her that easily. I figured it was some sort of a trap, so I hid the knife behind my back and confronted her. I raved about her manipulating my mind and displacing my father as alpha. I'm not sure she bought the act, but I knew I'd only have one shot at attacking her. I waited until she lifted a hand, getting ready to hurl magic at me, and I threw the knife before she could."

The memory of Geneva falling to her knees on Elfhame, bound and shackled, was a deeply satisfying one. It was even more impressive now that I'd heard the story of how it came to be. No offense meant to my new mate, but I'd genuinely assumed Dianthe had been behind Geneva's capture.

Cai frowned. "I'm pretty sure the fae bitch was trying to cut me in half. I managed to duck the wave of magic she let loose when the dagger hit, but a few trees right behind me were split straight through the trunks. The dagger hit her in the side, and I guess fae *really* don't like iron, because it incapacitated her even though it wasn't a mortal wound."

I shook my head in amazement. "Okay, wow. I'm not sure you really grasp how impressive that is."

Cai ducked his head. "*Impressive* would have been if I'd caught onto what she's been doing all these years, before it was too late. Manipulating the pack. Manipulating *me*."

"Still," I said—because I'd been a victim of Geneva's magical attack too, and I hadn't fared nearly as well.

"Anyway," he continued, "after that, I slung her over my shoulder and carried her to the blacksmith's hut. I had him bind her with iron. It wasn't that difficult. She was still weak from the dagger in her side, otherwise I'm sure she would have put up more of a fight."

"How did Dianthe find you?" I asked.

Cai shrugged. "I have no idea, honestly. She showed up while the blacksmith was putting the final touches on Geneva's shackles. She just strolled in like we'd arranged to meet there. She looked back and forth between me and Geneva a few times and said something like, *'Well, I guess there's not much for me to do here after all.'*"

A pained chuckle escaped me, as I tried not to think what might be happening to Dianthe and the others on Elfhame. "Sounds like her, yeah."

"She's something," Cai agreed. "I was glad she showed up, too. As you might imagine, I had a lot of questions for her. I wanted to know everything. Where you were, what was happening, why Geneva had returned..."

"Did she answer?" I asked, genuinely curious. Tamlain and Dianthe hadn't exactly been forthcoming with me, but I thought maybe they were finally learning not to hide so many things.

"Yeah, she did—in broad strokes, at least. She told me you were planning to confront Oberon to try to rescue Darby. Well, I couldn't stand the thought of you going into that kind of danger alone, so I demanded that she take me to you."

"I wasn't alone," I protested. "And you had to know how dangerous it would be for you to go there!"

Cai shrugged. "You're the wolf I should have mated. Darby is a member of my pack. You were both supposed to be under my protection, and instead I was responsible for you being exiled and Darby being kidnapped. And then Dianthe tells me you're about to face the most powerful fae in Elfhame? I had to help, if I could."

I shook my head slowly, still trying to take everything on board. "But Dianthe had to know you'd go crazy on Elfhame. Why would she agree to take you there?"

"Well," Cai hedged, "I may have minimized a few parts of our story to convince her to take me to you."

I raised my eyebrows at him in question.

"She asked me about the fate-bond. She seemed to think it would protect me from the madness of Elfhame, if our connection was strong enough."

"You didn't tell her that your father tried to have it destroyed?" I asked, appalled. "And that we've both slept with other people to further weaken it?"

For the first time, Cai looked a little guilty. "I might've downplayed both those aspects… a bit."

I groaned. "No wonder she looked so annoyed when you went off your rocker and started tearing through the crowd in the plaza."

He scrubbed a hand awkwardly through the messy hair at the back of his head. "That may not have been my finest moment, granted." His amber eyes met mine. "Do you think she was right, though? If I went back now, would I be protected?"

I hesitated, unsure. My hybrid heritage aside, I was no expert on Elfhame or fae magic. I had no idea if he would be protected, but I supposed the fact that he was protected from my powers on Earth now argued in favor of it.

"Maybe," I replied. "And I'm afraid we may have to test that sooner rather than later."

"Then let's hope Dianthe knows what she's talking about," he said. "Because I hate to say it, but my memories are pretty hazy after we jumped through the portal."

"Mostly it involved extreme mayhem," I told him. "Which… actually sort of worked, I guess — because everyone was so distracted by the crazy wolf in their midst that Tamlain was able to get to Darby."

It might have turned things in our favor, if the cards had fallen just a bit differently.

Silence fell between us, but it was surprisingly comfortable. I gently probed at the bond, which seemed to be growing stronger as time passed. I desperately hoped it meant Earth would now be protected from my powers.

When the wind had picked up earlier, it hadn't seemed as strong as usual. On the other hand, I hadn't really let go enough to test it properly. I didn't dare.

"Tamlain has this theory," I explained after a while, "that by mating with an inhabitant of Earth, it would cement my connection with the entire realm, not just my mate. In that way, he believes that my mate's world would be protected from the destruction I cause with my powers."

He blinked, clearly taken aback. "Wait. You mean… Earth is safe now?"

I shook my head, frustrated. "I'm not sure. I don't know how to test it. I made the wind blow earlier, but... not a lot? And the bond might still have been settling then."

"Do you want to try it?" he asked cautiously. "See if you can make a storm appear?"

I grimaced. "I don't think I dare. What if I start a storm but can't stop it? What if my friends on Elfhame get hurt? It's always worse in the other realm."

Cai wrapped his arms around me and tugged me against his chest. I stiffened—still unaccustomed to that kind of touch from others—but then I melted against him.

"We need to know, Ember," he said. "We're bonded now. I know you can feel it, because I certainly can. Keep it small for now, and I'll help you regain control if you start to lose it."

I nodded. "Okay. You're right. I know you're right."

Tamlain had told me once that a small disturbance I'd caused on Elfhame would only have caused a thunderstorm on Earth, not an apocalypse. I sat on the ground with my eyes closed, letting my fear for Darby, Dianthe, and Tamlain creep free of its prison. A gentle breeze brushed over me, wisps of hair tickling my ears. Yet even as I allowed my fear and anger freer rein, the wind settled and died away within moments.

My eyes flew open, taking in the calm wilderness surrounding me.

"It died down," I said stupidly, packing my emotions away in their box again. "The wind died down."

"Then I think that's your answer," Cai told me, tucking a stray lock of hair behind my ear.

I jumped up, filled with sudden, manic energy as it sank in. "That's it—that's my edge against Oberon. He can't use me as a weapon against Earth anymore! We need to get going, we have to figure out a way to rescue the others."

Through the mate bond, I felt Cai's mind pull back from mine, putting emotional distance between us.

"What is it?" I asked, frowning.

"Sorry, it's just—" He shook his head, as though trying to shake away a buzzing insect. "That male fae. Tamlain. You're really worried about him, and… you slept with him."

It wasn't as though he was accusing me—not really—but there was tightly leashed pain behind the words.

I met his eyes, not backing down. "You slept with a bunch of female shifters the night you rejected me, while I was locked naked in a cell, awaiting exile. Or did you think I didn't feel *every second* of that through the bond?"

Cai winced and looked away.

"Geneva cast a spell at me to force me into an unnatural heat," I said icily. This wasn't a conversation I wanted to have right now, but if we were having it anyway, I wouldn't be pulling any punches.

"It was terrible," I told him. "I felt like I was going to die—like my own body was in revolt against me. Tamlain could have taken advantage. He could have secured Elfhame's protection from my powers by bonding us when I was too out of it to stop what was happening."

Cai's shoulders hunched inward. His fists clenched, but I couldn't tell if he was angry at himself, or at Tamlain, or Geneva, or all of it together.

"Instead," I continued, "he helped me through it as best he could without mating me. I couldn't give consent, and he's an honorable man. But that doesn't mean he was willing to watch me suffer the torment of an unfulfilled heat."

A flicker of something washed across Cai's face too fast for me to pin it down. It might have been grudging respect, but I wasn't done yet.

"I won't apologize for what we did together," I said, biting off the words. "Not after what you did to me on that first, horrible night. So if you want this to work between us, you can just suck it up and move past it."

Cai looked very somber. He unclenched his hands and took one of mine between both of his. He was still holding himself at a distance within the bond. I watched him with wary eyes, ready to show my fangs if he tried to make this into an issue — metaphorically, and if need be, physically.

I hadn't forgotten the way his wolf had yielded to mine when I'd first returned from Elfhame with Tamlain.

He brushed his rough fingers across my knuckles, meeting my gaze directly and holding it.

"You love him." It was a statement, not a question.

I mentally stumbled, caught by surprise. This wasn't the fight I'd geared up for.

"I… care for him," I finally replied, weighing each word before letting it free into the world.

And that was undeniably true. I cared for Tamlain. But I didn't think it was any more than I cared for Darby, or for Dianthe.

Was it?

My uncertainty must have come through the bond, because Cai only nodded and said, "All right. We'll figure it out later."

I wanted to argue further, but all of this was a distraction. I needed to focus on getting us back to Elfhame. Part of me wanted to leave Cai behind on Earth, as far away from Oberon as possible—but the idea of being away from him so soon after we'd mated made my stomach clench painfully.

I can protect him better if he's close to me, I reasoned. *He won't suffer the madness again, I'm sure of it.*

And, perhaps more to the point, I needed the moral support. The idea of trying to storm Oberon's castle alone made me want to curl up in a ball and never come out again.

"Right. Do we have a plan?" Cai asked, making it clear he considered his presence at my side to be a foregone conclusion.

"Well," I began slowly, "there are no fae here to cast a portal for us, so I guess I'll have to do it on my own."

I hesitated, not sure how to continue without making it clear that I had no freaking clue what I was doing.

"Go on," Cai prompted.

I sighed deeply. "My powers can only wreak havoc on one realm now—Elfhame. My father is about to find that out the hard way. I just need to make sure that my magic can stretch across the two realms before I try to make a portal."

He didn't need to know it would be my *first* portal, right?

Cai nodded. "Makes sense. How can you test that?"

I glanced down at my naked body. Cai and I had been sitting casually next to each other, our shoulders touching. Standing, I gestured to my bare skin.

"Well, I can't really keep walking around like this."

"You can't?" he asked, raising an eyebrow. "Why not?"

I shot him a quelling look, and a hint of a teasing smile curled one corner of his lips, despite our earlier fight. With a slow, calming breath, I thought about the mental gymnastics Tamlain had taught me to summon my clothes. This time, they'd been left in tatters in the palace square on Elfhame. I could feel the phantom memory of Tamlain in my head, guiding me. I waved my hand in a slow arc down the length of my body.

My clothes reappeared around me, warm and fresh.

"Um… okay, wow," Cai said. "I think I've definitely missed out on some things since I saw you last."

"Stand still," I told him, concentrating and repeating the motion over his body. A moment later, he, too, was fully clothed.

He ran his hands across his undamaged shirt in awe. "Holy ancestors. I thought this shirt was a goner."

I quirked my lips in a crooked smile, feeling more connected to my fae powers than I ever had before. I'd never done anything on this scale, but I thought I understood the theory after recalling our clothes from the other realm. If the clothes could travel *from* Elfhame, Cai and I could travel *to* Elfhame.

Simple. It really was just a matter of concentrating on exactly what I wanted to happen, and then throwing magic at the problem.

I let the desire to be with Darby, Dianthe, and Tamlain fill me nearly to the point of bursting. As the power built in my body, I felt heat radiating from my palms. In some ways, it reminded me of when I'd instinctively thrown up the protective shield during the battle. But this time, I channeled all my power into creating a portal that would take us to the friends who needed us.

I lifted my hand in a circular gesture like I'd seen Tamlain and Dianthe use. Power poured out of my fingers, and the air in front of us caught fire.

TWENTY-FIVE

THE FORCE OF the power erupting from my hand made me step back. As I blinked in the suddenly bright light, I could see a massive portal, bigger and brighter than any I'd ever seen before, expand into existence right in front of me.

"I guess that answers that question," Cai said. "You can definitely make portals now. Gods above, I'm mated to a magician."

I scowled at him over my shoulder, afraid to turn away from the magic tunneling through reality for more than the briefest instant. I wasn't sure how long my baby fae powers would be able to hold it open.

"Stay close to me and follow my lead," I told him, stepping towards the opening leading to Elfhame.

"Just a second." Cai shed the clothes I'd just called for him and crouched, shifting into his wolf form.

I could feel his thoughts in my head as he assured me he'd keep his head this time. *I'm stronger as a wolf and will be more useful if this turns into a battle,* he told me through the bond.

I nodded, quickly looking back to make sure the portal was holding steady. "Okay. Good thinking."

With a deep breath, I passed through the flaming oval, stumbling a bit as I landed in a dim environment I hadn't expected. I didn't know at first if my friends were here, or if my plan to travel directly to them had failed. Then my shifter senses adjusted to the low light, and I took in a horrific scene.

Cai's fur brushed against my leg as he came through the portal after me. His wolf growled as he took in our surroundings. Darby and Dianthe were chained against the stone walls, the former appearing to be barely conscious. I wasn't sure if it was the madness of Elfhame affecting her, or whatever Oberon had done to her, but she seemed nearly incoherent.

Dianthe was conscious, and clearly angry as hell. She strained at her shackles, and I winced as I noticed the blood dripping from her wrists. She must have been fighting her chains so hard that the metal had cut into her skin.

Aside from a quick glance at the portal we'd just come through, her gaze was focused behind us. I turned to see what she was looking at and found Oberon standing in the middle of the room, with his guards stationed along the opposite wall.

He was studying several items on a small, dark table, as though my arrival with Cai didn't even rate as an inconvenience. Tamlain lay in a heap on the floor in front of him—bare-chested, burned, and bleeding. Like Darby, he appeared to be barely conscious. His blue eyes were open, but glassy. A faint flicker of recognition kindled in their depths as I stared at him, but otherwise he made no sign that he was aware of what was happening around him.

Oberon sneered at me.

"It appears I've sired a fool," he said. "It was madness to return here, little plaything. Unless you surrender yourself to me unequivocally, I will destroy everyone you love today. You will lose control, knowing that in doing so, you are responsible for untold destruction in the pathetic realm you call home."

I crossed my arms, staring him down. "Oh, is that what you think is going to happen now? Because I've got news for you."

Oberon waved away my words with a derisive sweep of his hand. "Capture her," he commanded, jerking his chin at the nearest guard.

The fae obeyed his king at once, stepping forward and drawing a heavy sword from his belt. Cai snarled in warning and leapt forward, placing himself protectively in front of me. Misgivings squirmed in my stomach as they squared off. Even as a wolf, Cai was vulnerable—his body so much more fragile than the near-immortal inhabitants of Elfhame.

The sword swung high, and I couldn't even get a yell of warning past the tightness in my throat. I didn't need to worry, though. Cai sprang effortlessly out of the way, so light on his feet that I barely saw him move. It occurred to me with a flash of surprise that I'd never actually seen my mate fight—at least, not while he was in his right mind.

The fae spun, swinging wildly at the beast before him, his blade missing a second time. Cai pressed his advantage and snapped at the fae's arm, teeth missing flesh by less than an inch.

Every eye was focused on the two combatants battling in the center of the dungeon. Even Darby's dark, blank eyes, which were barely open, seemed to follow the two as they spun and thrust and parried and snapped.

The guard's every attempt at a deathblow missed, as Cai twisted and leapt through the air. The wolf seemed to have wings on his feet, and I couldn't keep my eyes off the lithe, strong body of my mate. After so long feeling the sting of rejection and the constant weight of unworthiness, seeing the shifter I'd bonded fighting to protect me was intoxicating.

But why wasn't he going in for the kill? This deadly dance would only keep Oberon's attention for so long...

Then, Cai's strategy became clear. The guard was succumbing to exhaustion from the nonstop attacks and counterattacks. Each thrust and swipe from the large broadsword came a little slower. Cai continued dancing around the man, barely out of reach.

Finally, after a particularly poor swing, the fae's momentum carried him to the side, exposing his shoulder and back to the wolf. Cai lunged, knocking the guard to the ground and pinning him beneath heavy paws.

The wolf snarled, his teeth bared. Striking like a snake, he bit down hard on the fae's wrist.

Screams filled the chamber, echoing off the stone walls so it sounded like an eerie symphony of pain. With a crunch like a breaking twig, the fae's wrist snapped beneath powerful jaws, and the sword fell to the ground with a clatter.

Oberon growled in fury and turned towards his other guards.

Cai snarled in response, as though ready to attack the King of Elfhame himself. I pressed my hands together in front of my chest, reaching for every shred of magic inside me. I took a deep breath, and just as Oberon took one step in my direction, I let out a massive blast that exploded outward in all directions with me at the epicenter. As the field of energy passed over my friends, their iron chains shattered and fell in pieces to the ground.

I looked up, my eyes blazing with righteous anger, and met Oberon's shocked face. Apparently my rotten sire hadn't expected me to grow so powerful so quickly. *His mistake.*

Feeling my magic swirling around and through me, I lifted my hands and threw up individual shields around each of my friends, separating them from Oberon and his minions. Meanwhile, Cai moved away from his fallen enemy, rubbing his body along mine in a way that communicated his love and support. He was encouraging me, holding me up, telling me to be strong. Irrational tears of gratitude pricked at my eyes.

The sneer of disdain on Oberon's face was the final straw. Still maintaining the shields, I let every emotion that I'd been suppressing for weeks, if not months, boil up inside of me—all of the pain and rage over my exile, the abandonment by my pack, and the horror of learning who and what I truly was. Everything I had been pushing down in my desperate attempt to save Earth and Elfhame from my destructive powers now came flooding to the surface.

The strongest storm I'd ever conjured began to swirl and heave around Oberon's palace. In the dungeon, we couldn't feel the full force of the wind directly, but I could sense it howling through the streets above us.

I poured all my energy into the storm, feeling its effects through my magical senses. Buildings would collapse. Trees ripped up by the roots would go flying, smashing into anything that managed to stand against the terrible wind. I pictured the ground around the fae king's stronghold trembling, and knew that it would become real.

Oberon looked around in alarm as the walls of the dungeon began to shake, the palace crumbling above us. A low groan shuddered through the massive structure, as it failed beneath the strength of my power. A few of Oberon's guards cried out in terror, falling to their knees.

"You foolish cur!" Oberon roared, whirling to face me. "You will destroy the human realm in your pointless attack on me! *What of your home?*"

An expression that probably bore some distant relation to a smile stretched my lips back, baring my teeth. "Earth is safe. *I'm mated now*, asshole."

With a bellow of rage, Oberon started throwing spells at me. The blasts of magic landed against my skin with nothing more than a light slapping sensation. I had been expecting the attacks, so every magical blow he landed was absorbed and immediately poured into the storm raging around us.

A huge crack appeared over our heads, and the roar of the wind above us became audible as part of the ceiling caved in.

I looked around wildly, confirming that my magical shields were still in place, protecting Dianthe, Darby, and Tamlain, as well as Cai.

Tamlain was weakly trying to push himself to a sitting position, and Dianthe was staring around with a look of shock. Darby sat crumpled on the floor next to her, looking dazed and absent as the chaos swirled around us.

I needed to get them all out of here. My storm was going to bring this whole damned palace down, and I didn't want to have to worry about their safety while it was happening.

"Dianthe!" I shouted over the cacophony of wind and grinding stone. "Take Darby to the cottage in the forest!"

She met my eyes grimly and nodded her understanding. Crouching by the collapsed shifter, she cast a portal and dragged Darby forward into nothingness.

I moved in front of Dianthe's portal, ready to defend the connection until it closed. The last thing we needed was one of Oberon's men to follow them through to the cottage. It was the one safe refuge on Elfhame that I knew well enough to travel to. We just had to keep the wards around the forest in place.

I'd been distracted trying to ensure they got away safely, and Oberon took advantage of my inattention. He redoubled his magical attack.

"Cai!" I cried, knowing that my mate was my vulnerable point, and Oberon must have realized that by now.

The wolf darted behind me, his protective shield moving with him seamlessly. This time, the force of Oberon's magical blows pushed me back, heat searing painfully against my skin. I gritted my teeth, trying to maintain the power of the storm and to hold off his most damaging spells.

"You can't win against me, whelp," Oberon shouted over the thundering noise of storm and battle, his fingers curling into claws as he tried to blast me off my feet. "I made you, and I can destroy you just as easily!"

Out of my peripheral vision, I saw Tamlain push himself up and stagger against the table holding the tools of torture. Most of the items had fallen or been knocked to the ground, but he reached out and grabbed something sharp and deadly looking, holding it tightly in his fist.

I dragged my gaze away, knowing that it would be a mistake to draw Oberon's attention to the fae at his back. From the corner of my eye, I saw Tamlain stagger forward on unsteady legs. He grabbed Oberon by the shoulder and whirled the king around to face him, before plunging the iron-bladed knife deep into the king's chest.

Swirls of magical power erupted from the wound, and the king's attacks ceased as though someone had turned off a human light switch. Oberon slumped forward, mouth open in shock — falling to his knees as a crimson stain spread across his robes.

I dragged my rampaging emotions under control. Above us, the wind quieted. The structure of the palace — whatever part of it was still standing — groaned ominously.

Oberon was choking on his own blood. His expression was one of disbelief, as though he couldn't conceive of dying at the hands of his former general and his own bastard half-bred daughter. I grabbed the king's collar, pulling him upright before he could fall on his face. His head lolled back until he was staring at me, dazed and dumbstruck.

"You may have created me," I said, staring into the terrified eyes of the father I'd never wanted. "But you do *not* control me."

Message delivered, I released my grip and let him fall. He hit the floor with a wet thump, his rattling breaths filling the room. Blood dribbled from his mouth as he coughed. With a shaking hand, he reached up and wiped his mouth, then examined the stain of red on his skin. He still looked genuinely confused.

The last of the storm had already faded, but another huge chunk of the ceiling caved in. With a curse, I jumped back as part of the wall beside me collapsed. A pile of falling debris crushed Oberon's body, sending up fresh plumes of dust.

Cai pressed against my leg with an unhappy whine. I followed his gaze and saw Tamlain lying on the ground, his face completely bloodless. Another ear-shattering rumble above us made me look up quickly in alarm.

"We need to get out of here," I shouted.

With Cai at my side, I rushed over to Tamlain, already picturing the peaceful little cottage in the woods and mentally constructing the portal that would take us there. I threw out my hand in a circular gesture, feeling power flow through me as the glowing oval sprang into existence next to the fae's collapsed form. I reached down to seize him under the arms, unsure if I was strong enough to move him, but someone shouldered me aside. It was Cai, back in his human form.

He grabbed Tamlain's dead weight and hauled him through the portal. I darted through with them, just as the last of the palace's supports gave way. A cloud of dust and grit poured out of the portal's opening, and I quickly snapped it closed behind us.

The thunderous sounds of the palace collapsing were cut off in the same instant, but it still felt like the noise was echoing inside my skull. By contrast, the silence surrounding the peaceful cottage was profound.

My heart pounded, and my breathing came in ragged gasps. Cai settled Tamlain's body carefully on the ground. We were just outside the cottage door, and we were alone. I strained my ringing ears, and could just about make out the sound of Darby's hysterical sobbing and Dianthe's low, soothing voice coming from inside. After a few moments, the tentative sound of birdsong returned to the forest as the disruption caused by my unexpected portal faded into memory.

I met Cai's amber gaze, trying with minimal success to process everything that had just happened. He lifted a hand to the side of my face, his callused palm cupping my cheek in silent support. As one, we both looked down at Tamlain, who lay limp and unmoving on the forest floor.

TWENTY-SIX

MY HEART POUNDED against my ribs as I gazed down at Tamlain's body, lying still and quiet on the dried leaves surrounding the cottage. He couldn't be dead. There was no way that he could possibly be dead. Yet, his limp form didn't exactly inspire confidence.

"Tamlain?" I gripped his bare shoulder and gave it a tentative shake.

His head flopped from side to side, a dead weight—but there was no other response. Dreading what I might find, I lowered my face over his parted lips. To my everlasting gratitude, a gentle puff of air hit my cheek. He was breathing.

A strangled noise of relief escaped me. I sat up and looked at Cai.

"He's alive." The words sounded ragged and hoarse in my ears. Even though he wasn't dead, panic still threatened to overcome me. How badly was he hurt? What had Oberon done to him? The wind began to whip around us, whistling through the trees.

Before any tree limbs started breaking off, I reined in my tumultuous emotions and got myself firmly back in check. Panicking wouldn't help.

"We should get him inside." Cai said, drawing my attention back to him.

Once again, he was naked. *This was becoming a habit,* I reflected. I realized that I had been staring at him for too long and blinked my brain back into some kind of working order. A blush crept up my neck. I cleared my throat and waved my hand vaguely in his direction, concentrating on what I needed to happen. His clothes reappeared with a slight rustling noise.

"Useful trick, that," he said, looking down at himself.

Before I could summon a response, the sound of tortured wailing from inside the cottage rent the air. I whirled toward the door.

"Darby," I breathed, caught between competing crises. "Elfhame is still making her crazy."

Dianthe's soft, soothing voice murmured in counterpoint to Darby's pained shrieks. It sounded like she was unable to recognize friend from foe. She might have no idea that she'd even been rescued.

Cai crouched at my side. "Can you bring her back from the madness? Like you did for me?"

I bit my lower lip and glanced away. "I don't know."

"You can try," he said firmly, wrapping a warm arm around my shoulders. "I have faith in you."

"Why?" I asked, feeling utterly ill-equipped to deal with everything that still needed to be fixed.

Cai appeared to consider his words for a moment, his head tilted in thought.

"It was your wolf's love that drew me out of the insanity," he finally said. "And I'm pretty sure you love Darby more than you do some asshole alpha who rejected you and treated you like crap."

Our eyes met, and I could tell that he was beginning to understand the complexity of my feelings for him. He knew, just as I did, that our mating had an awful lot to do with my desperate need to tip the power in my favor against Oberon.

An uncomfortable squirming sensation twisted my stomach—because, yes, that had a lot to do with my decision… but I still had feelings for him. Feelings I didn't fully understand yet.

He knew that already, though. He was the son of a pack alpha. He understood duty better than most people, and he seemed determined to accept the reality of our bond if it turned out to be nothing more than that.

There *was* something more, though.

Unfortunately, this wasn't the time to have a long discussion about the future or our feelings for one another.

"I don't know what I did to help you, exactly," I said. "It was just instinct. I'm not sure I can do it again."

He turned me to face him, squeezing my shoulder. "You need to try to help your friend."

And he was right. Of course I did.

"Is that an order, alpha?" I joked.

Cai's amber eyes twinkled. "I wouldn't dare, after what I just saw in that dungeon. But it *is* good advice, and you should take it."

I couldn't argue with his logic and said, "Right. Let's get Tamlain inside and make him comfortable. Then I'll see about Darby."

Cai leaned down and pulled Tamlain's large frame over his shoulder. With one smooth motion, he stood with the fae in an awkward fireman's carry. I grimaced internally, knowing that Tamlain would hate how undignified he looked. Still, it would be worth it if he woke up and started bitching about it. I followed Cai through the door of the cottage.

Inside, I looked around the cozy front room, grabbing some blankets from one of the chairs. "Here, put him down on these blankets near the hearth. We should probably light a fire to keep him warm—he might be in shock."

"I'm on it," Cai assured me. "Go see about Darby."

I laid the blankets in a cozy nest on the floor and nodded. Following the anguished screams and whimpers down the hallway, I found Dianthe and Darby in the bedroom where I had stayed for a few hours when Tamlain first brought me to Elfhame. My friend was lying on the bed, thrashing back and forth while Dianthe restrained her gently by the shoulders.

The fae looked up as I entered, relief clear on her striking features. "Thank goodness you made it out of there," she said, standing up and embracing me. Darby curled onto her side in the fetal position, her screams subsiding to frightened whines.

I squeezed Dianthe back hard. "Tamlain is hurt. I don't know how badly, but he's unconscious. Cai is with him."

"I'll tend to him," Dianthe assured me. "You see what you can do for your friend. The madness is rooted deeply inside of her, Ember."

Somehow, I could sense that even from across the room. It felt like a thick, slimy tendril curling around Darby's mind. The wrongness of it filled my awareness in the same way the smell of rot could fill a person's nose.

"Thank you, Dianthe," I said. The fae gave me a strained smile and left the room to go see to Tamlain. I crossed to the bed and knelt next to it so I was at Darby's level.

"Darby," I murmured.

Half of her face was mottled black and blue from a beating she'd sustained while in Oberon's custody. One of her eyes was swollen shut. Her good eye flickered open for a moment before squeezing closed again. She gripped her hair with fingers that looked stiff and swollen, the knuckles bloody.

My throat tightened. My gentle friend had fought back despite the impossible odds, and I was so proud of her in that moment I could weep.

The more closely I examined her, the more injuries I found. Being as careful as I could not to cause her any more pain, I peeled off the disgusting, dirty prisoner smock she was wearing.

I tossed the offensive garment into the corner and brushed Darby's matted hair away from her face. Without a mate bond, I didn't know exactly how to reach her mentally, nor could I clearly picture what I'd done to call Cai back to sanity.

My wolf whimpered inside my head, desperate to help. I stilled, turning my attention inward. *My wolf.* Was that the answer? Could it be so simple?

"Darby," I ordered. "Shift into your wolf form."

As I said the words, I remembered how Bardulf had commanded my body to shift during the wolfbirth ceremony. I let a bit of fae power trickle through me as I issued the command.

Still whimpering, Darby blinked at me through frightened tears. Some deep part of her responded to me, though, because moment later her wolf form cowered on the bed, trembling and whimpering. I pulled off my clothing and shifted to match her, hopping onto the mattress with her.

While our emotional connection wasn't as strong as what I had with Cai, I could still clearly sense her mind and spirit through our pack connection. Being best friends and close companions for years had its advantages, apparently.

Something inside her wolf recognized something inside my wolf. She belly-crawled closer to me, our flanks rubbing against each other. Darby leaned against me, moaning.

I allowed serene and peaceful feelings to flood through our fragile pack-bond, passing into her. Slowly her inner turmoil quieted, and I led my friend back to the sanity of her human mind.

She sighed in utter relief, immediately growing drowsy after so many days and nights of torture. I could sense her gratefulness even without words, as she nuzzled her cold nose against my shoulder.

As soon as I felt her slide into a deep slumber, I pulled on my human skin and stood up. My mind slipped free of hers, leaving my protection against Elfhame's madness behind. I waved a hand and my clothes appeared without me having to put them on the normal way.

I smiled in satisfaction. That was one of my favorite new skills.

Grabbing a blanket from the foot of the bed, I spread it over the sleeping wolf, gently stroking the soft fur of her head. She sighed again, content but exhausted. I knew that there would be so much I needed to explain once she woke, but I couldn't worry about that right now.

From the darkest corners of my mind came the fears that I had been steadfast in ignoring. I couldn't stop mental images of Tamlain's death from filling my mind. I gritted my teeth. What would I do if he died? Would I be able to keep control and not destroy this entire realm in my desire for vengeance? Earth might be safe from me now, but Elfhame wasn't. Not remotely.

I didn't want to hurt innocents, but I feared my rage would be uncontrollable.

Pressing a soft kiss onto Darby's silky head, I straightened and quickly left the room, confident that she would sleep for hours now. As I entered the main part of the cottage, I was met by a bustle of activity. Cai was just reentering through the front door with a pail of water.

"Just got back from the stream," he explained, setting it down next to Dianthe.

She barely acknowledged him, except to snap, "Find clean towels."

Cai immediately disappeared into the back of the cottage. I heard the banging as he rummaged through cabinets and chests. A few moments later, he returned with a stack of fluffy white towels. He handed them wordlessly to Dianthe, who set them down and bent over Tamlain's motionless body.

I peered over her shoulder and saw that she was carefully cleaning a deep gash. Fresh blood welled up almost as fast as she wiped it away. Looking at Tamlain's grey and lifeless form, I wondered how it was possible he had any more blood to spill.

"Will he be all right?" I whispered, not wanting to interrupt her concentration.

"Difficult to say," she replied. "Fae are hard to kill, but he's been severely weakened both physically and magically. The next few hours will be key."

"This is Oberon's doing?" I demanded, knowing that Tamlain had once been Oberon's highest ranking commander.

With a disgusted snort, Dianthe nodded. "It is. His Royal Psychotic-ness even deigned to get his own hands dirty this time."

"Is there anything I can do to help?" I asked. I tried to keep the plea out of my voice, but I knew she heard it anyway.

She was silent for a moment, wiping the sweat away from her face as Cai stoked the fire next to them.

"Maybe," she finally replied, making my heart leap.

"What is it?" I said. "Dianthe, I'll do anything."

I could feel Cai's eyes on me, but I ignored the weight of his gaze.

"Were you in full control of your powers during the battle?" Dianthe asked.

The question was so unexpected that I was momentarily taken aback. "In control?" I echoed blankly.

"Yes."

I chewed on my lip for a moment before nodding. "I… think so? Tamlain guided me to my magic and showed me how to use it while we were hiding in the cave. But since then, I've been experimenting with my abilities."

"On your own?"

"Yes. Just by instinct, though," I clarified. "I don't claim to understand exactly what I'm doing, but if I picture something in detail and then throw magic at it, I can usually manifest whatever I was thinking of."

Dianthe nodded thoughtfully. She was silent for a few moments. When she finally spoke, her voice was sober.

"I have some minor skills in healing, but I'm completely drained right now. I don't know if I can save him on my own."

I took in her pinched expression. She'd been trapped in Oberon's brutal torture dungeon right along with the others, and she was just as exhausted as everyone else.

"I have this crazy idea," Dianthe continued, "to try to harness your magic to power my healing ability."

My brow furrowed, but a spark of hope kindled in my chest. "Harness it how?"

"It seems like you have a nearly limitless supply, unlike the rest of us. Together, we might be able to use it to speed Tamlain's healing."

Dianthe sat on the floor wearily, and I sank down beside her.

Cai came to my side and gently laid a hand on my shoulder. "Were you able to help Darby?"

I nodded. "Yes, she's sleeping now."

"Since you helped her, you should try to help Tamlain, too," he said.

I craned around, looking up at him in surprise. It was unusual for an alpha to try to protect or heal another strong male. Shifters had a deeply ingrained sense of letting nature take its course to prevent competition, or so Geneva had always told me. But... could I really trust *anything* that woman had told me, knowing what I knew now?

Still, it nagged at me. Why was Cai doing this?

His eyes held mine steadily, but I could see the conflict behind his gaze. I also saw the moment he put his own feelings aside. Cai knew I wouldn't be able to live with myself if I didn't try to save Tamlain, and he would see that I did so, no matter what.

Now, if I could just calm my own fears. I knew that once Tamlain recovered, there would be a very awkward, very uncomfortable situation to work through between all three of us.

But first, we had to heal him.

"All right, Dianthe," I said. "Let's make this happen. What do I need to do?"

We both knelt on the hard floor next to Tamlain's makeshift nest of blankets. He didn't even stir when I leaned over him, though his breathing hitched slightly for a moment before resuming its regular, shallow rhythm.

"Take my hand," Dianthe said, holding hers out to me.

I placed my hand flat against hers, aware that my nerves were getting the better of me. Clammy sweat dampened my palm.

She tangled our fingers together and squeezed for a moment. Then, with an encouraging nod, she turned my hand over and placed it palm-down over Tamlain's bare chest, covering his heart. In some deep part of my wolf's awareness, I felt a flicker of jealousy across my mate bond with Cai. Instinctively, I sent peaceful feelings through the connection in return, soothing him.

I'm mated to you. But I still have to help him.

A low sigh from behind me told me that my message had been received loud and clear. Cai relaxed incrementally, watching the proceedings.

Dianthe pressed her hand over mine as she lowered her head, concentrating. I could feel the power surge around us as she called it up from its reservoir. A brilliant light appeared in my mind.

Just as before, it was as though a path had been illuminated through my body and into Tamlain's. I simply had to follow it across the winding synapses of my mind.

Healing, it turned out, was a far more complex activity than retrieving clothes or even making shields during a battle. It was intricate and detailed. I had to focus all my energy on following the exact twists and turns, forcing my power through narrow places within me.

"Relax and let your power flow into him," Dianthe counseled. "Let me do the delicate part."

I'd closed my eyes at some point. It was easier to follow where Dianthe was guiding me without the distraction of sight.

"You're not relaxing," she chided. "You're thinking. Stop it, and let your instincts take over."

"Easy for you to say," I mumbled, annoyed.

I dropped my shoulders and rolled my neck, trying to loosen the strained and tight muscles. As I felt the knots relaxing, it became easier to allow my fae magic to push forward. Dianthe gripped my hand more tightly. Tamlain's skin warmed beneath my palm. I could feel the magic spreading outward from my touch.

I thought about everything that Tamlain had done for me. I thought about the guidance, the rescues, and how he'd preserved my free will and dignity as best he could when I'd been thrown into an unnatural heat. He was one of the truest people I'd ever known, and I couldn't bear the thought of losing him.

"It's working," Dianthe murmured.

I kept doing whatever the heck I was doing, until I became aware of Dianthe settling back on her heels with a sigh of satisfaction.

She started to pull away, but I caught her arm before she could.

"Fix your injuries, too," I told her, gesturing at her bloody wrists.

She hesitated before nodding.

Taking my hand, Dianthe guided my fingers to the places where the shackles had left raw wounds. One spot was torn so badly from Dianthe fighting her restraints that I wondered how she was even using that hand. When I touched her skin, I felt the jolt of my magic passing between us. I glanced up at Dianthe's face just in time to see her silent sigh of relief.

"That's so much better. Thank you," she said, repeating the process with her other wrist.

The skin knitted itself closed, leaving only dried blood and fresh, pink skin behind. She carefully rubbed the flaked blood away and massaged the newly healed skin.

"A little achy, but that will be gone in a day or two," she said with a smile. "You have an amazing talent for this, Ember."

I shook my head with an answering smile. "Good teachers, that's all."

A low groan startled us both. As one, we turned to look down at Tamlain. He stirred, the movement barely visible. Already, a healthier pink color was returning to his skin. His eyes fluttered for a moment before opening. He blinked rapidly, his summer-blue gaze unfocused in the dim light.

"Easy, cousin," Dianthe said, grasping his shoulder. "We're all here. We're safe, just rest now."

He grimaced, ignoring her admonition as he tried to sit up.

"Oh no, you don't," she said, her tone growing dangerous. "If I have to hogtie you, I will, you stubborn ass."

Tamlain settled back, but his eyes darted around the room until they found me. "The palace," he rasped. "You destroyed Oberon's palace. But Ember, what of the human realm?"

My gaze darted to Cai.

Tamlain didn't know about the mate bond. He must have been too out of it to understand when I'd told Oberon during the battle. I licked my lips, suddenly unsure how to explain what I'd done without making it sound like a betrayal.

TWENTY-SEVEN

"IT'S A BIT complicated," I hedged. "But I promise nothing happened to pose a danger to Earth."

Coward, my internal voice taunted.

Shut up, I told it. I wasn't remotely ready to broach the subject of my mating bond. Not until there was no other choice.

"Where are we?" Tamlain rasped.

His voice was weak, as though he'd screamed himself hoarse during his torture. I clenched my jaw at the mental image and tamped down the emotions that threatened to rise up inside of me.

"We're in the cottage where you brought me when we first arrived," I said. My hand still rested on his shoulder. Cai moved to my side. His stance was protective, edging toward possessive. I glanced at him darkly, trying to convey that if he went all caveman on me in front of Tamlain, he and I were going to have a problem.

The fae frowned, but didn't comment on the posturing. "How did we get here?"

Dianthe looked at me expectantly, wearing an expression on her face that clearly said, *go on, shifter—explain all of this.*

Moving my weight uncomfortably from foot to foot, I cleared my throat to buy a bit of time.

"Um, well… I sort of rescued you with a portal after I destroyed Oberon's palace."

My words seemed to hang in the air for an eternity. Tamlain blinked at me, as though he had to translate my words from some unfamiliar language.

"You destroyed his palace," he finally said, his voice slow and measured. "But Earth is still safe?"

I nodded and replied, "Yes, that's right."

"And you created a portal?"

"Yes."

"So you rescued the three of us?"

"Well, I mean—Cai helped, too." I said, hearing him huff in response to the rather backhanded compliment.

Tamlain's expression grew intense. "And yet, you are confident that the Earth is safe."

My stomach plummeted. I'd hoped that he'd still be too out of it to wonder about that, but of course the fae was healing quickly. His mind was as sharp as ever.

I needed to face this, even if it felt like preparing for a battle.

Just do it, I thought. *Get it over with.*

Dianthe was still staring at me in the flickering, insubstantial light from the fire. *Tell him the truth,* her expression warned.

"Tamlain," I said quietly, "I mated with Cai to test your theory about protecting Earth."

There was an uncomfortably long pause.

"I see. Did it work?" he inquired, expressionless.

I hesitated. Irrational guilt flooded me, sour in my stomach and throat. I was painfully aware that if Tamlain hadn't figured out the secret to my powers and shared it with me, I would have never taken that vital step to protect Earth and defeat Oberon. Tamlain was the reason why Earth had been saved, and I'd left him and the rest of his people out in the metaphorical cold—choosing my home's safety over his.

It was a slap in the face, and I knew it.

"Ember," Tamlain said, his voice slightly stronger. *"Did it work?"*

"Yes," I whispered.

He was quiet for a moment. Eventually, he nodded. "Of course you would test it, if it meant protecting your home. That was a strategically adept decision, and it worked out well for you. That's good."

I didn't know what to say to that. Was he giving me his blessing to be with Cai? Something about the idea twisted in my stomach uncomfortably.

But after that bland pronouncement, it appeared Tamlain wanted nothing more to do with the topic. Instead, he began asking questions about the details of the battle. When the whole story had been told, he nodded again. Even in the low light, he looked completely exhausted.

"So Oberon is truly dead, then." His eyes slid closed and his breathing slowed. "Well, that simplifies things, I suppose. We should be able to stay here unmolested for some time before we have to make any major decisions. It will allow us a chance to recover, if nothing else."

Dianthe crossed her arms. "Elfhame will be in chaos after the king's death. Anyone who saw what

334

happened in the dungeons is almost certainly dead. You're right—I don't think they will come looking for us."

Tamlain hummed agreement, his eyes still closed.

"Who will take over Oberon's position?" I asked. With him dead, I supposed the throne would likely pass to his heir, but I had no idea who that was. Did he have any children? Or rather, did he have any children other than me—a bastard half-shifter?

"His wife Titania will probably take control now," Dianthe said. She settled herself at the foot of Tamlain's bed, being careful not to jostle him. "She wasn't at the castle when the storm hit, since she and Oberon are currently estranged. I doubt she even knows what happened yet."

A loud rumble from the vicinity of Cai's stomach made me look around with a pointedly raised eyebrow. He was holding his hand over his abdomen, as though he could somehow quiet the noise.

A sheepish look spread across his face. "Um… sorry to ruin the moment, but I guess I'm pretty hungry. The rest of you must be, too."

"Yes," Dianthe said, pushing herself to her feet. "We'll need to hunt and gather supplies if we're going to be here for a while."

Cai stretched, and then looked Dianthe over with an appraising eye. "How good of a hunter are you?"

She gave him a cold stare in return.

I chuckled under my breath. "Believe me. You really don't want to cross her."

Cai's lips twitched in a poorly hidden smile. "Hmm. I guess she'll need to prove that to me, since I've mostly just seen her chained up in a dungeon."

"You're about to wish you never uttered those words," Dianthe said, a gleam of mischief in her eyes. "Sure you can keep up with me, Wolf Boy?"

"Oh, I'm sure," Cai shot back, and I rolled my eyes at both of them.

The two clattered around, readying themselves to leave. After offering brief goodbyes, they left and started along the winding trail beyond the front door. The soft padding sound of wolfish footfalls behind me made me turn away from watching them, my attention drawn to the darkened interior hallway. A pair of gleaming eyes greeted me as Darby, still in wolf form, made her way into the front room.

"Hey, sweetheart. How are you feeling now?" I asked, walking over to her and leaning against the wall as I spoke. I wanted her to feel welcome and comfortable, but not like I was hovering or trying to babysit her.

She stared at me, her canine expression unreadable.

"Did you get some decent sleep?" I tried again.

Still nothing.

"You could change back into a human so we can talk properly," I suggested, misgivings tugging at my heart.

Rather than shift, Darby shook her head violently back and forth. She grew unsteady and stumbled hard into the corner of the hearth.

"Darby!" I cried in dismay. "Are you okay?"

Legs shaking, Darby pushed herself to her feet and sat shivering next to the fire. She swiveled her head back and forth again, clearly saying no.

"Right," I conceded, holding my hands up in the air in surrender. "I get it. You want to stay a wolf. And that's okay. That's fine."

The wolf huffed.

"I understand," I assured her. "I really do. There's no rush. Take your time."

She didn't respond directly, instead padding silently back to the bedroom where Tamlain lay. I followed and watched with interest as she approached the bed and sniffed the air around him.

"Hello, wolf," he said evenly.

Darby continued to sniff around Tamlain for a few more seconds, before expanding her exploration to the rest of the cottage. I watched her without speaking, simply allowing her to investigate her surroundings. The quiet sound of her paws against the floorboards was soothing, and when I returned to check on Tamlain, his breathing had grown slow and deep.

Studying his profile in the dying firelight, I surmised that he was finally sleeping—the genuine, deep sleep of the bone-weary. He looked completely untroubled like this; the lines of strain falling away from his face, making him appear younger. I was certain I'd never seen him so relaxed before. It wasn't the first time he'd slept in my presence, but he'd always seemed tense and on guard, even in repose.

This, by contrast, was Tamlain with all his defensive barriers down. He looked… *peaceful.*

Darby whined, snapping me out of my fascinated reverie. She stood near the door, looking at me as though she expected me to do something.

"Darby? Is something wrong?" I asked quietly.

The wolf's gaze never wavered, but she didn't seem upset or frightened.

"What's going on?" I tried. "Do you need something?"

She looked over her shoulder, toward the front door.

"Oh," I murmured. "I see. I could go outside with you? I think Tamlain will be okay in here alone for a while."

Liquid amber eyes blinked back at me, reflecting the dying light of the fire. Without another word, I shed my clothing and pulled on my wolf skin, sinking into the familiar warmth of the black and white parti-colored fur across my body. Slipping past Darby, I headed to the front room and pushed the door open with my nose.

Darby's thoughts weren't as clear in my mind as Cai's when we were both in wolf form, but I could sense relief flooding through her. She was grateful for the chance to escape into Elfhame's wilderness for a bit.

We padded quietly through the trees, allowing the sounds of the forest to blanket our footsteps. Darby seemed content to follow me. Soon I broke into an easy trot, then a graceful lope. Darby kept pace with me and we ran together, the blur of the ferns flashing by as we ran faster and faster.

I had no clear idea where I was leading her, but found that I was heading inexorably towards the edge of the forest. When I could smell the grass in the meadow beyond, I slowed our pace to a walk. Darby came even with my shoulder, looking around curiously. The run had obviously done her some good. I couldn't blame her—it had done me good as well.

I sent her a hard glare, signaling her that she needed to stay put.

Obediently Darby sat, cocking her head at me as I moved a short distance away. I wanted to see without being seen, but I couldn't risk Darby crossing the boundary of the wards. That was one mistake I certainly wouldn't be making a second time. Crouching low, I slunk forward, using every ounce of my skill to be as silent as possible. If anyone was watching, they would never even notice I was there.

When I was as close to the edge of the trees as I dared, I slowly raised my head until I could peek through the bushes. The twin moons and stars twinkling above reflected so much light that I could see the desolation of Oberon's city clearly from my hiding place, even though the lights of countless torches no longer illuminated the palace.

There *was* no palace—only a giant pile of rubble stretching nearly a mile wide. Most of the capital city lay in ruins. I gulped, feeling a hot prickle of shame in my throat.

Sure, the bad guys were dead. Oberon could no longer hurt the ones I loved. But I couldn't shake the mental image of all the people—innocent people—who might have died right along with the guilty ones.

Was I a monster? In that moment, I thought that I probably was. There was no one else around—no guards standing watch on the other side of the wards. I rose and gave my wolf-body a sharp shake, knowing I needed to stop staring at that swathe of destruction and get back to Darby. If I stayed here, the guilt for what I had done in my desperation to save my friends would eventually eat me alive.

TWENTY-EIGHT

BY THE TIME I made it back to Darby, allowing her to greet me with playful nips on the chin, I'd successfully pushed my feelings back down into a neat little box—shut tight and buried deep in my heart.

With our paws flying over the forest floor, the journey back to the cottage seemed to take no time at all, for which I was grateful. Exhaustion was starting to weigh heavily on me. As we neared the small shelter, I could smell venison cooking over the hearth fire, the rich scent making my mouth water.

I slipped my human skin into place and waved my hand over my body, conjuring my clothes as though they'd never been gone. As I pushed open the door with Darby still in wolf form at my heels, Dianthe and Cai looked up. They'd been ladling steaming hot bowls of what appeared to be stew, and my stomach rumbled.

"That smells amazing," I said, inhaling deeply.

"It should," Dianthe said with a sly smile. "I did all the work."

"In your dreams," Cai shot back, not taking his attention off his own meal.

Tamlain sat propped against the wall, slowly lifting a spoon to his lips. He chewed thoughtfully on his mouthful and swallowed. "Where did you get all these vegetables, cousin? Are these leftovers from the last time we hid out here?"

"Some are, but after I took down the hart, I also scavenged these ramps from where they were growing wild on the edge of the forest." Dianthe replied, her tone growing smug.

Her statement drew another huff of irritation from Cai, but I noticed he didn't try to contradict her. Maybe my mate was smarter than I'd sometimes given him credit for.

He frowned at me. "What?"

I realized that a fond smile was tugging at the corners of my lips, and quickly hid it. "Nothing, just looking forward to the meal," I told him.

The food was delicious, the gamey meat and vibrant vegetables of the forest giving the stew a distinctive woodsy flavor. The hearty food in my stomach lulled me into even more of a weary stupor than before. After yawning for the tenth time as I sat by the fire, Cai finally pulled me to my feet and steered me towards the bedroom where Darby had slept earlier in the day.

"You should rest now," he said. "You're about to drop."

I allowed him to direct my steps without a word, my eyes barely open. He pushed me onto the bed and settled in behind me, spooning me with a strong arm draped over my waist. Before I even had a chance to process the unfamiliar feeling of a second body snuggled up to mine, I fell into a deep, serene sleep.

The following days proceeded in much the same pattern as the first—hunt, eat, and rest. By the third day, I was finally beginning to feel like myself again after the long weeks of constant stress and worry. It was starting to sink in that Oberon was gone for good. My life was my own again... and now I had a new mate to think about. I contemplated what that was likely to mean for both of us, in between animated conversations with Dianthe and lending my magic for additional healing sessions with Tamlain.

My noble fae had recovered remarkably well, and by the end of the second day, his condition was much improved. Still, Dianthe roped me in for continued healing sessions each night, and I wasn't about to complain. Even though Tamlain seemed tired, he still took time to continue my magical education during the process of channeling my power through Dianthe and into him. Gradually, the pair schooled me in controlling the healing myself, and seemed pleased at my progress.

They weren't the only ones. Recalling my clothing might be handy for a shifter, but that was nothing compared to being able to *actually heal injuries*. I was delighted to discover that my powers worked on Cai, too — and even on myself.

But while I might be content to lounge around the cottage for days on end, resting and recovering, not everyone was. One warm afternoon, Dianthe declared she'd had enough of hiding here, and left to try and get news from the city. A couple of hours later, I caught Cai pacing around the cottage restlessly. He looked up when he felt me watching him, his expression growing sheepish.

"I'm not used to just sitting," he admitted. "Being the son of the Greystalker pack alpha meant there was always something that needed doing. Having no responsibility to speak of feels really strange. I won't lie—I don't think I like it much."

I nodded as though I understood the feeling, even though I didn't. Being at the bottom of the pack had afforded me a lot of downtime. I'd mostly used it to sneak into the human world to buy junk food and get tattoos. It was *just* possible I wasn't the best person to empathize with wanting to work all the time.

"We could spar," Tamlain offered from the other side of the room, where he'd been tending the fire. His tone was casual… almost *too* casual.

I turned, wide-eyed, to see him brushing his hands off and appraising Cai with a thoughtful expression.

"I don't know if that's a good idea—" I started to say, but Cai cut me off with an excited whoop.

"Yes! You're on, fae! I'll try to take it easy on you since you're in such a weakened condition."

"Your concern is touching, but unnecessary." The words were dry as dust.

"We can make a friendly little competition out of it," Cai replied, scratching his chin. "What's your weapon of choice? Blades? Quarterstaff? Bare hands?"

"I think we can do a little better than street brawling, wolf." Tamlain waved his empty hand over the kitchen table, and two beautifully carven wooden practice daggers appeared there. They each had an intricate design—one a wolf, and the other, an eagle. Tamlain picked up the wolf one and handed it, hilt first, to Cai.

"No need to tax Ember's newly acquired healing skills with metal blades," said the fae.

Cai examined the wooden blade, and a slow smile spread over his handsome features. "That's still sharp enough to hurt."

"Of course," Tamlain replied, deadpan. "What would be the point of the fight, otherwise?"

Without further discussion, the two men headed outside onto the soft grass in front of the cottage. I glanced over at Darby where she'd been lolling in the corner, aware that my expression probably looked a bit shell-shocked. She gave me the wolfish equivalent of a shrug, and rose to follow the men out the door.

I joined them and found a comfortable spot in the shade, not at all sure I was ready for this, but determined to take in the show regardless. Darby plopped down close enough to me that I could sling an arm over her furry shoulders.

Cai and Tamlain removed their shirts. Unable to resist, I let out a low wolf-whistle in appreciation. Cai preened. Tamlain shot me a look of mild disapproval, though I didn't think there was any real heat behind it. Darby snorted in lupine amusement and leaned closer against my side, ears pricked.

"Yes, okay," I muttered. "I'll admit I could get used to this view. So sue me." The wolf's ribs shook, and it was absolutely one hundred percent worth it to know that Darby was enjoying herself, even if it was at my expense.

Tamlain and Cai were both gorgeous specimens. That was simply a fact. They were a study in opposites in many ways, but they complemented each other well. Tamlain was tall and well muscled, but leaner than Cai, who was built like a bull with rugged features and bulging muscle.

When it came to the actual fight, I had no idea what to expect. Tamlain had fae magic on his side, but I didn't know if he would use it in a simple sparring session. He was also recovering from terrible injury. Meanwhile, Cai was a young, strong shifter in perfect health. I guessed that they would be more or less evenly matched against one another.

I watched avidly as Tamlain bowed to Cai, who looked slightly confused at the formality. He was used to pack fights, which were usually more like the street brawls Tamlain had mentioned with such disdain. Still—I'd seen Tamlain take down the alpha wolf, Bardulf, with utter ruthlessness. He might not approve of brawls, but it didn't mean he couldn't fight that way if the situation called for it. Quite the opposite.

After a moment of awkwardness, Cai jerked his chin down in something like a bow of acknowledgement in return.

Tamlain crouched over the balls of his feet, holding his wooden practice dagger at the ready. The pair began to circle warily, taking each other's measure. Cai feinted low, making the first move, only to leap back when Tamlain lunged forward.

The shameless display of rippling muscles in the dappled sunlight made my mouth go dry. Evidently, I hadn't been prepared for the reality of Cai and Tamlain testing their strength against one another. And Cai, at least, knew it... the smug bastard. Every now and then he would glance at me, flashing me a sly half-grin.

"Show off," I murmured when he wasn't looking, not wanting to give him the satisfaction. By contrast, I didn't think Tamlain had the first clue what kind of effect he was having on me. All of his attention was on his opponent. His cool, calculating expression was every bit as appealing as Cai's good humored teasing.

Tamlain spun and ducked in, trying to get a hit on Cai's unprotected left side, but Cai caught his wrist, trapping it. Rather than attempting to pull away, Tamlain somehow got a leg tangled between Cai's and took them both to the ground. The pair rolled, each trying to gain the upper hand as they grappled, and I could no more have looked away than I could have flown.

I caught myself daydreaming about the artificial heat Geneva had spelled me with... and about the delicious way Tamlain had eased my suffering. Guilt flooded me almost immediately. I'd mated Cai, not Tamlain. Maybe that had been a strategic decision rather than an emotional one — but I was still mated. That meant that my mind should be on Cai, not anyone else. And I *did* desire Cai. He wasn't the monster I'd first assumed when he rejected me. I was hopeful we could have a good life together, once all of this craziness was over. Still…

I wish I could have both.

The wistful thought flitted through my consciousness like a cloud in a stray breeze. My breath caught, and I blinked, sitting up so abruptly that I dislodged Darby, who made a disgruntled noise in surprise.

Possibilities whizzed through my head like buzzing bees. Did I really want both? And… if I was mated to both of them, would that mean that Elfhame would be protected from my powers, as well as Earth? Was such a thing even possible?

My mouth was hanging open and I must have looked like a slack-jawed idiot. Fortunately, Cai and Tamlain were too focused on grappling with each other to notice my blank look of utter shock.

Eventually, brawn won out and Cai gained the upper hand. "Got you," he said with satisfaction, pinning Tamlain to the ground. "See? What did I say? I told you I could win against some pointy-eared elf that runs around in the woods."

"*Elf?*" Tamlain echoed in a tone of disbelief. An explosion of bright sparks erupted, and Cai went flying with a yelp. He landed on his back, looked over at Tamlain in disbelief, and then descended into deep-throated laughter.

"Fine. A pointy-eared *fae* who runs around in the woods," he amended, and laughed again.

Tamlain huffed and rolled smoothly to his feet. He crossed to Cai and reached a hand down, pulling him upright when he accepted it. I watched Cai brush himself off with good humor, thinking, *by the ancestors, could something like this actually work?*

Before I could convince myself that I was crazy and needed to go dunk my head in the river, Tamlain froze in place. My adrenaline spiked as I followed his gaze to an empty patch of grass that appeared to be dancing lazily in the warm afternoon breeze. A portal appeared, and Dianthe stepped out, looking harassed.

Darby and I both jumped to our feet.

"What is it?" I demanded. "Dianthe, what's happened now?"

She sighed. "It's Titania, Oberon's wife. As we expected, she's taken control of Elfhame's throne. She's summoning anyone who she thinks might have knowledge of the attack on the palace." Her eyes fell on Tamlain. "Cousin, she's asking for you specifically."

TWENTY-NINE

TAMLAIN LEANED BACK against the nearest tree trunk as though for support, his expression growing resigned. "I suppose that isn't unexpected."

I whipped around to stare at him, my mouth agape.

"What do you mean?" I demanded. "How could that have been expected? How could *any* of this mess have been expected?"

"Titania is no fool," Dianthe said in a low voice. "She will have heard rumors about Tamlain's defection and his fall from Oberon's good graces."

Fresh terror tried to grip my stomach. The strain of controlling it before I could whip up a storm in the forest brought back the weariness that had temporarily lifted from my shoulders over the last few days of respite.

Would this never end?

"Just stay here in hiding," I said in a rush, glancing back and forth between Dianthe and Tamlain. "Don't go to her. We can all stay here and—"

Tamlain's hand settled on my shoulder. Warmth spread through my chest at the contact, even as my stomach sank. I could guess what he was about to say.

"We can't hide forever, Little Wolf," he interjected.

I looked to Cai, searching for someone else to support my position. To my consternation, I could see the same determination mirrored in his face that was visible on Tamlain's. Two warriors, united in their determination to do battle head-on against all comers.

I couldn't give up so easily, though. Not when Tamlain's life was at stake.

"Earth!" I said. "Let's go to Earth, we can hide you there in the Greystalker packlands. Titania would never need to know you'd even left Elfhame. She can spend a lifetime searching if she wants to—"

I was interrupted again, this time by a low chuckle.

Tamlain was laughing quietly at me.

"*What*?" I snapped, offended by his response.

"I appreciate what you're trying to do," he said. "But it is my duty to face the consequences of my actions. I cannot flee from Titania."

Noble fucking bastard, I thought in disgust.

I turned to Dianthe. "What about you? What do *you* think of this?"

She hesitated for a moment, shifting her weight from one foot to the other. "I don't think hiding will be a… practical solution, shall we say. Not in the long run."

"I don't think she's looking for practicalities," Cai said wryly. "She's been getting too comfortable with miracles lately."

I threw him a dirty look, but he only smiled at me in understanding.

"Ember," he said, coming to my side, "I know you're worried about his safety. But we're in fae territory now. They know better than we do how to handle this situation."

Tamlain nodded in approval.

I narrowed my eyes at both of them. "One little wrestling match, and you two are the best of chums all of a sudden? Don't gang up on me, damn it!"

They wisely didn't reply. I took several deep breaths, forcing my feelings under some kind of control. Circling my shoulders, I stretched my neck from side to side to loosen the tension building there.

"Fine," I finally said. "So, you plan to do… what, exactly? Stroll up to Titania's front door and throw yourself on her mercy?"

Tamlain cocked his head to the side, considering me for a moment before he answered. "That does seem like the easiest way to figure out what she wants of me."

I gritted my teeth. "Then I'm going with you."
Silence fell.

"No," Tamlain said.

His tone held a sense of finality that made me angry. If he could choose to walk into a volatile situation that was most likely a trap, I could damn well make my own choice to follow him.

I squared up to him, hands on hips. "If you go, I go. This isn't a debate, Tamlain."

"Your presence would only complicate matters," Tamlain answered, not backing down.

"Or," I countered, "I could prevent her from flying off the handle and calling for your head on a pike."

"How?" Dianthe asked. The question sounded genuine, not sarcastic. I could tell she was at least open to what I had to say.

"If she decides to try something, I'll lay waste to her court, just like I did to Oberon's."

I tried to keep my voice firm, but the idea of hurting or killing more innocent fae nauseated me. I pushed the feeling down. If Titania was as smart as everyone insisted, she would know better than to call my bluff.

Cai snorted, drawing all eyes to him.

"She does have a point, you know," he said, gesturing towards me. "She's probably the most powerful being on Elfhame right now. Maybe even the most powerful being that has ever existed. If this Titania woman won't play nice with her..." His voice trailed away and he shrugged indifferently. "Well, it's her funeral, I guess. Ember can always go back to Earth and lay waste to the whole damn fae realm if she wants to."

Dianthe and Tamlain looked stricken.

"Yeah," Dianthe said, "I really hope you won't do that."

"Dianthe. You know I don't want to do anything like that," I said. "But the threat of it might come in handy."

Dianthe nodded but her expression remained tight and worried. "You probably *could* destroy our entire world, you know."

I didn't want to think about that. I dug in the dirt with my toe to avoid looking at anyone.

Dianthe sighed. "I suppose the shifters *do* have a point, though, Cousin. Titania would have to be a fool to take on someone as powerful as Ember."

Tamlain paced slowly toward the cottage, thinking. All eyes followed his progress. "No, I'm not convinced. Oberon wasn't always a fool. Titania may have changed as well. She does have the entire kingdom at her command, now. That's a powerful temptation."

"The fact that she asked for you specifically means she's well aware of Ember's existence, and of her power," Dianthe argued. "I disagree—she will not risk her people. She's far more sane than Oberon ever was."

"That," Tamlain said, his voice grim, "is certainly true."

After a few silent moments Tamlain finally let out a long sigh and nodded.

"Very well," he said, "I accept your ultimatum to accompany me."

I rubbed my hands together. "Good call. So, how should we play this?"

The discussion that followed took the rest of the day. After a lengthy debate, it was decided that I would go to the palace with Dianthe and speak with the queen. Once I received assurance of Tamlain's safety, then I would bring Tamlain and Cai to the palace through a portal. That way, Cai could provide extra security.

"I don't need a bodyguard," Tamlain grumbled. "Much less a babysitter."

"It would put my mind at ease," I told him.

"You're not thinking, Little Wolf," Tamlain said, frowning. "If Titania kills your Earthen mate, then the protection you've established will be destroyed. You're banking on the fact that she doesn't have the same motives as Oberon, but you forget that she has been his wife for centuries."

I frowned back. "But she's sane, Dianthe said. That's kind of a big difference, for starters."

Tamlain closed his eyes, as though searching for patience. "Ember, he needs to stay behind. It only makes sense."

Cai and I looked at each other and I immediately shook my head. I was not leaving my mate behind.

"No way," I said. "If he's with us, we can protect him. If he's here by himself, Titania could send someone after him and I wouldn't be able to do a damned thing about it."

The grudging look on Tamlain's face told me I'd scored a point. I knew I couldn't have won the argument *quite* that easily, but just as I was marshaling another defense of my plan, Tamlain and Dianthe fell silent, staring past my right shoulder.

I turned to find Darby standing a few feet behind me, pale and unsteady on two legs. She had a sheet wrapped around her body for modesty, her white-knuckled fingers grasping the edges of the fabric like it was a shield.

"I'm going, too," she said in a whisper, her voice hoarse from long disuse.

My instinct was to hurry forward and shepherd her back to bed for about a week's more rest, but something about the determined look on her face stopped me.

"Darby… are you sure?" I asked, moving closer to her.

She met my eyes and I could see a fire burning there. It was a look I hadn't seen since she'd charged forward after my disastrous wolfbirth ceremony, holding off shifters far above her in rank and dominance.

"I need to do this," she said.

I couldn't help it. A slow smile spread across my face. My dear friend was facing her fear, and I admired her deeply in that moment. Plus, I was relieved beyond measure to see her in human form again.

Putting my arms around her, I squeezed the bony shoulders hiding underneath the sheet she'd wrapped around herself. Her injuries might have been healed, but I knew the ordeal with Oberon had greatly weakened her.

Maybe this was exactly what she needed to get her confidence back. I'd insisted that I would meet with Titania, and that Cai come along, too. What right did I have to deny Darby?

Dianthe cleared her throat. "If this is the plan, we need to go over the details. There won't be a second chance at this meeting."

We broke apart to look at her. "You're right," I agreed.

As a group we moved into the shade of the cottage, sitting in a circle on the ground.

"Titania has taken over the Summer Palace as her new seat of power," Dianthe told us. "Since the Grand Palace is a bit, er... how should I put this?"

"Pulverized?" Tamlain suggested dryly.

I covered a wince.

"What's Titania like?" I asked, trying to deflect attention from my discomfort.

Dianthe and Tamlain glanced at each other.

"She's difficult to describe," Tamlain said.

"Capricious," Dianthe suggested. "But not usually in a malicious way. Intelligent. She lacks her husband's cruel streak, which may work in our favor."

I sat thoughtfully for a few minutes, pondering their words. I had an ominous feeling growing in my stomach, making me dread the upcoming interaction.

Might as well get it over with, I decided.

Sighing, I pushed myself to my feet. "Okay, I say we go now."

"Right now?" Cai asked, glancing at me. "As in, this minute?"

I grimaced, knowing he could read my hesitancy through our mate bond.

Dianthe shrugged and got up, turning towards Darby, who flushed scarlet.

"I, uh, don't seem to have any clothes," my friend said. "Probably not a great way to make an impression on a queen."

Smacking myself on the forehead, I walked over to her and gave her an assessing look. "Sorry, I should've thought of that earlier. Don't worry, I can fix that."

Conjuring brand new clothes was a little more difficult than summoning an existing pair. After two attempts, I managed to fit Darby with a pair of canvas pants, solid hiking boots, and a green button up shirt.

With wide eyes she stared at her new apparel, rubbing her fingers over the fabric in awe.

"That's amazing," she whispered. "How did you do that?"

"Magic. It's a *really* long story," I muttered.

"Thank you, Ember," Darby said, her round eyes shining as we stared at each other.

"Actually," Dianthe interrupted, "we should be wearing court attire for this."

I raised an eyebrow at her as she described the flowing dresses that the other fae women would be wearing in Titania's presence.

"I think that's probably beyond me," I admitted. "I've never worn anything like that, and I'd have no idea of the details."

"Allow me," Tamlain said. With a wave of one elegant hand, he called three dresses into existence, draping us in the shimmering, colorful fabric. Cai raised an eyebrow. I couldn't read his expression, but I was also distracted by the new clothing.

The warm crimson hue of Darby's dress seemed to bring more color into her face. She combed her fingers through her chestnut hair and twisted it into a knot at the base of her neck. Dianthe, now clad in emerald green, straightened the long red braid that fell gracefully over her shoulder.

"You look perfect, as always," Darby assured me as I struggled to brush my fingers through my hair, looking down at my sapphire blue gown.

I felt my heart swell in a way that even Cai had never managed to achieve. This beautiful soul that had been beaten and tortured because of me was my most precious friend. The ache deep in my chest nearly overwhelmed me as I threw my arms around her for the second time that afternoon.

I couldn't speak as we clung to each other, but Darby seemed to understand.

When we finally broke apart, we were both drying our eyes. I turned to Dianthe, who had silently watched the exchange with a soft expression on her face.

"Are we ready?" I asked.

Darby and Dianthe nodded.

Turning back to Cai and Tamlain, I glared down my nose at them, mock severe. "Try not to kill each other in some sort of territorial pissing match while we're gone, please."

Tamlain scowled at me, but Cai wrapped his arm around my shoulder and gave it a squeeze.

"I'll just make sure he stays in one piece," he promised, giving me a flicker of a wink.

Tamlain's scowl deepened, but he said, "Take care, all of you. Titania is not Oberon, but she is still powerful."

I nodded my understanding. "See you both soon."

With a wave of her hand, Dianthe opened a portal right in front of the group. As it expanded into existence, Darby yelped in surprise and huddled against my side, but she did not hide her face.

I put a comforting arm around her for a moment and whispered an encouraging word in her ear. She gritted her teeth and nodded her head, stepping forward first to pass through the portal.

Dianthe and I followed close behind her, emerging into the bright, warm sunlight before a set of dazzling silver gates. A pair of guards came to attention as we approached, the portal snapping shut behind us.

"State your name and purpose," one said in clipped tones.

"I am Ember Valentine of the Greystalker clan, messenger on behalf of General Tamlain. We're here to see Queen Titania." I replied, trying to sound like I knew what the hell I was doing.

I thought the guard would argue with me, but he immediately pulled the gate open and allowed us to pass through to the other side.

"Please follow me," he said, nodding to another guard who immediately stepped forward to take his place.

We walked towards the palace, the structure of which seemed to be made from living trees. The rich, dark brown wood shone as the trunks wove and wrapped themselves into tall pillars. Vines covered in thick clumps of bright purple and yellow flowers wove through the walls of the grand building. It was massive, and it felt as though the season of summer itself had somehow been formed into a castle for Queen Titania.

Our escort led us inside past yet more guards. The space we entered resembled a cathedral. Large windows opened towards the cloudless blue sky beyond. Strangely colored birds flew overhead, piping brilliant songs through the clear air. A faint, sweet scent wafted around us, reminding me of the honeysuckle that grew on Earth.

I looked at my two companions. Dianthe strode forward gracefully, looking neither left nor right as she approached the throne room that likely held Queen Titania. Darby, by contrast, was glancing back and forth with wide eyes. She smiled as two birds chased each other around the domed ceiling, twittering madly at each other.

It was so good to see her happy again. I only hoped this meeting went well, and didn't plunge us into a new round of danger and conflict.

Our guard bowed as he pulled open the door, gesturing us forward across the threshold.

Titania's throne room was just as majestic as the rest of the palace, if not more so. Large, glittering fountains emitted musical tinkling sounds as water cascaded down into the marble basins.

The queen herself was seated on a high backed throne, her chiseled features emotionless as she looked down at the short fae official speaking to her from the floor below her dais. I couldn't hear his words, but he seemed to be pleading for something. His hands were clasped together in front of him as if in prayer.

A small gasp made me look around at Darby. She was staring open-mouthed, but not at the queen. I'd been so distracted by all the grandeur that I hadn't noticed the two figures unobtrusively flanking the throne. My instincts prickled. These weren't fae, but rather shifters from Earth.

I didn't recognize either of them, and I wondered what in the name of sanity they were doing in the queen's palace on Elfhame. The one on the left was a middle-aged woman with long auburn hair, shot through with gray. The other was a young male, perhaps a few years older than Darby and me. As I looked at the male's face, it became immediately clear why Darby had gasped.

He was stunning, with well-defined muscles on display beneath his sleeveless tunic. His eyes were a brilliant, piercing shade of blue, perhaps a few shades paler than Tamlain's. His dark hair fell in waves across his forehead. All in all, he looked like one of the male fashion models that humans always liked to put on television.

I glanced back at Darby and found that she had frozen where she stood, her mouth still hanging open.

"Darby," I whispered, trying to capture her attention. She didn't move an inch.

"*Darby!*" I hissed—still to no avail. A discreet elbow to the ribs finally managed to break through her reverie.

"*Ow,*" she mouthed, glaring at me and rubbing her side.

I rolled my eyes and jerked my head towards the throne. "Come on, we're here to speak with the queen, remember?"

"Sorry," she said sheepishly, and fell into step next to me.

"We'll have to wait our turn for an audience," Dianthe whispered, as we came to a stop some distance away from the throne and the current supplicant.

But I was done with this whole fiasco. "No, we don't," I said. "Tamlain was summoned, wasn't he? And we're acting as his envoy. She'll see us now, because I'm out of patience."

Dianthe looked at me like someone might look at an unexploded bomb. "I can tell already that this is going to be an exciting day."

I waved away her words and strode forward.

The others followed as I pushed my way past other fae who were standing in line to speak to the queen. After ignoring several angry outbursts and smacking away a hand that landed on my shoulder, I reached the front of the line.

For the space of a handful of seconds, I watched as Titania continued to listen to her current petitioner's request, her beautiful features expressionless in the face of his abject pleading. Her haughtiness made my blood boil. My anger propelled me forward until I was standing just behind the man, who was now kneeling.

Whispers had broken out through the court attendees. Titania's eyes settled on me, cold and unreadable. I cleared my throat, and the pleas of the man on the floor in front of me stumbled to a stuttering halt. He looked up at me, terrified.

"Hello there," I greeted everyone, my voice raised. I let a slow, predatory smile spread across my face, and glanced quickly over my shoulder.

Behind me, I saw Darby staring at me with a dumbfounded expression. Dianthe, by contrast, had a hand pressed against her forehead in a classic facepalm—a combination of annoyance and resignation rolling off her in waves.

"You probably don't know me," I continued in a raised voice. "But my name is Ember Valentine—daughter of Skye Valentine of the Greystalker pack… and Oberon, former king of the fae."

I raised my hand and gave a sarcastic little *hello* wave in Titania's direction.

"I heard that you were looking for information on the destruction of Oberon's castle," I continued. "Well, spoiler alert—that was me. Yeah, I was the one who demolished it."

Gasps rang out among the crowd.

Good. I was tired of this game.

"So here's the deal," I said, my voice growing in intensity. "I'm here on General Tamlain's behalf, to talk about Oberon's death… and about what comes next for Elfhame. He's willing to come here and speak to you himself, but before he does, I require your assurance that he won't be harmed."

I glared at Titania, knowing that my expression showed just how close I was to burning it all down if I didn't get what I wanted. "Make your decision, Queen. But know this—if you don't play nice, I'll pull out a fresh can of whoop-ass and knock down this castle, too. Right here. Right now."

THIRTY

IN THE RINGING silence that followed my words, I felt my heart pounding with a mixture of barely controlled fear and defiance. I stared unblinkingly at Titania, who surveyed me with the same cold, expressionless look that she'd used while listening to the pleas of her subjects.

Light glinted against her crown, which was made of delicately twisted metal, burnished so thoroughly that it shone almost white against her long, silky red hair. The coronet was emblazoned with flowers that were obviously made from precious stones and crystals. It fit perfectly with the ambiance of the entire palace, which seemed wrapped in summer flowers. Sunlight filtered through the thick leaves of the trees outside, casting ever-moving shadows across the smooth stone floor of the throne room. The dancing illumination made me feel slightly dizzy.

Low mutters began to break out. I remained completely frozen, fists clenched, standing in the center of the hall.

Titania tilted her head to one side as though considering me. For an instant her facade cracked, and I saw genuine curiosity pass over her perfect features. It was so fleeting that I wondered if I'd imagined it.

There were more nervous coughs and titters from the crowd behind me.

"My beloved subjects," Titania said, never taking her eyes from my face. "We will resume court again tomorrow and I will hear the remainder of your petitions. Please leave us now."

The crowd began to silently disperse, long dresses and soft boots whispering across the stones as they filed out of the throne room. Allowing myself to glance away for a moment, I quickly scanned the echoing space, noticing that several extra guards had slipped in quietly and were standing near the back. They were not gripping their weapons, but they were clearly tense and alert.

I returned my gaze to Titania, and she motioned for me to come closer.

"Let us speak now," she said. "As you are no doubt aware, I am Queen Titania of Elfhame. You are, as you have said, Ember Valentine of the Greystalker Lands."

She held up two empty hands, palm up, as a gesture of goodwill. It was all I could do not to look skyward for patience. It wasn't that I didn't appreciate the offer of peace, but sometimes the pompous attitudes of the fae grated on my nerves.

"Yes, that's me," I answered in a curt voice, briefly mimicking the hand movement.

I glanced quickly at the two shifters standing on either side of her throne. The young male had the most striking eyes of anyone I'd ever met. They were so brightly blue that they almost seemed to glow from within. I was used to eye-shine off of animals in the forest, but this was far more piercing than anything I'd seen on either Earth or Elfhame.

How did he get here? Who was he? Were these the shifters from the story the others had told me about Titania and Oberon? The ones they'd fought over?

Questions whirled around my mind, bouncing around and clamoring for answers. The female shifter's eyes were not as unnaturally bright, but they did seem to be a similar color. As I studied the pair furtively, I decided that they could easily be related—mother and son.

Following my gaze, Titania nodded at each of the individuals in turn and said, "These are two of my most trusted advisors. They are here to counsel me in the governing of my people."

I filed that away, resolving to ask Dianthe later—but I barely had time to wonder about it before Titania continued.

"Now, Ember Valentine, please tell us more about why you are here."

I hadn't expected her to so baldly ask me to explain my purpose, so the speech I had been quietly rehearsing to myself was useless. It figured—I'd expected to have to argue to be heard, but instead I was being invited to speak openly about my errand.

Well, since she really wanted to know…

"As you have probably guessed, I am the bastard child your husband Oberon sired to seek revenge against you," I said, deciding to get the most unpleasant bit out of the way first.

I thought Titania would express anger or possibly disbelief at my words, but again I was wrong. She sat completely still, taking in everything I said with watchful eyes.

I plowed forward. "While I was still a pup, Oberon figured out that mixing fae and shifter blood had created a being of immense but uncontrolled power, and it wasn't long before it occurred to him that I could be used as a weapon against Earth. Instead of allowing that to happen, I took the necessary steps to protect my home. No matter what happens now, I will not destroy or harm Earth in any way. I am no longer a threat to my realm. Elfhame, however, is still vulnerable to my power."

Her watchful gaze didn't falter.

"Here's what I am proposing, Queen Titania," I said. "I'd like to develop some sort of mutually beneficial truce with you. But have no doubt—if you attempt to harm me or the people I care about, I will unleash my power again and lay waste to your kingdom."

Titania's eyes narrowed as I spoke. I could sense anger rolling off of her in barely controlled waves. I tensed, ready to act if she turned that quiet rage on my companions or me.

"My late husband certainly didn't lack creativity when it came to his cruelty," she said, her tone disgusted. I relaxed minutely, sensing that her anger was more for Oberon than for me. She took a deep breath, and continued, "Tell me, child, what would a truce look like between us?"

The venom in her voice when referring to Oberon was not present when she spoke directly to me. Oberon had been the one to pick this fight, but perhaps Titania didn't want to continue it?

"My demands are simple," I replied, keeping my voice measured. "I want no retribution, either for myself or my companions, for the destruction of the palace, or for any other crimes committed in the course of destroying Oberon. Total amnesty for all of us."

"Interesting. You believe you are asking much of me." Titania leaned forward on her throne. "But in reality, you are thinking too small, wolf child."

I blinked. *Too small?* I wanted nothing from this woman except to be able to live freely and ensure the safety of those I loved.

"I'm not sure what you mean," I replied.

Titania nodded as if I had just confirmed a suspicion of hers. "Tell me this, young one, how did you protect your planet from your powers?"

I hesitated. I hadn't really wanted to give Titania any information that she could use against me. However, I doubted that my secrets would stay that way for long, especially with a pair of shifters burning holes through my skull with their incisive blue gazes.

I cleared my throat awkwardly. "Uh, it's a little complicated. Shifters are sometimes born with a fate bond connecting them to another's soul. These come as matching marks and a deep, spiritual connection with the one fated to be your mate. We theorized that the power of the mate bond would solidify my link to Earth, thereby protecting it from my magic."

Titania gave a slow nod, digesting the words. "And this worked? You mated with someone on Earth and the entire planet is now protected from your destructive power?"

"Yes."

She sat back. "I see."

Silence reigned for a long moment as Titania considered this. Her eyes roved around the throne room and settled on a point just behind me.

"Dianthe," she said. "Come forward, my subject."

So she knows Dianthe. I pressed my lips together, forcing myself not to interfere until I got an idea of how this was going to play out.

Dianthe glided forward with graceful steps until she was standing next to me, her face expressionless. What was it with everyone here being so damn stoic?

"You were involved in this… incident?" Titania asked, choosing her words carefully. Her gaze bore into Dianthe, who remained unmoved.

"Peripherally, my queen," she replied.

"And your dear cousin? Was he involved as well?"

Dianthe cleared her throat and glanced at me for the briefest moment. "Yes, Tamlain was more directly involved, as you have no doubt already determined."

Titania shifted on her throne and steepled her fingers together. The female shifter at her shoulder leaned down and whispered in her ear. Titania didn't look up, but she gave a small nod in reply.

"And you, young wolf," Titania said. "Is Tamlain one of those that you wish for me to grant amnesty?"

The question made my stomach squirm. It was now or never.

"Yes, your majesty," I said.

The title rankled, but I supposed a little show of respect wouldn't go amiss. This quest was all about my friends' safety— Tamlain's especially. I would do whatever I had to do to secure it.

"A moment while I discuss this with my advisors," Titania said, turning towards the female shifter again. Both shifters leaned close to whisper with the queen, barely moving their lips. Even with my sensitive hearing, I couldn't make out their words.

"Is this going to work?" I murmured to Dianthe, never taking my eyes off the group on the raised dais.

She made a hesitant noise in the back of her throat. "I'm not sure."

Darby leaned in as well, her voice a bare whisper. "Why does she have shifters as advisors? How can they even be here without going insane?"

"Long story," I said. "I'll tell it to you later."

After a few moments, Titania turned back towards us, sitting primly on the edge of her seat.

"I have a proposal," she said, pitching her voice as though she wanted everyone present to hear her verdict. "But first, I must speak with

Tamlain in person. It is his amnesty in question, and I will not deal with an emissary on his behalf."

"Surely you understand our concerns—" Dianthe interjected, but Titania forestalled her with a raised hand.

"I do understand, child, but on this I will not yield."

I thought quickly. We had anticipated such a move, and I knew what I had to do.

"I will arrange for him to come here if, and only if, we have your word that he will not be harmed or captured. He must be free to come go from this meeting safely. Do I have your word?"

I allowed some of my power to bleed through during my final question. The wind picked up within the hall, blowing Titania's hair around her face. Leaves slapped against the glass on the fantastic windows, which showed darkening skies above the summer palace.

For the first time, Titania looked taken aback. She glanced around apprehensively. Her guards stepped forward.

She raised a hand to halt them, and at the same moment I allowed the wind to slacken. As the air settled around us, Titania took a steadying breath. "You have my agreement that Tamlain may attend this meeting—and leave it—unmolested."

"Your word?" I verified, raising my hand to open a portal.

"Yes, you have my word on it," she replied gravely.

"Dianthe?" I asked, looking at her for confirmation. "Is it safe? She's not playing me somehow?"

Dianthe never took her eyes of Titania, but tilted her head to the side for a moment, studying the fae queen closely.

"Yes, it is safe. She is not deceiving you."

I nodded and stepped forward. Waving my hand slowly through the air, I opened a portal through which I could see the side of the cottage. Two figures emerged, both wearing crisp, clean court attire that was honestly rather distracting.

Cai didn't speak, but he surveyed the area with narrowed, suspicious eyes.

Tamlain, by contrast, stepped forward and bowed, his pale hair nearly brushing the ground.

"My queen," he greeted in a deferential tone.

The corners of Titania's lips twitched. I couldn't read her expression. On the other hand, it was clear to me that while Tamlain held nothing but contempt for Oberon after his descent into madness, he still had respect for Titania. He did not consider her his enemy, and I took some comfort from that realization. If Tamlain could still respect this woman, even after everything that Oberon did, she couldn't be all bad.

"You, general, have much to answer for," Titania sighed theatrically, leaning back in her ornate chair.

I tensed. Maybe I'd spoken too soon.

Tamlain held his ground, answering in a grave and serious tone. "Yes, my queen, I do."

Titania lifted her chin. "Tell me—why have you associated yourself with king-killers, Tamlain? Especially after so many loyal years of service devoted to my husband."

Tamlain's voice was flat. "Forgive me, your majesty, but you are making a mistaken assumption. These people are not guilty of regicide. It was I who drove the iron blade through Oberon's heart."

The guards stirred, their ceremonial leather armor creaking as they reached for their weapons, seemingly in unison.

"Peace, guards," Titania ordered, quelling all movement with a look. "We do not owe this man retribution. We owe him our thanks."

And... *what*?

"Did I hear that right?" I whispered to Dianthe, trying not to move my lips.

"I think you did," Dianthe murmured back.

"Um," I replied. "Okay. That's... good?"

The queen must have caught something of our exchange. "Yes, young wolf, you heard correctly. My husband was quite mad, at the end. Tamlain has rendered this kingdom and his queen a service. He has demonstrated that his loyalty is to Elfhame and its people, not merely to one misguided fae ruler. He has likely saved us all with his actions."

Tamlain's face was utterly blank, and I got the impression it was because he was in total shock. He opened his mouth as if to speak, but nothing came out.

Fortunately, Titania didn't seem to require an answer.

"Given this new information, I have another proposal to offer," she continued, looking straight at him. "If you are amenable?"

Tamlain blinked once and then bowed his head subserviently. "Anything, Your Highness."

"I will form an alliance with Ember Valentine—one that will last until the end of both our days. I will also extend amnesty to everyone involved in the death of King Oberon and the destruction of his palace. On one condition."

Tamlain glanced at me, before quickly turning his attention back to Titania.

"What condition is that, my queen?" he asked.

Titania smiled, but there was a glint in her eye. "It's a simple enough request, General. Ember must mate with a fae as well as an earthen shifter, so that both our realms will be protected from her powers for all time."

THIRTY-ONE

ICE SETTLED in my stomach at the same time flaming heat began radiating from my face. I knew my cheeks had turned bright red, but I couldn't help the mortified reaction. Titania might as well have plucked the thought directly from my brain.

My secret. My deepest desire. Something that I hadn't even truly acknowledged to myself, except in the hazy world between sleep and waking. And somehow, Titania knew.

I wanted both of them. I wanted Cai and Tamlain.

Was I so obvious? Could this woman I'd known for, like, *five minutes* so easily see into the depths of my heart?

I gave myself a mental shake. No. It was impossible.

The queen of the fae didn't care about my half-realized fantasies. She wanted to protect her realm from my powers. And... apparently, she thought this might be a way to do it.

Was she right?

I threw a wide-eyed look at Tamlain, but he didn't appear to be faring much better than I was.

"I do not believe that shifter mating bonds work that way," he said.

He didn't say no, a voice whispered in my head. Also, I could swear there was a hint of pinkness darkening his cheekbones — complement to my full-face blush of embarrassment.

The female shifter standing at Titania's shoulder cleared her throat. "If I may, Your Highness?"

Titania waved an open hand, inviting her to speak.

"General Tamlain." The woman addressed Tamlain gravely. "You must remember that Ember is not only a shifter. She is half fae, which is how we ended up in this dilemma initially."

"This is true enough," Queen Titania agreed.

"What's more," the woman continued, scratching her chin thoughtfully as she considered me, "I believe that such a situation would help restore the balance between our two realms, as well as maintain the peace in a political sense."

"Restore the balance?" I asked, confused.

"From the moment of your birth," said the shifter, "Earth and Elfhame have been drawn towards each other, the veil between them straining at the seams. That is why your power can so easily flow between both places. Now that you are bound to Earth, and thereby providing your mate's realm with protection, there is still an imbalance pulling on Elfhame."

"And having a second mate bond would somehow fix that?" I asked.

The shifter tilted her head back and forth, as though unwilling to commit fully to the concept.

"Theoretically," she admitted.

"Theoretically," Dianthe echoed. "And you would throw the lives of two people into disarray to test your *theory*?"

"Three people, I think you mean," Cai muttered.

I winced, both at his words and at Dianthe's harsh tone, but I recognized she was simply trying to protect Tamlain, who still resembled nothing so much as a deer caught in the headlights of a human motor vehicle. Besides, she had a point.

Titania watched the exchange with a gaze that saw too much. "It is my duty to protect Elfhame. I will take whatever steps are necessary to secure my realm against this growing magical imbalance. A mate-bond seems a small price to pay."

"Look," Cai interjected. "I don't claim to understand all of this. But what about the risk to Ember? What if, by restoring the balance between the two worlds, you inadvertently take all of her powers away, or even harm her somehow? She's my mate, and I will *not* allow her to be endangered on the basis of an old woman's guess about what's happening."

I bit the inside of my cheek to hold back a smile, touched by the sincerity that I could feel through our mate bond. He wanted me to remain powerful, and not only because it benefited him. He wanted me the way I was—which was touching, since I was hardly the typical weak omega for an alpha wolf like him to dominate.

Of course, that warm, fuzzy feeling lasted for all of two seconds before the doubts crept in. *What if he just doesn't want to share me?*

It would only be natural. That's how alphas *were*, after all. I searched our mate bond, trying to sense possessiveness. It was present, but his suspicion and distrust was turned exclusively towards the queen. He did not trust her and was obviously concerned about my safety.

Something of his thoughts seeped through to me and I caught the last vestiges of his concerns.

… If she doesn't have her powers anymore, how can she defend herself against all these crazy fae? Titania could send some henchmen or an assassin after her.

As subtly as I could, I slipped my fingers into Cai's hand, which was hanging loosely at his side. I gave his fingers a gentle squeeze, which he returned without looking at me.

Unbidden, the mental images of the destruction I had caused passed in front of my eyes. I could see the demolished buildings, tossed around like children's toys in a box. I had torn down and ripped up trees, swept away rocks, bushes, and grass. Animals and people had been killed as my power poured out on the Earth and on Elfhame, uncontrolled. I knew Cai could sense those images, too.

I wouldn't be opposed to never causing a storm again. How many people had died because I was scared, or lost my temper? It would be a relief to know that could never happen again.

"Queen Titania," I said, "this is a decision that involves several people, all of whom should have a say in what happens. Can we have a night to discuss this?"

Titania made a magnanimous gesture toward us. "Of course, child. It is not a decision that should be made lightly. I will be happy to house you here at the palace, if you have need?"

I looked over at Tamlain.

He cleared his throat. "Thank you, Queen Titania. We appreciate your generosity. However, we would prefer to spend the night at our own lodgings. We will return here tomorrow with our decision."

Titania sat back in her throne. "As you wish. We shall reconvene this discussion at midday, in that case."

A moment later, she stood, and all of her guards snapped to attention. The entire royal retinue walked toward a small door in the back of the throne room, with her at the head. Both of her shifter advisors followed behind her, though the younger male glanced back in our direction. His gaze fell on Darby, who swallowed a tiny, nearly inaudible squeak of surprise.

"Come, Ember," Tamlain said, his voice giving nothing away. "Please cast a portal back to the cottage for us now."

I waved my hand but was so distracted that the portal collapsed upon itself before anyone could pass through it.

"Sorry," I muttered, trying again.

This time the gateway held, and we all filed through to the area in front of the cottage. As soon as I had passed through, I closed the portal with a flick of my hand.

The ringing silence of the forest was a contrast to my racing thoughts.

Dianthe turned around and gave me a piercing onceover. Then, she sighed, meeting Darby's wide-eyed gaze.

"Darby? What would you say about a late hunt near the edge of the mountains? I have a craving for goat stew, and I could use your help in catching one."

Darby glanced in my direction, with a look equally as knowing. "Yeah, I'd like that. Let me shift form and we can go."

They were tactfully giving us the privacy we needed to discuss our options. Darby touched my arm briefly before slipping into the cottage to change. A few moments later, she emerged as a wolf. Dianthe also went inside to gather a few supplies, before breezily informing us that the mountains were a long way from here.

"We can camp for the night and then come back tomorrow with our game," she said. "We'll save you some meat... probably."

"That sounds great," I replied, without much enthusiasm. *Awkward* didn't even begin to cover this situation.

Dianthe gave me a sympathetic smile and slung her bag over her shoulder. She and Darby jogged off into the trees, boots and paws barely making a sound. When I turned back toward the cottage, I found both Cai and Tamlain staring at me with varying degrees of misgivings visible in their expressions.

"Let's go inside and start a fire," I said.

After building up a merry blaze in the fireplace, we settled into low wooden chairs situated in a half-circle around the fire. I'd retrieved a blanket from my bedroom and wrapped it snuggly around my shoulders. Somehow this seemed to give me courage, as if the blanket could shield me from all the awkward feelings swirling through the room.

I turned towards Cai first. For better or worse, we were mated now. Even though our history was ugly, his opinion mattered when it came to this decision.

"What do you think about all of this?" I asked, not sure I was ready to hear the answer. He'd locked down the bond between us until I could barely feel it at all, and I had no idea what that signified.

He sighed before speaking. "Ember, this is ultimately your decision. I know I've hurt you… and badly. I allowed our mate bond to be burned out, and then desecrated what was left of it with other females. I know you only mated me to save our world, so I don't really feel as though I should have much of a say."

We sat in silence for several moments, everyone staring at the dancing flames. I pondered his words, sad that I couldn't find it in myself to dispute them. He was right. He *had* done all of those things. I'd be lying if I said that his original abandonment and betrayal didn't still sting.

Should that be a part of my decision, though? Surely, I needed to decide based on what was best for everyone.

"It's all true," I finally said into the quiet. "But I don't think we should make our decisions based on what happened before. We can't change all that. It's in the past. And sure, it sucked—but my inner wolf has never been more fulfilled and at peace than she is now."

Cai frowned. "How do you mean?"

"Now that we've mated," I clarified. "We are joined, and in her mind, the part of us that was destroyed when you rejected the bond has been made whole again. I believe we can heal and move on from what happened before, because *she* believes it. I believe you and I can have a good life together... but we have to survive all of this craziness first."

Cai still looked unconvinced. "I'm glad you feel that way about our future, but I still maintain that I gave up my right to dictate anything about your life when I rejected you. I have no place in this decision. If you decide to mate with Tamlain, I'm not sure how my wolf will react. But in the end, it doesn't really matter, does it?"

"I would say it matters a great deal," Tamlain observed. "Why would you believe otherwise?"

Cai threw him a wry glance. "Because obviously, you could kick my ass with magic any time and make my wolf submit. So if this is what Ember decides to do, and you force me to submit, I'll do it. I may be an alpha, but I was never *the* alpha—my father was. I know very well how to take orders."

I stared at Cai, and he looked back at me, unflinching. It was clear he was uncomfortable with the idea of being forced to accept this, but also that he'd thought it through pretty extensively. He really was leaving the decision up to me.

"That isn't how this thing is going to go down," I told him. "Assuming it happens at all. But I do appreciate what you're trying to say."

I looked over at Tamlain and watched him for several moments, wondering if he'd speak again without prompting. He was hardly moving, blinking infrequently, his blue-eyed gaze fixed on the depths of the fire.

"Well? What about you?" I asked eventually.

Tamlain drew breath, only to hold it rather than answering immediately. I couldn't read the expression on his face.

"Talk to me, Tamlain." I pressed. "You're fae, so I know I'll get the truth when you speak. How do you feel about sharing a mate bond with two shifters, in exchange for the protection of Elfhame?"

The words burned my tongue, because I didn't want him to do it for Elfhame. I wanted him to do it for *me*.

"Why do you automatically assume I am the best choice for this undertaking?" Tamlain asked, finally turning to look me in the eye.

I blinked. "Excuse me?"

Who else would I choose? I wanted to blurt. *Who else would even have me?*

"You seem to assume that I am the only option to mate with you. That is not the case. It could be any fae on Elfhame. The protection would be the same."

It was the truth, in a literal sense—but I couldn't imagine mating with any fae other than Tamlain. For me, there *was* no other option.

He was still talking, though. "I will not force either one of you into a situation that you are not comfortable with, and I will not insist on being the one to bond with you, if there is a better or more acceptable choice available."

"Tamlain..." I said, but he interrupted me.

"I will not take advantage of this situation, merely to satisfy the untested theory of the queen's advisor."

The finality in his voice sent a shiver of cold down my spine. I shook it off. He was being stupid and noble again, a trait that I both admired in him and found deeply annoying.

"You're being an idiot!" I flared, and then laughed bitterly at my own folly as I looked up at the ceiling, praying for patience.

Tamlain's slanted eyebrows furrowed in confusion, or possibly offense. "I *beg* your pardon?"

"*Idiot,*" I repeated, modulating my voice to something calmer this time. How could he have missed all the signs, when *freaking Titania* picked up on it in five minutes flat?

"Haven't you realized yet that I've wanted you since the day you refused to take advantage of my heat?" I threw my hands into the air in exasperation when his look of confusion didn't falter.

"You've... wanted me? All this time?" Tamlain asked. He sounded as though he were testing the words as he spoke them, like they were a new language to which he'd had very little exposure.

Cai stared at him. "You're kidding, right?"

"Oh, for fuck's sake." I ran my hands down my face as though scrubbing away cobwebs, and met the gaze of the world's most clueless fae head-on. "It was obvious enough to Titania. I'm really surprised you never noticed."

"Oh," Tamlain whispered, his gaze far away. "I suppose I should have seen that."

"You think?" I demanded, incredulous.

Noble, bloody, irritating, ridiculous male.

"I never took you for a fool, fae," Cai said. "Now, though, I'm beginning to have second thoughts about my mate's taste, if she's really attracted to someone this dense."

I flushed, and batted a hand at Cai to shut him up.

"I guess the real question now is whether or not *you* want *me*," I said. "Because I'm not going to force you to do this either. I can find someone else, if that's what you really want."

Cai looked as though he could have used a bowl of popcorn to eat, as he watched the back-and-forth.

I was trying to put a brave face on it, but this whole thing was killing me. What would I do if Tamlain looked me in the face and informed me that the safety of Elfhame wasn't enough motivation to make mating me a tolerable prospect?

The fae's frown deepened. "Do you really have to ask if I want you or not? *Truly*, Little Wolf?"

For the first time, his mask slipped enough for me to see the hidden pain and longing behind his eyes. I breathed in sharply.

"*Oof*," Cai said from the peanut gallery. "Felt that one through the bond. Tamlain—you know, you might've led with that part. Saved us all some time."

I glared at my mate. He raised his eyebrows, completely unrepentant.

Inside, I was still in shock. *He hadn't rejected me. He wants me. They both want me.*

Tamlain was looking at me with fragile hope in his eyes, covering an ocean of long-hidden desire. Great ancestors above, if that ocean had always been there, how had he managed to keep his desire under control when I was practically throwing myself at him, begging for sex?

How had I missed it? And to think I'd called *him* an idiot...

But... thinking about that unnatural heat we'd spent together might have been a mistake. Warmth began to spread through my body, even as a shiver went up my spine.

Cai shifted in his seat. He was obviously well aware of my arousal and was being affected by it. Sure enough, as I studied him more closely, I could see a faint flush of pink crawling up his neck.

He cleared his throat. "Okay," he said. "So we're clearly doing this. Next question—exactly *how* are we doing this? How does a shifter—or a shifter-fae hybrid—mate two people?"

We all fell silent. My heart thrummed excitedly in my chest, as I tried to imagine myself with both of these beautiful men, being pleasured by them at the same time. Hard on the heels of that thought came another, far less welcome one.

I have no clue what I'm doing, and I'm going to mess this up completely.

An idea occurred to me. It was a little bit crazy, and a little bit scary, and I suddenly wanted it more than I'd wanted anything in a very long time.

"Um, Tamlain?" I asked, my voice hesitant.

He looked at me with his eyebrows raised. "Yes, Little Wolf?"

I swallowed and asked, "Could you put me into heat? I mean, magically, like Geneva did?"

He tilted his head in consideration, as though the idea had never occurred to him.

"An interesting proposal," he said quietly. "I suppose it would be possible, yes."

"What would it take?"

He gave that a moment's consideration. "Pavia—or Geneva, if you prefer—used fungal spores imbued with magic. But she was always a potion-maker. I believe I could do it with a spell." He hesitated. "I've come to know your mind well during our training sessions, so I do not believe it will be difficult to find that place inside of you."

"Okay, great," I said, making to rise from my chair.

"Wait," Tamlain said, and I sat back down. We stared at each other for a long moment before he finally asked, "Are you certain this is truly what you want? *Completely* certain? Both of you?"

His gorgeous blue gaze pinned mine, making my heart flutter in my chest again. Through my mate bond I could feel Cai's desire building in response to my own, our lust feeding off each other's.

"I have to admit," Cai said. "Given what's coming through the bond right now, the idea is starting to grow on me."

Fresh urgency flooded my body. *Maybe I didn't need an artificial heat after all?*

"Yes, Tamlain—I do want to mate you," I told him. "I want you to join in the bond that Cai and I already have. And I want us to do it right here, right now."

THIRTY-TWO

CAI STOOD UP, coming to stand before my chair and reaching a hand down. After a moment of nervous hesitation, I took it and allowed him to pull me to my feet. The blanket slipped from my shoulders, falling to the floor.

"You're so much more than I deserve, Ember," he said, his hands coming to rest on my shoulders. "Every decision you've made has been to protect or save other people. You're allowed to make this final decision to protect Elfhame, because it's also what *you* want."

My breath caught. Cai turned me around to face away from him and stepped close, the heat of his body pressing all down my back. His arms looped around my stomach, holding me in place — both of us facing Tamlain.

"A world is at stake," Cai continued, murmuring the words against the shell of my ear. "You need to trust that Tamlain and I can workout our issues. We'll make this work for you, even if it's messy sometimes. Even if we don't get it perfect at first. Isn't that right, fae?"

Tamlain's stunning blue eyes met mine and held. He didn't have to say anything. His expression said it all. He rose from his seat on the floor, all lean lines and preternatural fae grace. My heart thundered as he approached, standing just inside arm's reach.

"Tonight, you will make me yours, Little Wolf," he said, never breaking eye contact. "Do you still wish me to spell you into heat?"

My mouth felt dry. I swallowed and nodded, knowing that this would be so much easier—so much *better*—if my stupid brain wasn't endlessly whispering doubts and worries inside my head. I had no uncertainty regarding what we were about to do—not really... only about my capacity to somehow screw it up.

"Yes," I said. "I want it. Please, Tamlain... do it now."

Cai's arms tightened, grounding me in a reassuring embrace from behind. The fate-bond thrummed between us. Would my bond with Tamlain feel the same? Or would it be different, because he was fae?

Tamlain closed the last step separating us. Smooth lips brushed my forehead. I closed my eyes, trembling, and he also brushed a kiss over each closed eyelid before straightening to his full height. Cool fingers settled on my forehead, brushing my hair back. His thumb came to rest over what the humans sometimes called the third eye, on top of the little furrow that had formed between my eyebrows.

His other hand stroked the hollow at the base of my throat before trailing lower. Even through my clothing, his touch between my breasts raised gooseflesh. My nipples hardened into points, abruptly and agonizingly sensitive. Tamlain rested his palm over my galloping heart. I felt him breathe in and then out. My lungs echoed the slow breath, falling into sync with him.

The cool, clinical mind that had guided me through my early, fumbling attempts at magic slid into mine. It was a completely different experience than my bond with Cai, which was all about emotion. My shining fae ran deft mental fingers through my mind, following and discarding pathways until he found one that led where we both wanted to go.

The wolf in me stirred, stretching, as Tamlain played my shifter instincts like a master musician coaxing music from the finest and most delicate of instruments. Liquid heat stirred deep inside me, molten sparks kindling to life beneath his skilled hands. It was nothing like the horrible, wrenching ache of Geneva's violent attack on my wolf's nature… just as I'd known it wouldn't be.

This was *my* choice. These were *my* men. I was a child of two worlds, and now, I would finally be anchored to both, as I had always been meant to. A low rumble of animal satisfaction rose in my chest. It was echoed in Cai's, as my growing ardor spread along our bond.

Tamlain's palm moved from my heart to my lower belly, over my womb—coming to rest a couple of inches beneath Cai's loosely clasped hands. As though a switch had been flipped, the heat inside me abruptly burst into flame.

I… *wanted.*

But there was something else that called to me, too—my wolf, demanding her freedom.

I slipped from between them, sliding out of Cai's embrace. My face was flushed; I could feel the warmth radiating from my skin as I looked at the pair of them—strength and grace, emotion and logic.

"If you both want me… then catch me," I whispered hoarsely. I let the wolf take over, magically banishing my clothing even as my body transformed.

The front door wasn't barred. I nosed it open, scenting the rich perfume of Elfhame's forests beyond, and ran. Within moments, I heard the sound of paws crashing through dry leaves and underbrush behind me. Two sets of running footsteps—and my wolf's heart sang. The trees blurred past me as I sprinted faster and faster, drinking in the evening air as the last rays of sun disappeared into shadow.

This place was my home every bit as much as Earth. I understood that now, and I could feel how that understanding would change everything. No wonder I'd caused such destruction—always trying to be in one place or the other, when I was clearly meant to be in both.

Part of me wanted to run forever, because running felt so good. The larger part was waiting to be caught. I knew from experience that Tamlain could have used magic to catch up to me in moments in the form of his great white wolf. But when my mates finally closed on me, they were running together.

Tamlain came up on my left side, and Cai's muscular gray form appeared on my right. Then they were nipping at me, bumping into my shoulders mischievously. The flat-out run became play, and finally devolved into wrestling. Soft, thick fur slid over my body, surrounding me on both sides.

The teasing touches further enflamed my instincts. I wanted to crouch on my belly and present for mating, there and then—but at that precise moment, Cai let out a growl that didn't sound so playful. Sudden insecurity transmitted through the bond. Cai's wolf could smell my readiness, and his instincts were taking over.

The small part of me that hadn't already succumbed to my sexual need sounded an alarm. I was preparing to send a pulse of angry censure down the bond when my wolf stopped me.

No. They must work this out here and now, if this pack of three is to flourish. We cannot force our shifter mate to ignore his instincts. Let the two of them figure it out.

It went against every fiber of my being, but I slipped away from between them, leaving Cai and Tamlain's wolves facing off in the clearing. I cringed inwardly, remembering what Tamlain had done to Bardulf, the Greystalker pack alpha. If he humiliated Cai in a genuine fight—or worse yet, injured him—how would Cai ever be able to feel comfortable with the three-way bond?

A whimper escaped my throat as I pictured everything falling apart—with me stuck in another magically induced heat while my supposed mates were too busy fighting to even think of satisfying me.

Have faith. That was my wolf again—and I had no idea how she could be so calm, given what was pouring through the bond. All of Cai's hidden worries about being replaced by Tamlain had come to a head when his animal form took over.

This was how alphas *were*, I thought miserably. How had I ever believed this could work?

The pair of them were still facing off in the clearing, circling each other warily. I whined in distress as Cai charged, certain that everything was about to end in disaster. The pair collided… and Tamlain rolled onto his back, his massive white wolf showing its throat to Cai's snarling gray wolf.

I shifted form, uncaring of my nakedness—my breath caught fast in my lungs. Tamlain could have destroyed Cai in a fight. Why had he submitted?

Cai and Tamlain shifted back to human form in near unison. Cai drew in a gasp and pushed away from the fae. Like me, he was naked—while Tamlain had magically reappeared in his buckskin and linen clothing when he changed form.

The look Cai sent me conveyed the depth of his mortification over his slip. "Oh, *shit*. Tamlain… Ember. I didn't mean to—"

I couldn't speak, too overwhelmed by my heat and by what had just happened.

Tamlain didn't suffer from the same affliction, however. He rolled onto one knee, resting his forearm casually on his other knee as he addressed the shifter male.

"Yes you did," he said, without anger. "Your wolf did, because that side of you needed to truly understand that I am no threat to you."

Cai sat down heavily on the mossy ground, rubbing a hand over his face.

"Right." He let out a short, self-deprecating laugh. "So much for my rousing speech earlier about making this three-way bond work."

Tamlain tilted his head. "*'Even if we don't get it perfect at first,'* I believe you said. And here we are, in all of our imperfection. But right now, your mate needs relief, alpha."

He was half-right. I *did* need the kind of relief he meant, and with increasing desperation. My sex ached and throbbed, longing for my mates to fill me up. But in another sense, I was already relieved. I was also well past the point of self-consciousness, because I stumbled forward and grabbed Cai's hand, dragging him with me into a messy, three-way embrace.

Tamlain made a surprised *oof* noise, falling on his ass beneath my unexpected assault. After a moment's hesitation, his arm came around me, holding me between himself and Cai.

"Thank you," I said. "Thank you both for trying to make this work."

"Mmm," Cai said, breathing in the heat-scent rising from my skin.

I got the impression he had no idea what words had just come out of my mouth. I couldn't really blame him—right now, I was no better off when it came to clear thinking. The press of his nose against my neck sent a full-body shudder through me. He followed it with lips and teeth, and I was lost.

"Clothes," I begged Tamlain, scrabbling without coordination at the same intricate leather laces that had defeated me the first time he had helped me through a heat.

But before I could make any progress, I was on my back and Cai was kissing and nipping his way down my body. I cried out as he buried his face between my thighs and began to devour me — tongue delving, lips sucking.

"There's plenty of time, Little Wolf," Tamlain said. He stood towering over me as I took in his upside-down form. His hands moved to his buckskin waistcoat, sliding laces free with slow precision. "We have the entire night, after all."

My sex clenched as the sense of his words penetrated. Cai licked into me, the flat of his tongue dragging up and over my clit. Just like that, with Tamlain's voice in my ears and Cai's mouth on me, my first release shuddered loose.

Spots danced in my vision, but I could see the half-smile on Tamlain's face well enough to tell that the expression was positively diabolical. His hands never wavered in their steady work, removing his complicated clothing, and it occurred to me with a fresh flush of urgent heat that when it came to these two, I might have seriously underestimated what I was signing up for.

THIRTY-THREE

PANTING, I WATCHED as Tamlain bared his body to me, one piece of clothing at a time. Cai was still nuzzling and licking at my oversensitive folds, drawing out little aftershocks that made me whimper.

Tamlain's loose linen shirt followed his buckskin vest onto the forest floor, baring a lean-muscled torso that I'd seen before—but only when he'd been covered with bruises and burns as he lay collapsed in Oberon's torture dungeon, and later, when Dianthe had recruited me to help heal him. At the time, I'd been too worried to drool over him.

Now, his skin was flawless, and he glowed like silver moonlight in the deepening shadows of dusk. I was going to have all of that pretty, just like I was going to have all of Cai's rugged alpha-ness. My mouth watered just thinking about it.

Some combination of my scent spiking and my lust transmitting itself through the bond drew a moan from Cai. I felt the vibration all the way up to the roots of my hair. Tamlain's soft boots and leather breeches joined the pile of clothing on the ground. Then, he was crouching next to me, running fingers through my hair, smoothing the strands on the bleached-blonde side away from my face.

"Look at you," he murmured. "Your eyes are all wolf. Which of us will you have first?"

He was asking as though that was a question I could answer; a choice I could realistically make. "B-both," I managed, swallowing another whine as Cai growled against my soaked flesh.

With a final light nip, he pulled away. "You take her, fae. Help her protect your world. That's why we're here."

"One reason, perhaps," Tamlain replied.

His hand trailed down my cheek, fingertips brushing the side of my neck as he stroked downward. As it had when he induced my heat, his palm rested flat over my racing heart, a grounding pressure. I gazed up at him, wondering what he saw when he looked into my eyes.

"If you wish to have us both, then you will have us both," he said. "Roll over, Little Wolf. Pleasure your mate with your mouth while you take your pleasure from me."

The image had me scrambling inelegantly onto all fours on the soft forest loam, practically pouncing on Cai as the need to taste him the way he'd tasted me overwhelmed me.

I can have them both, I thought, giddy. *I can finally have everything I want, here and now, all at once.*

I still had no idea what I was doing when it came to sex, and it didn't matter. I was in heat, my lust flooding through the bond to set Cai alight. Shoving him onto his knees, I pushed his legs apart to make room for myself and zeroed in on what I wanted. His woodsy, musk-laden scent flooded my senses as I licked up his length. His skin was salt and sweat and *male*. The pearl of liquid beading at his tip dribbled onto my tongue as I closed my lips around him. It was slippery and astringent, and I was going to have *more*. I was going to have *all of it*.

"*Ember*," Cai choked out.

His large hand cupped the nape of my neck, but it seemed to have more to do with steadying himself than controlling my movements. Whatever the case, it went straight to my wolf's instincts. I groaned around my generous mouthful.

A second hand settled between my shoulder blades before sliding down the length of my spine, mapping the vertebrae one by one, leaving my skin on fire in its wake. I was wet with need… dripping with it. The aching emptiness threatened to swallow me, even as I swallowed Cai's length.

"So beautiful," Tamlain said. His hands framed my hips. The hard length of his cock nudged against my folds, sliding forward to brush my clit, and back to tantalize my entrance. He repeated the deliberate movement over and over, as though he were in no hurry whatsoever — ignoring my increasingly desperate moans and whimpers around Cai's throbbing erection.

I couldn't take it. The next time his tip teased at my passage, I rocked back almost violently, sheathing him inside me. It felt like heaven. Full and hot, stretching me exactly the way I needed to be stretched. He was longer than Cai but not as thick, and he stroked my sensitive flesh in a different way than my shifter alpha had done when we'd mated.

"You're perfect, Little Wolf." Tamlain's voice had lowered to a velvet rumble. "Take what you need from both of us. Don't hold back."

By rocking backward onto Tamlain's cock, I'd slid off Cai's length until my lips only wrapped around his tip. I leaned forward, taking him deep again, the motion pulling me away from Tamlain in a delicious slide that only felt better when I reversed course once more. The hands on my hips suggested an easy rhythm, back and forth between them, each of them filling me up as I pulled back from the other.

It was perfect. I could do this all night and die a happy shifter. I could do this for the rest of my *life*. The pleasure built and built. I would ride it to the top of the cliff and leap off the edge joyfully. I would do that over and over until the burning need inside me was finally sated.

Time had no meaning, but the last hints of daylight had disappeared into night when Cai shuddered, spilling his hot release over my tongue. I sucked and swallowed greedily, feeling my own climax gathering. Cai fell backward into a loose sprawl, his softening cock sliding out of my mouth.

Strong hands urged me upright to straddle muscular thighs, my back supported against Tamlain's hard chest as he pumped into me with rolling thrusts of his hips. I half-expected him to bite me as shifter males did when they mated — but Tamlain was not a shifter.

And, as I still had to remind myself, I was only half.

His right arm cradled me against him, back to front, his hand once more resting over my heart. The fingertips of his left hand came to rest delicately over my temple and the side of my face, the electric feel of them steeped in his fae magic.

I couldn't have stopped my barreling course toward the edge of the cliff even if I'd wanted to — and I didn't want to. Tamlain was with me inside my mind again, but this time it wasn't just the cool logic of his thoughts that I felt. I also felt his heart, swelling with emotion.

For *me*.

He was sharing his feelings… *for me*.

A sob caught in my throat, even as my body and soul tried to take flight. All of my respect and gratitude — and yes, burgeoning love — poured through the bond. I couldn't control it; I wasn't really trying. I knew Cai would be getting it full-blast as well, so I also let my gratitude and fragile but growing care for him flow into the mix.

My orgasm crashed over me. Tamlain made a startled noise against the nape of my neck and convulsed, following me into bliss as our minds and souls tangled irrevocably through the link he'd opened between us.

Mate, I thought. *Mates.*

I was allowed to have this. I was allowed to love other people… to be loved by them in return. Tears streamed down my face, even as my body pulsed and clenched around Tamlain's cock, milking him for every drop.

"Of course you're allowed to have this," Tamlain whispered hoarsely against my ear. "Of *course* you are, Little Wolf."

I could feel the bond settling into place, easing in next to the one I shared with Cai—but I couldn't seem to stop sobbing. Cai rolled onto his knees, pressing me between his broad body and Tamlain's lithe one. Holding me protected between them. I cried shamelessly into his shoulder as Cai stroked soothing fingers through my hair, and Tamlain stroked soothing thoughts through my mind.

Maybe everything was finally going to be all right, now.

Once I managed to drag my emotional shit back together, my body helpfully reminded me that I was still in heat. This was absolutely not a bad thing. I had two powerful males at my sexual beck and call, both of them seemingly dedicated not only to making me come over and over, but also to pouring all of their feelings through the fragile new bond tying us together.

To a low-status outcast shifter like me, it was the most potent and addictive drug imaginable.

They took turns filling me up, making me gasp and cry out. Eventually, inevitably, the fire in my veins finally cooled, leaving me wrung out and too weak to so much as stand. I ached in places I hadn't even been aware I'd possessed... and that *wasn't* a complaint. Unfortunately, this was roughly the point in the proceedings where I realized that we were nowhere near a convenient river, or stream, or pond.

"We're going to end up glued together with sweat and spunk," I observed, making no move to wriggle out from between the two males.

Cai groaned, presumably in agreement—also making no move to do anything about it. A flash of dry amusement that didn't belong to me flitted across my mind. I blinked, still taken by surprise in the best possible way by this small glimpse into Tamlain's emotions. He flicked a hand lazily, and a tingling sensation washed across my skin. In its wake, the itchy, sticky feeling disappeared—inside and out. A thick blanket appeared around the three of us in the next instant, materializing from nowhere.

"Right," Cai said, sounding taken aback. "I think I understand what you see in him now."

I elbowed him, and he chuckled. Tamlain settled against my other side, still broadcasting mild humor through the bond. "Rest, both of you. We have a handful of hours before we must return to the cottage."

"And then to the palace," Cai said thoughtfully. "Think Titania's going to be satisfied? She'll leave Ember alone now?"

"I believe so, yes," Tamlain replied. "Now, sleep. I will keep watch against any night creatures that might stumble upon us."

Cai yawned widely, prompting me to do the same.

"Sounds good," he said. "Wake me if you need me to growl at anything, fae."

I wriggled into a more comfortable position between them, sleep sliding over me like warm honey within the safety of their arms. When I woke, it was to the sound of crackling flames and the delicious scent of roasting meat. Dawn had broken, and someone had gone hunting. It wasn't a huge bounty — something roughly the size and shape of a fat hare back on Earth. But it didn't matter, because my mates had made me breakfast, and today we were going to take the final step toward fixing the horrible mess that my deadbeat father had brought into existence when he'd sired me.

"Good morning," Tamlain said, sliding the meat off of the makeshift spit he'd erected over the campfire.

I stretched, feeling my joints pop. *Yep.* Still sore. Still wasn't even mad about it.

"Morning," I greeted around a yawn.

Cai crouched next to me and rubbed his cheek along mine, scent-marking me. I leaned into the contact, still soaking up the bounty of affectionate touch after so long spent without it. He handed me a weird fruit-gourd thing, lurid purple and with a couple of ragged holes punched in the top — possibly done with a pointed stick.

"Here," he said. "Tamlain says the juice is safe to drink."

I accepted it and tipped it cautiously to my mouth. The juice was tangy and a bit pulpy. I drank the rest of it with a noise of appreciation. Tamlain shared out the meat, and we all sat eating in easy silence for the next few minutes.

Cai eventually broke it, and I could feel his uncertainty through the bond. "I know I should have asked about this before the fact instead of after, but... is there a chance we made pups last night?"

I rubbed a hand absently over my womb, thinking about little male pups with Cai's amber eyes... little female pups with Tamlain's flaxen hair. "Probably not," I said. "I'm a hybrid. Hybrids are sterile."

I felt his disappointment through our connection for an instant before he muted it. It matched my own.

"It seems likely," Tamlain said. "I magically muted my own fertility, since we did not discuss such matters beforehand. But as Ember says, reproductive compatibility among the three of us is not highly probable."

I sighed. "And realistically, even if there were some way for me to have pups, I'm not sure it would be fair to them. What if they inherited my powers and we ended up right back in the same mess as before?"

Silence fell over the clearing, each of us lost in our own thoughts. Eventually, I shook myself free of the moment of melancholy. With a wave of my hand, I summoned my clothes from the distant cottage. I raised an eyebrow at Tamlain when I noticed that he must have already done that for Cai at some point, while leaving me naked. One corner of his lips twitched up—a hint of the same devilish expression he'd graced me with last night.

"Are we ready to depart?" he asked, innocent as anything.

Cai hopped to his feet. "Yes, let's get back. I won't be happy until this mess is properly sorted out."

He reached a hand down to me, helping me rise on rubbery legs and making sure I was steady. Tamlain extinguished the campfire with a gesture. I grabbed the blanket before he could banish that as well, folding it in half and draping it over my shoulders like a cloak. He opened a portal, and I stepped through it—ready to return to the cottage to catch Darby and Dianthe up on events, and prepare for our meeting with the fae queen.

THIRTY-FOUR

STARING AT THE cottage that had become something like a home over the past days, I waited for Cai and Tamlain to reappear behind me. With an elegant gesture of one hand, Tamlain willed the portal closed as soon as we were through. Even though I suspected Darby and Dianthe would already be aware of what we'd been up to last night in the forest, I felt a small amount of dread at the prospect of facing their knowing glances.

I told myself firmly not to be ridiculous. They were my friends, and they only wanted what was best for all of us.

Squaring my shoulders, I pushed through the front door, where I was met with the fading smell of their breakfast. The two were working together to clear up the last of the mess, and they looked up with matching expressions of expectation when we walked into the kitchen area.

Through my mate bond, I could sense a hint of a smug edge to Cai's attitude. I sent him a low, mental growl of warning not to embarrass me, and he immediately pushed the air of cockiness down. Even without turning, I could tell he'd dutifully arranged his handsome features into a solemn expression. Tamlain, cool as ever, merely walked in and began gathering supplies for our journey.

"Well?" Dianthe asked, glancing back and forth between us in clear expectation.

I cleared my throat awkwardly. "Erm... yes. I'm mated to Tamlain now, too."

A twitch of a smile tugged at Dianthe's lips. Darby nodded in satisfaction.

"Good," Dianthe said. "Now what? Back to the Summer Palace?" She raised a questioning eyebrow at Tamlain. He merely jerked his chin in my direction, deferring to me.

"Yes. I'm ready to return to Titania and give her the news," I said. "With luck, that should wrap up this entire awful affair, and we can finally get on with our lives."

Despite my confident words, I still had misgivings—but I pushed them away as best I could. Now was not the time to worry about the shape my *happily-ever-after* might take... or how *happy* it would actually end up being.

"Good," Dianthe said. "Tamlain, should we take some kind of gift with us when we return to Titania?"

Tamlain tilted his head in consideration. "Something to seal the peace treaty between Earth and Elfhame? I'm not certain."

Cai joined them as well, and they fell into a discussion of whether a gift was appropriate, but I couldn't find it within myself to join the conversation. Tamlain and Dianthe would know better than I would about fae customs.

"Ember," Darby said. She came to stand next to me, our shoulders brushing. There was something reassuring about her warm presence—

her friendship satisfied a different part of my soul that neither Tamlain nor Cai could ever hope to complete. "Have you thought about what happens after all of this is finished?" she continued quietly. "I mean... where are you going to live? And with whom?"

I sighed and shook my head. She'd zeroed in on precisely the thing I wasn't ready to face yet.

It must have shown in my expression, because she said, "Sorry, I can tell you don't want to talk about it."

"No, you're right," I assured her, touching her arm. "I need to. I just don't know how to answer those questions yet."

"It's going to be complicated," she said, perceptive as ever.

I rubbed at the bridge of my nose. "To put it mildly. What if Cai doesn't want to live on Elfhame? Or Tamlain doesn't want to live on Earth? How are we going to make this work?"

Even though our voices were low enough not to be overheard, both of my mates sensed my uncertainty through our bond. Tamlain excused himself from his conversation and joined us, stopping in front of me and ducking down to meet my lowered gaze.

"One step at a time, Little Wolf," he said. "For now, let us focus on this meeting with Titania."

Cai watched us carefully. I could feel his unspoken question through the mate bond.

"I'm just worrying about what you two will want to do about this three-way mating after the crisis is over," I told him, feeling heat rise up in my face.

"I'm the one who brought it up," Darby said. "Sorry."

Cai only smiled and shook his head. "What *we* want? Why are you worrying about that so much? Maybe you should worry about what *you* want for a change, Ember."

I opened my mouth to answer, but I couldn't seem to find any words. What *I* wanted? How was I supposed to answer that question? For me, life had always been about survival, not happiness. I'd given up on fairytale endings—and yet, here I was, on the verge of getting everything I'd ever desired. Or… possibly not.

"Just think about it," Cai said kindly. "That's all I'm saying."

I was still lost for words when Dianthe brought us back to reality. "Perhaps we should leave now. The sooner this is concluded, the better."

"Yes, let's go," I agreed, grabbing the suggestion as the lifeline it was. We went outside, where I breathed in the cool morning air and tried to clear my head. My eyes strayed back to the cottage. I was going to miss this place when I left for…wherever we ended up going.

With a wave of my hand, I opened a portal leading to the gates of the Summer Palace. We all passed through it, moving as silently as shadows.

Somewhat to my surprise, the guards seemed to be expecting us. One of them gestured to us to follow him inside, without a single word needing to be exchanged. We trooped after him to the throne room, passing other courtly fae—many of whom gave us speculative or appraising looks. I wonder how much they knew or had guessed about my presence here. I could feel heat rising up my face until Cai and Tamlain touched my hands at the same time. The feeling of both of them flanking me protectively bolstered my courage, and I held my head high as we passed through the murmuring crowd.

Despite the relatively early hour, Titania was already ensconced on her throne, though there was no sign of her two shifter advisors this morning. She wore a different gown than she had on the previous day, but the same delicate crown adorned her brow. She smiled as we approached, each of us dipping our heads in a respectful greeting as we reached the dais.

"Greetings, my friends," she said. "I am glad to see you have returned as promised."

"Greetings, Queen Titania," Tamlain said, while I silently wondered at what point during this process we'd supposedly become the fae queen's *friends*.

Titania nodded graciously to him. "Have you completed the task I requested of you, General Tamlain?"

That was certainly a nice way to ask if we'd bumped uglies last night, I thought, sensing Cai's appalled amusement through our mate bond. Unlike Tamlain, he didn't seem able to take these fae proceedings at all seriously. In some ways, I could relate.

"Yes, Your Highness," Tamlain replied, as though it didn't bother him in the least to tell the ruler of his world that he'd just had a smoking hot threesome with two wolves.

Titania sat back and tilted her head to the side. "Please forgive the discourtesy, but I will require some form of proof that Elfhame is truly safe before we proceed. You must understand that my world is more important than protecting fragile egos."

I was about to agree that the request seemed fair, but her next words sent a spasm of horror through me.

"Guards!" she called, a sudden chill entering her tone. "Arrest Dianthe and the female wolfshifter!"

With a clatter of armor, several guards marched forward, seizing Darby and Dianthe by the arms. Darby shrieked and immediately began to struggle, probably in the throes of a traumatic flashback. Her anguish shot through me like a bolt of lightning. Before any sense of reason could catch up, I lunged forward with a snarl, my temper boiling.

How could Titania betray us like this? *We'd done exactly what she wanted!*

I punched the nearest guard in the face as hard as I could, too incensed to even think about trying to channel magic in my attack. Darby had shifted into her wolf form and was cowering on the floor, half-tangled in her human clothing—alternately whimpering and snarling, teeth snapping at the guards surrounding her.

The merest wisp of a breeze wafted through the throne room, nothing more than if someone had waved a paper fan at my face.

"Guards, halt!" Titania's voice rang out.

I was still fighting and shoving, making my way towards Darby—desperate to free her from the fae surrounding her like statues. Just as I was about to slam into another one of them, strong arms wrapped around me from behind. Tamlain's voice hissed in my ear and in my mind.

"*Wait*, Ember. Just wait. Titania isn't going to harm your friend."

But Titania had *already* hurt Darby. I fought like a maniac against Tamlain's grip; letting the betrayal I felt pulse through our spiritual bond. He shuddered against my back, my emotion rolling through him… but he didn't loosen his hold on me.

The guard I'd punched dabbed at his split lip, though he didn't make a move to come after me while I was helpless.

"Stop. Peace, all of you," Queen Titania said. "No harm was meant."

"Go fuck yourself, you fae bitch!" I hurled back, still trying to shove Tamlain off of me.

Then Cai was standing in front of me, his hands raised palm-out in a quelling gesture. "Ember, please calm down. I think maybe it was a test."

"No!" I shouted, my throat raw. "She went back on her word! *She hurt Darby!*"

Tears of rage streamed down my face as I craned around, looking for my friend. Cai's large frame blocked my view as he stepped closer, cupping my cheeks in his hands and forcing me to look him in the eyes.

"Ember, *please*. Stop and think!" he urged.

I fell silent, staring at him. My breath escaped through clenched teeth as he and Tamlain tried to channel calm through the bond. He moved to the side enough for me to see Darby, hunched on her belly a few feet away from us—still in wolf form. She looked up at me, her ears tucked back flat against her head. Even at this distance, I could see she was shivering violently, but seemed otherwise unhurt.

My eyes flashed to Dianthe, who was also standing nearby. She was rubbing her wrist, glaring angrily at a guard who must have been holding her captive.

Titania stared at me, holding my gaze unblinkingly. "I rescind the order of arrest. Your friends are free and will not be molested."

I glared at her, not relaxing my tense posture in the slightest. For the first time that I had ever seen, the fae queen looked a tiny bit sheepish. Even when she was ordering me to mate with Tamlain, she hadn't looked so uncomfortable.

"Forgive me, all of you," she repeated. "I had to verify for myself that Elfhame was safe."

A chill passed through me as understanding finally penetrated my layer of rage. "You were never going to arrest them. You only did that to make me lose control."

The queen nodded apologetically and said, "Please take no offense. The protection of the fae realm is my duty, and sometimes that requires unsavory actions. Do not let this taint our new alliance. You kept your word, and I will keep mine."

Tamlain cautiously loosened his grip on me. I glowered at him over my shoulder, but he didn't back down from my angry gaze.

"Yeah, all right. Fine," I replied grudgingly. I was still shaking with outrage on Darby and Dianthe's behalf, but the rational part of me could understand why Titania had done it.

The theory that I was now harmless had just been put to the test in the most direct way possible. I'd completely lost my shit, and the palace was still standing. The realization sent an odd shiver down my spine.

"I do have one further request," Titania continued. "We must test all of the possibilities. It's still conceivable that Elfhame may not be protected from your powers while you are on Earth."

"What? Why wouldn't it be?" I asked, taken aback by her words.

She shrugged helplessly, in a decidedly un-queenlike gesture. "Ember, very little is understood about your hybrid magic. We can't know anything for certain except through direct observation."

"You believe there's still a risk to Elfhame while I'm on Earth, even though I have a mate bond with Tamlain?" I clarified.

"I believe it's possible," Titania replied. "There's really only one way to find out."

I let out a slow breath. "So, you want me to go to Earth and… what? Get pissed off about something?"

The queen raised a delicate eyebrow. "For lack of any better ideas, yes."

"That shouldn't be difficult," Cai offered.

I scowled at him. "Why do you say that?"

"You don't think you could find anything to pique your temper back with the Greystalker pack?" Cai asked dryly. "Anything at all?"

And… okay. Fair point.

"I probably could, yes," I allowed, hiding my annoyance. "But if I didn't make a huge storm here, then I'm not likely to do it from Earth, either."

The queen looked troubled. "You are most likely correct, but I still require proof."

I sighed in frustration and looked between my two mates. They both gave me their own version of a shrug, which wasn't terribly helpful under the circumstances.

"How will I know if it worked or not, if I'm on Earth?" I asked Titania.

She tilted her head, considering. "I propose that Tamlain remain behind on Elfhame, while you and the other shifters return to your homeland. Once there, you will allow some circumstance to anger you enough to cause a storm here. If there is any destruction, Tamlain will portal to your side immediately and let you know to calm yourself."

I frowned, weighing the odds that this was a ploy to separate us for nefarious reasons. After her deception with Dianthe and Darby, could Titania be trying to divide and conquer?

"How will you know for sure if there's a storm on Elfhame? I can't control where the destruction lands in another realm. I always assumed it was random."

A small smile flitted across Titania's face before disappearing as quickly as it had come. "I am Elfhame's queen. Suffice to say, if Elfhame is injured, I will know."

I threw Dianthe a questioning look. She frowned, indicating without words that she didn't love this idea either. Supposedly, fae couldn't lie, and I guess it hadn't truly been a lie when Titania ordered my friends arrested, only to rescind the order a moment later.

"I believe your experiment will prove conclusive, my Queen," Tamlain told her, bowing slightly from the waist. "I will agree to stay behind."

"But—" I started.

Tamlain held up a hand as we turned to face each other. It was a quieting gesture, but then he reached forward until his cool palm rested against my cheek. We stood like that for a long moment, oblivious to the world around us as his ocean-like calm seeped through the bond and into me.

"Trust me, Little Wolf," he breathed, so low that only I would hear his words. "Trust me, and trust our connection. We are strong together, and no realm can separate us."

Despite my apprehension, his words soothed me. I gave a small, reluctant nod, and he leaned forward to kiss my forehead before pulling away.

I took a deep, steadying breath. "Fine," I said. "Let's get this over with." My gaze took in Darby and Cai. "Darby? Can you shift back now, please? I'll fix your clothes for you."

After a moment, Darby's wolf form shimmered. I recalled her torn clothing with magic, and then lifted my hand, casting a portal leading to the Greystalker lands. Some part of me marveled at how effortless it was becoming to use my powers for things like this, when not that long ago my fae magic had seemed so foreign and out of control.

"We will see each other soon," Tamlain said, stepping away to give us space. "And when we do, all of this will finally be behind us."

"Soon," I agreed. "Dianthe? Look after him, please?"

Dianthe snorted. "I do my best, but you've seen how that tends to go."

Cai took my left hand and gave it a reassuring squeeze. Darby came to my other side, looking shaken and pale faced.

"We're taking you home," I told her. "Back to your family, where you'll be safe."

She blinked a few times, nodding even as she continued to tremble. Before we left the throne room, I threw one last appraising look at Titania, locking eyes with her.

Don't betray us, my expression said.

She must have understood, because she dipped her chin in solemn acknowledgement. With that, I ushered Cai and Darby through the portal into the familiar forests of the Greystalker lands, before reluctantly closing the sparking oval behind us. Silence fell, broken only by the familiar sounds of the forest where we'd all grown up.

Darby made an odd choking noise. I looked over to find tears streaming down her face. She had her eyes closed and was taking deep, long breaths, as though she was filling herself up with the familiar smells and landscape of the Greystalker lands.

Relief. Deep, profound relief. I could feel it, too. As much as I might resent many aspects of my youth growing up with the pack, a piece of me would always belong here in the Greystalker lands.

"Come on," I said to the other two, "let's go home."

Cai grinned and threw an arm around my shoulder. Darby came to my other side and I wrapped an arm around her, too.

Together we walked along the familiar forest paths, until the outermost pack dwellings appeared in our view. Curious eyes peered out at us from windows, apprehensive. A few people walking around outside acknowledged Cai with subdued greetings, but something was definitely off. Was it my presence?

"What's going on?" I whispered, glancing at my mate. "I thought they'd be happy to see *you* back, at least."

Cai looked around with narrowed eyes. I could feel his instincts prickling through the bond. He sniffed the air, and a soft growl escaped his throat.

"Something's changed," he said, his voice low and dangerous. "The alpha marks are all different."

"What do you mean?" Darby asked, sounding alarmed.

Cai shook his head. "My father. He's no longer the pack alpha."

My footsteps slowed as the implications of that set in, but Cai urged me forward. "We'll deal with whatever has happened in a bit," he said. "But we need to get Darby home first."

"I don't like this," Darby said, leaning closer against my side.

"Me either," I told her. "But Cai's right. Let's worry about getting you back to your family first."

As we approached Darby's dwelling, her footsteps sped up until she'd shrugged off my arm on her shoulders and hurried ahead. A small crowd had been gathering as we made our way through the town, following us at a distance. The commotion was enough to draw Darby's parents outside before we'd even had a chance to reach the door.

Darby's mother—a plump, middle-aged shifter with curvy hips and deep brown eyes—ran forward as soon as she recognized her daughter.

"Darby!" she cried.

They ran to each other, meeting in a crushing embrace and collapsing into sobs in each other's arms. Darby's father hurried after his mate, a few steps behind, wrapping his arms around both of them and holding tight.

He looked at Cai over his daughter's shoulder, ignoring me completely. "You saved her?"

"He helped, but it was mostly Ember," Darby managed tearfully. "She risked her life to save mine."

Her father looked at me with new eyes. "Thank you. Both of you," he said. "We'd feared the worst."

"If I could have a moment before you go inside?" Cai asked.

Darby's father paused, his face showing the same apprehension that had reflected on the other pack members hiding inside their houses.

"Bardulf's gone," Cai said. "Tell me what happened."

"There was a fight for the leadership," Darby's father said, his weight shifting uneasily from foot to foot. "I'm sorry, Cai, but your sire fell to Thelen Lycus. This is now the Lycus Pack."

My eyes widened. *Thelen* was in charge now? One of the gang who'd bullied me mercilessly throughout my puphood? Oh, *hell* no.

"Is my sire dead?" Cai asked, and I could feel how carefully he was holding the bond closed—preventing his feelings from leaking across to me.

"No," Darby's father replied. "At least, not that I know of. He fled into exile, though he was injured at the time."

Cai sighed in frustration, rubbing his forehead with tense fingers. "When did this happen?"

"Not long after you disappeared. The battle was decisive. I get the impression Thelen had been biding his time until he saw an opening to take over. He'd been preparing for that fight for a while."

"And the pack followed him afterward?" Cai asked, only to shake his head. "Never mind, of course the pack followed him."

I exchanged a glance with him, not needing the bond to know that we were in perfect accord on this. Thelen Lycus and his alpha-bitch Star in charge of this pack? Not in a million years.

"Well, alpha," I told Cai. "Now that Darby's back safe, it sounds like you and I need to pay Thelen and his hangers-on a friendly little visit."

THIRTY-FIVE

TENSION ROLLED OFF Cai in waves. I could sense his churning thoughts—second-guessing his decision to leave the pack essentially leaderless... debating whether following his alpha instinct to reclaim his family's territory would make things better or worse.

"Tell me—what sort of leader is Thelen?" he asked Darby's father.

The shifter grimaced and shook his head. "He's violent. Far more than your father ever was. His mate Star is even more vicious. They've been systematically running off many of the lowest ranked pack members, especially the loners that aren't part of a larger clan."

Anger flared inside of me at his words. *I* had been the lowest in the pack. After my mother was exiled, I'd had no one except Darby and that deceitful bitch Geneva Padfoot. Darby had always been the closest thing to my family. The idea that Thelen and Star were targeting people in similar circumstances made me feel ill.

"He can't do that." My voice shook with rage. I'd become so accustomed to pushing down my emotions that I was acutely aware of how close I was to an explosion of temper—but that was part of the reason I was here, after all.

Cai watched me cautiously, but made no move to calm me. He and I both knew the importance of this test, so I let the fury flow through me… though I made a point of keeping it at least somewhat tempered. No breath of wind stirred around us. Long moments passed, but Tamlain didn't appear from the other realm to stop me. I exchanged a glance with Cai, and he gave a minute shrug. Apparently, no decimation was occurring on Elfhame in response to my emotional outburst.

The part of me that wasn't thrumming with indignation felt a wash of relief.

It's over, I thought, feeling mildly giddy. *I can't be used as a weapon against either world. Tamlain's theory was right.*

"So, you've returned after all," a cold, familiar voice said from behind us. "Thought maybe you'd run off for good, Cai."

Cai and I turned as one, watching as the new alpha of the pack emerged from the trees. Thelen Lycus had his oily hair tied back into a low ponytail, his sharp features prominent in the low light of the forest. Behind him, I caught a glimpse of Star, his mate, casually leaning against a tree trunk.

"These are *my* packlands now," Thelen said, folding his arms and staring at Cai in open challenge.

My anger flashed again. If you'd asked me six months ago whether I would have lifted a finger to help my former pack, I'd have laughed. But something had changed. My wolf's hackles rose at the idea of our old tormenters controlling our packmates' lives. I knew she would back our mate against them or die trying.

Cai must have felt my wolf's temper threaten to snap through the bond. He sent a request for calm through our connection. Then he stepped forward without hesitation until he and Thelen were nearly nose to nose.

"I wouldn't get too comfortable," he said in a deceptively conversational tone. He sounded as though he didn't have a care in the world. Thelen's gaze flickered for the barest instant before he, too, masked his expression with casual insouciance.

"We'll see," he murmured.

Cai stared unblinkingly at the usurper. It was Thelen who looked away first, walking away and motioning for his mate to follow him back towards the center of town.

I moved to Cai's side, catching his hard amber gaze. "Um… I think Tamlain and I accidentally broke your pack. Sorry about that." I paused. "So, do you want to take them down? Because I kind of want to take them down."

Cai stared after Thelen and Star for a long moment.

"Maybe. I'm still trying to decide if yet another alpha fight will make things better or worse for the pack," he said. "Let's go see where Jace and Finn ended up. I want to talk to them."

I nodded. After giving Darby a long, tight hug of farewell, I rejoined my mate. We excused ourselves from Darby's father before heading down the main road together.

"Where would your father have gone?" I asked, thinking of the grizzled old pack leader who'd burned out my fate mark so callously.

"I'm not sure," he answered. "He was humiliated in two separate fights. As an alpha, there's really no coming back from that."

I took that on board, surprised at how difficult it was to picture this pack without Bardulf. I'd hated him for what he'd done to me... but he'd also been the controlling force throughout my puphood, bringing order to a chaotic group of shifters with an iron fist.

"I'm betting Jace and Finn will be at Jace's parents' place," Cai said. "They'd need to keep their heads down, since Thelen knows we're friends."

I followed him through the darkening trees, winding in and out of patches of dense forest. Every now and then a dwelling would appear in the wild landscape, its windows dancing with the warm light from a cooking fire within.

We approached a den that I had passed by on countless occasions, even if I'd never had cause to speak with the inhabitants.

Cai knocked on the door in a complicated pattern that sounded like a code. It opened sharply a few seconds later.

There stood Jace, tall and slightly uncoordinated in his movements. His mouth fell open as soon as he saw Cai. Then he lunged forward, crushing my mate in a massive bear hug.

"You came back!" He sounded choked. "*Finn!* Cai is here! I can't believe it! I can't believe you're here!"

Cai wrestled himself free of his friend's tight embrace with a breathless laugh. "Jace—enough, man, I can't breathe!"

A second figure appeared in the doorway. I recognized Finn, another one of Cai's oldest friends.

Finn stared back and forth between both of us, a look of naked relief on his pleasant features. He shook hands with Cai for a moment before he, too, pulled Cai into a tight embrace.

"Where in perdition's name have you been?" As they broke apart, his excitement bubbled out of him in a torrent of words. "You just disappeared! No one knew where you'd gone, or what happened. You will *not* believe what it's been like here since you left! Have you heard about your father? And about Thelen? Cai, this shit *cannot* be allowed to stand."

Cai held up a hand to stem the flow of Finn's words. "Whoa. One thing at a time. First you need to hear the truth about what happened to me. And, more importantly, the truth about what happened to Ember."

Jace nodded. "Come inside. We'll talk."

We followed the pair into the pleasant dwelling, to a room with enough seats for all of us.

"You two want something to drink? Or eat?" Jace asked.

"No, we're good for now," Cai told him, and launched into an abbreviated version of recent events.

Finn and Jace listened raptly, frowning at some of the more outrageous parts of the tale. When Cai got to the part where we were mated, though, they exchanged a glance.

"Thought so," Finn muttered.

"Yeah, no offense, man—but that was pretty much inevitable," Jace agreed.

"Why do you say that?" I asked, frowning at them. "I was exiled. You were there when Bardulf burned out our marks. Hell, you two took me to the cells that night."

Jace looked troubled. "Believe me, I remember. I've always heard that mate bonds are stronger than pretty much anything. Bardulf could try to burn it out of you, but even then, we didn't believe it would really work. And that was before we knew you were actually a magical bad-ass."

Cai and I exchanged an uncertain look.

"Yeah—I mean, it was obvious that you were drawn to each other from the beginning," Finn agreed, leaning back in his chair. "It really was only a matter of time before you two fu—"

"*Anyway,*" Cai cut him off. "That's enough about that. Once we were sure that Ember mating me meant Earth would be safe, we went back to rescue the others on Elfhame. Ember destroyed Oberon's castle with her powers. He died, and his wife Titania took over. She hated Oberon's guts, so she offered a truce if Ember also agreed to mate a fae, meaning Elfhame would be protected as well. So, we... uh... did that."

Silence stretched.

Jace cleared his throat. "You mean you're, like... co-mated or something? With a *fae*? Is that even a thing?"

"It is now," Cai said, in a tone of finality.

I'd been keeping silent, curious as to how Cai would choose to tell the story. Now, I spoke up. "Let's just say my relationship status is complicated. But it worked, and both realms are safe. Which brings us back to Thelen and this pack. I'm with you, Finn—this situation can't be allowed to stand."

Jace looked uncomfortable. "We haven't had a series of challenges like this against a sitting alpha in decades. So soon after Bardulf, we could be setting a dangerous precedent."

"Is that why you haven't challenged Thelen yet?" Cai asked.

"No," Jace replied, heat spreading over his face. "That was because he's too powerful for either of us. We've been very much hoping all this time that you'd come home."

Finn nodded his agreement. "Truth. Though if you didn't, and if things got too bad, we'd been talking about taking Thelen out together, and becoming joint alphas somehow. I don't know if that could even work—but we weren't going to let him trash this pack completely."

Cai bowed his head for a moment, clearly moved by the pair's words.

"It's good you're back, though," Jace teased. "Finn didn't want to risk getting his good looks all scarred up in a fight."

"Yeah, major tragedy there," Cai said. "No wonder you held off."

Warmth grew in my chest at this intimate glimpse into Cai's life and relationships. I thought of Darby, and it occurred to me that a person's friendships said an awful lot about them. Thelen and Star's crowd had always been focused on who they could hurt. Cai's friends were focused on how they could help — even if it meant going up against an alpha wolf who was too powerful for either of them alone.

"We're in agreement, then? We're going to get Cai's pack back?" I asked, looking between the three friends.

They nodded solemnly.

My sudden urgency had nothing to do with Cai being the rightful alpha of the pack, and me, as his mate, being second in command. No, while Cai had been sharing the abbreviated story of recent events, I'd been obsessing about Thelen chasing off the shifters he considered weak and worthless. Even with her family to protect her, Darby might have been on that list, if she'd been here.

In many ways, I'd been directionless for most of my life. But now, something was bubbling up inside me, and it wouldn't be denied. It was time for pack culture to change, and I was determined to use my position as Cai's mate to make the Greystalker pack a safer, more welcoming place for wolves like Darby and me.

We could do this, I thought with dawning excitement. We could make real changes happen. Things could be better under Cai's leadership. He understood how awful it had been for me and the wolves like me. He would make sure things got better, and I would help him.

"... and at least a formal challenge would be better than what that crazy fae bastard did," Finn was saying, drawing my attention back to the conversation.

"Sorry, what?" I interrupted, shaking my head.

He glanced at me, blinked, and repeated, "I was saying that Cai should issue a formal challenge against Thelen instead of just unleashing a can of whoop-ass on him out of the blue."

Jace rubbed at the back of his neck. "Finn thinks it would make the transition to a new alpha smoother if we follow the old traditions. But I don't know if I agree."

"Okay. Why not?" Cai asked.

Jace shrugged his broad shoulders. "Gives him too much time to prepare. He's a slippery bastard, and his old crew is pretty loyal to him."

Cai frowned. "Do you think he could split the pack?"

"I guess it's possible," Jace said.

With a scowl, Cai moved to a window and stared off into the darkness of the forest. "I don't want to see this pack shattered into pieces."

"He might not be able to find anyone willing to follow him that far," I offered. "I can't imagine anyone really loves his leadership style all that much."

"True," Jace allowed.

Through the bond, I could sense Cai weighing the possibilities in his mind. After a few moments he looked up, meeting our gazes one by one.

"I'll issue a formal challenge," he said. "I think the risk of him splitting the pack is minimal. Even if a few decide to leave, the majority will remain loyal to whoever wins the battle."

"Want me to go deliver the message?" Finn asked.

"Yes, tell him I'll meet him in the town square to settle this at dawn."

Finn nodded and headed for the door.

Cai watched him go, slightly apprehensive. "Maybe I should have gone with him. I'm not sure I trust Thelen to treat him fairly, as the messenger."

"He wouldn't dare do anything," Jace said. "Finn will make sure there are witnesses when he delivers the challenge. Alpha challenges are deep-rooted in pack law, including the safety of messengers."

I hoped he was right.

"What do you need to do to prepare?" I asked Cai.

He shrugged. "Just some sleep. It's been a long few days."

"You two should stay here tonight," Jace said. "We have a spare room."

Jace's family greeted us warmly when he ushered us into the kitchen for something to eat—though I could see their confusion at my presence by Cai's side after I'd supposedly been exiled.

"You're the rightful alpha, Cai," Jace's mother said. She gripped his hands tightly between her own. "Everybody knows it. I'm glad you've returned to put things right. Doubly so if it means Jace and his friend won't be forced to fight Thelen."

We accepted food and drink with murmurs of thanks, then spent the rest of the night curled up together in a cozy nest on the floor of the spare room. It was reassuring to be wrapped tightly in Cai's arms, but my mate bond with Tamlain throbbed and ached without his presence. For the hundredth time, I wondered how in the two realms I was supposed to make this crazy situation work.

We're a family now, I thought sleepily, my eyes drifting closed. *A broken, confused, and deeply strange family – but a family nonetheless.*

It was still dark outside when Cai woke me up, his lips pressing over the bite mark he'd put on my neck when we'd mated. We joined Jace and his family at the table and ate breakfast, though the nervous butterflies in my stomach didn't do much for my appetite. Cai, too, ate lightly. He was silent, chewing each morsel with a focused expression on his face. No one else was speaking much either, other than to confirm that gossip about the upcoming battle had spread far and wide throughout the entire pack.

"I'm sure everyone will be there to watch," Jace said.

So, no pressure then, I thought wryly.

We walked together towards the meeting place, with Jace and Finn on Cai's left, and me on his right.

"Don't let him get at your left side; that's not your strong side," Finn counseled.

"I know, Finn," Cai replied patiently.

"Remember the last time we really brawled?" Finn asked. "I almost got you down by knocking your front paw out on that side."

"The key word being 'almost,'" Jace said.

"I did better against him than you did, asshole," Finn shot back.

Jace scowled at him. "What? You're crazy. I lasted way longer in that fight."

Finn scoffed. "Dream on."

Cai let the verbal tussle flow past him, making me think the pair were only doing it to distract him from his worries. As soon as we made it to the central square, I looked around and raised an eyebrow. Jace had been right. It looked like every single member of the pack had turned up to see the outcome of the battle. Some looked excited, others frightened. Everyone was staring straight at us. It made my neck prickle.

Cai wasted no time shifting into his wolf form. He was massive, his amber eyes shining as he surveyed the pack. Most looked down and away, intimidated by his alpha spirit.

"So, the usurper has come to be taught a lesson," Thelen announced, stepping into the center of the square. "I look forward to demonstrating exactly what I did to his weakling of a father." He transformed into a wolf as well, not quite as tall as Cai, but just as broad and muscular.

The tension grew in the crowd. I stood to one side with Finn and Jace, chewing on the inside of my lip. There was a breath of stillness before the two wolves launched themselves at each other. Cai leapt, slamming into Thelen's side. I was sure the other wolf would crumple under the blow, but he simply rolled and Cai's momentum carried him over the top of Thelen, tumbling in a cloud of dust.

Both wolves were back on their feet in the blink of an eye. Their claws scraped deep gashes into the earth as they lunged towards each other a second time, their chests colliding.

Several people gasped as snarls ripped through the air. Cai had Thelen by the neck, his long fangs pulling him towards the ground. Thelen whipped his head around, their skulls crashing together with a crack as loud as a gunshot.

I swallowed a whimper as the flash of pain transmitted through our mate bond. Gripping my head, I swayed slightly at the echo of the blow.

Cai shook his head, getting unsteadily to his feet. Thelen, too, looked dazed—rubbing at his face with one of his paws.

"That's the problem with a head butt," Finn muttered. "Hurts you just as bad as the other guy."

Cai recovered quicker and propelled his shoulder into Thelen, sending the other wolf sprawling on the ground. Cai pounced on top of him, pinning him to the ground as he tore chunks of skin and hair from Thelen's body.

Blood covered Cai's muzzle. I balled my fists together, wishing the fight would just *end* already.

"Cai's going to win," Jace said, loud enough for others around us to hear.

A murmur of agreement spread outward through the crowd of onlookers. Just then, an enraged shriek tore through the air as Star, Thelen's mate, came rushing towards us. Her hands were outstretched towards me like claws, a look of rage distorting her pretty features.

"What the—?" Finn said as the female wolf reached us.

"*I won't let you ruin this, you bitch!*" she yelled, seizing my arm and trying to throw me to the ground. Rage bubbled up in my chest for the space of a heartbeat as I remembered every time she'd made my life torture. But that wasn't the way to win this fight. After a single, staggering step, I set myself, using my fae powers to lock my feet in place, immovable as a statue.

Star stumbled, losing her grip on me. She regained her balance and gaped at me. "How... how are you *doing* that, you fucking freak?"

She twisted and kicked out, trying to dislodge my feet from the ground. That was never going to happen. I gave her a flat look, feeling my magic flowing through me, rooting me to the forest soil.

"Yield," I commanded, my voice resonant. Alpha power, long submerged, buzzed through my veins.

Star gasped, falling to the ground at my feet beneath that invisible force. Dimly I was aware that the fight between Cai and Thelen was still raging, but half of the crowd was now watching the conflict between us instead.

Star panted as she stared up at me, wide-eyed. I didn't blink, pinning her down on the ground with my gaze.

"You know what I would like to do to you?" I said, coming closer as she cowered. I nudged her with the toe of my boot, and she whimpered, curling into the fetal position on her side.

"Please, let me go," Star begged, raising her hands and rolling onto her back. Even in her human form it was clear she was showing me her belly. "What *are* you?"

I ignored the question. "I'll tell you exactly what I want to do. I would just *love* to take a knife and hack off all your hair, like you tried to do to me," I said, projecting my voice so the onlookers could overhear. "I would love to shame you, just like you always shamed me when I was young."

. Star trembled, averting her eyes from my righteous anger. She rolled her head to the side, exposing her throat.

"But I won't," I said, lifting my foot from her shoulder and stepping back.

I looked up and found Cai standing triumphant over Thelen, who lay bleeding and defeated on the ground at his feet.

"You and your mate are finished… and I won't become another bully to replace you," I told her.

Cai shifted into human form, sweating and battered. His chest rose and fell in rapid pants. "Thelen!" he said, projecting his voice for the crowd. "This battle is finished! You and your mate have been defeated. You have submitted to me as the rightful alpha of this land. Depart now in disgrace, and never return."

Star threw one last terrified look at me and scrambled away. Thelen had transformed back into his human form in a heap on the ground. He was a bloody mess as Star dragged him clumsily to his feet. With a last, hateful look at us, they stumbled away through the trees, vanishing from sight.

"Someone follow them," Cai ordered. "Make sure they cross the boundary and don't come back."

Wild applause broke out through the spectators, even as several people shifted form and loped after the beaten pair. Everyone had been hoping for Cai's victory, it seemed.

Finn and Jace slapped Cai on the back. He winced at his bruises, but there was a satisfied smile on his face as his friends congratulated him on his victory.

A sudden electric crackling noise cut through the sounds of celebration, as a portal erupted into existence in the center of the square.

I drew in a sharp breath, expecting Tamlain to step through. Uncertainty flooded me. Had I been wrong? Had my anger caused damage on Elfhame after all? Or had he sensed our victory through the bond and come to join our celebration?

My confusion turned to horror as Geneva Padfoot stepped through the portal. An expression of sheer hatred twisted her features as her eyes locked on mine. Before anyone could react, she hurled a flaming ball of magic directly at Cai, who stood frozen in shock.

THIRTY-SIX

"NO!" I SCREAMED as Geneva's ball of magic flew toward Cai. Without thought, I threw out my left hand in a desperate bid to cast a shield in between Geneva and my mate. My reaction was too slow, and I was only able to catch the edge of the crackling energy mass. It struck Cai in the shoulder. He spun under the impact and collapsed to the ground, where he lay twitching and jerking.

I turned slowly back toward Geneva, rage pouring through me like an uncontrollable flood. Flexing my hands, I reached out for the weather, wanting to bring a pile of trees crashing down on top of the fae bitch. I lifted my arms, hoping to feel the swell of wind, but only the mildest breath of a breeze lifted my hair.

Rage and terror, my best weapons, were gone.

Geneva cackled, looking at my empty hands.

"Without the forces of Mother Nature you really aren't of much use, are you?" She asked. "Don't worry, little creature. Maybe once your mate is dead, you'll get your power back."

With a snarl, I lunged for her, calling up the lesser magical skills I still possessed. She parried my attacks with infuriating ease, twisting her hands and arms in an intricate dance of defense. But unlike me, she could apparently multitask.

I was forced to duck as she sent a blast of power towards my head that would have surely sent me careening into the trees behind me. Landing on my stomach in the soft earth, I cast power downward, sending a spray of mud, leaves, and bark in her direction. She turned away, but not before getting a face full of dirt that left her coughing and choking.

Pressing my advantage, I scrambled forward, intending to physically tackle her to the ground. As I rushed towards her like a human rugby player, Geneva brought her hands together with a clap that echoed through my skull and sent me sprawling again. It felt like I'd been standing at ground zero when a bomb went off.

Blood trickled from my nose, but at least my arms and legs still seemed to be working. I pushed myself to my feet, trying to ignore the way my ears were ringing. Calling on my remaining energy, I sent fiery bolts of power pelting in her direction. The brilliant light illuminated the village square with weird shadows. Yet despite my best efforts, my blows were deflected harmlessly into the ground.

I reached out and tried to call her boots toward me, the same way I retrieved my own clothing from a distance. I jerked my hand in a grasping motion, putting every ounce of mental energy into calling her footwear to me with her feet still in them, wanting to see the fae flat on her back, groveling in the mud.

She sliced the air in front of her, casting her own protective shield between us.

With a wordless shout of frustration, I jumped forward, transforming into a wolf in one smooth motion—landing on my heavy paws and tearing up the earth underneath me to reach her.

Something flickered in her cold eyes as I dove forward, my jaws going for her throat. She spun away with the gracefulness of a deer, and I skidded to a stop as my teeth closed around nothing but air.

We squared up, panting and glaring at each other. I snarled and snapped my teeth, running at full speed towards her again. This time I anticipated her feint and was able to bash into her with my shoulder. As soon as our bodies collided, however, I felt a horrible shock through my system that made me gasp and whimper in pain.

Geneva had fallen to the ground but was instantly back on her feet, walking towards me with death in her eyes. My body transformed back to human. Rolling to my feet, I waved my clothes back into existence and stood tall despite the pain, my hair blowing wildly around me.

"How dare you trespass here, witch?" I hissed, allowing my newfound alpha power to flow through the words.

She flinched in response, her eyes widening—but she didn't back down. We circled each other warily, never breaking eye contact.

"You were always such a pathetic pup," she sneered. "I was loyal to Oberon, my king—ever his most faithful servant. Yet you were too self-absorbed in your own misery to even look around you! You could've had control of your powers years ago, but you were too weak to take it. You could've stood at your father's right hand, but no! Instead you destroyed him. And for that, I will see you suffer."

She punched the air, sending a wild burst of energy at me. I raised my hands, a shield exploding into existence in front of me. As the energy struck my barrier, I could taste her bloodlust through the mingling of our magic.

"You won't defeat me," I snarled, hoping like hell it was true. "*Bitch.*"

Geneva laughed—a shrill, hysterical note behind the sound. "You think I'm here for you? I don't need to best you in battle to bring you low, girl. I've already defeated you by dealing a mortal blow to your pathetic excuse for a mate."

A chill skittered down my spine. Cai couldn't be dead—if he were, surely I'd have felt it. If he'd been dead, I'd have been able to call up a storm here on Earth. But… he wasn't moving. Was he still breathing?

"Why *do* this?" I demanded.

Her tone grew disdainful. "That mangy shifter boy captured me and locked me in iron chains. You weren't supposed to mate him. Oberon wanted you as his weapon against Earth, and that one ruined his plan!" She raised a shaking finger to point at Cai.

Around us, pack members had been fleeing in all directions as the fight raged. They'd come to see an alpha battle—not… *this*. Families pulled their pups into the shelter of the trees, vanishing from sight.

I tried to go to my fallen mate, only to be brought up short when Geneva cast a force field in front of me. Jace, Finn, and Darby converged on Cai instead, standing guard over his prone figure. Darby fell to her knees, running gentle hands over his injured chest and shoulder. She looked up at Geneva, eyes hard with defiance and anger.

Affection for my friends surged inside of me, only to be strangled by fresh terror. My magical energy was nearly exhausted. I couldn't break through Geneva's barrier to get to them. One magical blast in their direction, and nearly everyone I loved could be dead.

Geneva could destroy all of them at once.

I clenched my fists. "You were in love with him, weren't you?" I shouted, desperate to draw her attention away from the group huddled a short distance away from us. "In love with your king — with Oberon?"

Geneva looked up in surprise, uncertainty flickering across her face. "What? Don't be preposterous, you foolish pup!"

Had I touched a nerve?

"There's nothing preposterous about it," I said, moving slowly sideways so that I stood directly between her and the others. "You were loyal to a madman for years. You had a good life here on Earth. Why throw it away like you did? Was he really that good in the sack?"

Geneva's face went purple as she sputtered with outrage. I took advantage of her momentary distraction to turn my focus inward.

Tamlain! Help me! I poured every bit of my fear and desperation into the mental cry. It echoed along the untried mate bond connecting us, resonating like a struck gong. Even so, I had no way of knowing if he could hear me across the boundary between realms. I had to keep Geneva distracted—had to keep her from attacking my friends as well as my mate.

I threw a weakened bolt of energy in her direction, just to keep her attention centered firmly on me. She swatted it away as if my attack was nothing more than an annoyance.

Her eyes remained glued to me, seething with anger. "You dare besmirch your own father that way, whelp? I should cut out your tongue and force feed it to you. That would teach you a lesson."

"Oh yeah," I replied, raising an eyebrow. I lifted my sleeves to reveal the tattoos covering my arms. "You know, you were the closest thing I had to a proper mother figure. Obviously your guidance and life lessons really made an impact on me."

An explosion of sound rent the square. A portal flamed open at my side. Tamlain stepped through it, his sword drawn and his long cloak billowing. Rage crackled around him in a tangible aura as his brilliant blue eyes took in the scene.

"*You,*" was all he said, his gaze pinning Geneva like an insect under glass.

In the next instant, he went for her—striking with the speed of a venomous snake.

Go to Cai. Tamlain's voice echoed through our mate bond. *Heal him, Little Wolf. Hurry — his life force is fading.*

I jolted as though I'd received an electric shock. Geneva had let the barrier separating me from the others fall when Tamlain appeared. I immediately rushed towards Cai, even as Geneva pulled a short sword from her belt to meet Tamlain's attack. With a flick of her wrist, the blade exploded into blue-white fire.

I didn't have time to worry about their fight — I would have to trust in Tamlain's ability to defeat her, or at least hold her off. I fell to my knees next to Cai. I could hear the almighty clashes of Tamlain and Geneva's blades in the background, but my attention was solely focused on my mate. His life was draining away before my eyes.

"No! Cai, you need to hang on!" I begged, brushing away Jace's grip as he tried to shake Cai back to wakefulness.

Thinking about the way I'd helped heal Tamlain after the battle with Oberon, I placed my hands palm down on Cai's muscular chest. He was barely breathing, and his heart rate felt faint and erratic.

I summoned all the energy and power that I could muster, remembering what it had felt like to bring the entire castle down on top of Oberon. I reached deep inside myself, pouring magic through my hands and into Cai's body, desperate to knit his internal injuries together after Geneva's magical attack.

With a gasp, I felt the energy disappear into a dark, bottomless well inside him. I could sense him scrabbling to escape the nothingness that was dragging him down. I pitched forward, almost collapsing on top of him as I tried in vain to fill the endless chasm with my healing power.

Strong hands grabbed my shoulders as a cold sweat broke out across my face. I vaguely recognized Jace and Finn supporting me from either side.

"Cai," I whispered, the sound as weak as if I, too, were vanishing into the darkness. "Cai, don't leave now. Please come back."

As I focused all my energy on saving my mate, time became meaningless. I might have been kneeling on the dirt for a minute, or an hour, or a month. I didn't know. All I knew for sure was that everything was fading away from me. A heavy, sweet sedation began to settle over my mind and body—making me feel like I was being pulled irresistibly downward, toward the center of the Earth.

The more energy and magic I poured into Cai, the further away from me he seemed to be. I pried open bleary eyes, looking around at the fuzzy outlines of the shifters still standing guard over us.

"We're losing him," I slurred, exhaustion pushing on me as the depths of his injuries threatened to pull me down, too.

"You can't!" Finn snapped, sounding like he was speaking from miles away. "You've got all this crazy fae magic! You have to save him!"

"Please, Ember!" Jace urged. "You can fix him. You have to!"

I turned my head, searching for my other mate, but never releasing Cai or relenting on the power flowing into him. Tamlain was the one person who could save us both.

"Tamlain," I whispered, my voice faint as my eyes slid closed.

No! I couldn't sleep now. I had to concentrate.

With a great effort, my eyelids fluttered open. I shook my head, trying to clear the rolling, dark fog gathering at the edges of my vision. I needed Tamlain. He would have enough power to pull us both back from the abyss, but he was still locked in deadly combat with Geneva.

I couldn't distract him now, or we might *all* die at her hands.

Faintly, I could sense magical attacks and counterattacks careening wildly around us. A tree on the edge of the clearing burst suddenly into flame, and Darby shrieked in alarm. I blinked at the hazy tableau of destruction, everything in the world slowing down as the space between my heartbeats grew longer and longer... just like Cai was falling away from me, and the gap between us was growing.

Shush-shush. Shush-shush. Shush-shush.

My thudding heart sounded very far away. Was this what it felt like to die?

I tried to take a deep breath — to refocus myself and pour even more power into Cai — but it felt like my lungs had been flattened. Was someone sitting on my chest?

Across the square, a sharp crack of sound split the air, as loud as a human gunshot. I ducked my head instinctively, only to turn and see through my darkening eyes that a building across the square had split down the middle.

Light flashed in all directions as Tamlain and Geneva fought. I could sense the strain of the battle through the mate-bond with Tamlain, but also his cold satisfaction as he pounded his enemy with relentless attacks.

This was what my lethal fae warrior was made for. If only I had his strength.

"Ember! Wake up!" a male voice called. Jace or Finn—I couldn't tell them apart anymore. It was all far away and unimportant. Hands were shaking me, and I felt my head flopping uselessly from side to side.

Then Darby's soft voice whispered in my ear.

"Don't you dare give up, Ember Valentine," she said, quietly, but with great force. "I need you. I *need* you to be here. You're my best friend—please don't leave me alone."

Nothing but those words could have roused me. Lifting my chin I forced my eyes open to find her familiar face watching me with worry. She was kneeling next to me, her arm wrapped protectively around my shoulders as Jace or Finn, I still wasn't sure which, kept me propped up from behind.

"I need you," she whispered again, our eyes locking. "And you need Cai. *Keep fighting.*"

"'M still here," I slurred. "Not leaving."

With an electric crackle, yet another portal opened up just a few yards away from us. A figure stepped through, but with my blurring vision, I couldn't make out if it was friend or foe.

THIRTY-SEVEN

A FLOOD OF armored warriors erupted through the portal. For a moment, chaos descended on the town square as fae weapons bristled and war screams echoed through the trees. It took a few seconds before I could make sense of the scene. Then, I caught sight of a familiar figure in the midst of the confusion, but wearing very *unfamiliar* garb.

I blinked in shock. "*Titania*? W-what?"

I could barely believe my eyes, but it was the queen herself, dressed in full shining armor, the light glinting off her silver breastplate. She still wore a crown, although this one was part of a gleaming battle helmet.

I watched as another figure whirled and darted through the battle with the gracefulness of a hunting cat.

It was Dianthe, coming to our rescue at Titania's side.

This was too much for my failing body and brain, and I felt my strength completely leaving me. I slumped next to Cai, the world swimming alarmingly around me. Everything was tilting sideways, and I clawed desperately at the ground, terrified that I would slip away into the endless void yawning beneath me.

In my wavering vision, I watched Titania's guards forming a circle around Geneva, who glared at them warily. She straightened from her battle crouch, letting her hands fall to hang limply by her sides.

"Surrender, witch!" called one of the guards. Around her, several warriors drew bowstrings and aimed spears directly at her heart.

"This battle is not about me. Look to your new allies, *Queen*," Geneva said, lifting her arms slowly. Her smile was a twisted thing.

"Stop her!" Titania commanded, just as Geneva clapped her hands together.

An energy wave exploded outward, blasting into the guards surrounding her. They stumbled back, but most of them immediately regained their footing and lunged toward her. The moment of distraction was still enough to let her open a portal and dive through it.

I watched all of this through half-lidded eyes. I was sinking slowly into a warm darkness. It waited to welcome me with open arms. Maybe I would be able to join Cai there.

"*Ember!*" Tamlain slid to his knees beside me and pulled my upper body onto his lap, supporting me. He patted my cheek lightly, as though trying to revive me.

It did nothing to drive back the encroaching darkness. "I couldn't save him," I whispered, tears sliding down my face. "I couldn't save Cai. I poured everything into him, but he just slipped away from me. It wasn't enough. I wasn't enough."

"Ember, don't speak. You're very weak, we need to heal you." Tamlain's voice was urgent. He cast around, as though looking for someone.

"Don't," I croaked, hating myself for my weakness. My *uselessness*. "I'm not worth it. I failed."

"You didn't fail. Your other mate still lives. I will see to Cai after I see to you, Little Wolf." Tamlain sounded as though he were suddenly very far away, speaking through a tunnel.

Wait. Cai was still alive? I shook my head weakly. "No, Cai first."

Tamlain let out an exclamation that sounded like an expletive.

"Dianthe! I need your help!" he yelled across the clearing. "*Now!*"

A moment later Dianthe's face swam in front of my eyes, a glowing haze surrounding her like a halo.

"Wow," she said grimly. "No offense, but you look like the backside of a pig right now, Ember."

I groaned and coughed, my breath catching in my lungs. "Help Cai."

Dianthe exchanged a look with Tamlain. She shuffled around on her knees to get a better look at Cai's fallen body. "Yeah, yeah. I'll save your mangy friend, don't worry."

"Mate," I reminded her stubbornly.

"Whatever. He's still mangy."

Dianthe and Tamlain each laid a hand on one of Cai's shoulders. They both closed their eyes and bowed their heads as if in prayer. A frown of concentration passed over Tamlain's face.

I didn't move, exhaustion and terror keeping me rooted firmly to the ground. As I watched, beads of sweat broke out across Tamlain's brow, rolling down his face as he strained to achieve whatever he and Dianthe were trying to do for Cai.

Finally, Dianthe let out a gasp. They both looked up at the same time, identical grim expressions on their faces.

"What is it?" I rasped, trying to sit up. My shaking arms would not support me, and I flopped pathetically back down on to the ground. "What's wrong? Is he dead?"

"No," Dianthe answered. "Not dead, Not yet, anyway."

Yet? Did that mean she and Tamlain couldn't heal him either? My fear must have shown on my face, because Tamlain took my hand and leaned over me.

"We will try to save him, Ember," he said. "But Geneva didn't just injure him. She spelled him magically to prevent healing."

Dianthe sounded as worried as I'd ever heard her. "I think you are sadly overconfident in our abilities, Tamlain."

I turned toward her. She had both hands over Cai's chest now, and a soft glow was forming beneath her palms.

"I will keep pouring life into him—otherwise he'll die," Tamlain said. "But you must find and unravel the spell inside him, Cousin."

I could do nothing more than lie there, desperately hoping for a miracle. Dianthe hesitated and looked up, her expression uncertain.

Tamlain met her eyes. "Dianthe, please. I have faith in your abilities. Search out the draining spell and reverse it."

"Draining spell?" I asked.

"Geneva put a spell on him that prevents healing by shunting any energy in his body into the void—even magical energy," he explained. "It will drain him of all of his life force. We must act quickly."

I stretched out my hand and placed it on Cai's chest. Letting my eyes slip closed, I forced a blast of my own waning life energy through him, trying to feel what Tamlain had described. His muscles jerked beneath the burst of power, and a guttural groan escaped his lips. But Tamlain was right— none of it actually stuck. It slid straight through him and away into nothingness.

"Ember, don't—you're too weak," Tamlain said. He moved to kneel at Cai's head, placing two fingers on each of Cai's temples. "I will force power into him while you search, Dianthe—but do it quickly. I don't know how long I will last."

"No, wait," Dianthe said, frowning. "Ember— give him one more blast of energy, exactly like you just did. It lit him up inside, and I was able to see the trail of Geneva's spell for a few seconds."

I wanted to groan in exhaustion, but I couldn't spare the energy. "Sure, no problem." It sounded like someone had used industrial sandpaper on my throat.

Dianthe gave me a strange look. "Less talking. More doing. Quickly, now."

"I can help," said a soft voice from over my shoulder. "Can you pull life force from me and feed it into Cai to keep him alive while you work?"

Darby. She sounded resolute.

"Use us, too." That was Finn. I craned my head to see him and Jace flanking my friend.

"Thank you," Tamlain said. "I will let you know when I need your energy."

"Right, let's do this," Dianthe said. "Ember, get ready to hit him with everything you've got so I can see what I'm doing inside him."

I took a few deep breaths, steadying my hand on Cai and drawing every ounce of my life force in to the center of my chest. I formed a mental image of a blue-white ball of power, just behind my sternum, pulsating and ready to blow.

I could feel heat forming underneath my palm. With one final deep breath, a bolt of the same blue-white energy exploded from my skin and directly into Cai's chest. With my life force desperately depleted, my head fell to the ground next to Cai's, and I knew no more.

***

My consciousness returned long before I regained any control of my muscles. For a while, I lay against a pleasantly soft surface, trapped inside my own skin. Was I in a bed? It seemed like it. Hopefully, that was a good sign.

I floated for a while, simply feeling the softness of the sheets and blankets—not wanting to examine the aches wracking my entire body, or the vaguely queasy feeling swimming in my stomach.

Some good amount of time later, I found that I could blink my eyes if I concentrated. It took a while to bring my blurry vision into focus, but I was definitely in a bed. Soft light filtered through a window nearby. I couldn't roll over or move my head to see the rest of the room—I was still too weak.

I was alone inside my mind, and a slow sense of dread rose inside me at the realization. What if I examined my mate-bond and found that the others were truly gone? What if Cai had died from the spell, and Tamlain had died while trying to save him? It couldn't be true. It *couldn't*. How could I possibly survive having my soul-bonds torn out a second time?

Shh. The soft whisper stroked across my roiling thoughts and fears like gentle fingertips, soothing.

Tamlain? I reached toward the ghostly voice.

I am here. You must rest, beloved. Try not to worry—all is well.

"Cai! What about Cai?" I whispered, trying to sit up. I failed, but my weak, uncoordinated movements caused my arm to brush against something lying next to me.

No... not something. *Someone.* A body, warm with life. I managed to roll my head on the pillow, only to find Cai stretched out on the bed next to me. A blanket had been drawn over both of us, covering him to his chest. He was still pale, but his eyes were moving rapidly beneath closed eyelids, and his breathing was soft and regular.

He was asleep. Not unconscious—just asleep and dreaming. My breath stuttered in my chest, relief flooding me.

Yes, Tamlain's disembodied voice assured me through the bond. *He has not yet awoken, but he is *sleeping soundly while he recovers. No doubt it will be a few days before he feels like himself again.*

I looked around, swallowing a slight feeling of hurt that Tamlain wasn't here with us. But that was petty of me. He'd risked his life to save Cai. For all I knew, he'd been sleeping and recovering when my panic through the bond woke him up. I consciously let a sense of gratitude wash through me and into our shared connection.

Thank you, I sent, with all the sincerity in my heart. *Thank you for saving him.*

I could sense Tamlain's surge of fondness, and I reveled in it.

It was Dianthe whose magical talents saved him, he sent, *but I will pass along the message to her. She's already grousing about having exhausted herself to save some mangy shifter mutt with an attitude problem, as she puts it.*

Amusement warmed me. Assuming Cai recovered fully, Dianthe would never let him live this down. As though my thoughts had summoned her, the door to our room opened and Dianthe stepped inside. She smiled broadly upon seeing that I was awake.

"Finally back in the land of the living, eh?" she asked, coming around to my side of the bed. "Do you feel up to eating something?"

I grimaced as I tried again to sit up, my stomach pitching and rolling as the world spun around me.

"Uh," I replied, letting gravity win another battle as I slumped back to the mattress. "Not just yet. Sorry."

She laid a hand on my shoulder and gave a supportive squeeze. "Take it slow, in that case. You just went completely white while trying to sit up."

With my eyes closed I murmured, "Too bad 'curdled milk' isn't a great color on me."

She chuckled, settling on the edge of the bed next to me.

I swallowed, remembering what Tamlain had told me just now through the bond. "Thank you," I said, feeling around so that I could pat Dianthe's knee. She grabbed my hand with her own and tangled our fingers together.

"You're welcome," she said. "Erm, what am I being thanked for, exactly?"

I snorted, peeking at her through a crack in my eyelid. "What do you think? You saved the day. *Again.*"

Dianthe waved away the words. "Well I wouldn't have been able to stand watching you mope around if something had happened to that one—even if he is irritating. And not a very good hunter," she added smugly.

"I'll tell him you said that," I threatened, but we were both grinning. Then I sobered. "I was pretty out of it, admittedly… but did I really see Titania, Queen of the Fae, riding to our rescue with a bunch of royal guards? And if so, what happened with Geneva?"

"The queen and her guards pursued the witch back to Elfhame," Dianthe said. "I don't know if they caught her. Tamlain knew something was badly wrong when you called him through the bond. He portaled to Earth immediately. I…

persuaded Titania that it wouldn't look good if she left you and your mates twisting in the wind right after she'd agreed to ally herself with you. As soon as we could organize a decent fighting force, we came to help. But I don't think the queen is comfortable spending more time on Earth than absolutely necessary."

I blinked, taken aback by the idea that I was apparently allied to the Queen of the Fae now. "Oh. Um… *wow*. Okay." After a few moments, though, I could no longer keep the next question to myself. "Where's Tamlain now?" I asked, trying to see into the hallway through the room's door.

Dianthe huffed. "After you and Cai were injured, Finn brought us here to this empty house and told us we could use it while you two were healing. But then there was some kind of disturbance at the edge of the settlement—a couple of shifters trying to claim they were the ones in charge. So he had to go deal with that. Since then, he's been splitting his time between sitting with you two, and making sure no one else gets any ideas about taking over while Cai is unconscious."

I scowled, trying to make sense of that.

"Wait. Two shifters? A male and a female?" I asked.

She shrugged. "Yes, I think so. Not really my department, so I didn't ask for details."

I flopped back on the pillow. "I bet it's Thelen and Star," I said to the ceiling. "Holy shit. I wonder if they found out somehow that Cai was injured?"

Dianthe's weight shifted on the bed. "Who are Thelen and Star?"

"They're the shifters who took over as alphas when Cai left Earth to help us on Elfhame. We got back here afterward, and Cai had to challenge Thelen to a fight to get control of the pack again."

There was a pause before Dianthe said, "Huh. That sounds incredibly tiresome. I suppose it explains some things, though."

I looked curiously at her. "What do you mean?"

"Tamlain seemed unusually eager to deal with them. He's not generally the type to pick fights if it can be avoided," Dianthe replied with an indifferent shrug.

"What do you mean, *pick fights*?" I asked, flashing back to Tamlain's battle with Bardulf.

A mischievous smile twitched Dianthe's lips.

"Well," she replied slowly, "first Tamlain went and met them at the edge of the packlands. Then he invited them back to the town square, where he had an epic two on one fight with them."

My eyes widened. *"He did what?"* I immediately delved along the mate-bond, but Tamlain's end had gone suspiciously quiet.

My concern must have showed clearly on my face, because Dianthe rolled her eyes at me. "Ember, you worry too much. He was fine."

"He could've been hurt!" I exclaimed. "Or killed!"

"Pfft. Not a chance," she said dismissively. "But your shifter friends thought they had him outnumbered, so he went easy on them at first."

I covered my face with my hands, both in irritation that Tamlain had rushed into such a situation, and to hide the growing amusement on my face. How I wished I'd been there to see Tamlain stomp that pair into the ground...

Dianthe continued her rundown. "After he let them get a few blows in to make them overconfident, he blasted them with magic until they were both lying in a crumpled heap on the ground, begging for mercy."

I couldn't help the bark of laughter that escaped my lips. "Holy ancestors. I can't believe I missed that."

"Oh, it was really something," Dianthe said, a light of amusement in her eyes. "Tamlain hit them with a spell to turn their skin bright green—and their fur, too, when they tried to shift into wolf form. Then he ordered them to be taken back to the boundary of the packlands and expelled again on pain of death."

I blinked. "I am so disappointed I didn't get to see that."

"With luck, they'll decide to test me and return," said a familiar voice from the doorway.

Dianthe and I both looked around to find Tamlain standing casually, leaning one shoulder against the doorframe.

I couldn't have stopped the slow grin that lit my features if I'd tried.

I didn't try.

"Tamlain," I said.

"I did consider blue instead of green," he mused, pushing away from the door and strolling towards the bed. "But I believe green is traditionally associated with envy in both our cultures. I thought it was appropriate, since they were coveting power they clearly hadn't earned."

Dianthe ceded her place on the edge of the bed to him. He sat, looking down at me with a soft smile. This time, I finally managed to drag myself upright so I could throw my arms around his shoulders. He leaned forward, pressing a kiss to my hair.

"I'm so glad you're back," I said into the crook of his neck.

Strong arms wrapped me up and held me close. Vaguely, I was aware that the world was still tilting and swaying, but his embrace kept me anchored.

"I wasn't far away, love," he answered in my ear. "I wouldn't want to be far away from you now. As I said, all is well."

At his words, the old insecurities flooded my stomach. I pushed away enough that I could meet his eyes.

"Is it, though?" I asked. How would the three of us navigate this strange new future? Where would we live? *How* would we live? Tamlain was fae. Cai was a shifter. I was somehow both, and in a way, neither. There would always be a divide, a split in our family. Who would be the one to make a sacrifice?

A groan interrupted my spiraling panic before Tamlain could pick it up through the bond. Tamlain, Dianthe, and I turned as one to stare at Cai, whose eyelids were fluttering.

"Cai?" I gasped, rolling towards him. "Cai? Can you hear me?"

"Yeah," he croaked. "Ugh. Crap. What time is it?"

Beyond the fact that it was light outside, I had no idea.

"Just after five in the evening," Tamlain offered.

"Ember, you're upset. What's wrong?" Cai asked, his words slurring a bit.

I blanched. "You felt that?"

"Some of it." He swallowed and licked his lips. "Enough to make me worry."

I shook my head. "It's nothing. You don't need to think about it right now."

"It's all right. I'm too out of it to be terribly troubled about much of anything," he replied with a crooked smile. "But seriously, I told you this before, and I meant it. Stop worrying about what everyone else wants. Worry about what *you* want for a change."

I stared at him in something like consternation, as I tried to herd my thoughts into some kind of order.

"What I truly want?" I asked, my gaze moving from Cai to Tamlain and back again.

They nodded, their expressions encouraging.

Deep breath.

"Okay," I said, thinking about Thelen and Star... about my terrible experience growing up in a pack that despised me. "Here's what I really want. I want to make the Greystalker lands a haven for abandoned and abused shifter pups. I want to be a beacon of hope for the outcasts, the loners, and anyone who doesn't feel like they fit in. I want us to make it so that everyone who needs a place to call home can find one here."

"Everyone?" Tamlain asked quietly. "Not only shifters?"

I chewed my lower lip for a moment and nodded.

"Everyone," I confirmed. "Not just shifters. There's plenty of room, and we all need to learn to work together, anyway. I want this place to be a haven for whoever needs safety and support."

Tamlain and Cai shared a long look over my head.

"Then that's what we'll do," Cai said, reaching for my right hand.

Tamlain reached for my left. I clutched them both, feeling our unity in that moment hum through the bond, while Dianthe crossed her arms and smiled a pleased little smile at the three of us from the doorway.

EPILOGUE

One year later

"*UGH*, WHERE ARE they?" I complained, pacing back and forth across the room. I'd been restless and irrationally anxious for the last two hours, tension cresting and ebbing in my body like waves.

"They'll be here soon," Darby said patiently. She grabbed my wrist as I passed, bringing me to an abrupt halt and looking me squarely in the eyes. "They're coming back, and I promise they'll make it home before your heat actually starts, okay? You're only in pre-heat right now — it's going to be hours yet."

I closed my eyes and took a deep, steadying breath. "Okay, you're right. I know you're right."

She rolled her eyes at me. "Yes. I *am* right. So just keep breathing, please."

"Yeah, yeah," I muttered, but I did make an effort to tone down my whole 'crazy bitch in heat' vibe.

The classroom where we were standing still smelled faintly of lumber and fresh whitewash. The entire school building was new, built against the side of a steep cliff in the mountain. The youngsters — fae children and shifter pups, and even a couple of human kids — were outside on the new playground, laughing and shrieking with glee as they played a rousing game of tag.

Darby and I had just met with a group of fae teachers visiting from Elfhame. We were trying to recruit them to educate the students here about magic and folklore. This had been our second meeting with them, and I was pretty sure they were finally coming around to our point of view.

Many of the fae children in our care had very little control over their powers, and some refused to use magic at all after suffering trauma or loss. I was convinced they needed to understand the theory behind their magic so they could grasp it better, giving them command over their instincts.

A slow sense of warmth spread through me from my mate bond, distracting me as I focused inward. I smiled in relief, sensing that Cai and Tamlain were returning from their most recent journey to Elfhame.

What they were doing there was important. Vital, even.

We'd been hearing disturbing rumors that an ancient and powerful fae mage was stealing vulnerable kids and using them as slaves. While that kind of thing might have slipped under the radar when Oberon was king, Queen Titania had imposed terrible sanctions against anyone found to be buying and selling children on her world.

Unfortunately, there were still rogue fae on Elfhame who resisted the queen's command. Even more unfortunately, that number included Geneva, who'd managed to slip free of Titania's net and scuttle under a rock somewhere. No one had seen or heard from her since her attack on Cai. It was possible she'd poke her head up someday to cause more trouble, but for now I had more immediate concerns.

I was on the brink of my heat. The tell-tale tremors and sweating were starting to make themselves known—although Darby was right that it would be several hours yet before I was truly incapacitated. It was regrettable that my mates had been called away to deal with the mage when I would rather have had them here, but helping children in trouble was more important than my personal convenience or wishes.

This was our life now. Flitting back and forth between Elfhame and Earth, rescuing and caring for the vulnerable in both realms, all while managing to squeeze in an amazing sex life in between.

Madness... but the best kind of madness.

I jerked my head, motioning Darby to follow me out of the classroom.

"Let me guess," she said, amused. "They're on their way right now?"

"Yep. Let's walk and talk. What else do you think the teachers will want?" I asked as we slipped outside, heading for the alpha dwelling.

"We've already got most of the supplies they'll need," Darby answered thoughtfully. "But if they decide to try new techniques with the kids, we may need to obtain other things for them on short notice. It'll be interesting having such a drastic difference in teaching styles from our regular shifter staff."

I nodded. "I agree. I think we're doing the fae children a disservice by denying them access to their own people."

"We haven't been *denying* them," Darby corrected. "We just weren't making it enough of a priority to facilitate connections with other fae."

"No, you're right," I said. "But they don't have access to fae teachers like their peers on Elfhame do, and they should."

She shrugged. "True. And now they will, assuming this group comes through for us."

As we spoke, we wandered up the path towards the home I shared with Cai and Tamlain whenever we were staying on Earth. My body was starting to ache, discomfort creeping through my bones and muscles to settle deep inside me, *wanting*.

I chewed on the inside of my cheek, trying to distract myself from my symptoms. I'd need to hold it together for a little while longer until Cai and Tamlain returned. Then I could sate my shifter appetites to my heart's content.

Darby pushed open the front door and led me inside the huge den, where Cai had grown up with Bardulf, and where he now lived as the leader of the pack. *The alpha's residence.* Sometimes it still felt surreal.

"Surprise," Cai's wry greeting reached me from the sitting room, and something inside me jolted pleasantly. I sucked in a breath and hurried to the door, drinking in the welcome sight that greeted me. Then I rushed forward, embracing both Cai and Tamlain.

"I didn't expect you back yet," I said, rubbing my face against their chests — shamelessly wallowing in their scents as my inner wolf rumbled her approval.

Tamlain touched my cheek, lifting my face to his for a kiss. It took all my willpower to allow him to pull back without immediately pouncing on him.

"We found the children," he reported. "It was true that the mage was using them as slaves to feed his magic."

A growl coiled low in my chest. Even after all this time, I still couldn't get used to the idea of adults abusing children in such a terrible way.

"Did you get them settled in at the bunk house?" Darby asked, saving me from having to string words together.

Cai shook his head. "We didn't bring them back. For once, we were able to return all of them to their original families, happily enough. The mage has been turned over to Titania for punishment, and after that, we were free to slip away early." He grinned. "So here we are."

He ran his hand possessively down my side, tracing along the curve of my waist.

I groaned in longing, the sound unnecessarily sexual considering poor Darby was still standing right in the room with us.

She only laughed. "I'll let you three have some privacy, shall I?" she said with a smirk, backing out of the door with a small wave and closing it behind her with a decisive click.

Anticipation washed through me the moment she was gone, and I could already feel my heat kicking in beneath the influence of the two most amazing men in all the realms. How could I have ever gotten so lucky?

"Little Wolf—you look like the cat that got the cream." Tamlain pulled me in for another filthy kiss. Our lips slid together passionately, and then Cai came up behind me to nip at the bite mark he'd left on my shoulder when he'd mated me. Crushed happily between the pair, both of whom now had their mouths all over me in every glorious way, I could only pant with desire.

"Wait, wait," I said, holding my hands up before I grew too lost to stop myself. "No offense, but you both look like you've spent the last two days rolling around in a pig sty. I like a bit of *eau-de-male* as much as the next she-wolf, but there are limits."

Cai frowned, then sniffed dramatically at his armpits—only to make a slight coughing noise. "Damn. You know, you might have said something earlier, fae."

"I was trying to be polite," Tamlain muttered against my skin, still distracted by the hinge of my jaw. To be fair, I was pretty distracted by what he was doing, too. A shiver went through me and my knees felt weak. It was hard to concentrate or keep my mind clear under his evil ministrations.

"A bath," I gasped, tilting my head to give Tamlain better access to my throat.

"Hmm?" he asked, never taking his lips from my skin.

Cai wasn't helping. He'd returned and was rubbing his hands up and down my stomach, caressing me through my clothes.

"A bath," I repeated, with more force this time. "Now. Both of you."

"Both of us? It's a really big bath, you know. How about all three of us?" Cai asked, a slow smile spreading over his ruggedly handsome features.

"Mm, creative problem solving," Tamlain murmured against my pulse point. "I approve."

"God, yes," I said, sagging between them. "Someone carry me to the bathroom, please. A bath would be good, because I have a feeling this is about to get really, *really* dirty."

finis

For more books by this author, visit
www.otherlovepublishing.com

www.ingramcontent.com/pod-product-compliance
Lightning Source LLC
Chambersburg PA
CBHW030657190726
48286CB00001B/62